THE WOMAN HE MARRIED

BOOKS BY WILLOW ROSE

Standalones

My Husband's Mistress

Detective Billie Ann Wilde series

Don't Let Her Go

Then She's Gone

In Her Grave

Find My Girl

Emma Frost Mysteries

Itsy Bitsy Spider

Miss Polly Had a Dolly

Run, Run, as Fast as You Can

Cross Your Heart and Hope to Die

Peek a Boo, I See You

Tweedledum and Tweedledee

Easy as One, Two, Three

There's No Place Like Home

Needles and Pins

Where the Wild Roses Grow

Waltzing Matilda

Drip Drop Dead

Black Frost

THE
WOMAN
HE
MARRIED

WILLOW ROSE

Bookouture

Published by Bookouture in 2025

An imprint of Storyfire Ltd.
Carmelite House
50 Victoria Embankment
London EC4Y 0DZ

www.bookouture.com

The authorised representative in the EEA is Hachette Ireland
8 Castlecourt Centre
Dublin 15 D15 XTP3
Ireland
(email: info@hbgi.ie)

ISBN: 978-1-80550-298-2
eBook ISBN: 978-1-80550-297-5

PROLOGUE

The wine glass feels cool in my hand. I admire the delicate curve as if appreciating a fine piece of art. The cleaning lady I'm about to hire is seated opposite me. Her name is Marie. Her chestnut hair is neatly pulled back into a low bun, and her eyes are a deep shade of green. Serene, she watches with a quiet attentiveness. I sense a flicker of nervousness in her posture, though; her fingers fiddle with the hem of her modest floral blouse. I take a deep breath. I want her to feel valued and respected, as she seems like a person who takes pride in her work. And I need her to like me.

"I need you to spy on my daughter-in-law," I say, speaking low, my words barely audible over the soft ticking of the grandfather clock in the corner. I rub the etched crystal goblet in a smooth, circular motion with a cloth, its intricate patterns catching the dim light. When Marie first walked into the room, I'd seen her eyes bulge at the selection of antique glassware I'd laid out on the polished mahogany table. The collection is a dazzling array of cut crystal vases, delicate flutes, and ornate decanters, each piece telling a story of its own, each one a test of her skill.

Every time I interview a new cleaner, I set out these treasures, carefully chosen for their rarity and fragility, to see how gently they handle them, to see if they can appreciate their beauty as much as I do. But this time, with Marie, I've taken things a step further. I've bypassed the usual pleasantries and jumped straight into the questions I really want to ask. There's something about her demeanor—her steady gaze and firm handshake—that makes me feel I can trust her with this other delicate task. She has a quiet confidence. Whatever it is, it has led me to this moment, where I find myself confiding in her, hoping she will be the ally I need.

"Things aren't quite right," I continue.

She remains composed, blank. She seems trustworthy, quiet, discreet. Not one way on the surface and quite another underneath. I can't have another of those women in my house. My daughter-in-law—Elizabeth—is one of those women. Pretends to fit, but she doesn't.

And that's where Marie comes into the picture. The petite woman in front of me seems perfect.

There's the smallest furrowing of Marie's brow. She's easy to read, at least.

I think of Elizabeth's feigned smiles, the way she checks her watch at family events. All those secrets she harbors, ready to spring on my son when he's least prepared.

"I need you to get close to her, have her trust you," I say, and I pause, letting the words hang between us.

The room's silence amplifies the tension. The only response is her stillness. She's like a statue. Her presence, unremarkable and plain, has a way of settling in without disrupting the order of things, blending seamlessly into the background. That's what makes her perfect for this task. That's why I chose her. She has a way of seeming almost invisible.

Marie shifts a little, her lips parting as if to speak, but then she hesitates. A flicker of doubt crosses her face, and for a moment, I wonder if she's going to protest and walk out. My eyes drift to her worn bag, the frayed edges whispering tales of hard times. I remember the lack of references she had. I know she needs this job. I have had her background checked and know that she's in financial distress. I know a lot about her, but she doesn't need to be aware of that. She just needs to be desperate enough, and I believe she is. Reassured, I see the resolve return to her eyes.

Finally, Marie speaks, her voice steady yet soft, "I still want the job."

"Are you sure?" The doubt in my voice is intentional, designed to provoke her. To make her insist she can.

"Yes, Mrs. Wilson," she says. Her words are careful, voice soft. "Of course."

I watch her hands, can see she's nervous in my presence. I smile tightly, as though this exchange is perfectly ordinary.

"I simply need you to watch her," I clarify. I can see Richard in my mind. So busy, so in love. So *trusting*. "I'll want to know what she does, who she speaks to. Do you understand?"

From the moment I met Elizabeth, I had a strong suspicion that her intentions were less than genuine. It was one of those sunny afternoons when Richard proudly brought her home for the first time. As they walked through the door, hand in hand, my son's face was lit up with pride as he introduced us. Elizabeth flashed a smile that seemed almost too rehearsed, her eyes hidden behind the perfect frame of hair cascading over her shoulders. She was impeccably dressed, exuding an air of elegance that seemed both charming and calculated.

As we exchanged pleasantries, my motherly instincts whispered caution. There was something evasive in her eyes, a fleeting shadow that passed like a cloud on a bright day. Over time, this feeling has only intensified. Elizabeth has always been secretive, and more than once, I've stumbled upon her in hushed conversations over the phone, her voice lowered to a conspiratorial whisper. I can't quite put my finger on it, but I worry that her affections for Richard are motivated by his wealth. It's for my son's welfare that I find myself increasingly uneasy, unable to shake off the gut instinct that she is more interested in his money than in him, a feeling that began at that very first meeting.

"Richard's father, my husband, is a prominent politician. Joseph demands a spotless family image, insisting that our personal lives remain as impeccable as his public persona. This is important. I must maintain an illusion of perfection. To Joseph, our social standing is paramount, and any blemish on our reputation is unacceptable. If anything is amiss, it's expected that I make everything right. Do you understand what I'm telling you, Marie?"

"I do," Marie says. She appears unconcerned, though there's an alertness in her eyes. "I understand exactly."

"But you must be careful. Elizabeth is very smart. These past years I have lost my son completely to her, and I don't trust her. I'm sure she'll be very friendly toward you, but I want you to remember that she's..." I search for the right word, wanting to get Marie onside and be honest with her. But wanting to make sure she takes the job. "Untrustworthy."

"Look, Mrs. Wilson. If I may," Marie speaks quietly. "You're employing me. I'm sure you know your son best—"

"She doesn't love him." I break Marie off. "You can't trust her, no matter how nice she seems, do you understand?"

Marie sits with perfect posture, as though a string pulls her upwards. Her hands rest in her lap, folded, the picture of modest compliance. I wait, letting silence drape itself over us, and I see her glance at the door, perhaps measuring the distance, before her eyes return to the task at hand. I place the cloth on the table. She shifts in her seat.

"I've been a cleaner for years. I know how to keep secrets. I know how to watch people," she says. She takes a deep breath. "I'm happy to watch her for you."

"The Wilsons have standards," I continue, relieved. It's one of my favorite words. Standards. Often completely overlooked by the new generations. I reach for another glass, the stem fragile between my fingers. I notice Marie's eyes follow with that curious mix of wariness and absorption, like a child learning a new language. She blinks, an act so small yet somehow revealing the layers beneath her carefully composed exterior.

"Elizabeth doesn't meet those standards; she simply doesn't belong." I rub the cloth on the glass in steady circles, watching Marie's face for the slightest shift, the smallest twitch. But she doesn't seem intimidated by me, so she should be fine with Elizabeth.

"You understand how important this is, don't you?" I don't look at her now; my gaze is fixed on the glass. It's perfect, not a blemish. I want the same for my son, and Marie knows it. Her head tilts, a soft movement, a mimicry of uncertainty. Then the nod, barely perceptible, just enough to confirm her comprehension without committing too much.

Marie's presence is a shadow cast by nothing at all. She seems to absorb the space around her, yet I know she doesn't miss a single detail. This quality is why I chose her. She is my invisible weapon, one Elizabeth will never suspect. I lean back a little, making sure to appear satisfied, but still holding her with my eyes.

"You'll begin right away." It's not a question. I push the glass toward her, watching as she takes it with slim, tentative fingers. I realize I've left fingerprints; small smudges marring the surface.

Marie lifts the glass, turning it, her movements becoming more assured as she repeats what I showed her; with the cloth, removing the smidge I left. I lean forward, letting the authority in my posture convey the gravity of the situation.

"Every detail, Marie," I insist, my voice as soft and strong as a silk thread. "I need to know everything. I will pay you extra if you do well. I will pay you a lot."

My eyes lock onto hers, waiting for a sign, something to tell me she is up to the task. Her expression doesn't change, though. She doesn't flinch or hesitate. I lean closer, so close I can see the shadow of the wine glass reflected in her gaze. My hand brushes against the edge of the table, feeling its solid reassurance beneath my palm.

Her nod comes again, this time more pronounced, more confident. I relax, just barely, watching as she places the glass back down. Her hand lingers for a moment, and I see no impression of her thumb left on the crystal as she removes it.

It's perfect.

I lean back, smoothing the cloth once more over the tabletop. Marie mirrors me, her movements growing bolder, her eyes less cautious. I see the understanding in her now, the silent communication that passes without a word. It is complete, this exchange of intent, and I know I have set the game in motion.

"Let me show you around the house," I say. "Mrs. Wilson is out for now but will appreciate that you're acquainted with the house before she gets back."

The room feels still, suspended in a moment of perfect clarity. I watch as Marie rises, the chair barely making a sound as it moves across the floor. She stands there, a figure of quiet determination, and I know she has absorbed everything she needs. She gives me one more nod, and I return it, allowing the corners of my mouth to lift in the briefest hint of satisfaction.

The echo of our footsteps follows us as I lead Marie down the long hallway of my son's house. I have told him I was going to get him a cleaning lady. Elizabeth said she didn't need one, since she works from home, as a consultant, but I insisted. People usually don't fight me when I insist.

The walls are lined with Elizabeth's careful attempts at refinement, art pieces and family portraits. I feel Marie's presence behind me, absorbing each detail. In the front sitting room, I point to the armchair where Elizabeth often sits to read. Marie's eyes narrow as she follows my gesture. I move to the bookshelves, the low table, drawing her attention to the pattern of Elizabeth's day-to-day existence. She gives small, thoughtful nods.

"This is where she sits most mornings," I say. She's at lunch at the country club at this moment, with her best friend Sarah Thomson, as she always is on Tuesdays. That's why I chose today. The upholstery on the chair is pristine, no sign of wear. As expected, Elizabeth keeps her throne in perfect order, just like the rest of her so-called domain. I pause, ensuring Marie has registered this critical point.

"You'll want to make note of her routines," I add as I watch Marie's eyes linger on the neatly arranged pillows, the surfaces too neat for comfort. My daughter-in-law is always present in these rooms, though it's rare that anyone truly sees her. I sense Marie is beginning to understand this paradox.

We move together through the space. Marie's gaze lingers on the stack of untouched magazines, another of Elizabeth's flourishes.

"You will come every morning and clean the house from top to bottom, while observing her. Her movements and routines are predictable for the most part," I continue, my voice as measured as my pace. "But that doesn't mean she's not hiding anything. I need you to look out for little details, things that seem suspect."

I stop in front of a cluster of frames, the family portraits Elizabeth arranged as if they could fill the space between her and the rest of us. They're too symmetrical, too sterile. I point, my finger hovering over the one with Elizabeth and my son.

Marie's words come, quiet and careful. "And Mr. Wilson?" she asks, the question carrying more than curiosity. It's insight, clever and dangerous.

I pause, the echo of her voice hanging like a challenge. She watches me, waiting.

"He must never know about our little arrangement," I reply, the truth undeniable and exposed. I see her nod.

The walls feel closer, the portraits watching, judging. Marie moves ahead, taking the lead with a subtlety that surprises me. "I'll see what I can find out and report back to you once a week. I won't let you down," she says, and we shake hands.

The air is thick. I watch her slip out the front door, as silent as she entered, and in her absence, the space feels larger, emptier. The curtains feel heavy between my fingers, their ornate pattern blocking most of the late-afternoon light. I pull them back just enough to see the driveway and the figure walking toward the minivan. Marie is pulling out her key and unlocking it, her posture relaxed, unconcerned.

I'm certain my son is in danger. It's what I wanted to tell her, what I wanted to say, but couldn't. I didn't want Marie to worry about her own safety. The soft thud of the van door closing is like a punctuation mark on my doubt. She pauses briefly, her face unreadable, before the engine starts. I clutch the curtain, fearing what the light reveals. I watch from the window as she drives away, hoping I'm not too late.

The room is hushed, my thoughts the only noise. I loosen my grip on the curtain, then tighten it again, the rich fabric a reminder of all I've built and all that might unravel.

My son is caught in Elizabeth's web, unaware of the silk tightening around him. I think of their marriage, the polish that disguises the damage. Richard, a reflection of his father, trusting and blind. Elizabeth, always self-contained, her smile never quite reaching her eyes. I feel the panic rise in my chest like the swelling summer heat.

I move from the window, trying to shake the sense of helplessness. The house is too quiet, the tick of the clock a cruel echo of passing time. My steps are slow, uncertain, as I consider what might come next.

THREE MONTHS LATER

ONE

MARIE

Police cars are never a good sign. I see five. Neatly parked outside the Wilsons' estate as I drive up in my minivan. Their light bars are off. A couple of officers are standing outside. All the signs of trouble. And here I am, arriving for work. Marie Clements, best in the cleaning-turned-spy business. Nothing is supposed to get by me. But now something is in my way. I almost turn around. Almost. But how can I?

Something in my chest contracts, then flutters into a series of rapid beats. I turn off the ignition and sit in silence, the engine ticking beneath the quiet. Should I go in? Or go home? I shift my focus to the polished marble stone path ahead. I can't go back now, so I walk toward the front door and pause. The police cars stand in precise formation, as if someone thought to make them presentable for company. An officer stops me at the door.

"Excuse me, ma'am, what's your business here?" he asks, his tone firm but polite.

"I work here," I reply, trying to keep my voice steady.

He scrutinizes me for a moment.

"I'm the maid," I clarify.

He looks me up and down and nods. "All right, go on in."

I draw a deep breath, steady myself and push my way through the front door.

Inside the foyer, the atmosphere is tense. I stand near the entrance, carefully surveying the room. Everything is in perfect order—except for the presence of three officers and some concerned-looking civilian dressed police men. The usual quiet elegance of the house is gone, replaced by the soft murmur of low voices and shifting feet. Dirty feet, whose dirt I will have to clean. I move slowly, hoping to remain unnoticed. Elizabeth stands at the center of the room, gracefully fielding questions from several of the officers. Her demeanor is polished, but even from my distance, I can see the edges fraying.

Elizabeth wears her poise like armor, even now. She gestures delicately with manicured hands, but something is missing in her usual elegance, some crack that threatens to expose more than she wants seen. My eyes follow her, watchful and steady. Her voice rises above the soft hum.

"Of course, we're all very concerned," she assures, and I hear the tension threaded through her measured words.

Elizabeth's eyes move across the room, and she sees me. "There's Marie, our cleaning lady," she says, a hint of relief in her voice. The cluster of people turns, almost in unison, as if she had choreographed the motion. The officers glance in my direc-tion, appraising me. I brace myself as they approach and lift a smile as I lock eyes with Elizabeth.

"Marie Clements?" asks the older officer, dressed as a civilian in shirt and tie, but with a badge attached to his belt.

I nod, softening the gesture so as not to appear too eager.

"I'm Detective Mitchell. Mr. Wilson has been reported missing," he says. "Do you know anything concerning his whereabouts?"

The news startles me. Missing? A man like Richard doesn't simply vanish. I move my head to the side, finding Elizabeth again, now standing like a marble figure, frozen and lovely on the other side of the room.

"We understand you work here regularly," the detective says. "Were you here on Monday when he was last seen by Mrs. Wilson?"

I answer carefully. "Yes. I was here till late in the afternoon. I usually stay till six unless Mrs. Wilson tells me to stay later."

"Did you see Mr. Wilson?"

I hesitate. I am trying to remember. "He came home around four. Mrs. Wilson left to go shopping for a present for a friend's birthday. He was in his office when I left for the day. I didn't want to disturb him."

The older one writes something down. "And did you notice anything unusual?"

I shift my weight, fidget with the strap of my bag. "Not at all. It seemed like an ordinary day."

They press on with their questions, and I offer agreeable replies. No, I didn't see him leave. No, he didn't seem upset. No, I can't think of any reason he would disappear. All the while, I watch Elizabeth. Flawless, even from this distance, but I know what to look for. The faintest crack, a nearly imperceptible fraying. I can see the strain in the tightness of her mouth and the way her eyes focus on some far-off point, not daring to blink.

I answer again, the same calm words repeated in different forms. Their attention shifts back to Elizabeth, where they believe the real answers must be. I take a slow breath, feeling the release of pressure in my chest.

I hear the distinct sound of high heels, purposeful and sharp. Jane Wilson enters, her eyes narrowing as she takes in the scene. There's something both theatrical and commanding in her presence, as though she expects her mere arrival to prompt immediate resolution. I wait, unwilling to miss the performance.

Her gaze meets Elizabeth's in a pointed exchange, and then she speaks, her voice steady and critical.

"What about the beach house?" she asks, as if she's been here the whole time, the suggestion tinged with accusation. "Should we check there?"

"We've already contacted the police in that area, Mrs. Wilson," one of the officers assures her. "They have knocked on the door, but no one answered. They're keeping a lookout in case he should show up there."

"I can give you a key and you can go inside and look for yourself," Jane says.

"That's not within our jurisdiction, ma'am."

Jane huffs a bit, clearly unconvinced, her brow furrowing in mild frustration. I watch as her arms cross defensively, her fingers tapping against the fabric of her sleeve in a calculated rhythm that seems to mirror her inner turmoil. She hasn't spotted me yet, her gaze focused elsewhere. I take a cautious step back into the shadowy corner of the room, my heart pounding like a drum. The dim light casts long shadows on the walls, and I can feel the coolness of the air wrapping around me like a cloak. My own breath catches as I observe her, trying to read the conflicting emotions playing out across her features.

"A mother knows these things, and I sense something is very wrong. Richard has missed important business meetings, and that is not like him. I simply think," she says, each word crisp and weighted, "well, we have certain standards that must be maintained."

"We're doing everything we can," Elizabeth replies, the effort of control audible. "My husband has been gone for longer periods of time before. I'm sure my mother-in-law is overreacting. Now if you would all please leave."

"No one is leaving," Jane says. "I'm telling you something isn't right."

Elizabeth sighs. "I'm sure he is fine."

"Fine?" Jane repeats, arching one eyebrow. "Of course you'll say that."

"What's that supposed to mean?"

"You tell me. My son is not fine. He doesn't answer his phone, he didn't even take it wherever he's gone; you found it in his office. He hasn't been home in two days, and you haven't even bothered to call the police. *I* had to do that. He could be lying dead in a ditch somewhere, he might have been mugged or attacked, and all you can say is, 'he's probably fine'?"

"Hey, I'm worried too," Elizabeth says. "I just meant that it has happened once before. Remember?"

Jane snorts. "Once. He was with that woman for a brief time, Elizabeth, and he has told you how sorry he was a million times. I can hardly see how..."

"Ladies, ladies," the tall officer interrupts. "Let's calm down."

"How am I supposed to calm down when my son is missing?" Jane says. "My one and only child."

"And my husband," Elizabeth adds. "A grown man. Let's not forget that."

My eyes take in the familiar foyer, now strangely alive with a quiet panic, as I watch from the sidelines.

Elizabeth's clear, controlled voice cuts through the confusion. She holds herself with practiced poise, a perfect picture of composure. The unease beneath her elegant exterior betrays her, though.

"It's important to stay calm," Elizabeth says. Her words are deliberate, each syllable measured.

The police talk among themselves, one glancing at a notepad.

Elizabeth turns, and her curtain of polished blonde hair sways. "The police are doing everything possible," she insists. "We have to be patient."

I admire the way she attempts to remain the consummate

hostess, even now. From my vantage point, I see the effort it takes.

* * *

I make myself small and move quietly through the house, each step an act of graceful evasion. Under the guise of cleaning, I weave in and out of the tension, never fully present, always nearby. Elizabeth and Jane's muffled voices drift from the other room, rising and falling like the tide. I pause to adjust the angle of a picture frame with the same care and precision with which I catalog the strained relationships and thick silence around me. Invisibility is my most valuable skill. Secrets come easily when I am not there.

Their words reach me in fragments, sharp and edged with uncertainty. "You don't know him like I do," Jane insists, her voice tinged with authority. "You never did."

I wipe a shelf slowly, my eyes scanning the room for what's out of place, what doesn't belong.

"I know him better than anyone," Elizabeth counters. Her attempt at confidence is threaded with doubt. She knows I'm here but not that I am listening.

The argument carries on as I move about, its rhythm familiar and repetitive.

"Clearly you don't," Jane replies, each word a small, calculated incision. "Look where we are."

I dust the top of the piano, arranging the music sheets.

"I'm handling it, Jane," Elizabeth says, but I hear the cracks. "We have to give it time."

"You're not doing enough, Elizabeth. Something is very wrong." Jane's tone is heavy with accusation. I hear a tremor of genuine fear.

I slide from room to room, a quiet, unobtrusive presence,

collecting words like prized trinkets. Their voices follow, a constant hum.

"Let's just wait," Elizabeth says. "The police…"

"Richard could be anywhere! Why aren't you doing more?" Jane's words chase Elizabeth's like a hound on a fox.

I dust a mirror, its surface cloudy, and catch their reflection in it. They are blurred outlines, moving with the tension of the unresolvable.

"Everything will be fine," Elizabeth repeats, but her confidence is as thin as the film of dust I wipe away.

Jane's response is immediate and sure. "I don't believe you," she says, cutting through Elizabeth's attempts at calm. "I don't think *you* believe you. Either that or you did something to him."

"Jane!" Elizabeth snaps, her voice finally breaking through the careful control.

"Are you upset with me, dear?" Jane's voice is thick with insincerity. "Or with yourself?"

"No, but if you would be quiet long enough for me to actually speak, then I could tell you what I told the police: that I found a letter on his computer saying he left me," Elizabeth says. "That's why I'm not more upset. He left me, Jane."

"He did no such thing," Jane snorts. "Why didn't he take his phone, huh? Or his clothes? Why didn't he take anything that belongs to him? Why didn't he tell *me*? His own mother?"

"He wants to start fresh, a new life, the note said."

"I don't believe it for a minute. You could have written that note for all I know. Detective, please don't believe anything this woman is saying."

I pick up the fragments of their conversation, bits of dialogue they leave behind. I place them in the right order, like ornaments on a shelf.

Preparing myself for the moment Jane might come talk to me.

TWO

JANE

In the foyer, I stand with my hands clenched at my sides. "I would have handled this far better than you."

Elizabeth, impeccably dressed in a tailored designer outfit, with every hair perfectly in place, adjusts her stance and tilts her chin upward. Her reply is measured. I pace, my footsteps echoing on the marble floor. Marie, polishing a vase near the entrance, fixes her gaze on the unfolding confrontation. She doesn't blink. A nearby clock ticks audibly. My questions grow sharper.

"Please, Mrs. Wilson," the detective tries. His voice is too patient, too reasonable. "We're doing everything we can. He hasn't been gone that long."

"Not gone that long?" My voice pierces through the foyer, cutting the air like glass. "My son has been missing for two days. She didn't even bother calling you. I had to do it. Do you understand who we are? Do you have any idea how this will reflect on us?"

Detective Mitchell gives me a nod that's almost a bow. "We do, ma'am. That's why we're taking this very seriously. There are people out there looking for him right now."

"I simply don't think," I say, my tone more exacting than a slap in the face, "that you're doing nearly enough." I let that linger, unsatisfied. "Don't you agree, Elizabeth?"

Elizabeth meets my gaze with a steady calm that only infuriates me further. Her voice is serene, condescendingly so. "I think we should let the police do their work. After all, he did leave a letter saying..."

"Again, with the letter. I'm telling you, I don't believe this so-called letter is from him at all. And what do you call this?" I gesture around the room at the officers, at Elizabeth, at Marie, and at the silent crowd waiting for me to fall apart. "Standing around while Richard is out there? He could be hurt."

"Ma'am, we are..." Detective Mitchell tries.

"You're not taking this seriously," I say. "You have no idea the kind of pressure we're under. His father is a senator as you very well know. He could have been kidnapped for a ransom. Or to hurt my husband's image. I will not have this family dragged through the mud because of your inefficiency. I'm not losing my boy, my one and only child, because of you."

"Really, Jane." Elizabeth's voice has a steely undercurrent now. "He's a grown man, not a child. There's no need to—"

"There's every need," I interrupt, relentless. "Every need. He could be anywhere. Anything could be happening to him."

Elizabeth moves as if to approach me, then thinks better of it and stays where she is. Her composure only aggravates me further, her indifference like a bruise that won't heal. "This isn't helping anyone," she says quietly.

"Not helping anyone?" My voice is incredulous, a knife-edge of rage. "It would help me, Elizabeth, if you could muster some concern. It's my son we're talking about. The love of my life. He is everything to me, don't you understand? Everything."

She says nothing. She says it with a pointedness that is louder than my yelling.

Detective Mitchell tries to intercede. "Mrs. Wilson," he begins.

But I am not to be placated. "Why aren't you worried? Why is everyone just standing here?"

I look to Marie for support, but she stays silent, her hands folded, eyes watching every move with the vigilance of a hawk.

Elizabeth lifts her chin, choosing her words with excruciating precision. "I simply think, dear, that getting worked up like this won't do anyone any good."

"I'm worked up?" The word burns in my mouth. "Why aren't you, Elizabeth? Your own husband is missing, and you look as if you're waiting for a bus."

Another ripple goes through the room, but no one dares speak it aloud this time. My sense of decorum has failed. My insistence, they seem to think, is embarrassing. I can't help but wonder if Elizabeth's tone, dripping with false sweetness as she calls me "Dear," is meant to provoke. It irritates me. Our usual banter is marked by a playful wit, but today it seems she has taken an unexpectedly condescending turn. Perhaps it's her way of asserting dominance, or maybe she's just testing my patience, but the shift in our dynamic is palpable.

"I assure you," Elizabeth says with an infuriating coolness, "I'm every bit as concerned as you are."

"I don't see how," I snap. "Richard is my son. No one knows him like I do. I don't understand how you can stand there like it's nothing."

"We've been through this before, Jane." Her tone is so maddeningly restrained I want to shake her.

"No, Elizabeth," I say, my words firm and uncompromising, the truth she won't acknowledge. "We haven't. If we had, you'd know how to handle it."

This time, Elizabeth flinches. Her eyes narrow, the first sign of a crack in her perfect facade. A sense of victory should fill me, but it doesn't.

I stalk to the side table, grab a photograph of Richard from it, and thrust it toward her. "This is the man you're supposed to love. Where's your devotion? Your concern?"

Elizabeth remains silent, her face impassive, as if anything she might say is beneath her.

My voice rises, unbidden, echoing through the room. "Why are you doing this to me?" The question hangs in the air, slicing through the whispers and muted conversations around us.

"I'm not," Elizabeth replies, though her voice wavers, lacking its usual conviction. Her posture remains steady, a statue amidst the chaos.

"Where's your heart?" I demand, my voice cutting through the murmurs of the officers moving around us, their footsteps creaking on the wooden floors.

"You know exactly where my heart is, Jane," Elizabeth insists, eyes flicking to the framed photograph of Richard on the mantelpiece.

"Oh, yes," I say, bitterness coating my words like a thick fog. "I do."

The clock ticks ominously in the background, marking the passage of time. The police officers open drawers, whispering among themselves. One of them speaks briefly with Mitchell, nodding before moving on.

"None of you understands," I declare, feeling like a queen on a battlefield, my voice rising above the rustling of papers and the low hum of voices. "None of you can do what I can. He needs me."

The room is alive with movement and hushed urgency, yet Elizabeth remains a solitary figure, unmoving, her eyes locked with mine as if we are the only two players in this unfolding drama.

I press the photograph to my chest, feeling the gentle rhythm of my own steady heart beneath it. Memories flood back as I recall the last time I embraced my son, his warmth still lingering in my mind. It was on Sunday; he came over for dinner, alone, no Elizabeth. I had gotten used to that. I actually enjoyed it more than when they came together. She was always in such a hurry to go home and would seem miserable while at my house. The last time I saw him was when he left that night. I can still see him walking to his car, his smile bright and full of promise. I can almost hear his laughter mingling with the rustling of the palm trees, bringing him to life in my thoughts once more.

"I don't see how," Elizabeth says. She no longer sounds as certain as she did.

"He's out there," I say, "and none of you know what to do about it." My voice rings through the room. Elizabeth remains perfectly composed. I can see the tiny muscles around her mouth tightening. She lifts one elegant hand as if to forestall my words, but I have too much momentum now.

"You just don't care." The heat of my accusation is unbearable even to me, but she won't break. Not yet. Not quite.

"This is madness." Elizabeth's voice, again. "We need to keep our heads."

"That's the difference between us," I say, vicious and cutting. "I have heart."

The clock is loud, and the room is too full and too silent. I hold the photograph up again. "I know him better than anyone."

The detective I've ignored tries again, feeble and helpless. "We're doing our best, ma'am. Maybe if you could give us some more information?"

"I've already provided you with the names of all his friends and people working for him, including that unfortunate girl he crossed paths with that one time. I also mentioned his company, Bluestone Innovations—a name you should be well-acquainted with if you could just put in a modicum of effort. Bluestone Innovations is a pioneering force in the realm of advanced technology solutions, specializing in artificial intelligence, robotics, and sustainable energy systems. For over a decade, they have not only led the industry but have also revolutionized how businesses integrate technology into their operations, consistently setting the gold standard for excellence, innovation, and groundbreaking advancements."

The words are like bullets. But I am not done. "Yes, I am well informed about my son and what he does. I know his every move. I usually track his phone, but he didn't take it... he didn't take it with him and that has me worried. He always takes his phone everywhere. He always texts me good morning and calls me on his way home from work, ending the day with a good night text before bed. Every day. That's how devoted my boy is to his mother."

I see one of the officers raise her eyebrows. We're close. She wouldn't understand. "He could have forgotten to take his phone, Mrs. Wilson—"

"You heard her," I say, gesturing toward Elizabeth, ignoring her. "She thinks I'm unreasonable. Is that right, Elizabeth?"

My voice echoes off the marble.

Elizabeth doesn't move. I watch the careful composure of her face and know what it costs her to keep it. "I didn't say that."

"Didn't have to." I let the words sink in. "Everyone knows what you meant."

"Jane, this isn't—"

I speak over her, refusing to let her regain control. "You don't know what you're doing, and you refuse to admit it. He needs me."

"Please," Elizabeth says, softer now. "This isn't helping."

"Helping you?" I say, a challenge. "Or helping Richard?"

I wait, and she offers no reply. It's just like her. No backbone. No loyalty.

The photograph stays clutched in my hands. My voice floats back to them, repeating my mantra over and over again. "You don't know him like I do."

Elizabeth raises her head. She doesn't need to say it. She doesn't need to because I know what she thinks, and she's wrong. "Richard will come back, Jane. He did the last time he cheated on me, remember? He will be back."

But I can hear her doubt. Her uncertainty that she won't give me the satisfaction of seeing.

The officers look to Elizabeth, their discomfort plain and unapologetic. Marie stands to the side, taking it all in, letting nothing show. Her careful silence is her strength. Elizabeth's eyes drift over the assembled group, each of them waiting for her to lose control or prove herself more human than she is.

Their murmurs start again, as soft as the shadows cast by the clock's advancing hands. Elizabeth moves to speak to the detective, but even I can tell she has no faith in his authority. She might as well be speaking to the wind.

"We will be in touch," Detective Mitchell says, closing his notebook and walking out.

I follow the detectives toward the landing, turning to look down on them. Richard is gone, and it is only a matter of time before everyone sees what she cannot. The police are leaving, one after the other, oozing out of the house.

Elizabeth's head tilts toward Marie. I see her lips move, asking a question I'll never hear. I need to speak to Marie, but I can't do it now. The only card I have left in my deck is Marie. I hope she knows something.

* * *

The door to Richard's office closes softly behind me, the click of the latch echoing in the stillness. I am physically separated from them now, yet the air is thick with the lingering tremor of their hesitations, their unspoken questions, and the unyielding fear that perhaps I am right. This office is where Richard was last seen, a space that still vibrates with his energy. It's almost as if he is here with me, his presence palpable in every corner.

In my hand, I clutch the photograph like a dagger piercing my heart. In the image, Richard stands tall, his piercing blue eyes full of life and curiosity. His sandy hair is lightly tousled, a testament to his carefree spirit, while a warm smile graces his lips, exuding an infectious charm that has always been his trademark. The sight of him, captured in this moment of time, is both a comfort and a cruel reminder of his absence.

My eyes close. The world shrinks. Only Richard is important now.

My boy. My precious little boy.

THREE

MARIE

The moment I step into my dimly lit apartment, I make a beeline for the cluttered desk nestled in the corner. The space is a mess of papers and half-empty coffee cups, but tonight, I'm throwing caution to the wind by leaving everything out in the open. My heart races as I glance at my well-worn notebooks that have been my constant companion for the last three months. Each page is filled with meticulous notes, chronicling Elizabeth's every move. I am tasked with reporting these observations to Jane every week.

I pause, a pang of guilt washing over me. I snuck out of the Wilsons' home earlier to avoid Jane. We hadn't exchanged a word before I slipped away, and I wonder if Jane has noticed my absence. I need to make sure I clarify this in my next report to her, and I practice what to say. I had a family emergency? No, that's too much. I felt like I was in their way? Yes, that's better. I can't lose Jane's trust, but everything has changed now Richard is missing.

I remember when I first met him at the house. It was the third day I worked there. Due to his busy schedule, he is never home much. One day as I entered the house, I was surprised to find him there, standing in the kitchen, a cup of steaming coffee in hand. His eyes widened in surprise, but then he smiled warmly. Elizabeth was there too, all eyes on me as I entered.

"This is Marie, the new help," Elizabeth said, setting her mug down on the marble countertop. Then she faced me. "This is my husband, Richard. Please, don't let him get in your way."

"Nice to meet you," I said and lowered my eyes. Richard is a very handsome man and seeing him there, being unprepared for his presence, made me blush.

"Likewise," he said. "I know I'm not around much, but if you ever need anything, just let me know." It was this simple, considerate gesture that endeared him to me, and I always looked forward to the rare occasions when our paths would cross.

It was undeniably strange when Jane approached me with the peculiar request to spy on her daughter-in-law. Naturally, the proposition struck me as odd, and I did briefly flirt with the idea of declining. But that hesitation lasted only a fleeting moment. The substantial sum she offered was simply too tempting to pass up, especially considering the mountain of debt I had accumulated during my ill-fated marriage to Carl.

In the weeks that followed, I found myself deeply entrenched in the role of an unsuspecting observer. Marie, my alter ego, had already passed on snippets of information to Jane —tidbits about Elizabeth's daily routines, her social circles, and her occasional shopping sprees. As I gathered details, I couldn't help but notice the unwavering affection Jane held for her son, a love that was obvious in every anxious inquiry she made about his well-being and happiness. Eventually, I spied for her because I could see my reports reassured her.

I remember one afternoon, sitting with Jane as she leafed through a photo album, her eyes misting over memories of her son's childhood. Her voice trembled with emotion as she recounted tales of his youth, the pride and love evident in every word. It was then that I began to understand her motivations, her desire to protect him from any perceived threat, even if it came from his own wife.

Don't get me wrong, Elizabeth is kind. Nothing I've seen has made me worried for Richard.

But now he's disappeared it has made me wonder.

A stack of articles is next to the notebook. Neat, perfectly clipped rectangles, each one detailing an element of Elizabeth's life. At least, the parts she tells the world. "Gated Community Elects New President." "Young Couple Heir to Wilson Fortune." "Perfect Wife on Charity Mission."

She certainly has benefited from marrying into this family.

Perhaps Jane was right all along.

I shift in my chair and tuck a loose strand of hair behind my ear. There's something I haven't told Jane.

The afternoon Elizabeth came back from New York, two weeks ago, when I saw her frowning at her phone. And then there's the guest three days ago she didn't want me to see. The man that came to the house and sat with her in the kitchen drinking coffee. The conversation that ended when I walked in. Who was that man? Why did he stop talking when he saw me?

At the time, I didn't want to worry Jane.

What if I reported what I saw, and Jane confronted Elizabeth? I worried I'd lose my job. The money. The security. But now I'll have to tell her.

I arrive at Jane's house for my weekly report, taking a moment to admire the grandeur of her surroundings. The mansion is a stunning example of classic architecture, with ivy climbing gracefully up its stone facade and large windows that gleam in the afternoon sun. Situated in the prestigious gated community, it shares the same refined neighborhood as Richard and Elizabeth. The air is filled with the scent of blooming jasmine from the scrupulously maintained gardens, and a gentle breeze rustles the leaves of towering oak trees lining the driveway.

This meeting was arranged last week during a brief phone call. Jane insisted on the importance of discussing our progress in person, and I was more than happy to oblige. As I approach the entrance, the heavy oak door opens with a soft creak, revealing a uniformed staff member who offers a courteous nod. I step into the elegant foyer, greeted by the rich aroma of polished wood and the distant sounds of classical music playing softly from another room. The presence of the staff member is a stark contrast to Elizabeth's more casual home, where I am typically the one opening the door and the only music playing might be the hum of a radio in the kitchen.

The house is much bigger than Richard's. I'm just glad I don't have to clean it. I smile as I sit down in her living room. Jane doesn't acknowledge me. Her silver hair catches the light, creating a halo effect that seems entirely at odds with her nature. She gestures toward the spiral notebook with one perfectly manicured finger. "Go ahead."

I open the book and begin my report. My voice adopts the clipped, professional tone I've perfected for these meetings. But I'm more nervous than before. I wonder if Jane knows anything about Richard's whereabouts. Will she tell me if she does?

"Elizabeth left the house at nine fifteen on Tuesday morning. She told me she was going to her charity committee meeting, but I followed her as per your instructions as she drove to the Palmetto Coffee Shop instead. She sat in the back corner booth for approximately forty-seven minutes. I sat in a booth behind her, where she couldn't see me."

Jane's pen moves across her leather-bound notebook. The scratching sound makes my skin crawl.

"She received a phone call at nine thirty-two. She looked around the coffee shop before answering, then spoke in a hushed tone." I swallow. "She kept her hand over her mouth while speaking."

"Did you overhear anything?" Jane interrupts.

"Just fragments. 'Not yet' and 'I need more time.' When the server approached, she ended the call abruptly."

Jane nods, making another note. The sunlight falls across her face, highlighting the deep lines around her mouth—parentheses that bracket years of disapproval.

"Continue."

"After the coffee shop, she visited the bank on Harper Street. She stayed inside for twenty-three minutes. When she emerged, she was carrying a small envelope that she immediately placed in her handbag."

Jane's eyes narrow. "What kind of envelope?"

"Small, white."

My mouth feels dry. I'm not sure why I'm noticing these details for Jane. Why I'm helping her build this case against Elizabeth. None of this suggests she's done anything to Richard, does it? And she's always been nice to me. But I still need the money. Desperately.

"Good." She makes another note. "The bank visit is new. Anything else unusual?"

I flip to the next page in my notes. "She's been carrying her husband's cufflinks in her purse. The silver ones with his initials."

"Richard's cufflinks?" Jane's voice loses its cool edge for just a moment, revealing something raw underneath—grief or rage, I can't tell which.

"Yes. She takes them out when she thinks no one is watching. Rolls them between her fingers. She seems... fixated on them."

The memory surfaces: Elizabeth sitting on the garden bench, on the night after the cops had left, staring at the silver cufflinks in her palm, her face a mask of something complicated

—regret? Fear? Guilt? I've been watching her for months, very closely, and still can't read her expressions.

"She makes phone calls when she thinks she's alone," I continue. "Always from the guest room. Always with the doors locked."

Jane leans forward. The light catches on her pearl necklace —a gift from her husband, I remember she once told me. The Wilsons and their dynasty of perfect marriages, perfect tragedies.

"You haven't mentioned that before. Another man?" Jane's mouth curls with disgust.

"I don't know," I say as doubt is gnawing at me. "The calls seem to upset her. Last Thursday, I saw her hanging up the phone and then immediately rushing to the bathroom. She was sick."

Jane's pen stops moving. "Guilt can do that to a person."

An unspoken accusation: Elizabeth killed Richard.

"There's more," I say, turning another page. My fingers tremble, and I pray Jane doesn't notice. "Yesterday, I found a receipt in her trash. For a burner phone purchased last week."

Jane's face remains impassive, but her knuckles whiten around her pen. "That is probably the phone she uses for her secret calls. I have gotten her statements from AT&T and they don't show any unusual activity. This is good. Go on."

"She keeps a small notebook in her desk drawer. I only glimpsed at it briefly, but there were dates and times written down. One date was circled—the day of Richard's disappearance. She was meeting someone that afternoon when she left the house, but it didn't say who. She told me—and the police— she was going to get a birthday present for a friend."

My stomach churns as I say this. I've been breaking into Elizabeth's desk, reading her private notes, all to feed Jane's conviction that her daughter-in-law is a murderer. What kind of person does that make me? Not a very good one, that's for sure.

"She was lying, then. I see. This is excellent. You've done well," Jane says.

"There's something else," I say, hesitating. "Something that I don't understand."

Jane's eyes fix on mine, unblinking. "Explain."

My throat constricts. "Sometimes, when she thinks she's alone, she talks to him. To Richard. Not like he's gone, but like he's hiding. She says things like, 'How much longer?' and 'I can't keep doing this. Please come home.'" I pause. "Why would she say that if she knows what happened to him?" I venture.

Jane's pen scratches again, more forcefully. "Maybe to anyone who listens," she says dismissively. "Maybe she knows you're hearing her, or that I am. She wants us to think she's missing him, that she doesn't know what happened to him. I told you she's cunning. Or it could be madness. Either way, it confirms what we already know."

What we know? So, Jane does think Elizabeth has done something. The doubt gnaws at me. What if she's wrong? What if this elaborate surveillance operation is just feeding Jane's hatred of a woman who never quite fit into the Wilson family mold?

"The cufflinks," Jane continues, cutting through my thoughts. "Did you notice if they were damaged in any way?"

"No," I say. "They looked pristine. She polishes them, I think."

"A keepsake of her crime," Jane murmurs, more to herself than to me.

Really?

It's not my place to judge. Only observe and report. I keep reminding myself of this, repeating it over and over like a mantra. I must keep my focus on the prize ahead. My freedom, a life free from debt. It's what I want. I have my own problems to deal with. I can't care too much about these people, even if it's hard not to. My hand trembles as I turn to the final page of my notes. Jane notices.

"Are you unwell, Marie?"

"Just tired," I lie. "I've been watching the house at night too, since Richard disappeared. As you requested."

Jane nods, satisfied with my dedication to the cause. She doesn't know that my nighttime vigils have yielded the most troubling observations—the ones I'm not sharing with her.

Elizabeth, standing in the garden at 3 a.m., looking up at the stars with tears streaming down her face.

Elizabeth, placing fresh flowers in the vase by Richard's photograph every morning, her hand lingering on the frame with something that looks remarkably like love.

Elizabeth, startling at every knock on the door, as if she's waiting for someone—or afraid of someone.

None of these fit Jane's narrative of a cold-blooded killer who dispatched her husband for his money. But I keep these thoughts to myself. Jane will only say it's a performance on her part. To make us believe her innocence.

"What about the safe in the back of the bedroom?" Jane asks. "Has she accessed it?"

"Not that I've seen."

Jane's fingers tap decisively on the table. "Richard kept important documents in that safe—perhaps evidence that would incriminate her."

"Maybe," I say, noncommittal.

"I want you to find a way to open it."

I look up, alarmed. "I don't know the combination."

"Figure it out." Jane's tone brooks no argument.

My heart pounds in my chest. Breaking into a desk drawer is one thing; cracking a safe is quite another. The line between surveillance and criminal activity blurs further.

"I'll try," I say, knowing my hesitation is showing.

Jane's eyes narrow. "Is there a problem, Marie? Are you having second thoughts about our arrangement?"

The threat is veiled but unmistakable. Jane holds power in this town—and over my life specifically.

"No," I say firmly. "No second thoughts."

"Good." Jane closes her notebook with a soft snap. "Because we're getting close. I can feel it."

She leans forward, and I catch a whiff of her expensive perfume—something with sandalwood and spice, assertive and unyielding.

"Keep up the good work," she says, her voice dropping to a near whisper. "We're getting close to the truth."

The way she says "truth" makes my skin crawl. As if truth is something you can shape to your liking, a malleable thing to be molded by power and persistence. I'm sure that's how she sees it.

I nod, knowing I'm caught in a dangerous game between these two women. Jane with her cold calculation, Elizabeth with her secrets. And me in the middle, unsure which one I should fear.

"I'll report back on Friday," I say, closing my notebook. I decide in the moment not to tell her about the man visiting Elizabeth. I don't feel good about it. I don't feel good about myself right now.

Jane nods, dismissing me with a flick of her wrist. As I stand to leave, she speaks again.

"Marie?"

I pause, my hand clutching the notebook too tightly. "Y-yes?"

"Remember who you work for."

It's not a reminder. It's a warning.

"Of course. I always do," I say.

Jane repositions herself in her high-backed chair, spine straight as a ruler, not a single silver hair out of place. I'm no longer comfortable with what I'm doing, I think to myself, but I can't afford to show any hesitation now, not with Jane's eyes dissecting my every move.

"I expect a more thorough report on the phone calls next time," Jane says. Her voice is smooth, polished like the silverware displayed in the cabinet behind her. "The numbers she dials, the duration, the exact words, if possible."

"Of course." I stare into the porcelain mug on the side table next to her. The tea inside has gone cold, untouched during my report. Just like my conscience, growing colder by the day.

You're being dramatic, Marie. You're only doing your job.

"And the safe," Jane continues. "I want to know what's in it by the end of the week."

"That might not be possible," I say, instantly regretting the pushback when her eyes narrow to slits.

"I don't pay you for excuses, Marie."

I don't remind her that she barely pays me at all. At least not yet. So far, she has only given me one big check, and I'm still waiting on the next. I'm totally and completely in her power. She can refuse to pay me. There's nothing I can do. No contract, no agreement. She can fire me tomorrow and I will have no claim on the money she promised me. Jane knows exactly how precarious my situation is—she engineered it that way when she offered me the job. The creditors are knocking on my door daily, when they're not calling me. I need to get rid of this debt, so I can move on. When she came to me, I grabbed the opportunity with both hands.

Now those same hands feel dirty.

But there's no turning back now.

"I'll do my best," I concede.

Jane's mouth curves into something adjacent to a smile. "I know you will. You're resourceful. It's why I chose you for this."

The compliment lands like a weight on my chest. I'm not special; I'm convenient. Working on the property, privy to the household rhythms, and—most importantly—dependent on Jane's goodwill.

My mind drifts back to Elizabeth. Yesterday, I watched her through the kitchen window, standing at the sink. Her hands trembled as she took a phone call, her eyes clouding with that same anxiety I've noticed before. She'd twisted her wedding ring—a massive diamond that caught the sunlight—and then reached for her handbag, pulling out that silver cufflink again.

"Can I get more time?" she'd whispered into the phone. Then, more urgently, "It's getting complicated. I think I'm being watched."

Who was she talking about? Me? Jane? Someone else entirely?

And then there was that moment when she'd startled at a noise from the garden, her hand flying to her throat, eyes wide with unmistakable fear. Not the reaction of someone in control, of someone who'd orchestrated her husband's death. More like someone afraid they might be next.

"Marie." Jane's sharp voice pulls me back to the present. "You're distracted."

"Sorry," I say quickly. "Just thinking about the best way to access the safe."

Jane studies me, her gaze penetrating. I keep my face neutral, a skill I've honed over months of these meetings.

"Richard always used significant dates for his combinations," she offers finally. "My birthday, for example, or the year I was born. Try that first."

I nod, wondering if Jane realizes the contradiction in her theory. If Elizabeth killed Richard, why wouldn't she have already opened the safe using those obvious combinations? But I keep this thought to myself.

"What exactly are we looking for in the safe?" I ask instead.

Jane's expression hardens. "Evidence," she says simply.

"Of what, specifically?"

"I never told you this, but it's important you know now. Richard knew... things concerning Elizabeth's past. He found out that she wasn't who she claimed to be."

This is new information. Jane has implied that she believes that Elizabeth killed Richard for his money, for the freedom to live as a wealthy widow. The suggestion that Elizabeth had secrets predating her marriage introduces a different motive entirely.

"What did he find?" I ask.

"I just need you to get me the evidence." Jane stands, signaling that our meeting is over. "That's what was worth killing him for."

I rise too, feeling the weight of my notebook in my hands. Jane takes three precise steps toward her desk, her movements mechanical, controlled. Everything about her is contained—her emotions, her grief, her rage. It makes her even more terrifying.

"One more thing," she says, not turning to face me. "Elizabeth mentioned visiting her sister next weekend. I might ask you to follow her. If she goes."

"To Chicago?" I can't keep the surprise from my voice.

"She won't be going to Chicago," Jane says with conviction. "She doesn't have a sister there. It's another lie."

My throat tightens. "How do you know that?"

Jane finally turns, her eyes cold. "The evidence I suspect is in the safe stems from before their marriage. I had Richard hire a private investigator when they started dating. He never told me the results till last year when I pressed him for answers, starting to suspect something was off about her. He finally told me that Elizabeth Wilson was born Elizabeth Keller in Tallahassee, not Chicago as she claims. And she never had a sister. Only a brother. And it has come to my attention recently from my own private investigation into this Elizabeth Keller, she was once arrested for domestic violence against her first husband. She has been married before, something she conveniently never told us or Richard, as far as I know. But there is more, and this is when it gets bad. She was once arrested for attacking her ex-husband with a fire poker. Charges were later dropped by her ex-husband, but the arrest report is still there. Richard never would allow me to see the evidence he found, but I very much would like to have it, to build my case against her and show the police what a liar she has always been. It really is no wonder I don't trust her. She's full of secrets and lies. And she might be dangerous."

The revelation lands like a punch. If Elizabeth has been lying about something as fundamental as where she's from and whether she has a sister, what else might be fabricated? And the arrest for assault? This doesn't sound like the same woman I've been watching. Jane's confession, meant to prove she's right, has somehow made me wonder.

Jane moves to her desk, opens a drawer, and withdraws an envelope. I take the envelope, feeling the thick stack of bills inside. I wonder if I'm in over my head here. After all, I am just a cleaning lady with a considerable debt. Is this really worth it?

Do I have a choice?

"Jane," I begin, uncertainty creeping into my voice. "Are you sure this is necessary? The police say he probably just left her for—"

"The police," Jane interrupts, her voice dripping with disdain, "are incompetent. They saw a stupid letter and stopped looking. Anyone could have written that on his computer. I know my son. He would never leave me."

The conviction in her voice is unshakable.

"Don't let her out of your sight," Jane says, her voice lowering to a near whisper. "We're on to something here."

The phrase echoes in the vast room, bouncing off marble and glass. I nod once more, clutching the envelope along with my notebook, and turn toward the door.

My footsteps are muffled by the plush carpet as I cross the

room. I feel Jane's gaze on my back, assessing, always assessing. My hand trembles as I reach for the ornate door handle, but I force it steady. Any sign of weakness in this house is fatal.

"Marie," Jane calls just as my fingers touch the cool brass.

I turn, keeping my expression neutral. "Yes?"

"I do appreciate your loyalty in this matter." Her voice is honey over steel. "When this is resolved, I'll see to it that you're properly rewarded. I might even be able to get you a steadier job. I'm on the board at the country club. I could get you a management-level position, if you do this well."

The bribe is transparent but effective. A real career, financial security, a way out of the gatehouse and Jane's direct control. All I have to do is help her destroy a woman who might be innocent.

Or might be a murderer.

"Thank you," I say, the words ashen in my mouth. Behind me, I feel Jane's eyes tracking my movement, calculating, assessing. I wonder what she sees—a loyal informant or a potential liability?

I wonder which one I actually am.

FOUR

JANE

In a stark white room, empty but for a table and two chairs, I sit upright, back straight, hands folded, across from Detective Mitchell, who studies me from behind wire-framed glasses.

"Mrs. Wilson, your relationship with your son seems... unusually close."

I say nothing, waiting. The table between us is metal, cold, and clinical. He leans forward, pen in hand, a patient look on his weathered face. I asked for this meeting. I want to know how far they are in finding my son. So far, they have done nothing. They keep insisting he probably just left his wife, abandoned Elizabeth because he wanted out of her life. After all, they were going through a rough patch and were seeing a counselor. But I refuse to accept that. My son is missing, and every fiber of my being screams that his wife is to blame. I tell them this with a voice that cracks under the weight of fear and desperation. She did something, I know it in my heart, and I need them to understand that. The thought that she might have murdered him and buried him in the backyard torments me. Or what if she hired someone to do it, to make him disappear forever? The image of him being taken to the swamps, left for the gators to devour, fills me with unbearable anguish. I am desperate for them to see what I see, to feel the urgency and terror that consume me. Tears brim in my eyes as I plead with them to understand. Please, they must see the truth.

But they don't care. "No body, no crime," they keep repeating, as if it's a mantra that absolves them of responsibility. Besides, they have other more urgent cases that demand their attention—cases with tangible evidence and visible victims. They claim they lack the resources to search for someone who doesn't want to be found. Meanwhile, I am desperate for them to interrogate Elizabeth, to dig deeper into her alibi, and maybe even arrest her. As the detective's relentless questioning continues, I can feel the tension in the room, thick and suffocating, like a storm about to break. I don't understand why he isn't listening to me. Why he seems suspicious of me all of a sudden.

"You told us you have him tracked? That he calls every day, and texts you every morning and night. Perhaps you'd like to elaborate?" he suggests, his gravelly voice rough against the sterile silence. The chair beneath me is hard, unyielding, but I remain poised. He watches me with deep-set eyes that presume too much. The very notion that he can sit there and question a mother's devotion. As if he would understand anything about it. The air is dense with his insolence and the faint, persistent scent of bleach. I tilt my chin, fix my gaze on him. Words must be chosen carefully here, though his feeble attempts to insinuate something improper are painfully transparent.

Richard, I think, as if the single thought is enough to keep him safe.

"Richard is my son, Detective," I say the obvious truth. "He cares about his mother. He's a good boy. Always has been. Nothing wrong with that." Each word falls precisely where I place it, carefully measured and deliberate. Mitchell tilts his head, the corners of his mouth curving slightly as if to suggest he's made some clever discovery. He knows all too well the power the Wilsons hold in our community. My husband's influence is vast; he golfs with the mayor, and our connections are weaving through every aspect of our town like an unbreakable web. I know the chief of police personally. I am going to ask for his help.

My heart is loud in my ears, a wild metronome counting out my silence. *Richard, Richard, Richard*, it drums. My precious son. The light overhead flickers, but I do not flinch. Mitchell sets his pen down, steepling his fingers as if in prayer. I resist the urge to smile at the irony.

"We're curious about Richard's relationships," he says. "Particularly with his wife. Elizabeth." The name lands on the table like a small grenade. I do not blink. "We understand things have been... tense. They have been seeing a therapist."

My expression remains serene, but inwardly I am wondering who he's been talking to.

"Could he have simply left her?" he asks. "Like the letter said. People do that sometimes. Was it that bad between them that he was thinking of leaving her?"

"Not without telling his mother," I reply firmly. "Richard always tells me where he is."

Mitchell leans back, taking a breath before continuing. "We interviewed Sarah Thomson, Elizabeth's closest friend. She didn't have much to add, but we also spoke with some of Richard's colleagues—David, his work partner, and a couple of family friends, the Johnsons. During these conversations, a few names came up, and one of them mentioned an affair that Richard might have had."

I feel a tightening in my chest as Mitchell looks at me intently.

"Do you know anything about who she is?" he asks gently, his eyes searching mine for a hint of acknowledgment. "You said he tells you everything. Did he tell you who he was with when he cheated on his wife?"

I hesitate. This is a difficult question. He didn't tell me, but I saw where he was when tracking his location. I do that a lot. Look at Find My Phone, to see where he is, what he is up to. Many times during the day. When I caught him going to the same address again and again over the course of a few weeks, I knew he was up to something. I confronted him and told him to end things. It didn't look good on our family.

"No, he didn't."

"So, there are things he doesn't tell you after all," he says.

Mitchell leans back in his chair, the worn leather creaking under his weight, as he scribbles notes on his yellow legal pad. His technique is as subtle as a bull in a china shop, each stroke of his pen loud and deliberate. I have sat across from more formidable inquisitors at my dining table, such as my Aunt Margaret, whose piercing gaze could extract confessions with a single look, or my old college professor, Dr. Wallace, who could unravel the most guarded thoughts with his relentless questioning. But I humor Mitchell, offering him the benefit of my patience. Perhaps I do take on more of the burden of protecting Richard than others might. But what choice does Elizabeth give me?

Richard has always been sensitive and nervous, traits that became evident early on, even at school, where he would shy away from group activities and struggle with anxiety over exams. His teachers often noted his reluctance to participate in class discussions, preferring instead to sit quietly at the back, absorbed in his own world. This vulnerability has compelled me to shield him from the harshness of life, a task that grows more demanding each day.

"My son's happiness and safety are of the utmost importance," I continue, my voice a study in calm resolve.

Mitchell's eyes flit up, watching me watch him. His chair creaks as he shifts, and I imagine Elizabeth sitting in mine, crumpling under the weight of such questions, her weak voice stumbling through hollow replies. She doesn't deserve to be a Wilson. Not in name. Not at all.

I remember when Richard had just met her. He would do anything for her. There was a storm approaching from the west, the air charged with thunder and threat. We watched it roll in, and I told him we were safe inside, but he followed her outside anyway. She wanted to dance in the rain. "We both got soaked, Richard!" Elizabeth laughed. He caught a dreadful cold from that escapade, and while he lay feverish and weak, it was I who nursed him back to health.

Meanwhile, Elizabeth, with an air of indifference, laughed with strangers on the phone, her voice light and carefree, as if the world beyond her was inconsequential. I realized then, as I do now, that I had been right from the start. I always sensed a coldness that seemed to lurk beneath her charming exterior. Her selfish nature was evident, and I was certain it would eventually hurt Richard. Her laughter was like a siren's call, alluring yet dangerous, and I feared it would lead him astray, away from me and into her uncaring grasp.

Mitchell's voice cuts through the memories. "You and your son," he says, underlining each word with a verbal pause. "You've always been... close?" He wants to understand what he never will. Elizabeth will do anything to preserve herself. I must do everything to preserve Richard. For myself. For him. My desperation has the perfect disguise.

"Why does that surprise you, Detective?" I ask, raising a brow. Let him ponder. "We've never had cause to doubt our loyalty to one another."

Loyalty, Richard, I think. *Do you hear? To me. Not to her. She's nothing but a fluke, a phase in your life that will pass. But you refuse to see it. You refuse to see her for what she is. That's why I am doing what I must.*

The only sound is Mitchell's pen clicking against the table, a steady, mechanical rhythm. He jots down another line. His eyes flicker toward mine, and I see the questions rolling around inside them. Who did you think was to blame? For all of it. Who did you really want to protect? The clock above the door ticks. The light overhead hums, a luminous threat waiting to ignite. My certainty flares, then burns to ash and flares again. Everything I say must carry one meaning alone: that nothing matters but my son.

"Some might say, Mrs. Wilson," Mitchell begins, choosing each word as if it were precious, "that you've done more to hold on to him than most mothers would."

I nod slowly, feigning contemplation. Let him believe he's made an impact, that his words have pierced through. But within my mind, a louder voice will rise, drowning him out, drowning everyone out until there is only Richard. And me. Just the two of us, in our own world.

Mitchell's voice is laced with a sly undertone. "One might even say," he muses, "that Richard's struggled quite a bit... with separating himself." He pauses, the insinuation like a shadow. His eyes search mine, tentatively probing, as if he's gauging whether I share his unspoken suspicions. Perhaps he's subtly suggesting that my concerns about Richard are unnecessary, that my worries are misplaced.

I should laugh. I should let the sound bounce off the walls, should let Mitchell see what little effect his words have on me. But I do not. Marie's words are in my head: *I'm sure you understand, dear,* she heard Elizabeth say on the phone one day. She didn't know Marie was listening to her conversation in the kitchen, and she kept it that way, hiding behind the door. Marie told me she heard her as she fumbled for words, for reasons to justify herself. *I simply don't love him, I never did.* That's what she said.

No, dear, I think now. *I am sure you don't.*

She seriously said those words, like it wasn't important, like she was talking about the price of eggs. And then when I told

Richard, she spun around three sixty and denied ever having said anything like that. And he believed her, of course he did. He always believes her over me.

"A mother is always concerned," I reply, measured, unflinching, "when a son takes up with someone beneath him."

Mitchell's brows rise imperceptibly. I will not say any more about it. About Elizabeth's moral failings. Despite the last three months of Marie watching Elizabeth, I have no evidence she's done anything to Richard. And I know my suspicions will just make Mitchell wary of me. Mitchell waits for me to say more, but my silence is deliberate.

"And she has been arrested before," I add. "For violence against her ex-husband. If you look into her background, you will know. She was under a different name back then, Elizabeth Keller."

"This is news to us," the detective says.

"It makes her capable of violence," I say.

He says, "Be that as it may. We still have reason to believe that he simply left of his own free will. That will be all for now," but does not understand that it will never be all, not until Richard is with me again.

I stand slowly, smoothing my skirt with a firm, steady motion, while maintaining unbroken eye contact with Mitchell. I collect my things—a neat folder and a pen—and arrange them precisely in my arms. I look at the detective. My steady gaze remains on him. Every word, every breath has been for Richard, my precious son. My mind races ahead of me, already planning, already shielding, already obsessed with the perfect measures for his perfect protection.

I reach for the handle of the door across the room and pause, remembering our numerous social engagements—dinners with dignitaries, charity galas, and the annual ball at the governor's mansion. The chief of police, a frequent guest at our soirées, might lend an ear to my concerns about Richard.

"Could you please let the chief know I wish to speak with him before I leave?"

Mitchell's brow furrows, and he replies, "I believe the chief is currently away on business, ma'am, but I shall inquire about it."

I must not lose ground. Not again. I turn the doorknob, its chill like a ghost from the past. I refuse to shiver. I will not give him the satisfaction of thinking he has read me. Each gesture, each movement, is controlled, is intentional, is part of my orchestration. I think of Richard, of his smile when he was a boy, of his smile when Elizabeth was not around to ruin it. My control never faltered then, and it will not falter now.

"It was a pleasure, Detective, now go find my boy," I say, the slightest edge of dismissal in my voice. I do not ask to be shown out. The room, the building, the world beyond it—I have navigated more treacherous terrains. I leave, my words delivered like an invitation. Then I turn, deliberate and resolute and step through the door.

The hallway stretches before me, wide and empty. Each step propels me closer to Richard. I imagine him on the other side of the endless space between us, his laughter ringing in my ears, the way it used to when we played hide and seek in the garden. Each footfall is the tick of a clock, winding down the distance to his safety. Elizabeth always accused me of controlling time. She never understood the lengths I would go to.

The lengths I *will* go to.

Mitchell's warning is still in my ears: *We must follow procedure.* Yes, Detective. But not Elizabeth's. Not yours. Only mine. My shoes tap the polished floor with the sound of certainty resonating around me, echoing back to me. I let the echo spread, hoping it reaches Richard, reminding him where he belongs. Let it erase every other voice he thinks he hears.

I remember the warmth of his small hand in mine, the way his eyes lit up with curiosity and trust. Those memories flood back, painting a vivid picture of the beautiful bond we shared. No one knows him like I do. I will have him close again.

But as I walk, a realization creeps in. To find him, I might need to investigate. The thought lingers, and I decide I must speak to Marie again. She's the one who can watch Elizabeth, and her insights could be crucial. No one comes between me and my son.

No. One.

FIVE

MARIE

I stand before Elizabeth's vanity in the bright, rigorously organized dressing room, my heart pounding as I swipe dust from each delicate porcelain figurine and polish the large mirror with a soft, damp cloth. Moments later, Elizabeth enters—a graceful figure settling onto a nearby stool—and places her designer handbag on the glossy side table. Her eyes, warm yet troubled, rest on a framed family photograph as she begins, "Jane won't get off my back," she says to me. "Ugh, I'm so exhausted."

There's a subtle tremor in her voice that I've come to recognize after countless days spent together in her house. As I continue my work, I adjust a stray lock of hair from my face and lean in a small way, compelled to offer more than a silent nod this time.

"Is it the same all the time?" I ask softly.

Elizabeth's eyes flash with a mixture of vulnerability and resolve. "I know you don't know her, but... it's just a lot. Especially now that Richard has left me. I used to be able to have him defend me against her. I know she believes something happened to him, but I'm pretty sure he just had enough. Of all of us. In my therapy session yesterday," she confides, her voice lowering, "I told her that the constant probing makes me feel like I'm never truly seen—not just by Jane, but by everyone. In this family, I'm nothing but Richard's wife. That's it. And one that has failed to birth him an heir on top of it." She stops. "Sorry..."

I reach over, placing a comforting hand on Elizabeth's. "Don't apologize. I remember what it's like having a mother-in-law. Carl's mother was overbearing too," I reply, my voice softening as I share more of my past. "When I first married Carl, his mom would call me every day, questioning everything I did. It was suffocating. I felt like I was constantly under a microscope. But you know, over time, I learned to stand my ground."

Elizabeth looks up, her eyes filled with curiosity. "How did you do it?"

I smile. "It wasn't easy, but I started setting boundaries. I realized that I had to define my own role in the family. It took time, but eventually, she came to respect me. You've told me about Jane before, and I remember thinking how similar our situations seemed."

Elizabeth nods, her expression softening. "I remember that conversation. It was the first time I felt like someone truly understood."

I hesitate for a moment, unsure if I should continue. I take a deep breath, deciding to be vulnerable. "You know, Elizabeth, I hope I am not too blunt, I don't want to overstep, but I also don't want you to feel alone."

Elizabeth's lips curl into a small smile. "I know. It means a lot, Marie. Truly."

The room holds its breath as Elizabeth takes off her Jimmy Choo heels and puts them away. "I wish she would just leave me alone," she says. I note the tremor in her voice—small but telling. I continue dusting, letting her words settle.

I set the cloth down, take a moment to adjust a loose lock of hair from my face, and offer more than a silent nod this time.

"She can't help herself, I suppose," I say, choosing my words like stepping stones across an icy pond. "She misses her son."

Elizabeth's shoulders tighten, a small movement, almost imperceptible. "Jane always suspects that I am up to something," she replies with a sigh, a mix of resignation and defiance. "That I'm this villain who is conspiring against her. And I think she enjoys it. I told my therapist it feels like I'm never enough for her." She pauses, and in that pause, I see the shift again. The deflection. "That she resents me in his life," she adds, whispering Richard's presence back into the room. I feel the heaviness of his absence in her words, the unspoken accusation that lies beneath them. "That I don't belong with him."

"Is that what you feel too?" I ask, the question escaping with a hint of familiarity, something more than my role should allow. "That you don't belong?"

"Sometimes," she admits, her voice trembling, a rare lapse in control. She looks at the photo again, her expression wistful. "I just don't know how long I can pretend everything is perfect."

I pause in my work, letting my hands still on the vanity's polished surface, feeling the warmth of the exchange like a breath against cold glass.

"I guess I don't have to now that he's left."

There's a new sharpness in her gaze, but also a vulnerability that suggests she wants to trust me, needs to trust someone. "I told the therapist that," she adds, more composed. "That he'd grown so distant these past many months. I guess he was planning his escape. From what I don't know. I mean, I knew we had problems, but we were working on them."

I absorb her words, feeling the careful balance of my professional detachment and something more tangled, more human. I know Jane will want to hear about this. About every nuance.

"You're strong, Elizabeth," I say, testing the words like a foreign language. "Stronger than you realize."

She breathes out, a long sigh that feels like the release of something pent up, something close to despair. In this moment, she doesn't look like a woman capable of violence. "It's exhausting, all of it," she says, almost to herself.

I nod, watching her closely, witnessing the delicate unspooling of the emotional truths she's tried so hard to contain. She stands, and for a moment, she seems like she might reach out. But she doesn't.

"I have kept you from your work, Marie," she says, her voice softening in a way that suggests she really means it. "I'll let you get back to it. Enough of my sob stories."

She pauses before me, and then she turns and leaves the room.

Alone again, I pick up the cloth, noting the tremor in my hands.

Later, I walk into Elizabeth's modern kitchen, where sunlight streams in through floor-to-ceiling windows and casts a warm glow on the gleaming surfaces. I see a steaming teapot on the marble countertop and two delicate porcelain cups placed on the polished wooden table. Elizabeth is smiling at me.

"I made us some tea," she says. "Care for a cup? You've been working so hard, you deserve a break."

"Thank you," I say. We do this from time to time, but I'm careful not to assume Elizabeth and I are friends. Sometimes she just wants to sit in silence or tell me about the gossip among her friends. I watch her as she brings out a dish of cookies for us to munch on. It's hard for me to see the woman Jane has described. Elizabeth doesn't come off as cold and calculating, and the first time we had tea was the first moment I wondered if I was really doing the right thing spying on Elizabeth for Jane.

Elizabeth stirs sugar into her tea with a thoughtful frown. "I feel like Jane's always here, even when she's not," she says, a touch of exasperation in her voice. "Like she's watching everything we do, always making sure I live up to her expectations of who I'm supposed to be, what kind of wife I'm supposed to be to her precious son. Even now, I can't shake it off. I should be mourning the end of my marriage, and all I can think about is Jane."

"It's difficult," I offer, watching her closely. "You can't catch a break. You will never be good enough."

Elizabeth looks up, her eyes meeting mine with a sharpness that borders on desperate. "So true," she agrees, a tightness in her smile. "Me wanting to please her, and Richard always wanting me to make his mother happy, it gives her the upper hand, all the time. And that's what she loves: the constant control."

"Elizabeth, if you don't mind me asking—what did Richard say in his note? His disappearance has been on my mind, and I wonder if... well, I'm worried about you." I say his name with the softest touch, feeling the room constrict around it.

Elizabeth's hand stills, the spoon motionless in her cup. The hesitation is unmistakable, a slow, deliberate breath. "I..." She searches for words, for control, and I see her struggle. "I wish I knew more about why he left. His goodbye note was so vague. All it said was, 'I must find my path, one that leads away from here. I need a fresh start. Please understand.' How am I supposed to understand that?"

The admission is reluctant, pulled from somewhere deep. Her composure slips just enough for me to glimpse the chaos beneath. "Every day without him," she continues, her voice flattening into something dangerously close to despair, "deepens the ache, and I fear we're both drowning in uncertainty. Frankly, I don't know what to do. How to move on from here. I tell myself he left me, because that's what the note said. But part of me wonders whether it's true or not."

"I can't imagine," I reply, my voice measured, feeling my way through the intricacies of her emotion and my own growing suspicion. "How are you holding up?" I watch her for any signs, any cracks that might reveal more than she intends.

Elizabeth exhales softly, a small surrender. "Some days," she says, her tone a blend of exasperation and sorrow, "I think I'll wake up, and it will have all been a bad dream." There's a distant look in her eyes, as if she's watching that dream slip further and further away.

"Then I realize," she adds, more controlled now, "the nightmare is real. Jane's coming here every day, always there to remind me." Her gaze sharpens, a quick return to the present. "It never ends."

The porcelain rattles as she sets her cup down, a sound that startles both of us in the hushed room. I think of Jane's words, what she told me about Elizabeth's past. None of it lines up with the woman who sits before me.

"You've been so strong through all this, Elizabeth," I say, trying to gauge the sincerity in her fleeting smile.

"I don't feel strong," she replies, a quick laugh escaping—a laugh that doesn't quite belong. "I feel lost."

I listen to the distant murmur of passing cars and the soft hum of the refrigerator, each sound underscoring the isolation that words can't touch. My concern for her mixes with a sense of trepidation; the more she reveals, the deeper I find myself entangled in her web of uncertainties. I feel terrible that she feels watched. When I'm the one watching her.

"You've done all you can," I say, noticing how her eyes quickly look elsewhere, as if searching for escape from a truth she can't face. I recall watching Elizabeth over the past months as she tried to get close to him, offering warmth and love, only to witness him withdraw, retreating into his own private world time and again. His office became his refuge that he would shut her out of. Richard, with his mysterious presence, remained an enigma even to those closest to him, leaving Elizabeth struggling with the intricacies of their connection. As I observe her now, I feel the weight of those memories pressing down on her.

"Have I?" she questions, the words almost a challenge. There's a vulnerability now, one that dares me to believe her, to understand her plight. "It never feels like enough."

I want to assure her, to ease the burdens that weigh her down, but I feel my words catch, uncertain and awkward. "The not knowing," I offer, "must be so hard." My voice betrays the emotion I try to keep hidden. "It's been almost a week now, and you still have no idea where he is?"

"Some days, it's unbearable," she confides, her composure returning as if it never left. "Some days, it's a relief." The frankness of her admission startles us both, but she covers it quickly. "I mean, the not having to pretend for Jane's sake," she clarifies.

I watch her, absorbing the subtleties in her tone and the shifting expressions that pass over her face. I wonder if she knows just how much she's revealed—or how little.

"Thank you, Marie," Elizabeth says after a brief silence, a note of genuine warmth in her voice. "For listening. For caring."

I nod, the motion feeling small and inadequate against the complexity of what we've shared. The sun continues its path across the kitchen, casting long shadows that seem to stretch the minutes into hours. Elizabeth stands, her movements once more composed and deliberate. She leaves the room, her steps echoing like unanswered questions. I remain at the table, letting the final sips of tea grow cold, the tangled threads of our dialogue weaving themselves into a fabric of doubt and complicity.

. . .

I take out my notebook and sit in the guest bedroom—a quiet sanctuary where I can process the day's revelations. I settle at a simple wooden desk under the watchful glow of a small lamp. Slowly, I open my notebook and start writing, but then I stop. Do I really want to keep doing this? Jane is expecting a report from me this Friday. She will be even more on alert since Richard is gone, and she will want every little detail from me. But do I want to give them to her? To serve her Elizabeth on a platter?

I must give her something. If I want to keep getting paid.

I begin to write, capturing every nuance of Elizabeth's words and actions: the subtle tremor in her voice when she spoke of Jane's questions, the way her eyes darkened at the mention of Richard. I record with care, knowing each detail will become part of the story I must deliver to Jane. The pen moves across the page, a steady scratch that both calms and unsettles me. It is my duty to report everything, but as I write, I feel an unease growing—an awareness that the truth is as slippery and elusive as the ink drying beneath my hand. Will Jane read things into this that aren't there? Am I betraying Elizabeth?

This is your job. It's what you were hired to do, I tell myself. *You can't afford to have second thoughts.*

I pause, listening to the relentless ticking of the nearby desk clock, each tick marking not only time passing but another layer of complexity in the narrative unfolding around me. I reflect on my own position, my role in the web of secrets and suspicions. Am I merely an observer, recording the lives of others from a safe distance? Or have I become something more entangled, more complicit in the very stories I'm trying to unravel? Each word I write seems to pull me deeper into the fabric of Elizabeth's world, a world where every emotion is double-edged, every confession laced with ambiguity.

I think of Elizabeth, her poised demeanor, her carefully chosen words. Is she as lost as she appears? She was, after all, once arrested for violence against her ex-husband. Is she hiding her real self? I find it harder and harder to believe. I write down everything she said, everything she left unsaid.

I worry about what to tell Jane, how to convey the intricacies of the situation without losing myself in the process. Will she see what I see? Will she believe it? Will she still trust me? The pressure of knowing too much and yet never enough presses down on me, a weight that grows with every word I write. I feel the boundaries of my role collapsing, leaving me uncertain of where I stand. Am I helping to uncover the truth, or am I merely adding to the layers of misunderstanding and mistrust that bind us all?

My own position becomes increasingly blurred, the neat lines I once drew between myself and the Wilsons smudging into a hazy confusion of motives and loyalties. The turmoil inside me remains unsettled. I realize I can't share everything with Jane. I must withhold certain details to protect Elizabeth. But what if she finds out?

SIX

JANE

Her notebook lies on the table between us, a seemingly innocuous worn spiral with an ink stain on the corner. Yet to me, it carries the weight of damning evidence, or at least I hope it does. We have decided to meet in a café this time, a strategic choice since my husband, the senator, is home, deftly managing the media frenzy surrounding Richard's disappearance. He's been skillfully redirecting questions, dismissing rumors, and maintaining a facade of calm, all while secretly probing if his son has truly run off with someone. I can see the worry lurking behind his composed exterior, but I can't bring myself to share my suspicions until I have concrete proof of Richard's whereabouts.

"Mrs. Wilson," Marie begins, her voice barely above a whisper, as though the words themselves are too fragile for the bustling café air. "I've written everything down." Her fingers nervously trace the edge of the napkin, her eyes darting furtively to the side, wary of unwanted listeners, as if the casual café crowd harbors spies in disguise.

Earlier, I had asked Marie to be more friendly with Elizabeth, hoping to glean some valuable insights. Despite her efforts, Marie now reports on her progress—or lack thereof—with a hint of regret. "I tried to get closer to Elizabeth, just like you suggested," she admits, her voice tinged with frustration. "But it takes time."

"Of course. It's only natural."

"And accessing the safe was another matter entirely. I couldn't even get near it. Elizabeth has locked the door to Richard's office and told me not to clean in there. I am afraid of losing her trust if she catches me trying."

I sigh. "Okay, anything else?"

A tremor runs through her clasped hands. I note the way she keeps them folded, perhaps trying to stop the shaking, perhaps aware that I notice. The room's dim light bathes us in conspiratorial shadows. I take it she doesn't have anything for me. Nothing new. She just wants money, so she pretends to have something.

"Richard is missing. Does she talk about him at all?" My words land heavy, a challenge wrapped in false sympathy. She flinches but recovers quickly.

"She does, but only when I ask about him, and then she gets this odd look in her eyes when his name comes up," she says with a firmness that wasn't there before. "Just... vague. Distracted. I think she misses him, to be honest."

Distracted, indeed. I've always suspected that Elizabeth hides more than she shows. It's just like her to have secrets she never shares with the family. But this time, I intend to uncover them all. I lean forward, let a finger tap lightly on the table.

"The other day she had flowers delivered to the house," she suddenly says. Her eyes search mine, gauging my reaction, perhaps uncertain if this detail is significant. "Irises. And there was no card. She asked me who brought them. I said it was a delivery guy, and he didn't know who they were from, just that they were for her."

Her words pick up speed, the doubt that was in her voice

replaced by eagerness. "And when I brought them in, she looked... startled."

I give a slow, calculated nod, as though reluctant to agree, as though Elizabeth's deception wounds me more deeply than anyone can imagine. "Startled, huh?" The warmth of betrayal spreads through me, unwelcome and yet entirely expected. "She knows her lies can only last so long."

Marie shifts in her seat, and I sense her commitment wavering. She's been working in that house for months now. I wonder about her and if I can still count on her. She's seen Elizabeth's kindness, the one she only pulls out when she needs to. She's heard Elizabeth's lies, but does she believe them? The soft murmur of other patrons surrounds us, a gentle symphony of civilized society, oblivious to the drama of the privileged and powerful.

"It's hard not to feel sorry for her, Mrs. Wilson. I know this is a difficult time for all of you, but she's always been so—"

"Manipulative," I cut in, my voice firm, my authority undisguised. "You're not the first to fall for it, dear. I simply hope you're the last. Don't believe her lies, don't fall for her deception."

A look passes across her face, a fleeting shadow that tells me I may have overplayed my hand. But she lowers her eyes to the notebook again, touches it with the tip of her finger, and I see her mind working—see her real loyalties fall into place. Richard is missing, and Elizabeth's pretty mask will soon crack. Marie will be there to witness it, knowing she did her part.

I reach across and touch her hand, as though bestowing my benediction, and feel her skin go clammy beneath my fingertips. "Elizabeth isn't being truthful. She's so cold and indifferent to the fact that Richard is missing. Have you noticed that? I promise you. You're doing the right thing," I assure her, and her response is a weak smile that can't disguise her relief. We are conspirators, after all. Unlikely ones, but perfectly matched. "Now. Tell me what else you have in your little notebook."

She does. With an efficiency that might rival my own, she describes Elizabeth's perfect demeanor, the mask that everyone but me takes at face value. Marie's hands have stopped trembling, and my finger has stopped tapping. Her voice is steady now, no longer a whisper but not so loud that anyone in the civilized café might overhear.

"Sometimes I do wonder if she's even sad he is gone," Marie says, a small frown crossing her otherwise unremarkable face. "She goes about her day, doing her usual chores, meeting friends for lunch or getting their nails done, like nothing was wrong."

I smile without smiling. "How very like her."

Marie's nervousness has nearly vanished, replaced by something like confidence. Her shoulders, narrow and birdlike, are set with determination, and I can see that she's chosen her side. At least for now. She still belongs to me. "I just... I don't understand how she can be so calm, Mrs. Wilson."

"She won't be calm for long." The words come out sharper than I intend, but Marie doesn't seem to mind. She nods, and I know she's still mine.

We sit in silence, though it's not the kind that presses on nerves or lays claim to secrets. This is a silence of complicity, the pause before the axe falls. Marie picks up the notebook, holds it for a moment as though cradling something precious and fragile. I half expect her to add something, to bring up Elizabeth's kindness one last time, but she doesn't. She understands what I expect, and she's determined not to fail. She clutches the notebook to her chest and looks me in the eye.

The moment stretches between us, elastic and uncertain, until Marie leans even closer, her eyes furtive and her voice dropping to a conspiratorial hush.

"There's more," she breathes.

Her words are smoke and mirrors, and my heart clenches with an expectation I refuse to call hope.

"Yes?"

"I remember more about the man who came to visit Elizabeth recently," Marie continues, her voice barely above a whisper.

My eyes widen, the possibilities swirling in my mind, each one dangerous in its own way. "Yes?" I murmur, though the question is unnecessary, and Marie knows it.

"He was rough around the edges, wearing a white T-shirt and jeans," she explains, her eyes narrowing as she recalls. "Looked like a working-class man. He had stubble and unkempt hair, like he didn't care much about appearances. But they were very loving toward each other."

I lean forward, my suspicion growing as my fear begins to subside. "What else did you hear?"

Marie hesitates, then continues, "They were whispering, but I caught snippets. She called him 'love,' and he promised he would come back soon. It sounded like... like they were involved in something more than just a casual acquaintance."

My heart beats faster, the suspicion now a steady drum in my chest, as I realize the implications of Marie's revelation.

I catch my breath, let it tremble just enough. "Odd," I say, my tone edged with curiosity, suspicion, dread.

Marie blinks, surprised by my candor or by the oversight itself. "They sat in the kitchen and spoke quietly. Seemed surprised when realizing I was still there."

"I knew it. I knew she was doing stuff behind my son's back."

Good job, I think, marveling at the way this unremarkable creature has managed to insert herself into Elizabeth's life. But my gratitude is conditional. I need more from her before she earns it. "Was Elizabeth relieved to see him?" I ask, the question casual but my gaze sharp. "Or did she seem on edge?"

Marie hesitates, searching her memory, trying to piece together a mosaic that I already see clearly. The soft murmur of the other patrons swells around us.

"Both, maybe. At first, she looked relieved, but then..."

My fingers drum the table, quick, impatient, relentless. "But then?"

Marie leans back, regaining composure. "He was there for over an hour. When he left, she looked... upset."

"Over an hour?" I echo, as though each minute is a nail in the coffin of Elizabeth's innocence. Marie nods, and I see her waver, torn between loyalty to the present company and a lifetime habit of self-preservation. "Did he say anything specific?" I prod, and her reluctance crumbles. She wants to be on the winning side, after all.

"I couldn't hear what they talked about. Just bits and pieces." Her voice lowers, softer than before, straining to remember, perhaps straining to forget. "Something about it being too much and not what he signed up for." She watches me closely, eager to know if the fragments are valuable.

It is enough. More than enough. Elizabeth is as careless as she is cruel. And Marie is my best weapon against her, at least until the police take my claims more seriously. I hold my breath a second longer than necessary, then let it out with theatrical precision. "This is more than I imagined," I say, allowing a hint of gratitude to soften my voice. "You've been very helpful."

Marie's eyes light up with relief and—God help us both—pride. "I didn't want to worry you, Mrs. Wilson. Not without knowing more."

"You've done exactly the right thing." I reach for her hand again, like a queen rewarding her favored subject. "This changes everything. We know she's capable of violence, and now she has a motive."

A pause, heavy with things unsaid, and then Marie's composure slips for the first time. Her confidence is paper-thin.

She wonders, perhaps, if she's betrayed the wrong person. "I don't want to cause trouble," she says, the plea almost inaudible beneath the café's soundtrack.

"The truth isn't trouble, dear." I make my voice gentle, almost kind, and watch as the words settle on her like a balm. "Richard's safety is all that matters."

She exhales, the sound half sigh, half confession, and I know she'll play her part to the end. She needs the money to get her life back on track, and I need her more than she'll ever understand. "If I think of anything else, I'll—"

"Yes. Do." I release her hand and rise, the movement graceful and measured despite the growing storm within.

She follows suit, clutching her notebook as though it's a shield against Elizabeth, against me, against the tangled web we're both now caught in.

She slips out the side door, leaving me to gather my purse, my resolve. She's afraid, but she shouldn't be. I'm not her enemy.

I make my way through the café, my thoughts racing ahead to a place they've been so many times before. To Elizabeth's lies and what it will take to unravel them. To Richard's whereabouts and what it will take to bring him back. A man came to visit her. Who was he? A lover? My heart beats with renewed suspicion and fear giving way to cold determination.

I will find out. And I'll get my son back.

SEVEN

MARIE

Her voice follows me, even after I leave. It clings to the thick air and wraps itself around my thoughts. On my way back, through the gated neighborhood, I pass the playground. The small one near the clubhouse. I walk through the park. Children shout and scatter like colorful beads spilled from a bracelet. They clatter and bounce, and their mothers orbit them like forgotten gods. There's something strange about this familiar world, something a little askew. Like stepping off the treadmill to find the floor has lost its grounding. Maybe it's just me. My eyes dart as I walk, jump from the bird on the wire to the swing with the twisted chain, and I spot Elizabeth's best friend Sarah Thomson sitting on a bench, watching her children play. I see the red tricycle and the yellow slide. Sarah came to the house the other day, and I heard them talk in the living room while I dusted the blinds. I remember the cautious way she folded her hands while speaking to Elizabeth.

"I can't believe he just left like that, with nothing but a simple note," I heard her say. Her voice sounded genuine, like she was concerned for Elizabeth.

"Are you really that surprised?" Elizabeth said. "I mean, I'm not. This is the only way he can get away from that mother of his."

It's a crisp afternoon, and I step off the paved path. The wind whistles through the nearby trees. I follow the sound and make my way to the bench where Sarah sits. She looks at me like I'm a stranger, but one she's expecting to meet. Her gentle smile is a beacon in the low hum of conversation.

I stop a moment before I sit. "I'm Marie," I say. "I clean for Mrs. Wilson. We met at her house?"

She looks up at me, then smiles. "Oh yeah, Marie. I remember you."

"Can I sit?"

"Of course."

I settle next to her, ensuring my posture is open yet unobtrusive. My hands in my lap, my head tilted just so. I lower my voice and lean in. "You're close with Mrs. Wilson, right?"

"Yes, we've been friends for a few years, ever since they came to the area. I brought her a basket of wine and fruit when they moved in, and we've been meeting up for coffee or wine every now and then, when possible."

"I'm worried about her. It's an awful thing what happened with Richard," I say. "He's such a nice man. They seemed like a good couple."

She shrugs. "Like most of us, they had their problems."

"You know, I've always sensed something unusual about Richard's closeness with his mother," I say, fishing for her reaction. Her eyes remain steady on mine, measuring and weighing me as I speak. "It's like there's an intensity there that goes well beyond typical familial concern. It must bother Elizabeth. I know it would be hard for me to deal with."

"Absolutely," she says, her gaze drifting toward a delicate rose bush. "I remember the last charity auction we attended. There was an awkward heaviness in the way they interacted. Completely leaving Elizabeth out of their conversation, ignoring her. Made me feel bad for her. It's like those two speak a language she doesn't even know." Her voice wraps around me, and I listen closely for each subtle cue, every inflection and unspoken pause. I nod along, careful to keep the rhythm of our words in tune.

"To be honest, I always thought their relationship was a little strange," she tells me, her words carried in the thick afternoon air. "There's something odd about a mother being so obsessed with her son after he's married and gone, right? It's like she refuses to let go of him."

So, I'm not the only one thinking this way. My gaze remains steady on her, my body language as unthreatening as I can make it. I know I shouldn't be speaking to Sarah, but I need to find out who I can trust: Elizabeth or Jane. "And then there's Elizabeth —she's been so guarded, so careful in her own way. She seems lonely. Do you think she has anyone to talk to, besides us?"

A brief pause, and my heart holds its breath. She follows with a hesitant laugh, "I don't think I should be talking to her cleaning lady about details like that."

I laugh along with her, the sound awkward but convincing.

"Of course not. I went too far. I'm just curious."

Her next words arrive in a candid whisper that sends a chill of revelation through me. "To be honest, I wouldn't blame her for seeing someone else. Richard cheated on her too."

"Really?" I say.

"Oh yes," she continues, her certainty growing. "Their relationship has struggled ever since. Elizabeth found it hard to forgive him, whereas I do believe the mom protected him and said boys will be boys."

The longer we speak, the more the words pour from her, the more it feels like the beginning of something, the unraveling of a long, tangled thread. As our conversation deepens, the sounds of the playground—children's playful shouts, the rustling leaves —become a strange soundtrack to the peculiar incidents and subtle cues we exchange. With each revelation, a question gnaws at my mind: have I trusted Jane wrongly all this time? The thought weighs heavily on my conscience, especially as I consider the implications for Elizabeth. If I've misjudged Jane, I might have unwittingly put Elizabeth at risk by passing on sensitive information.

"Richard loves these glasses," Elizabeth says later the same day as we polish crystal, and I can't stop thinking about the first time I stood by this dining room with Jane. How it all started. I never imagined the woman Jane hated would be helping me clean her own house. My hands tremble, but Elizabeth's do not. We are as alone and together as two people can be.

"Do you miss him?" I ask. I set the glass aside and reach for another, hands quick and unsteady, attempting to match the even pace of her careful movements.

Elizabeth doesn't respond immediately. She crosses and uncrosses her legs, but the graceful motion can't hide the quiet sorrow that leaks into her voice.

"No, that was a silly question," I say. "Of course you do."

"No, it's okay. I don't mind your question. Yes, I miss him deeply," she says, but there's no emotion in her voice. "I feel as though a part of me is missing every single day. I know we had our issues, but he's still my husband."

"Naturally."

Marie and Elizabeth. I see us from a distance, our conversation a private whisper in the expanse of this extravagant space. Elizabeth would normally be immersed in planning her next charity event, organizing every detail with her characteristic flair. Lately, though, her usual activities have been overshadowed by the unsettling absence of Richard. She's taken time off work. She was supposed to go away, visiting her 'sister', but she said she couldn't go with Richard gone. She canceled her doctor's appointment, the reminder card still pinned to the fridge, untouched. Instead, her days are consumed with phone calls to the police, her voice steady yet tinged with desperation. She has spoken to Richard's colleagues, her inquiries met with sympathetic yet unyielding responses. Friends have visited, offering words of comfort, while she fields an endless stream of calls, each one a potential thread of hope or despair. The aura of her vibrant social life now dimmed, replaced by a pervasive sense of uncertainty and concern.

Her long, measured pause weighs the air around us. The shadows of old betrayals begin to rise, flickering in the dim light. "When Richard cheated," she says, each word carrying the weight of my suspicions, "Jane protected him. She said it was me that was at fault. That I wasn't enough of a wife for him."

The room feels full of ghosts. The light catches the crystal we polish, casting fractured rainbows that seem to dance with the specters of the past.

"I feel it every day. His betrayal. Jane's blame. It never leaves," she says, her voice a whisper that echoes through the room like a haunting melody. "I've been trying to find out more about who he was having an affair with," Elizabeth continues, her determination tinged with a hint of desperation. "I've heard whispers from friends, snippets from colleagues. Detective Mitchell called earlier. He said he's closing the case, but I can't let it rest. I need to know the truth."

Her words drift into the silence, mingling with the shadows and the secrets they hold.

I glance at her, careful to hold her gaze, afraid of what I'll find if I look too closely. She returns the look with soft eyes, but I don't know whether to see them as filled with certainty or regret.

"Did Jane ever say anything to you?" Elizabeth asks, holding a crystal glass to the light. Her unsteadiness appears in the furrow of her brow and the lines that crease her forehead.

The graceful, statuesque figure no longer entirely composed. "About me?"

The question startles me. I can't lie to Elizabeth. I nod, my hand brushing against hers as I reach for a fresh polishing cloth. The contact feels intimate, immediate. As if it contains the distance between us, the deepening sense that something important is unfolding here.

"Like what?" she asks. "Did she ask you to keep an eye on me for her?"

A nervous laugh slips out before I can stop it. I see myself, a flash of movement in the reflection of the large bay window. I'm waiting for her laughter too, and as it finally erupts, it's a great relief. "I'm sorry," I say, my voice breaking with the effort to hold it together. "It's just—well it feels almost like we're in a soap opera." I hear the incredulity echoing around us, filling the ornate room. "Why would she ask that?"

"Because she thinks I might be seeing someone else, I guess? For all I know, she probably believes that's why I wanted to get rid of Richard."

Elizabeth sets the glass down carefully. Her slender fingers tap against the mahogany coffee table, keeping time with her thoughts. "Do you believe her, Marie?" she asks, as if searching for the honesty she claims to find in me. "Do you think I'm seeing someone else?"

A swell of emotion fills the room, rising through the plush antique furniture and into the elaborate chandelier. I feel its intensity as it crashes down around me. My hesitation must show. It's more than I intend to reveal.

Elizabeth leans back, lets out a slow breath. Her certainty softens into resignation. "I don't know what to believe," she admits. "I don't know if I even trust myself to know any more."

We continue polishing, and the repetitive motion, the quiet intimacy, eases the tension between us. I allow myself to hope that this is a turning point, that her newfound vulnerability is a sign that she believes in me. I allow myself to hope.

I pause in my work, my fingers tracing the intricate patterns of a glass vase.

"I trust you," Elizabeth says suddenly, the unexpected confession landing like a blow. "I do. I trust you more than her." Her eyes find mine, and her lips pull into a small, genuine smile.

Her words surprise me. They take hold of me and fill me with a mixture of hope and fear. I like that she trusts me. I want her to. I like her. I like her more than I like Jane.

"You can trust me," I say, sounding surprisingly certain.

EIGHT

JANE

I can almost smell Richard's hugs in the air, the way they lingered long after he let go. His bedroom stands untouched since he disappeared. I remember our conversation a few months ago, sitting on the porch swing, the sun setting behind us.

"Elizabeth and I haven't slept in the same room since the affair," he confessed. I could see the pain etched on his face, a mixture of regret and longing. That moment stays with me, a vivid reminder of the rift that had grown between them. I always thought my sweet, sensitive boy would find someone to love him, and had accepted Elizabeth because I thought she would make him happy. Even if she wasn't my choice of bride. How wrong I had been.

I touch his shirt to my face, breathe it in.

I spot movement outside. Detective Mitchell's car rolls up the drive, and I watch from the window as he gets out. He heads toward the kitchen.

My hand trembles, a small betrayal of my nerves, before I take a deep breath to steady it and make my way downstairs. The stairs creak under my weight, echoing in the otherwise silent house. I settle into the plush armchair in the living room, my eyes scanning the patterns in the rug beneath my feet, while I wait. The detective is in the adjoining room, his low voice carrying as he questions Elizabeth. I insisted he come, to probe into the details of this mysterious lover of hers. The detective's demeanor had hinted at his skepticism, and I could sense his frustration with the situation. He even told me he had closed the case, but I told him to reopen it. That new evidence had come to light. I told him what Marie told me, and I reminded him who I was and especially who my husband was. He told me that my social standing and my veiled threats to leverage meant little to him. Yet he still came. My phone call to the chief earlier probably helped him change his mind.

But the interview doesn't last long. Suddenly, Mitchell appears in the living room, his eyes searching my face.

"How did it go?" I ask.

He sits down across from me and takes out his notepad.

"How are you holding up? Mrs. Wilson told me you've been visiting every day?" He leans back, casual as an old friend.

"And will continue to until my son returns."

"That's quite a commitment."

I nod, adjust my grip on the shirt. "I've always been committed."

"And Elizabeth? You two getting along?"

"She's my daughter-in-law," I say, but my tone answers the question he really asked.

"Still no word from him?"

"Not since he vanished." The word has more bite than I intend. "Might I ask why you're here, talking to me? I thought you came to talk to her. I told you she has a violent past, and a lover, a motive to get rid of my son. Did you ask her about this? Isn't that why you are here?"

His pen scratches at the page. "Is it?"

"Are you talking to me so you can rule me out?" I say, allowing myself a smile.

"Would that be wise?" he asks, his pen pausing mid-word.

"You know as well as I do how these things look." I meet his eyes, unblinking. "Family tensions. Estrangement. It all makes for a good story."

"And this is all just a story?" His eyebrows rise, a small signal flare.

"A bad one, and I'll be relieved when you find the proper ending."

"And you're certain you had nothing to do with it?" His tone changes, ever so slightly.

"Is that what she told you?" I feel my composure slip for a moment, but he doesn't pounce.

"I hear different things from different people," he says. "You are protective of Richard, aren't you? Always have been?"

"Is that a crime?"

"Sometimes it can be," he says, not missing a beat.

"Then perhaps you should arrest Elizabeth first," I suggest.

"An interesting angle," he replies. "You've been protective of your son for a long time. Before he even married Elizabeth, if I'm not mistaken."

I hold his gaze. I know exactly what he is talking about, what Elizabeth has told him. Trying to make me look bad. Me. The only one who truly cares for Richard. "Not every mother would pay off a girl to stay away from their boy. Just the committed ones."

"Amanda Gibson. Karen Schultz. Terri Matheson." The names come out rapid fire, shots at a firing range.

"And your point?"

"My point is, you've driven away a lot of people, Mrs. Wilson. Girlfriends that your son liked, maybe even loved?"

"You have no idea what kind of women they were," I tell

him. "I did what was necessary. For my son's sake. He didn't know what was best for him. I did."

"And Elizabeth? Was that a necessary marriage?"

"That's a question for Richard, not me." I shift, the wood of the chair biting into my shoulder blade. "They got married behind my back. She tricked him, wound him around her little finger. He'll do anything she asks for. It's so pathetic."

"Sounds like you're jealous?"

"Of her? Nonsense. I'm his mother. No one can ever take my place. They're just married. That's why we invented divorce."

"So, you didn't approve of them getting married?" he presses. "Maybe you still don't."

"What I think doesn't matter. Richard made his choice, and I accepted it."

"Not according to Elizabeth," he says. "She seems to think you have it out for her."

"And you believe her?" I ask, not hiding my scorn.

He scribbles something down. "I think she seems scared. Of you."

"She should be," I say.

"Why?"

I say nothing. It's a hollow exchange when silence can do all the talking.

"Thank you for your time," Mitchell says, standing up slowly, like he might sit back down. "I'll be back with more questions," he says, giving me a nod as he leaves.

I sit there, alone, the house breathing around me. I close my eyes for a moment, let the silence swell. It sounds different with each passing day, like it's trying to tell me something new. I open my eyes, hear the words the detective said in my mind.

"Family tensions. Estrangement. Protective of Richard." I whisper them like a prayer, let them drift back down where they came from.

They have no idea. I grip Richard's shirt tighter. I miss him.

I sit, watchful, Richard's shirt like a doll in my lap. I hear Elizabeth's voice. I'm sure of it. She is talking, it seems, to everyone except me. I step into the hall, and their conversation becomes clear. It's Marie she's confiding in. They seem very close now. Is it too close? I slump against the wall, the reality a weight I can no longer hold up. Is this what Elizabeth planned?

Elizabeth is speaking too softly. I don't like it. Her voice has the wrong note of confidence. Like she's whispering secrets to the help. "She knows what she's doing," she says. "I'm not sure I do any more." She's not talking about herself. I'm certain of that.

Marie's response is low, soothing. "You're doing exactly what you should. Everything's under control." She doesn't sound like a cleaning lady.

I move closer to the door, their figures becoming clear as I watch from a side angle. Marie leans in, her head tilted as if sharing a secret. Elizabeth glances nervously in my direction. I step back, hold my breath.

"I'm sure Richard is safe somewhere," Marie says.

"But the police, I don't like how they come here and insinuate that I somehow hurt him. I think it's all her plan."

"Jane?"

"Yes. She's had it in for me since the beginning. This is her way of getting rid of me. I'm sure of it. She is behind it all. She's the one who is hiding him somewhere, maybe so she can be alone with him at last. Their relationship was never healthy. She's trying to blame this all on me, I'm telling you."

I hear Elizabeth, the false tremor in her voice. How quickly she moves from panic to reassurance. I can barely watch. Their easy conversation, as though I'm no longer a part of their world. Or at least I'm the enemy. My nails dig into my palms, the pain an anchor. I step away, go back to Richard's room, let them think I'm not onto their betrayal.

I close the door without a sound, just in case they can hear me. Just in case it alerts them to how much I already know. Marie is calling her employer "Richard" now. She must think they're equals.

The thought exhausts me, all its implications. I rest my head in my hands, close my eyes until the spinning stops. I was the one who told her to get close to Elizabeth, to find out what she knows.

Maybe this was Elizabeth's plan all along, to divide and conquer. Marie seems more loyal to her every day. And if Mitchell believes them, so will everyone else. He seemed very skeptical of me, more so than her. Why is that? Did she poison his mind against me? Did she do the same to Marie?

The shirt is back in my grip. I didn't even notice reaching for it. Richard, if you can hear me, I love you like no one else can. Elizabeth doesn't love you. She's having an affair, I'm certain of it. I can tell by looking in her eyes. I see the guilt. She's happy you're gone. I knew she would be. She's happy to be rid of you so she can be with her new lover. She just wants the money. My money. But I will make sure she doesn't get it. I have found secrets in her past before, and I will continue to dig till I get the entire truth of who she really is. I have sent my private investigator to Tallahassee and am waiting for him to report back any moment now. I have tasked him with finding the ex-husband, so I can finally get to the bottom of who she really is. After what she did to him, I'm sure he has lots to tell.

I look at the closed door, half expecting Marie and Elizabeth to come through it any second. A glimpse of me in this state, and they'll know they're winning. They'll know their plan is working. But I have a plan of my own, a strategy they won't expect. Richard and I belong together. We will always be together. I will find him.

I've already begun my search. I've spoken to several of his colleagues, probing for any hint of his whereabouts. I've spent hours at his office, sifting through paperwork and scrutinizing every corner for clues. I've approached the therapist Richard and Elizabeth saw, but she won't speak to me. I even drove to the beach house, hoping for a trace of him there, a forgotten shirt or a note left behind. I was in a hurry so only checked the master bedroom, but that's where his things would be if he was there, I figured. I had asked Marie to snoop around the safe in their Cypress Estates house for any evidence, but that lead fizzled out. Now, I'm considering hiring the same private investigator Richard once used to uncover Elizabeth's past. I will make them see.

One day, they'll all see.

NINE

MARIE

The single bulb overhead stutters, casting erratic shadows across my collection of notebooks. I sit cross-legged on the floor of my apartment—a generous term for this cramped single room with its peeling wallpaper and constant smell of mildew. Tears blur my vision as I flip through pages of detailed observations: "Elizabeth woke at 6:43 a.m. Tea instead of coffee. Wore the blue sweater again. Third time this week. Called someone at 7:15, speaking in hushed tones." My handwriting is neat, detached. The words of someone who has made a career of watching without being seen.

I trace my fingers over a sentence I'd underlined three times: "Elizabeth cried in the garden for seventeen minutes after Jane left. Kept looking at photo on her phone."

The memory returns with painful clarity—Elizabeth's shoulders shaking as she perched on the stone bench among Jane's prized roses, her face a mask of raw grief. I'd watched from behind the hedge, documenting her pain for Jane's consumption.

My stomach twists with shame. Seven notebooks filled with Elizabeth's private moments, her vulnerabilities cataloged and delivered to Jane. All for what? Money. Security. The chance to exist in the periphery of wealth that would never be mine.

"I'm sorry," I whisper to the empty room, to Elizabeth's ghost that haunts these pages.

Three weeks before Richard went missing, things changed. I'd been dusting the library shelves when Elizabeth entered, not noticing me—the invisible help—in the corner. She sank into the leather armchair and pulled her knees to her chest, making herself small, vulnerable. Then came the phone call.

"I can't keep doing this," she'd said into her cell phone, voice cracking. "I'm afraid she knows. Jane is watching me. I need a way out."

I'd frozen, feather duster suspended in midair, hardly breathing. The raw desperation in her voice stirred something in me I thought had died long ago—empathy. Recognition. I knew what it was to be stalked, to be accused, to be afraid.

Later that week, I'd found Elizabeth alone in the kitchen, staring into a glass of water. Our eyes met, and for once, she truly saw me.

"Do you ever feel like you're drowning, Marie?" she'd asked, her voice soft. Not the voice of employer to employee, but one broken person to another.

I should have nodded and excused myself. Instead, I sat down across from her.

"Every day," I'd answered.

She'd smiled then—a small, sad thing—and for a moment, we were just two women sharing the weight of secrets too heavy to carry alone.

Now, I gather the notebooks into a pile, my decision crystallizing. I can't be Jane's eyes any more. I can't keep betraying the only person in that house who's shown me genuine humanity.

I retrieve the metal trash can from beside my makeshift desk and place it in the center of the room, away from anything flammable. My hands shake as I find the matches I keep for my single luxury—scented candles that briefly mask the damp smell of my living quarters.

One by one, I rip pages from the notebooks and drop them into the can. Each sheet represents a betrayal, a moment stolen from Elizabeth's life and handed to Jane on a silver platter. The first match flares to life between my fingers, a tiny sun against the dimness.

"I'm done being Jane's puppet," I whisper as I drop the match.

The paper catches quickly, curling and blackening at the edges. Orange flames lick upward, consuming my sins. A strange lightness fills my chest as I watch the fire grow, eating through months of surveillance. The acrid smell of burning paper fills the small room, but I don't open a window. Let it suffocate me. Let it cleanse me.

I'm so entranced by the flames that the sudden trill of my phone is a distant echo. The pages of my notebook crackle in the wastebasket, bright orange tongues dancing across my secrets. My phone buzzes again, more insistent this time, slicing through the haze.

I snatch it off the table. The screen reads UNKNOWN CALLER.

"Hello?" My voice trembles.

A rough, impatient male voice answers. "Marie." He pauses, as if savoring the moment. "We need the money."

I press the phone closer to my ear, heat from the trash can painting flickering shadows on the walls. "I-I don't know what you mean."

"Don't play dumb." Another voice, deeper and harsher, cracks through. "Carl said you'd try to stonewall us."

Carl. The name hits me like a punch. My ex-husband—the one who vanished two years ago, leaving me with empty accounts and maxed-out cards.

"I haven't heard from him in years," I manage, edging away

from the inferno in the can. "I don't know where he is or what he's done."

"Not our problem," the second voice says. "Carl borrowed twenty thousand from us. Interest's bumped it up to thirty. You've got seven days, Marie, or next time he won't be the only one who disappears."

My chest tightens. "I don't have that kind of money. The debt isn't mine—Carl took everything when he left."

Silence. Then the harsh inhale of breath, like he's tasting the fear on the line. "We'll be back in touch. Don't try anything clever. We always find what we're looking for."

The click of a hang-up.

The dial tone hums in my ear. I drop the phone, my knees hitting the floor. I press my palm to my pounding chest, the firelight catching my tears as I realize there's nowhere to hide, and no one coming to save me. I have to get the money, somehow.

The single bulb continues to flicker overhead.

I curl into myself on the floor, each breath painful. The room tilts and spins as memories flood back of him. Carl. His name alone still has the power to hollow me out, to reduce me to the shell I became in those final months together. Five years ago, I was different. Before the debts. Before the lies. Before I learned that love could be the sharpest weapon of all.

I met Carl at the Westbrook Annual Charity Gala, where I was working as a server. The venue glittered with wealth—crystal chandeliers, women draped in diamonds, men in tailored suits that cost more than my monthly rent. I moved between them with skilled invisibility, balancing trays of champagne flutes.

"You missed a spot," a voice said, warm and teasing.

I turned, startled, to find a man watching me. Not one of the wealthy donors, but not staff either. He occupied that comfortable middle space—well-dressed but not ostentatiously so, confident but approachable.

"Excuse me?" I said, clutching my empty tray.

He smiled, pointing to a champagne drop on my sleeve. "Just there. Hazard of the job, I imagine."

I should have nodded politely and moved on. Instead, I found myself smiling back. "Occupational hazard. Like paper cuts for office workers or..." I paused, studying him. "What is it you do?"

"Financial consulting," he said, extending his hand. "Carl Dawson."

His palm was warm against mine, his grip firm but not dominating. "Marie," I replied, not offering my last name. Staff weren't supposed to fraternize with guests.

"Marie," he repeated, as if testing how my name felt on his tongue. "When do you get off work tonight, Marie?"

Two weeks later, he brought roses to my apartment—not the predictable red, but a dozen in sunset orange that matched the scarf I'd worn on our first date. "They reminded me of you," he said, pressing his lips to my forehead. "Unusual. Beautiful."

Carl noticed things. The way I tucked my hair behind my ear when nervous. How I preferred the corner table at restaurants to watch people. My habit of collecting small, smooth stones from places I'd visited. He made me feel seen in a way I hadn't been since childhood—before I learned that being noticed often led to being hurt.

"You're different," he told me one night, his fingers tracing patterns on my bare shoulder as we lay in bed. "Most people are so wrapped up in themselves. You actually observe. You understand."

I preened under his praise, never suspecting that what he admired was precisely what would make me valuable to Jane years later.

The first sign came six months in—a stack of betting slips tucked into his pocket, discovered as I was hanging his coat in my closet. When confronted, Carl laughed it off.

"Just a hobby, baby. A group of us from work have a friendly pool going. Nothing serious."

I believed him because I wanted to. Because his smile still made my stomach flip, because he brought me thoughtful gifts and remembered every anniversary, because he called me his "little spy" with such affection when I noticed things about strangers in restaurants.

Then came the credit card bills. The missed rent payments. The increasingly elaborate explanations for why we needed to dip into my savings "just until next month." Each transgression was followed by such genuine-seeming remorse, such passionate promises to change.

"I'm getting help," he'd say, his eyes brimming with tears that never quite fell. "I swear, Marie. This is the last time."

It never was.

The memory that burns brightest came thirteen months into our relationship. I'd discovered our joint account emptied—five thousand dollars gone, money I'd been saving for years before Carl. I confronted him in our kitchen, my hands shaking as I held the bank statement.

"It's just a temporary setback," he said, his expression morphing from the man I loved to someone I barely recognized. His charm vanished, replaced by something hard and calculating. "I'll win it all back!"

"You're sick," I whispered, backing away from him. "You need help."

"What I need," he snarled, snatching the statement from my hands, "is a girlfriend who supports me instead of attacking me when I'm down."

I stared at him, suddenly seeing with perfect clarity how his manipulations had worked on me. How I'd been trained, like one of Pavlov's dogs, to anticipate his needs, to walk on eggshells around his moods, to blame myself for his failures.

"I want you out," I said, surprising myself with my steadiness.

His laugh was ugly. "Out? This is my apartment too, baby. My name's on the lease. And who's going to pay the rent if I leave? You, with your little waitressing job?"

The final blow came two weeks later. I woke to find his side of the bed empty, his closet cleared out. On the kitchen counter, he'd left his key and a note:

Sorry it didn't work out. Good luck with the bills.

By then, there was nothing left to take—he'd already emptied our accounts, maxed out credit cards in my name, even pawned my grandmother's locket while I was at work. What I didn't realize until debt collectors started calling was that he'd also taken out loans using my information, my good credit history.

Now, five years later, I'm still paying for loving him.

I push myself up from the floor. The room sways as I crawl toward the bathroom, leaving handprints in the ashes of my burned notebooks.

The fluorescent bathroom light is harsh, revealing every detail of my reflection without mercy. My eyes are those of a hunted animal—wide, glassy with fear.

"Thirty thousand dollars," I whisper to my reflection. The number is impossible. My salary from the Wilsons is generous for household staff, but most goes to paying down Carl's old debts. What little I save each month would take years to reach that amount.

Unless.

Jane's words from last week echo in my mind: *You've been invaluable, Marie. Your observations about Elizabeth have confirmed my suspicions. There will be a substantial bonus for you when this is all resolved.*

A substantial bonus. Jane Wilson doesn't think in small amounts.

"I need Jane's money," I tell my reflection, my voice raspy. "I have no choice."

Elizabeth's face flashes in my mind—her quiet dignity, her haunted eyes when she thinks no one is watching. In that moment by the kitchen window, when she asked if I ever felt like I was drowning, I'd recognized a kindred spirit. Someone else trapped in circumstances not entirely of her making.

But thirty thousand dollars in one week.

My shoulders slump as the reality of my situation settles like a weight around my neck. I will have to continue reporting to Jane. I will have to keep watching Elizabeth, documenting her movements, her conversations, her private moments of despair.

I will have to betray the only person in that house who has shown me a shred of human kindness.

I splash cold water on my face. The decision feels like swallowing glass, but it's made. Survival first. Morality is a luxury for people who don't have men with scarred faces threatening to kill them.

Tomorrow, I'll go back to the Wilson estate. I'll resume my role as Jane's perfect, invisible spy. I'll rebuild the trust I've cultivated with Elizabeth, all while documenting her secrets for Jane's consumption.

And I'll hate myself with every carefully recorded word, while looking for a way out of this.

TEN

JANE

I grip the steering wheel too tightly, my knuckles white against the black leather as I drive through the dappled sunlight of the Cypress Estates. The perfectly manicured lawns and towering oak trees mock the chaos in my mind. It's been thirteen days since Richard disappeared—thirteen days of unanswered calls, police reports filed with reluctant officers, and Elizabeth's infuriatingly composed voice telling me not to worry. My son doesn't just vanish. Someone knows something. The thought circles in my head like a vulture as Spanish moss sways in the afternoon breeze, casting shifting shadows across my windshield.

The neighborhood is quiet for a Saturday. Too quiet. I don't live on the same street as my son, but I always take the road past their house on my way home. I've been driving these streets every day, searching for what, I'm not sure—a sign, perhaps, or some clue the police overlooked. The detectives keep saying there's no evidence of foul play, that successful men sometimes need a break from their lives.

But they don't know Richard like I do.

I round the corner toward Richard and Elizabeth's house,

my eyes automatically scanning their driveway out of habit. I expect to see it empty, like the hollow shell their home has become in my son's absence. Instead, I slam on my brakes.

A line of luxury vehicles stretches down the street—a silver Bentley, two BMWs, a Range Rover with custom wheels, parked like shiny tokens of wealth leading directly to my daughter-in-law's doorstep.

"What on earth is going on?" I whisper to the empty car.

My pulse quickens as I crawl past, peering through the passenger window. The front of the house looks presentable, as always—Elizabeth never lets appearances slip. A valet in a red vest stands at attention near the grand entrance, checking his watch with experienced nonchalance.

The realization blooms inside me like an ink drop in water, spreading its darkness through my veins.

A party. She's hosting a party.

I park haphazardly across the street, not bothering to straighten between the lines. My hands are suddenly cold, but I feel a warmth in my chest, an uncomfortable heat that I recognize as rage.

The walk to the house feels endless. Each step on the herringbone brick pathway tightens the knot in my stomach. The closer I get, the more I hear it—laughter floating from the backyard, the delicate clink of expensive crystal, the gentle notes of a string quartet playing something classical and utterly inappropriate.

I don't bother with the front door. I follow the sounds around the side of the house, past the pruned hydrangeas that Richard planted last spring because Elizabeth insisted blue flowers would complement the facade. My son, who couldn't tell a hydrangea from a hosta, spent a weekend digging in the dirt to please her, because the gardener wouldn't be there till after the weekend, and Elizabeth had to have them in the yard *now*.

The backyard opens before me like a theater stage set for a production I wasn't invited to attend. White linen-covered tables dot the expansive lawn. Ice sculptures catch the afternoon sun, sending prisms of light dancing across the gathering. Men in summer suits and women in designer dresses cluster in small groups, their faces animated with the kind of carefree joy that feels like a personal insult.

A banner hangs between two oak trees:

CYPRESS ESTATES CHILDREN'S HOSPITAL BENEFIT

Children's Hospital! As if she cares about children. She couldn't even give Richard one, despite his gentle hints about wanting a family. Something cold and hard forms in my throat.

"Would you like some champagne, ma'am?" A young server in a white jacket appears at my elbow, offering a tray of flutes filled with bubbling liquid.

"No," I say, not looking at him. My eyes are scanning the crowd, hunting.

And then I see her.

Elizabeth stands near the rose garden, a vision in pale blue silk that makes her blonde hair shine like polished gold in the sunlight. Her posture is perfect—shoulders back, chin lifted at just the right angle to appear interested but not eager as she listens to a silver-haired man gesturing with his drink. She laughs at something he says, a practiced sound that reaches her lips but not her eyes.

I've always been able to see through her performance. Richard never could.

She turns, giving instructions to a staff member, her manicured hand making a graceful gesture toward the bar area. Her diamond bracelet—Richard's fifth anniversary gift to her— catches the light. Not a hint of worry lines her face. Not a suggestion that her husband is missing. Not a single visible sign that her world isn't perfectly, infuriatingly intact.

My body moves before my mind can catch up. I'm cutting across the lawn, past startled guests who glance at my casual clothes—I didn't bother changing out of jeans and a blouse for my daily search—with subtle disapproval.

"Elizabeth." Her name comes out sharper than I intended, slicing through the pleasant conversation around her.

She turns, her expression shifting from hostess smile to careful neutrality when she sees me. "Oh. Hello. I didn't realize you'd be joining us today."

The silver-haired man and his companion exchange glances and discreetly step away, sensing the sudden shift in atmosphere.

"Joining you?" My voice rises despite my attempt to control it. "Is that what you think this is? A social call?"

Elizabeth's eyes dart around, assessing who might be watching. Always concerned with appearances. "Perhaps we should talk inside."

"How can you stand here, looking like that, when Richard is missing?" I hiss, loud enough for nearby guests to hear. The words feel hot in my mouth, burning to be released.

Her perfect composure cracks, just a little. A tightening around the eyes, a brief compression of those expensively glossed lips.

"This event has been planned for months," she says quietly. "The hospital committee—"

"I don't give a damn about your committee!" The nearby conversations halt. A waiter freezes mid-pour. "My son is gone, and you're throwing a party like nothing's wrong."

"It's not a party, it's a fundraiser," she corrects me, her voice still measured but strain beginning to show. "And lower your voice, please."

"Lower my voice? Are you embarrassed? Worried what

your friends will think when they realize you haven't bothered to look for your husband?"

Elizabeth takes a step closer, her eyes like blue ice. "That's not fair. I've been cooperating fully with the police. They told us—"

"Us? There is no 'us' here. He's my son," I say, my voice rising with each word. "Mine. You could never understand him the way I do."

The silence that follows feels physical, a weight pressing down on the manicured lawn. Guests have stopped pretending not to listen. The string quartet has paused between pieces, leaving my words to hang in the still air.

Elizabeth stares at me, something complicated moving behind her eyes—hurt, anger, and something else I can't name. For a moment, I see the crack in her perfect veneer, a glimpse of genuine emotion that makes me almost regret my words. Almost.

"Richard is *my* husband," she says finally. "Don't you ever forget that. And I am dealing with his absence in my own way."

"By ignoring it? By pretending everything's fine?"

"By not falling apart." Her voice drops lower, meant only for me now. "Unlike some people."

The implied criticism stings more than I care to admit. I open my mouth to respond but notice the circle of onlookers that has formed around us—wealthy neighbors and friends of Elizabeth's, their expressions ranging from embarrassed fascination to thinly veiled judgment.

And then I see her—Marie, the cleaning woman—standing near the kitchen door. Unlike the others, she doesn't pretend not to watch. Her eyes are fixed on us with an intensity that feels inappropriate for household staff. She doesn't flinch when I catch her gaze; instead, she tilts her head, as if analyzing the scene from multiple angles. There's something in her expression—not quite sympathy, not quite curiosity, but a calculating interest that sends an unexpected chill down my spine.

Elizabeth follows my gaze, sees Marie watching, and makes a small, dismissive gesture with her hand. The cleaning woman doesn't move immediately, her eyes lingering on me for a beat too long before she retreats into the house.

"I think you should leave," Elizabeth says quietly, her voice steady though her cheeks are still flushed with emotion. Her attempt to maintain composure is evident, even as the tension lingers. "You're upset, understandably so. You're making people very uncomfortable. This isn't helping Richard."

"And this is?" I retort, sweeping my arm dramatically to encompass the entire gathering. The area is filled with the murmur of hushed conversations, with guests casting curious glances in our direction. "This charade?"

For a brief moment, I catch sight of a couple of familiar faces among the crowd, their expressions a mixture of concern and judgment. A pang of self-awareness tugs at me, and I lower my voice. My eyes flicker down to my jeans, the fabric now feeling tight and constricting. A small part of me recognizes the truth in Elizabeth's words; the realization that I might be embarrassing the family settles uneasily in my mind.

"Life continues," she says simply, her voice steady and resolute. "The police are doing their job. Richard wouldn't want everything to stop because he's taken some... time away." She pauses, looking at me with a firm gaze, and adds, "Remember, I had already committed to all of this before Richard disappeared. I'm just continuing to fulfill my duties as a wife, as he would have wanted. It's important to keep things moving forward, for both of us."

The implication in her words—that Richard left voluntarily —feeds the fire in my chest. "He didn't just walk away. Something happened to him."

Elizabeth sighs, a sound so dismissive it makes my hands twitch with the urge to shake her. "We don't know that."

"I know my son."

"And I know my husband." Her eyes harden. "Perhaps better than you might think."

A challenge. What does she know that I don't? What secrets did Richard share with her that he kept from me? I don't believe her. He would never.

For a moment, doubt creeps in. Then I remember Richard's face the last time I saw him—distracted, tired, his smile not quite reaching his eyes when he kissed Elizabeth goodbye. He wasn't happy. And she either didn't notice or didn't care. I consider telling her what I know. That she's not who she says she is, that she's been married before and arrested for violence against her ex-husband. But I stop myself. My private investigator is still in Tallahassee, and I don't want to blow his cover or ruin his investigation. She can't know I'm digging into her past. She can't know he is there.

I've said enough. More than enough. The guests have heard, have seen Elizabeth's true colors—her callous disregard for Richard's absence, her determination to maintain social appearances at all costs. She will get what's coming for her. The truth will come out soon enough.

"Enjoy your party," I say, my voice dripping with disdain, as I glance around at the elegantly dressed crowd. My heart clenches with a mix of anger and humiliation, knowing I wasn't invited to this grand affair. The realization stings, and I can't help but wonder if Elizabeth orchestrated this deliberately. Did she ensure I looked scruffy and out of place in front of these important guests, to tarnish my image? Is this all part of her calculated plan?

As I turn on my heel, head held high despite my rumpled appearance, a thought gnaws at the back of my mind. Could Richard's sudden disappearance and my relentless search for him be playing into Elizabeth's hands? Is she using this situation to make me seem like I'm unraveling, losing my grip on reality? The pattern feels alarmingly familiar, echoing past moments when I've felt manipulated. I walk away, each step fueled by the burning need to prove Elizabeth wrong and find Richard before the whispers grow louder.

The crowd parts silently, no one quite meeting my eyes. I feel their stares on my back, hear the whispers begin before I'm out of earshot. Let them talk. Let them wonder why Elizabeth Wilson is hosting a charity event while her husband has vanished.

As I reach the side of the house, a movement catches my eye. Marie again, watching from an upstairs window, her unremarkable face unnervingly focused on my retreat. Our eyes meet briefly before she steps back from the glass, disappearing into the shadows of the house.

The encounter leaves me unsettled in a way I can't quite define. There was something in her gaze—recognition, perhaps, or understanding—that felt too intimate for a woman who simply cleans their floors. Was she watching me like she was supposed to be watching Elizabeth?

I push the thought aside as I walk to my car. My hands shake as I grip the door handle, the adrenaline of confrontation beginning to fade. In its place comes a strange mix of emotions —embarrassment at causing a scene, satisfaction at having exposed Elizabeth's callousness, and underneath it all, the constant, gnawing fear for Richard.

Why doesn't she care that Richard is missing? Why isn't she out there searching for him every minute of every day?

I slide into the driver's seat and start the engine, catching a glimpse of myself in the rearview mirror. My eyes are bright with unshed tears, my face flushed. I look unhinged, exactly how Elizabeth wants others to see me—the overprotective mother, unable to accept that her grown son might have reasons for disappearing that have nothing to do with her.

But she's wrong. Something has happened to Richard. I feel it in my bones, in the hollow space that's grown in my chest since the moment I realized he was gone.

As I pull away from the curb, I glance back at the house. The party continues, the moment of disruption already being smoothed over by Elizabeth's social graces and the distraction of free-flowing champagne. How quickly they forget.

But I won't forget. And I won't stop looking. Richard is my son, and I'll find him with or without his wife's help. Now all I have to do is wait for what my investigator finds out. Then I will have all I need to take her down.

The thought steadies me as I drive away, leaving behind the superficial concerns of the Cypress Estates for the real world where my son has vanished without a trace. In that world, parties don't matter.

Only Richard does.

ELEVEN
MARIE

I wasn't scheduled to be here this late, yet the debris from last night's party was overwhelming. Elizabeth expects me gone by 6 p.m., with the house left pristine and immaculate. But today, I've lingered, still scrubbing and tidying well into the evening, my rubber gloves clinging to my hands at a quarter past six. It's the stubborn rings left on the bathroom counters that have kept me here, or so I tell myself. In truth, I haven't finished yet, and Elizabeth will likely assume I've already departed.

The party was an exhausting affair, especially for Elizabeth, who had felt awful about hosting it in the first place. Despite everything going on in her life, she selflessly put herself last to ensure the evening went smoothly for her guests. As I cleaned, I couldn't help but think of her determination and grace. Elizabeth had orchestrated this event, not just as a social gathering, but as a strategic move to support Richard's business endeavors. She and Richard had discussed how this party could help him make crucial contacts in the industry, potentially opening doors that had previously remained shut. Her intentions were clear, and her resolve was admirable; she wanted nothing more than to see Richard succeed, even if it meant pushing her own needs aside.

The long hours of scrubbing seemed a small price to pay in comparison to what Elizabeth had gone through to make the event happen.

The bathroom gleams under the recessed lighting, all marble and chrome that I've polished to a mirror finish. My reflection fragments across the fixtures—a slice of mousy hair here, the curve of my unremarkable chin there. I've made myself invisible enough that she rarely notices when I'm present, let alone when I should be gone.

I run my fingertips along the edge of the claw-foot tub, checking for any residue. There isn't any. There hasn't been for the past twenty minutes, but I keep wiping anyway, ears attuned to the sounds of the house. The tick of the grandfather clock downstairs. The hum of the refrigerator. The subtle shifts of an empty home settling into evening.

When I hear the crunch of tires on the gravel driveway, I freeze. This must be the person who texted Elizabeth this morning about a late meeting. The message popped up while her phone lay on the counter as I wiped down the kitchen. I wasn't snooping, not really. The screen lit up and my eyes simply... registered the information.

Elizabeth is alone, having returned from her tennis lesson an hour ago. I heard her moving around downstairs, the gentle clink of ice in a glass, classical music turned low.

The car door closes with a soft thud rather than Richard's usual decisive slam. Still holding the cleaning cloth, I shift toward the bathroom window, angling myself to see without being seen. The evening sun casts long shadows across the manicured lawn, and through the filmy curtain, I make out a figure—tall, male, but definitely not Richard.

This man moves differently. Where Richard strides with purpose, this man approaches the house with an unhurried confidence, his leather jacket casually slung over one shoulder. It's him again. The same guy.

I let the curtain fall back into place and slip off my rubber gloves, placing them silently beside the sink. My shoes are already off—I always work in stockinged feet, both for comfort and for the quiet it affords me. Moving to the hallway, I position myself at the top of the stairs, where the angle allows me to see the foyer without being visible from below.

The doorbell doesn't ring. Instead, there's a pattern of knocks—three soft, one firm. A code, perhaps. A familiar signal.

Elizabeth appears in my limited field of vision, moving with a grace I've always admired and resented. Her blonde hair falls loose now, not in its usual controlled twist. She's still in her tennis clothes—white skirt, fitted top—but there's nothing athletic in the way she approaches the door. Her movements have a deliberate quality, like an actress who knows she's being watched.

When she opens the door, the change in her is immediate and startling. The careful poise she maintains around Richard, around me, around everyone melts away. Her face transforms with a smile I've never seen before—unguarded, genuine. She steps back, allowing him to enter, and they embrace in the foyer.

It's not the brief, perfunctory hug of acquaintances. His arms encircle her fully, one hand splayed against her back, the other cradling her head. She fits against him easily, her body relaxing into his as if returning to a familiar shape. They hold the embrace long enough that I feel an uncomfortable heat rising in my cheeks—embarrassment, or something else I don't care to examine.

When they finally separate, their hands linger on each other, reluctant to break contact completely. In the slanted evening light, I catalog details with the exactitude that comes from years of observing: his light hair neatly trimmed but with a wayward curl at his temple; the crisp white of his shirt contrasting with sun-browned skin at his throat; the way Elizabeth's fingers trace a path down his arm before reluctantly letting go.

"It's so good to see you. I wasn't sure you could make it," she says, her voice carrying up the stairs in the quiet house. It's her voice but transformed—warmer, lower, with none of the controlled pleasantness she uses with Richard or the polite disinterest she directs at me.

"I managed to rearrange some things," he replies, and even in these few words, I detect an accent I can't quite place. "It's been too long."

I shift to maintain my vantage point as they move toward the kitchen, their bodies oriented toward each other like compass needles finding north. Their arms brush as they walk, and at one point, his hand finds the small of her back in a gesture so natural it must have happened countless times before.

Something twists in my stomach—not quite envy, not quite judgment, but a complicated blend of both. I've spent three months in this house, cleaning their spaces, observing their lives, collecting the small details they think no one notices. I've seen Elizabeth and Richard grow increasingly distant, occupying the same enormous house like strangers in a hotel. I've wiped Richard's lipstick-stained tumblers after late nights, knowing the shade doesn't match anything in Elizabeth's carefully organized vanity. Their marriage has been failing in plain sight, at least to anyone paying attention. And now Richard is gone. Has been away for two weeks.

But this—this is different. The Elizabeth walking beside this stranger isn't the cool, controlled woman who instructs me about special cleaning products for the marble or leaves rigorous notes about dinner party preparations. This Elizabeth moves differently, inhabits her body differently. She seems both younger and more fully herself, her hand briefly catching his, fingers intertwining for a stolen moment before they reach the kitchen doorway.

My throat tightens with something that might be disapproval or might be something more complicated. I know things about the Wilsons that they don't realize. Things I have kept even from Jane. I know that Richard keeps a separate phone in his briefcase that Elizabeth doesn't know about. I know that Elizabeth takes twice the prescribed dose of her anxiety medication on days when Jane visits. I know that they haven't shared a bedroom in at least the past year, though they maintain the fiction when company is present.

As they disappear into the kitchen, I hesitate at my perch at the top of the stairs. The responsible thing would be to quietly gather my cleaning supplies and leave, pretending I was never here. That's what they pay me for—thoroughness and discretion, presence without existence.

But curiosity—or something darker—pulls me down the stairs, one careful step at a time. My stockinged feet make no sound on the hardwood. Years of moving through homes without disrupting their atmosphere have made me good at this —this skillful invisibility, this skilled eavesdropping.

I pause at the bottom of the stairs, listening to the murmur of their voices from the kitchen, the occasional soft laugh from Elizabeth that sounds foreign to my ears. Deciding quickly, I move along the hallway, placing each foot with care. The wall sconces cast enough light to navigate but leave convenient shadows where I can pause if needed.

As I approach the kitchen, their voices become clearer. They're sitting at the small breakfast table—not the formal dining room where the Wilsons usually entertain, but the intimate nook where I sometimes see Elizabeth alone with her morning coffee, staring out at the garden with vacant eyes.

I position myself just outside the doorway, in the shadow of the hall. From here, I can see a slice of the kitchen—enough to observe without being seen. My pulse quickens, hands suddenly damp. My mouth tastes metallic, and I recognize the familiar feeling of crossing a line I've established for myself, of going from observer to intruder.

But I don't step back. I don't leave. Instead, I adjust my position, angling to better hear their conversation as it flows into the hallway, intimate and unguarded in the gathering dusk.

The table soon holds two steaming mugs of coffee and their clasped hands, fingers intertwined with the ease of old habit. Elizabeth has her back partially to me, but I can see her profile, softened in a way I've never witnessed before—her perpetual vigilance replaced by something raw and unguarded.

The man sits facing her, his back straight but relaxed. In the warm kitchen light, I can study him more carefully—early forties perhaps, with features that wouldn't stand out in a crowd but arrange themselves pleasingly. It's a face that reveals itself slowly rather than announces itself immediately. His thumb traces circles on Elizabeth's wrist as they talk, a gesture so intimate I feel like I should look away but can't.

"I needed this, more than I expected," Elizabeth says, her voice carrying to where I stand frozen in the hallway. She's leaning forward a fraction, her free hand cradling her mug but not drinking from it. "After this week with Jane..."

"Still making those little nasty comments?" he asks with a familiarity that speaks of long-standing knowledge of Elizabeth's mother-in-law. "Just ignore her," he murmurs, and they share a look of such perfect understanding that I feel a strange hollowness open inside me. I can't remember the last time anyone looked at me with that kind of recognition.

Elizabeth sighs. "That's what I have been trying to do. But it's not easy, you know? I can't get rid of her. At least not yet."

"Of course not."

My fingers press against the wall, steadying myself. This isn't just an affair. This man knows the family, knows Jane. The complexity of the situation pulls me further into the shadows as I strain to hear more.

"How are you holding up?" the man asks, and there's no jealousy in his tone—only what sounds like genuine concern.

Elizabeth's shoulders lift in a small shrug. "The same. I feel numb, to be honest." She pauses, takes a sip of her coffee. "It's not like Richard and I were close any more. We were like actors in different plays who somehow ended up on the same stage. We had our lines down perfectly, but none of them connected."

The man nods, and I notice a fleeting sadness cross his features. "Sounds awful."

"But I'm..." Elizabeth starts, then stops. Her hand tightens around his. "I'm better now that you're here."

He raises her hand to his lips, pressing a kiss to her knuckles. The gesture is so tender, so uncalculated that I feel heat rise to my face. In three months of working for the Wilsons, I've never seen Richard touch Elizabeth with such care.

"I still think you should tell her," the man says softly. "It's been too long, Liz. These stolen hours—"

"I can't do that now," she interrupts. "Not with everything else. It's too early."

"It's always something," he says, not unkindly.

This catches me by surprise. This isn't some recent development, then. Whatever is between them has history, depth. I shift a little, my foot nudging a decorative table in the hall. The small brass figurine atop it wobbles, and I freeze, heart hammering as I catch it before it can fall.

In the kitchen, their conversation pauses. I press myself against the wall, barely breathing.

"Did you hear something?" Elizabeth asks.

"Probably just the house settling," he replies. "These old places are always talking to themselves."

There's a moment of silence, and I wonder if one of them

will come investigate. But then Elizabeth speaks again, her voice now pitched lower, making me strain to hear.

"I miss you every day, Daniel," she says, and I finally get his name. It fits with the person simply named 'D' in her phone.

"I know," he says. "I feel it too. But you're the one who wanted clear boundaries after what happened. And I've respected that. You got married and asked me to stay away."

My fingers dig into my palms, nails leaving half-moons in the flesh. This isn't a casual affair. This isn't even a romance. This is something older and deeper than Elizabeth's marriage, something that predates her life with Richard. Could it be the ex Jane mentioned?

Elizabeth stands abruptly, turning away from the table. Her movement gives me a clear view of her face for the first time since they sat down. There are tears tracking silently down her cheeks, but her expression is one of profound recognition, as if she's finally seeing something that's been in front of her all along.

Something shifts in Elizabeth's posture—a straightening of her spine, a lifting of her chin. I recognize this transformation; I've seen it happen countless times when she prepares to face the outside world. It's her armor coming back on, piece by piece.

"Will you stay and have dinner with me?" Elizabeth asks.

"Sure," Daniel says.

"That would be nice, especially since you came such a long way."

I retreat silently down the hall, away from the kitchen, my mind racing. This isn't just gossip. This is the kind of information that could shatter the careful facade of the Wilson family. Jane Wilson, with her obsession with appearances and family legacy, would be devastated. Richard—cold, distant Richard who nevertheless plays his part in the family drama—would face public humiliation. It would hurt the senator's reputation.

This is worse than Richard having an affair; Elizabeth doing so embarrasses them.

I wait until I hear the water running in the kitchen sink before running upstairs. My mind is churning with what I've witnessed, what I've learned. This information feels dangerous, volatile. In the wrong hands, it could devastate multiple lives.

Or it could be exactly what someone like Jane Wilson would want to know.

My phone feels suddenly heavy in my pocket. I slip my hand around it, tracing its edges as I consider my options. I don't owe Elizabeth Wilson anything. Her problems are not my problems. Her secret life is not my concern.

And yet.

I've seen something real tonight—something truthful in a house where truth seems in short supply. Elizabeth Wilson isn't just the distant, privileged woman who leaves me notes about special cleaning products. She's someone caught between the life she has and the life she wants, someone who's been silently carrying decades-long love and regret.

I pull out my phone, anyway, staring at the dark screen. Jane Wilson has always treated me with a kind of dismissive politeness that rich women reserve for the people who serve them. But she said she would pay me richly for important information; she told me this many times, always followed by a little speech about loyalty and discretion, making sure I told her and only her.

Richly.

My thumb hovers over the screen. I could walk away. I could pretend I never saw this, never heard any of it. I could continue cleaning their bathrooms and changing their sheets and polishing their silver, maintaining my role as the invisible witness to their lives. But this is wrong. This man being here is wrong. This is exactly what Jane is paying me to report back to her. And it's the kind of stuff that will give me an extra bonus from her. One I desperately need. And, if I'm honest, I'm disappointed in Elizabeth. Seeing her with this man, I suddenly worry she's not being truthful with me. That I can't trust her after all.

So, I unlock my phone and pull up my contacts. *Jane Wilson.* I press her name and raise the phone to my ear, already stepping toward the front door, already crafting the careful, concerned way I'll present this information.

"Mrs. Wilson? It's Marie Clements." I pause, lowering my voice to a respectful murmur as I stand silhouetted in the dim hallway light. "I have something important to tell you about your son's wife. But it's going to cost you."

TWELVE

JANE

I drive down the street, fast. I know I'm speeding, but even the police will have to understand the importance of my mission, should they stop me. Marie called me: as I was downtown shopping, she said someone was with Elizabeth, a man. He came to the house. She said she was certain it is the same man she was with earlier. I must see it for myself, with my own eyes.

I press the accelerator harder, my knuckles white against the steering wheel. The manicured lawns of Cypress Estates blur past my window, their perfect symmetry a mockery of the chaos I suspect is unfolding at Richard's house. My heart beats against my ribs like a trapped animal, driven by something more potent than concern—a mother knows when something is amiss.

The security guard at the gate nods with deference as I speed through. He knows better than to stop Jane Wilson for pleasantries. I've cultivated that understanding over decades with the fastidiousness of a master gardener. The tires of my Bentley crunch over the pristine, shell-lined drive that winds through our community. Each house sits like a fortress of propriety, hiding whatever secrets lie within.

My daughter-in-law has always been a disappointment. A

woman with the completely wrong background, with nothing to offer my son—not even a child. Yet, she had a way with Richard that none of the others had. I remember the others well, all those prior women who came into my son's life. A few whispered rumors about them in the community were enough to send them packing. I would invite them over for tea, where I would subtly criticize their upbringing, their manners, or their ambitions until they felt small and insignificant. Most would leave, their confidence shattered, while I would persuade Richard to part ways with the others.

But when I tried the same tactics with Elizabeth, she remained steadfast by his side. I spoke of her modest family, her lack of refinement, and her inability to bear children. I orchestrated social gatherings, where she was intentionally left out, hoping she would feel unwanted and leave. Yet, she never wavered. Elizabeth faced my challenges with grace, and no matter the obstacle I placed in her path, she held on to Richard with a quiet strength that I had not anticipated.

But she has no idea who she's up against.

The house appears in view—my son's colonial revival, the largest in this section of the community. I slow as I approach, surveying the scene. The silver sedan still sits in the driveway, out of place among the manicured hedges and imported Italian planters I selected myself. More telling than this stranger's car is what's missing: Marie's modest Toyota is nowhere to be seen.

Good. The girl followed my instructions precisely. I told her to leave. I didn't want her cover blown. I need her there, to continue keeping me updated. Marie didn't question me. She never does. The girl understands her place, unlike so many of the help these days.

I park around the corner, out of sight from the main house. No need to announce my arrival. My heartbeat steadies as I slip into the familiar rhythm of control. I reach into my purse, extracting my spare keys. Richard objected when I had copies made, but I reminded him that mothers require access in emergencies.

This, I decide, qualifies.

The backdoor key slides into the lock with a satisfying click. I step onto the flagstone patio, my heels making no sound on the smooth surface. The smell of gardenias hangs in the humid air—my favorite. I insisted on planting them despite Elizabeth's objections, saying they tend to drop petals that will only end up in the pool.

The house seems unnaturally quiet, holding its breath. My legs feel stiff as I cross the slate floors of the sunroom. I'm not young any more, but I move with purpose, with the dignity that has carried me through four decades as the matriarch of the Wilson family. Through the living room, past the portraits of me hanging on the wall, and toward the central hall. All the while, I strain my ears for voices, for evidence.

There. A murmur from the kitchen. Low, intimate tones.

I ease myself along the wall, inching closer to the partially closed kitchen door. The voices become clearer—Elizabeth's soft, breathless cadence, and another, deeper voice. Male. Unfamiliar.

"I wish we could have been together more over the years," the man says, his words striking me like physical blows. My breath catches in my throat, hot anger rising beneath my carefully applied blush.

"We still have time," Elizabeth replies. "The future awaits."

My fingers press against the cool wall, seeking stability as the room seems to tilt. The future? What future could Elizabeth possibly envision that doesn't include my son? I've spent my life ensuring the Wilson legacy continues unblemished, unchallenged. I refuse to let her ruin it.

A laugh now, rich and easy, belonging to the stranger. "You always were the optimist."

"One of us had to be." Elizabeth's voice carries a warmth

I've rarely heard from her. A warmth she certainly never directs at me.

I edge closer to the gap in the door, angling for a glimpse. All I can see is a portion of the kitchen island, the gleaming marble top I selected from an Italian quarry. There's food on the table, a roast and potatoes, along with empty plates. Elizabeth's hand rests there, her wedding ring catching the light. Beside it, a larger hand, tanned, with dirt beneath the fingernails. Not the manicured hand of Richard's social circle.

"Do you ever regret it?" the man asks. "Marrying into all this?"

A pause, weighted with what I imagine to be her consideration. I hold my breath.

"Richard is a good man," she finally says, but the hesitation tells me everything I need to know.

"That wasn't my question."

Another pause, longer this time. My ears ring with the effort of listening.

"I regret the distance," she says eventually. "Between us. Between me and... everyone."

The man sighs. "That was your choice, Lizzie. You could have reached out."

Lizzie. Nobody calls Elizabeth that. Nobody would dare use such a common diminutive for a Wilson wife.

"After what happened with you? With the drugs and the stealing..." Her voice trails off.

Drugs? Stealing? What is this? She's with a man with a history of drug use and theft. A man who represents everything the Wilsons stand against.

And she's invited him into my son's home.

"I'm clean now," the man says with quiet dignity. "Five years. I have a job, an apartment. Nothing fancy, but it's mine. Earned it honestly."

"I'm proud of you," Elizabeth says. "I just wish..."

"That you didn't have to keep me a secret?" There's an edge to his voice now. "Afraid I'll embarrass you in front of your country club friends?"

"It's not that simple," Elizabeth protests. "Jane would never understand. She has very specific ideas about family, about who belongs and who doesn't."

My name in her mouth feels like a violation. The presumption that she knows me, understands me, when she's spent years hiding behind a facade of obedience. My face burns with an uncomfortable heat that I recognize as betrayal.

"Richard is under her thumb in ways I can't even begin to unravel."

Under my thumb? My son is a leader, a man of substance and character. I've raised him to uphold standards, to recognize quality, to maintain traditions that have served our family for generations. That's guidance, not control.

"You could leave," he suggests, and my heart seizes. "Just pack your bags and go. Start over."

"With what?" Elizabeth asks, and I hear genuine fear in her voice. "Jane controls everything—the money, the social connections. Even the house is in a trust she oversees."

I feel a moment of vindication. Those arrangements weren't about control—they were about protection. Protecting the Wilson legacy from exactly this sort of threat. Protecting my son. From someone who might try to take advantage, to steal what we've built.

The conversation lulls into tense silence. I stand frozen, processing this new information, recalibrating my understanding of the woman my son married. It's even worse than I thought. A secret lover with a troubled past. A potential threat to everything we've built. The press will have a field day with this scandal. He must have done something to my son.

My hand tightens around my car keys, the metal edges biting into my palm. The pain focuses me, clears my thoughts.

Whatever this man wants—money, recognition, access to our family—he won't get it. I've spent too long cultivating the Wilson reputation to allow it to be tarnished by association with a former drug addict.

I push through the kitchen door with enough force to send it crashing against the wall. The sound reverberates through the room like a gunshot, freezing Elizabeth mid-sentence. She stands by the granite island, her face draining of color as her eyes lock with mine. Beside her, a man I've never seen before—dressed in jeans that have been worn for work and a faded button-down that's seen better decades—straightens up, his posture defensive. The granite countertops gleam under the recessed lighting I selected, the perfect backdrop for the scene of betrayal unfolding before me.

"How can you do this to my son?" The words tear from my throat, sharp as surgical instruments.

Elizabeth flinches as if I've slapped her. The man beside her shifts, angling his body in front of hers—protective, familiar. The gesture only feeds my certainty.

"Jane," Elizabeth stammers, her hands fluttering nervously against the counter. "I didn't expect—"

"Clearly." I scan them both with a gaze I've perfected over decades of charity board meetings and country club politics. A look designed to flay. "How long have you cheated on Richard?"

The accusation lands with physical force. Elizabeth's mouth drops open. The stranger's eyebrows shoot upward, then furrow in confusion before his expression morphs into something like grudging understanding.

"Cheated?" Elizabeth repeats, her voice rising. "What are you talking about?"

"Do not insult my intelligence." I step further into the room, claiming the space. This kitchen—with its Sub-Zero refrigerator and imported Italian marble—is territory I funded, territory I designed. "Richard is gone for two weeks, probably lying dead in a ditch somewhere, and you immediately invite this... person into his home?"

The man shifts uncomfortably, running a hand through hair that hasn't seen a proper stylist in years. He clears his throat. "Ma'am, I think there's been a misunderstanding—"

"I'm not speaking to you," I snap, not sparing him a glance. "Elizabeth, answer me. How long?"

Elizabeth's shock gives way to something harder, a steel I didn't know she possessed. "This is Daniel," she says, her voice steadier than her hands. "My brother."

"Your brother?" I infuse the words with every ounce of disbelief I can muster. "The brother you've never once mentioned in years of being married to my son?"

"Yes." She straightens, standing taller. "My brother, who I haven't seen in seven years. My brother, who I didn't tell you about because I knew exactly how you would react."

The man—Daniel—offers me a tight smile. "Pleasure to finally meet you, Mrs. Wilson. I've heard a lot about you."

"I doubt that very much," I reply coldly. I take in his appearance with deliberate thoroughness. The worn boots. The calloused hands. The watchful eyes that remind me, uncomfortably, of Elizabeth's. "Elizabeth has no brother. We thoroughly vetted her family before the wedding."

Daniel laughs, a short, harsh sound. "Vetted? Like she was a show dog or a political candidate?"

"Daniel," Elizabeth warns.

"No, it's fine," he says, crossing his arms. "I'm curious what the great Jane Wilson thinks qualifies as 'vetting' a human being."

My jaw tightens. "We ensure that anyone joining the Wilson family meets certain standards. Standards that clearly would have excluded you."

Elizabeth moves around the island, putting herself between

us. "You had no right to burst in here like this. No right to spy on my conversations. This is my home."

"This is Richard's home," I correct her. "A home provided by Wilson family money. Money that comes with certain expectations of behavior."

"Like what? Not having a family of my own?" Elizabeth's voice rises, and I see a flush spreading up her neck. "Not having relationships outside your approved list of country club wives?"

Daniel places a hand on her shoulder. "Lizzie, maybe we should—"

"No." She shakes off his hand. "I'm tired of hiding. I'm tired of pretending I have sprung fully formed from nothing just to be Richard's perfect wife." She turns back to me, eyes flashing.

"Daniel is my brother, my only living family since our parents passed away. He struggled with drugs after the car accident that killed them, spiraling into a dark place that ultimately led him to prison for theft. Those were tough years, and I felt as if I was losing him too. But he's been clean for five years now, and he's turned his life around, dedicating himself to his craft as a skilled carpenter. I kept him a secret from you because I knew you'd react just like this—treat him as if he were something diseased, something to be hidden away.

"I remember when Richard met him after he came out of prison. He took one look at Daniel and told me he wasn't allowed in the house. That moment drove a wedge between Richard and me, and now, after all these years, Daniel shows up trying to mend broken ties, to be a part of my life again. So yes, I keep him a secret. I hardly think you can blame me for it. I think I have every right to."

I take a step back, momentarily thrown by her vehemence. In all these years, I've never heard Elizabeth raise her voice. Never seen her defy me openly. The change is disturbing, like finding a crack in what I thought was solid marble.

"You have got to stop coming over like this," Elizabeth

continues, her words gaining momentum. "I don't feel safe even in my own house. You use your key whenever you want, you rearrange my furniture, you criticize my decorating, my choice of friends, you question my clothing choices—it must stop. I only hosted the hospital fundraiser to keep up your image. You're welcome, by the way."

Daniel watches this exchange with evident satisfaction, and I resist the urge to slap the smug look from his face. Instead, I smooth my hands over my skirt, gathering my composure.

"I see," I say, my voice deliberately modulated. "Your brother reappears after years of absence, and suddenly you find the courage to attack me. Interesting timing."

"This isn't about courage," Elizabeth retorts. "It's about basic respect. Something you've never shown me."

"Respect is earned," I reply. "And hiding a criminal relative for the entirety of your marriage doesn't suggest honesty worthy of respect."

Daniel steps forward, his movement fluid despite his workman's frame. "Mrs. Wilson, with all due respect, you don't know the first thing about my sister or what she's been through."

"I know that she married my son, took the Wilson name, and accepted everything that comes with it." I turn my gaze on him fully now, assessing. Up close, the family resemblance is undeniable—the same high cheekbones, the same stubborn set to the jaw. But where Elizabeth has cultivated a polished fragility, this man radiates a rough-hewn confidence. "The Wilson name doesn't associate with felons."

"Ex-felon," he corrects, his tone mild but his eyes hard. "And I didn't come here to associate with the Wilson name. I came to see my sister."

"After seven years of absence," I point out. "What changed? What do you want?"

Elizabeth makes a small, angry sound. "Not everyone has an agenda, Jane. Some people just want to reconnect with family."

"Everyone has an agenda," I counter. "Particularly people who suddenly reappear when there's inheritance money at stake."

Daniel laughs again, but this time the sound holds genuine amusement. "Is that what you think this is? A play for Wilson money?" He shakes his head. "Lady, I don't want your money. I don't want your name. I don't want anything from you except to be allowed to have a relationship with my sister without your permission."

"Daniel found me," Elizabeth interjects. "Through social media. He's been sober for five years. He has a life, a career. He's not here to cause trouble."

I move to the kitchen island, trailing my fingers along its perfect surface. My mind races, calculating threats, assessing damage control options. If Richard were to discover this deception—this brother Elizabeth has been seeing behind his back—it could destabilize everything. Richard values honesty above all else, a trait he inherited from his father.

"How convenient that he shows up just as my son disappears."

"I don't have to explain myself to you," Elizabeth says, but her renewed confidence wavers.

"No," I agree. "But you'll have to explain yourself to Richard. If he ever comes back."

The implied threat hangs in the air. We all understand what I'm saying: I will tell Richard if she doesn't.

Daniel steps closer to his sister. "Lizzie has nothing to explain or apologize for. She didn't commit any crime. She didn't hurt anyone. She simply loved a brother who made mistakes."

"She lied by omission for years," I correct him. "To her husband. To her family."

"To you," Daniel says pointedly. "She was afraid of you, not Richard."

His perception unsettles me. I glance at Elizabeth, who doesn't contradict him. Has she truly spent five years being afraid of me? The thought is both gratifying and disturbing.

"I think you should leave," Elizabeth says, her voice quiet but firm. "We can discuss this another time, when we've all had a chance to calm down."

"Calm?" I arch an eyebrow. "I'm perfectly calm, Elizabeth. I'm simply concerned about what your brother's sudden reappearance means for my family's stability."

"My reappearance doesn't mean anything for your family," Daniel says. "I'm here to see my sister, period. I'm not interested in your money, your social standing, or whatever else you think needs protecting."

"Everyone wants something," I insist. "It is quite suspicious that you should show up right as my son goes missing, I must say."

Daniel's face darkens. "I don't owe you any explanation as to why I'm here. And as for wanting something from you? I built my business from nothing while paying restitution for my crimes. I did it honestly, which is more than I can say for how you're treating my sister right now."

Elizabeth moves to the refrigerator, pulling out a bottle of water. Her hands tremble as she twists off the cap. "Jane, please. Not now. Please just leave me alone."

"This isn't over," I say, gathering my purse from where I placed it on the counter. "But I'll give you time to consider how you want to proceed."

I turn to Daniel. "If you genuinely care for your sister, you'll understand that reconnecting with you presents certain... complications for her position."

"Her 'position'?" Daniel repeats, incredulous. "She's not a chess piece, Mrs. Wilson. She's a human being with the right to have relationships outside your approval."

"Of course she is," I say smoothly. "And her choices have consequences, as I'm sure you've learned in your own life."

Elizabeth sets down her water bottle with enough force to splash liquid onto the counter. "That's enough. I want you to leave, Jane. Now."

I study her, noting the heightened color in her cheeks, the unusual firmness in her stance. This newfound rebellion is Daniel's influence—it must be. In all these years, I've never seen this version of Elizabeth. It's concerning. Potentially dangerous to the carefully balanced dynamics I've maintained.

"Very well," I concede, moving toward the door. "But consider carefully what you tell your neighbors and social circle. Richard has worked extremely hard to build his reputation in this community. A brother-in-law with a criminal history could be... problematic."

"Are you threatening my sister?" Daniel asks, his tone deceptively mild.

"Not at all," I reply. "I'm simply stating facts. In our circle, associations matter. Elizabeth has enjoyed the benefits of the Wilson name for years. Those benefits come with responsibilities."

"Get out," Elizabeth says, her voice barely above a whisper but charged with emotion. "Get out of my house, Jane."

I pause at the threshold, surveying them both one last time. Daniel stands protectively near his sister, his presence a new variable in an equation I thought I'd long since solved. Elizabeth, usually pliant and accommodating, glares at me with undisguised hostility.

"We'll speak soon," I say, making it sound like both a promise and a threat. I'm still waiting for an update from my investigator, but once I get it, she won't know what hit her.

As I walk through the house toward the front door, my mind churns with contingency plans. The warm Florida air hits me as I step outside, heavy with humidity that instantly wilts my carefully styled hair. I glance back at the house—my son's house—feeling an unfamiliar sense of uncertainty. For the first time in years, I face a situation I didn't anticipate, can't control.

Elizabeth's criminal brother has an apparent influence over her that I never suspected. The foundation I thought was solid has developed a crack, and I'm not entirely sure how to repair it. I feel defeated. I thought I had her, but I will get her. Next time.

I straighten my shoulders as I walk to my car. The Wilsons have weathered worse challenges than an ex-felon carpenter with familial claims. I'll handle this threat as I've handled all others over the years—with precision, determination, and whatever force necessary to protect what's mine.

Richard.

THIRTEEN
MARIE

I watch her as she leaves. Jane storms out of the door, slamming it behind her in her usual theatrical fashion. She gets into the Bentley and takes off. Then I put the minivan in gear and drive up to the driveway, and park. I had left my phone in the house when rushing out of there and need to get it back. I didn't want to be in the middle of whatever was going on between Jane and Elizabeth. I prefer to stay out of it and prefer that Elizabeth doesn't find out that I called Jane, and risk blowing my cover. I really wish I didn't have to spy on Elizabeth, but the money is so good, and I still am not quite sure that Jane isn't right in her suspicion about her. Especially after seeing her with that man earlier.

I slip back into the house like a ghost, the door clicking shut behind me with barely a sound, using the key Elizabeth has given me so I can get in and clean even when she's not there. The Wilson home breathes differently when it thinks no one is listening—creaks and sighs that it wouldn't dare make when being watched. I left my phone upstairs, where I must have put it after calling Jane and gathering my cleaning supplies. Such a careless mistake. I'm never careless.

The foyer stands empty now, Jane's lingering perfume—something expensive with notes of jasmine—the only evidence she was ever here. I exhale slowly, releasing the tension that always builds in my shoulders when that woman is present. The disapproving tilt of her mouth follows me even when she's gone.

My hand brushes the smooth banister as I begin my ascent. The third step creaks, as it always does. I know all the sounds this house makes, all its secrets and telltale signs. The Wilsons have lived here for five years, but I understand their home better than they do after just three months of employment.

"Know their spaces, and you'll know them," my mother used to say. She often imparted wisdom with an air of mystique, her eyes twinkling like she held the secrets of the universe. This was one of the few useful things she taught me, amidst her tales of growing up in a small coastal village, where she had learned the art of understanding people by the way they arranged their homes. She believed that a room could whisper the true nature of its inhabitant, revealing hidden desires and unspoken dreams. Whether it was the diligent arrangement of books on a shelf or the choice of colors in a room, she saw it as a reflection of the soul. Her ability to read these silent cues was unparalleled, and it was this wisdom that she passed on to me, a lesson that has shaped my understanding of others ever since.

I climb with measured steps, keeping to the right side where the wood beneath is most solid. At the landing, light filters through the tall windows, casting long rectangles across the hardwood floor. Elizabeth told me she had insisted on these windows despite Richard's concerns about privacy. "I need the light," she'd said during my second week.

My phone sits exactly where I left it, a sleek black rectangle that contrasts with the rich, polished walnut of the console table. The surface gleams under the soft overhead light, casting subtle reflections. Beside the phone, a shimmering silver frame captures a moment in time: Elizabeth and Richard on their anniversary trip to the idyllic island of Santorini last year. The photo shows them standing against a backdrop of azure seas and whitewashed buildings, their arms wrapped around each other with smiles that radiate warmth and happiness. Yet, beneath those seemingly genuine smiles lies a different story. Elizabeth once confided in me during a quiet afternoon over coffee, revealing that they had returned three days earlier than planned, enveloped in a chilling silence, not speaking to each other. It was during this trip that Richard had confided in her about his affair, marking the beginning of the unraveling of their once-solid marriage. The photo, frozen in time, belies the turbulent reality that simmered just beneath the surface.

I pick up my phone, the screen lighting up with two missed calls from my landlord. The rent check. I'll need to drop it off tomorrow. Once Jane pays me. My fingers hover over the screen, then move to the silver frame instead. I straighten it, adjusting its angle by perhaps two degrees. Elizabeth will never notice, but I will know it's perfect now.

The house settles around me with a soft groan of wooden beams. These old Florida mansions in Cypress Estates look modern and pristine, but they hide their age poorly. Like the women who live in them.

I stand motionless, listening. Traffic hums distantly beyond the gates of the community. A lawn mower drones three houses down. The central air conditioning cycles on with a gentle whoosh. I catalog each sound automatically, an old habit that's served me well.

My thumb swipes across my phone screen, clearing the notifications. I shouldn't linger, but something holds me here. The upstairs hallway stretches before me, doors to the various rooms. The master bedroom at the end, always immaculate because Elizabeth can't stand disorder. The guest room to the right, next to the nursery that still stands empty. The home office where Richard retreats when the silence between him and Elizabeth grows too loud.

I know each room intimately. I've dusted every surface, straightened every drawer, folded every piece of clothing. I've read the titles of their books, noted which ones have cracked spines and which remain untouched for show. I've emptied their trash cans, finding the evidence of lives they try to hide: wine bottles in Elizabeth's bathroom bin, crumpled papers with figures and desperate calculations in Richard's office waste basket.

The house is full of stories that the Wilsons don't realize they're telling.

My fingers curl around my phone, its case cool against my palm. I should leave now.

Yet I linger, drawn to the framed photographs that line the hallway wall. The visual history of the Wilson family, carefully curated to show only their best moments. Wedding photos with Elizabeth and Richard, younger, she's looking radiant and uncertain beside Richard, who looks full of hope. Holiday gatherings where Jane's presence dominates every image, her hand always on Richard's shoulder, her eyes always watching Elizabeth.

The frames are dusty on top. I'll need to take care of that.

My feet make no sound as I turn toward the stairs.

I pause at the top of the stairs and look down into the foyer. From this height, I can see the exact arrangement of furniture, the careful positioning of art pieces that Elizabeth selected with her designer, only to have Jane rearrange them a week later. Nothing is out of place. Nothing except the Wilsons themselves, who never quite seem to fit inside their perfect home.

I know Elizabeth cries in the guest bathroom because the master bath echoes too much. I know Richard keeps a bottle of whiskey hidden behind the gardening supplies in the garage. I know Jane has a key to their house. I know because I watch. I listen. I remember.

The light changes as I walk down the stairs, the foyer suddenly darker as a cloud passes over the sun outside. Through the tall windows flanking the front door, I can see the manicured lawn and the curved driveway where Jane's Bentley was parked just thirty minutes ago. The driveway is empty now. The sedan is gone as well. The man must have left.

I take a final look around the foyer, making sure everything is as it should be. The crystal vase on the entry table holds fresh flowers I arranged earlier. The mail is sorted neatly beside it. The slate floor gleams with the polish I applied last week.

Everything is perfect. Everything except—

A sound breaks the silence. Faint but unmistakable.

I tilt my head, listening more intently. It's coming from the back of the house, from the kitchen perhaps. A soft, uneven sound that makes my skin prickle with recognition.

Someone is crying.

My feet are already moving, drawn toward the sound. The crying grows louder, more distinct. A woman's sobs, broken and raw.

Elizabeth.

My pulse quickens as I approach the kitchen doorway. I walk inside. How can I not? How can I ignore her? I did this.

The kitchen light casts a soft glow over Elizabeth's hunched form. She sits at the marble island, her face buried in her hands, shoulders shaking with each sob. I pause at the threshold, one hand still gripping my phone. This is Elizabeth undone—not the polished socialite who hosts garden parties, but a fragile creature coming apart at the seams. I should retreat, pretend I never saw this moment of weakness. Instead, I clear my throat.

Elizabeth's head snaps up. Her mascara has created dark rivers down her cheeks, and her usually perfect blonde hair hangs limply around her face. For a moment, she stares at me with naked confusion, as if I'm an apparition that doesn't belong in her kitchen.

"I thought you left," she says finally, her voice hoarse from crying.

I hold up my phone, a peace offering, an explanation. "I came back. I forgot my phone upstairs." The device trembles in my grip. Not from fear—I don't fear Elizabeth—but from the unexpected intimacy of this moment. I've seen Elizabeth cry before, of course. Small, elegant tears during sad movies or when reading particularly moving thank-you notes from her charity events. Never like this. Never raw and messy and real.

"Oh." She wipes at her face, smearing the mascara further. It's the kind of mistake Elizabeth never makes. She's always careful about her appearance, especially in front of the help. Even me.

I should say something comforting. That's what normal people do. "Is everything all right, Mrs. Wilson?"

A laugh escapes her, bitter and sharp like breaking glass. "No, Marie. Everything is not all right." She takes a shuddering breath. "And please, how many times must I ask you to call me Elizabeth? Especially when we're alone."

"Elizabeth," I correct myself, though the familiarity feels wrong in my mouth. Distance is safer. Distance is control.

She stands suddenly, moving toward me with an unexpected urgency that makes me step back instinctively. But I'm not quick enough. Her arms wrap around me, her body pressing against mine in an embrace that crosses every boundary I've carefully established in this house.

"I'm sorry," she mumbles into my shoulder. She smells like expensive salon products and salt. "I just—I needed—"

I pat her back awkwardly, my hand making small circles between her shoulder blades. This isn't in my job description. I clean her house. I prepare her meals. I spy on her and report to her mother-in-law.

I don't hold her while she falls apart.

Yet here we are.

"It's all right," I say, feeling terrible for her, and for what I've done. I feel the slight tremble in her frame, the warm dampness of tears soaking through my shirt.

After what feels like an eternity, she pulls back, not meeting my eyes. "I'm sorry," she says again, retreating to the island. "That was inappropriate of me. You must think very poorly of me."

"It's fine." I remain where I am, uncertain whether to approach or leave. The script for this scenario isn't one I've rehearsed. "Would you like me to make you some tea before I go?"

Elizabeth shakes her head. "No. Thank you." She tugs a tissue from the box on the counter and dabs at her eyes, further smudging her makeup. "Jane was here."

"I know." The words slip out without me thinking this through. I just gave myself away. I need to fix it. "I mean... I saw her rush out of here, when I came back." I take a cautious step forward, placing my phone on the counter. A commitment to stay, at least for now.

"She just walked right in here, you know. She always does that." Elizabeth crumples the paper towel in her fist. "I never know when she'll be watching me. I'm never safe from her controlling eyes."

I nod, encouraging her to continue, though I already suspect what comes next. Jane Wilson's thinly veiled hostility toward her daughter-in-law is hardly a secret. "What did she say to upset you so much?" I ask, my tone carefully neutral. I'm just the maid, after all. Just the help. Not a confidante.

Elizabeth's eyes fill with fresh tears. "She said—" her voice breaks, and she takes a steadying breath. "She thought... she thought I was having an affair. But my brother was here. I have no privacy, Marie, none whatsoever."

Her brother?

What have I done?

"Maybe you can ask her to not use her key when she comes over? To ring the doorbell? Or maybe even call first before she comes over?"

Elizabeth scoffs. "Yeah, wouldn't that be nice. But fact is... she's right."

"About what?"

She takes in a deep sigh. "That I'm draining the life out of Richard. That if I was a proper wife, he wouldn't—" She stops, pressing her lips together.

"Wouldn't what?" I can't help asking, though I know I shouldn't.

"Have reasons to look elsewhere." The words come out in a whisper. "He wouldn't have left me. I think about it every day, you know? Why did he leave me?"

I look at her, unsure whether this is part of her manipulative plan. To make me believe she thinks Richard just left, that nothing has happened to him. To get me on her side. If so, then Elizabeth sure is a good actress.

"I'm sure that's not true," I say automatically, playing my part. The supportive, discreet maid who doesn't notice the cracks in the marriage she tends to daily.

Elizabeth stares at me, her eyes suddenly sharp through the tears. "Isn't it? You're here more than either of us. You see everything." She gestures broadly at the kitchen. "These walls are closing in on me, Marie. This perfect house with its perfect furniture and its perfect facade." She wraps her arms around herself. "I don't feel safe in my own home."

The confession hangs between us, heavy with implication. I consider her words carefully. Is she afraid of Jane? Or is it something more nebulous—the fear of her life continuing to unravel, perhaps?

"Why don't you feel safe?" I ask softly.

She shakes her head, a jerky movement that sends a tear sliding down her cheek. "Jane has always hated me. From the day Richard brought me home. I wasn't from the right family, didn't have the right background." Her laugh is bitter. "Five years of marriage, and she still treats me like I'm temporary. Like she's just waiting for Richard to come to his senses. Maybe she's even the one who has sent him away so she can get rid of me. I wouldn't be surprised. She can be very cunning." Her gaze is unsettlingly direct. "Sometimes things are missing. Small things. A pair of earrings. My favorite scarf. Sometimes they move to places I didn't put them."

My pulse quickens. This conversation has veered into dangerous territory. What is going on here? Has she lost her mind?

"Are you accusing me of something?" I keep my voice level, professional.

Elizabeth's expression shifts suddenly, the suspicion draining away, replaced by a desperate hopelessness that's somehow more unsettling. "Not you, her. Jane. Jane wants me to look bad. I think she's moving things, to make me feel like I'm going insane," she says, her voice barely audible. "I think she's the one who sent me those flowers. She's trying to mess with me."

I blink, genuinely taken aback. "What?"

"The earrings turned up in my jewelry box. The scarf in my closet." Her hands are shaking now. "I didn't put them there, Marie. I swear they were gone. I would never—" She breaks off, covering her mouth with her hand.

I process this information carefully. Someone is moving items, then putting them back. Messing with Elizabeth's possessions and her mind? Who would do that?

Would Jane?

If so, then that's really messed up.

For a moment, we stand in silence, the kitchen suddenly too

small, too intimate. I see Elizabeth differently now—not just as my employer, but as a woman trapped in a gilded cage, surrounded by people she can't trust.

"I should go," I say finally, reaching for my phone. "You need to rest. Things will seem clearer tomorrow."

"Don't," she says quickly, her hand shooting out to grasp my wrist. Her grip is surprisingly strong. "Please don't go yet. I-I don't want to be alone when Jane comes back."

"Jane is coming back today?" This is unexpected. Jane typically visits once a day.

Elizabeth nods miserably. "I fear that she will. To spy on me. She'll say she's just looking for Richard, but I know her. She's driving me crazy. That's her whole plan, Marie. To drive me nuts. Maybe even have me admitted somewhere. To get me out of Richard's life."

"Elizabeth," I say firmly, "that's nonsense. Jane is just being overprotective of Richard, as always. No one is that devious."

She looks at me through tear-spiked lashes. "Oh, you clearly haven't met my mother-in-law," she says with a sniffle, then adds, "well, maybe you're right. I am getting carried away. Please, won't you stay for a while? I get so lonely here."

I glance at the clock on the microwave. Nearly eight. I don't have anywhere to be. I guess my empty apartment can wait.

"I could stay for a little while," I offer.

Relief washes over Elizabeth's face. "Would you? I'd pay you extra."

"Of course." Money isn't what I'm after, not in this moment at least. I feel terrible for what I've done, responsible for how she's feeling.

She releases my wrist and steps back, suddenly self-conscious. "I should clean up," she says, gesturing vaguely toward her tearstained face. "I must look a fright."

"A quick splash of cold water and no one will notice," I assure her, falling back into my role as the efficient helper.

Elizabeth nods, then pauses. "Marie?"

"Yes?"

"I hope you don't think I'm crazy." She stops, struggling to find the words. "I guess I'm just paranoid these days. I have a lot on my mind."

"It's totally understandable," I say smoothly.

"Thank you." Her smile is fragile but genuine. "I don't know what I'd do without you."

As she leaves the kitchen, heading upstairs to repair her appearance, I allow myself a moment of stillness. The Wilson household is unraveling faster than I anticipated. Elizabeth is cracking under pressure. Jane is playing some sort of game. And Richard—well, Richard is the unknown variable in this equation.

And me? It seems I once again have made Elizabeth's life miserable. When will I ever learn?

I move to the cabinet and pull out cups for tea, hoping it will make her feel better. My mind works through possibilities, contingencies, scenarios. Someone is moving items, creating distrust, isolating Elizabeth. Someone with access to the house, with knowledge of its routines and residents.

As I pull tea bags from the drawer, I consider my own words: *No one is that devious.*

I fill the kettle with water and put it on the stove. My reflection in the stainless steel stares back at me, ordinary and forgettable. Just as I've designed myself to be.

"Oh, Elizabeth," I murmur to the empty kitchen. "I'm afraid, you'd be surprised if you only knew the real truth."

FOURTEEN

JANE

The late-afternoon sun slants through the blinds of my study, casting tiger-stripe shadows across the polished mahogany of my desk. I've arranged Elizabeth's background files in neat stacks—medical records on the left, employment history in the center, known associates to the right. When my private investigator calls from Tallahassee, I answer on the first ring, my free hand already hovering over a fresh legal pad.

"Mrs. Wilson," the investigator's voice crackles through the line, deep and matter-of-fact. "I've got that information you requested on Elizabeth Keller, now Wilson."

"Go ahead, Mr. Delaney." I uncap my fountain pen with my teeth, the silver cap cool against my lips. I've been waiting for this call all day.

"I've been looking into her background, as requested. Found something interesting from about eight years ago, before she moved to Jacksonville. Back then, she went by Elizabeth Keller, as you've informed me about. She was married to Thomas Barrett and became Elizabeth Barrett."

I write this down, underlining the surname twice. "Continue."

"There was a domestic violence incident. Pretty ugly, from what I gathered. Between Elizabeth Barrett and her husband at the time."

A small smile tugs at the corner of my mouth. I press the phone closer to my ear, as if proximity might extract the information faster. "I knew something like this happened, but not the details. Tell me what you learned."

"The neighbor who witnessed it said there was screaming, things breaking. Police were called twice to that address," he explains methodically. I can hear him flipping through papers. "First time, no charges. Second time, different story."

I tap my pen impatiently against the legal pad, leaving small blue dots that grow darker with each tap.

"The second call came about three weeks after the first. According to the police report, officers arrived to find the husband with wounds on his arms, and a black eye. Place was trashed. Claimed she came at him with a fire poker during an argument."

The information ignites something in me—a tiny dart of pleasure, until I remember who is at risk here. What has she done to my darling boy?

"Any arrest reports? Restraining orders?" I press, wanting to nail down the concrete details, the things I can use.

"Yes, to both. She was arrested that night, spent about twelve hours in county lockup before posting bail. Temporary restraining order was issued, keeping her away from the residence and the husband."

I scribble furiously, the script of my handwriting growing sharper, more angular with excitement. "And this restraining order—what happened with it?"

"Dropped about six weeks later. Husband withdrew his complaint, declined to pursue charges. Pretty common in domestic cases," Delaney says, his voice remaining neutral, professional. "But here's where it gets interesting, Mrs. Wilson."

I lean forward in my chair, the leather creaking beneath me. "I'm listening."

"I spoke with the landlord of the apartment they shared. After they both moved out—separately, of course—he claimed he found blood on the walls that had been painted over. Not just a little, either. Said it looked like someone had tried to cover up a crime scene."

My breath catches. The pen stills between my fingers. "Blood? Did he report this?"

"He did, but by then both Elizabeth and the husband had cleared out. Police investigated, but without either party to question, it didn't go anywhere."

I close my eyes briefly, savoring this development. In my mind, I can see Elizabeth—her perfect clothes, her cultivated grace, her rehearsed smile that never quite reaches her eyes—standing in a blood-spattered room, calmly painting over evidence of her rage.

"I need concrete evidence, not just hearsay," I tell him, my voice steady despite the excitement coursing through me. "Get me copies of the police reports, arrest records, court documents for the restraining order. Anything with an official seal that can't be dismissed."

"I'm working on that now," Delaney assures me. "Should have the court documents tomorrow. Police reports might take another day or two."

"What about medical records? Hospital visits?"

"Nothing I've found yet for her, but there are records of the husband visiting the ER twice in the three months before the incident that led to her arrest. Broken wrist once—claimed he fell while running. Split lip and concussion another time—said he walked into a door."

Classic excuses. I tap my pen against my lips, thinking. "And Elizabeth's contacts from that period? Friends, coworkers, family?"

"Still tracking those down. She seems to have cut ties pretty thoroughly when she left."

"Of course she did," I murmur, more to myself than to Delaney. "Clean break, clean slate. New name, new city, new victim."

"Pardon, Mrs. Wilson?"

"Nothing," I say quickly. "Just thinking aloud. And the husband? This Thomas Barrett? Have you located him?" I ask, turning to a fresh page on my legal pad.

"That's another thing, Mrs. Wilson," Delaney adds, his tone shifting. "The husband she allegedly attacked? He disappeared three months after the restraining order was dropped. Never found."

The words hit me with physical force. My breath catches, and for a moment, the room seems to tilt. I grip the edge of my desk to steady myself.

"Are you suggesting...?" I begin, but can't finish the thought. The implications are too enormous, too perfect for my purposes.

"I'm not suggesting anything, just reporting facts," the investigator says, maintaining his professional distance. "Thomas Barrett was reported missing by his employer when he failed to show up for work three days straight. His car was gone. Search parties found nothing. Case is still technically open, but cold."

I stand abruptly, the chair rolling back behind me. I move to the window, watching the gardener below as I process this information. The shears in his hands glint in the sunlight with each cut.

Snip. Snip. Problem eliminated.

"And Elizabeth?" I ask, my voice carefully controlled. "Was she questioned?"

"According to the police reports I've seen so far, yes. They found no evidence connecting her to his disappearance. By then, they were living separately. She had an alibi for the weekend he went missing—was staying with a friend, who corroborated her story. This was shortly before she left town and changed her name. When she arrived in Jacksonville, she was Elizabeth Turner."

Of course she had an alibi. Of course there was no evidence. Elizabeth wouldn't make such elementary mistakes.

"The timing seems... convenient," I observe, watching a hummingbird dart among the roses below. Here and gone in an instant, like Thomas Barrett.

Like my Richard.

"Convenient is one word for it," Delaney agrees, the first hint of opinion creeping into his tone. "The police certainly thought so, but couldn't prove anything."

"Keep digging," I instruct him, turning back to my desk. "I want everything—medical records, police reports, interviews with anyone who knew her then. Friends, coworkers, neighbors. Someone must know something."

"I'll do my best, Mrs. Wilson, but it's been eight years. People move on, memories fade."

"Not all memories," I say, thinking of Richard. Of how Elizabeth looked the night before he disappeared—flushed, agitated. Of the hushed argument I'd overheard between them. "Some things stay with us forever."

"I'll call when I have more," Delaney promises.

After ending the call, I sink back into my chair and open the bottom drawer of my desk. I remove a crystal decanter and pour myself a small glass of brandy, my hand trembling as I replace the stopper. The amber liquid catches the late-afternoon light, glowing like a warning signal.

I rarely drink before dinner, but some revelations demand immediate fortification. I take a small sip, letting the heat bloom in my chest as I consider the implications of what I've learned.

Elizabeth Barrett. Domestic violence. A restraining order. Blood on walls. A name change. A vanished husband.

And now, my vanished son.

The pieces are falling into place. Elizabeth has a pattern—violent outbursts, followed by erasure and reinvention. I think of her face, always composed, always slightly guarded. The way she flinches when doors close too loudly. How she avoids conflict at all costs, until she doesn't.

I've known from the beginning that something was off about her. The way she ingratiated herself with Richard, her careful study of our family dynamics, the charm that never quite reached her eyes. Richard called my concerns "paranoia" and "jealousy." If only he had listened. Did Richard know all of this? Are details of Elizabeth's arrest hidden in his safe? Why would he want to protect her?

I pick up my phone to call Detective Mitchell, then hesitate. I need to be strategic about how I present this information. Coming on too strong might make me appear biased, vindictive—the stereotypical mother-in-law who never approved of her son's choice. But if I'm too hesitant, the detective might not grasp the significance. Might tell Elizabeth what I know. This knowledge is power.

Perhaps I should confront Elizabeth first? Watch her face when I mention Thomas Barrett and her former name? Catch her in a lie and then report that to Mitchell?

I take another sip of brandy, mentally mapping out my approach. The tangible evidence—police reports, court documents—should come first. Then the husband's disappearance, presented as a concerning pattern rather than an accusation. I need Mitchell to see the connection himself, to come to his own conclusions about Elizabeth's capacity for violence.

I'm so absorbed in my planning that the sudden ring of my phone startles me. Brandy sloshes over the rim of the glass, staining my notes with small amber drops. I set the glass down hastily and check the screen.

Detective Arnold Mitchell.

My heart rate accelerates.

"Perfect timing, Detective," I say, answering with a calm I don't entirely feel. The brandy burns in my throat, lending warmth to my voice. "I was just about to call you."

"Mrs. Wilson," his gravelly voice comes through the line, professional but with an undercurrent I can't quite identify. "I wonder if we might meet in person. There have been some developments in the case."

My pulse quickens. "Developments?"

"I'd prefer not to discuss this over the phone. Would tomorrow afternoon be convenient?"

I straighten in my chair, mind racing. What has he found? Has Elizabeth slipped up? Or is this about Richard's disappearance?

"Yes, that would be fine," I reply, striving to keep my voice steady.

"Tomorrow, then," he says and disconnects.

I set the phone down gently, like it's something precious and fragile. Outside, the sun has dipped lower, casting longer shadows across my desk. The gardener has finished his work, the hedges now perfectly trimmed, not a stray branch in sight.

Tomorrow afternoon. By then, I'll have decided exactly how much to reveal about Elizabeth's violent past—and exactly how to ensure Detective Mitchell sees her for what she truly is.

FIFTEEN

MARIE

I step onto the porch of the Wilson beach house as the sun bleeds its first light across the horizon. My cleaning supplies weigh down one hand, keys jangle in the other. The house has stood empty for months—Jane mentioned this when she hired me, that it would need cleaning twice a month, her voice clipped with the nonchalance of someone accustomed to owning multiple properties they rarely visit. It used to belong to the family but was given to Richard and Elizabeth as a wedding gift. Elizabeth doesn't like it because Jane decorated it, and so she never goes there. It's dusty and smells moist, and I know I have a job cut out for me. The metal of the key feels cool against my fingertips as I slide it into the lock, and something else—an uncomfortable heat that I recognize as anticipation—rises in my chest.

The door gives a low, protesting creak as I push it open. Darkness greets me, thick and still, as if the house has been holding its breath. I fumble for a light switch, my fingers tracing unfamiliar walls until I find it. The overhead fixture sputters to life, casting a weak, yellowish glow that barely penetrates the shadows clinging to the corners.

"Hello?" I call out, though I know no one will answer. The sound dies quickly, swallowed by the emptiness.

I set my cleaning caddy down with a soft thud. The house smells of disuse—that particular blend of dust, stale air, and the faint, lingering scent of whatever cleaning product was last used here. Beneath it all, something else: the subtle musk of expensive furniture left to sit untouched, of money that allows spaces to remain vacant.

My footsteps echo as I move deeper into the house. Each step is measured, deliberate. I'm not in a hurry. No one expects me to finish quickly—Elizabeth specifically said to "take all the time you need" when she told me to go yesterday after I was done at her house. Her voice had been tight, controlled, like she was reciting lines rather than having a conversation.

The hallway stretches before me. I trail my fingertips along the wall as I walk, partly to guide myself, partly to ground my nerves. The wallpaper feels cool and lightly textured—some expensive pattern that probably cost more than I make in a month.

My heart thumps steadily against my ribs. Not from fear, exactly. From purpose.

I reach the end of the hallway where it branches in two directions. Left leads to the guest rooms and a bathroom. Right leads to the master suite. I turn right.

The floorboards don't creak here—everything in this house was built too well for that—but I still step carefully, my shoes barely making a sound against the hardwood. The silence presses against my ears, broken only by the soft sound of my own breathing.

I pause outside the master bedroom door. It stands a little ajar, a slice of deeper darkness visible through the gap. I press my palm flat against the wood and push gently. The door swings inward without a sound.

"Just a cleaning job," I whisper to myself, though we both know that's a lie.

Elizabeth asked me to clean the beach house, as she does several times a month. However, this visit, I'm searching for more than just dust bunnies. A previous time I was cleaning here, Richard unexpectedly showed up. He claimed he was only there to pick up a few items, and I took him at his word. Yet, through a barely open door, I witnessed him opening the safe in the master bedroom and placing some documents inside. He seemed anxious, and I suspect he was concealing secrets in there. Maybe it will contain information that can help reveal where he is? Or at least something I can give to Jane and earn myself another bonus?

I need all I can get to make sure those goons won't come to my door again.

The master bedroom is larger than my entire apartment. Even in the dim light filtering through the windows, I can make out the king-sized bed dominating the center of the room, a chaise longue positioned near floor-to-ceiling windows that offer stunning water views. Two nightstands flank the bed, both empty except for simple lamps. The room feels impersonal, like an upscale hotel suite rather than someone's intimate space.

I don't turn on the lights. Not yet. Instead, I move to the windows and draw the curtains fully closed. Only then do I reach for the bedside lamp, twisting the switch until a soft glow illuminates the room.

The air is musty, with undertones of the expensive cologne Richard favors. I inhale deeply. My fingers twitch at my sides. I should be dusting, vacuuming, changing sheets. Instead, I scan the walls.

There—above the dresser. A painting of a sailboat on calm waters, tasteful but generic. Nothing special except for its placement, centered on the wall at perfect eye level.

I cross to it, my steps no longer those of a cleaner but of someone with intent. Up close, the painting is unremarkable, probably chosen to match the nautical theme rather than for any artistic merit. My fingers tremble as I reach for the frame.

It lifts easily away from the wall, hinged on one side. Behind it, just as I suspected, a wall safe stares back at me. Brushed steel, digital keypad. Newer than the house itself.

"What secrets are you keeping here, Richard?" I murmur, running my fingertips over the cool metal surface.

I know him better than he realizes. I've cleaned his office at the main house, seen the way he absently taps rhythms when he's thinking. Four numbers, always the same pattern. The same four digits he punches into his phone before making calls he doesn't want anyone to overhear.

I haven't come this far to hesitate now. I lean closer to the safe, hyperaware of every sound in the empty house. My reflection stares back at me from the glossy surface of the keypad.

Four numbers between me and whatever truths the Wilsons are hiding. Four numbers before I decide what to do with what I find.

The house creaks around me, settling into the night. Outside, waves must be lapping against the shore, though I can't hear them through the well-insulated walls. I'm alone with the Wilsons' secrets, and they don't even know my name. To them, I'm just Marie the cleaner, invisible until something needs tidying.

I trace one finger over the keypad, not pressing yet, just feeling the slight resistance of the buttons.

"Time to clean house," I whisper and begin.

My fingers hover over the keypad, the combination a rhythm in my head. Four digits that Richard uses for everything —the year his dog died. Not his mother's birthday. Not his wife's birthday, not his anniversary. I punch them in slowly, deliberately, each press of a button sending a jolt up my arm. The safe answers with a soft click, the sound almost disappointing after all this buildup. I pull the door open and peer inside, the scent of paper and metal wafting out like the breath of secrets long held.

The safe is neat, organized. Of course it is—this is Richard's space, and Richard keeps everything in its place. Folders labeled with dates, a small jewelry box, what looks like a passport, and a stack of documents bound with a black clip. I reach for these first, my heartbeat quickening. The paper feels expensive beneath my fingertips, heavy and textured.

"Let's see what you're hiding, Richard," I whisper, spreading the documents on the bed.

Financial records. Pages of them. I scan quickly, my eyes catching on numbers with too many zeros. Banking statements, transfer notices, loan agreements. I have seen this before, and my breath is caught in my throat. The story they tell is clear enough—Richard Wilson, successful businessman, pillar of the community, has a gambling problem.

A serious one.

I flip through more pages, my breath catching. Here it is—proof of what I suspected. A series of wire transfers from Jane Wilson's personal account to Richard's over the past three years. Large sums, each followed by payments to entities with vague, corporate names. But I recognize some of them from what my ex-husband left me with. Front companies for exclusive gaming establishments, the kind that don't advertise and don't forgive debts.

Mother dearest has been bailing him out. Repeatedly.

"Keeping your son on a leash, Jane?" I murmur, taking my phone from my pocket to snap discreet photos of the most damning pages.

I'm careful not to disturb the order of the papers, replacing each exactly as I found it.

I almost miss the iPad, tucked against the back wall of the safe. It's an older model, plugged into a charging cable that snakes through a small hole drilled in the back of the safe. Interesting—a permanently charging device, hidden away but kept ready. This isn't for casual use.

I disconnect it and press the home button. The screen lights up immediately—no password required. Either Richard is careless, or he considers the safe security enough. I tap on the mail icon first.

Richard's emails fill the screen, organized into folders with Jane's characteristic exactitude. I recognize his email style from messages I've glimpsed while cleaning—terse, formal, to the point. I scroll through quickly, looking for anything relevant, then pause when I spot a folder simply labeled "Mother."

My finger hovers over it for a moment before I tap. Dozens of conversations appear, dating back three years. I select one from two months ago.

From: Jane Wilson
To: Richard Wilson
Subject: Elizabeth's Charity Gala Involvement
Richard,

I've been observing Elizabeth's plans for the children's hospital gala. While her enthusiasm is commendable, I'm concerned about her inexperience leading to embarrassment for the family. The Prestons have chaired this event for years—they have the connections to ensure proper attendance.

Perhaps suggest she step aside and assist rather than lead? You might remind her that her strengths lie elsewhere. I've taken the liberty of speaking with Margaret Preston, who agrees this would be best.

Your mother

I swipe to the next email.

From: Richard Wilson
To: Jane Wilson
Subject: Re: Elizabeth's Charity Gala Involvement
Mother,

I'll speak with her tonight. Thank you for your foresight, as always.

Richard

Cold, calculated undermining. I remember this—Elizabeth had been excited about chairing that gala, had mentioned it while I dusted her living room. A week later, she was just "helping," her smile tight when she mentioned it in passing to the gardener. I'd thought nothing of it then.

I scroll through more emails, a pattern emerging. Jane's messages always the same: identifying ways Elizabeth is stepping beyond her assigned role, suggesting Richard "manage" his wife, offering helpful "alternatives" that diminish Elizabeth's position. Always framed as concern, as "for the best." And Richard, obedient son that he is, always agrees. He has to, right? Or no more money.

From: Jane Wilson
To: Richard Wilson
Subject: Holiday Dinner Arrangements
Richard,

I notice Elizabeth has been discussing hosting Christmas this

year. While I appreciate her initiative, I'm concerned the
disruption to tradition will upset your father's cousin Ellen,
who, as you know, is quite traditional and rather fragile these
days.
I think it best if we maintain our usual arrangements at my
home. Perhaps suggest to Elizabeth that she could be
responsible for the table settings? She has good taste in
such things, and it would give her a specific role to focus on.

Your mother

I check the date—almost three months ago, right when I
started working for her. I remember Elizabeth working for
weeks on holiday plans, making lists, calling caterers. Then
suddenly it all stopped. She spent three days in bed with
"migraines." Richard brought her tea that I prepared, his face a
mask of concern.

I close the email app, my hands trembling with anger. Poor
Elizabeth—surrounded by people who should protect her, yet
constantly undermined. I knew Jane was controlling, but seeing
the systematic way she manipulates both her son and daughter-
in-law makes my stomach turn.

I notice a notes app and tap it open. Files neatly arranged
by subject: "House Maintenance," "Club Memberships,"
"Financial Planning," and there—"Emergency Contacts."
Innocuous enough, but something about its placement at the
bottom of the list catches my attention.

Inside is not a list of phone numbers but an address. A property in Savannah, Georgia, listed under "Mother's Retreat."
There's a security code, notes about a caretaker who visits
weekly, and detailed instructions for "discreet arrival." The final
line reads: "No discussion with E under any circumstances."

I take photos of this too, my mind racing. A secret property

Elizabeth doesn't know about? Does Jane know about it? Do the police?

The sound of a car door slamming outside jerks me back to reality. I check the time—I've been in here a long time. Too long. I quickly replace the iPad exactly as I found it, making sure the charging cable is positioned correctly. The financial records go back in their folder, everything arranged exactly as I found it.

I close the safe door, listening for the soft click of the lock engaging. The painting goes back into place, my fingers smoothing the edge of the frame to ensure it sits perfectly against the wall. I step back, scanning the room. Nothing out of place, no sign I was ever here.

Grabbing my neglected cleaning supplies, I quickly dust the visible surfaces, run the vacuum over the carpet in broad stripes. Professional. Thorough. Just doing my job.

I'm wiping down the bathroom counter when I hear footsteps in the hallway—light, measured steps I recognize immediately. My heart slams against my ribs, but I don't pause in my movements. I've done nothing wrong. I'm just cleaning.

"Marie?" Jane's voice is soft but carries clearly through the doorway.

I turn, cloth still in hand, forcing my expression into one of mild surprise. My heart pounds in my chest. I didn't know she was going to come here. Is she checking up on me? I was looking for evidence to give to her, but I can't share what I found. She can't know I found any of this. It will destroy my position, and her trust in me.

"M-Mrs. Wilson. I didn't hear you come in."

Jane stands in the bedroom doorway, a silhouette of perfect posture and contained energy. Her hair is pulled back in a low ponytail, her linen pants and silk blouse casual in a way that you know it's designer and expensive. Her eyes scan the room, missing nothing.

"Elizabeth told me you were cleaning the beach house today. I thought I'd see how you were doing," she says, her tone revealing nothing.

I gesture to my cleaning caddy. "Just finishing up the bathroom. The main areas are done."

She steps into the room, moving to the center where she can see everything—including the painting above the dresser. Her gaze lingers there a moment too long before returning to me.

"Did you touch anything?" she asks, the question casual but her eyes sharp.

"Only to clean," I answer, meeting her gaze steadily. "Everything's spotless now."

"I meant beyond cleaning," she clarifies, her head tilting slightly. "Did you move anything? Richard is very particular about his things."

The air between us feels charged. Why would Richard care if I've moved his things? Doesn't Jane think something terrible has happened to him?

"The painting was a bit crooked," I say, watching her face closely. "I straightened it. Because it was dirty behind it," I add, leaving the statement deliberately ambiguous.

Something flickers in her eyes—concern? Relief? I can't tell.

"I see," she says finally. "Well, thank you for being so... thorough."

I nod, beginning to pack up my supplies. "It's my job to notice details, Mrs. Wilson."

"Yes," she agrees, her voice softer now. "I suppose it is."

I move past her into the hallway, feeling her eyes on my back. The weight of what I've discovered sits heavy in my chest —not just the secrets themselves, but what they might mean for Elizabeth. For all of them.

"Will you be staying here tonight?" I ask, pausing in the hallway.

"No," Jane answers. "Just checking that everything is good.

Looks like you did a great job. I'm sure Elizabeth will be very satisfied, even if she never comes here."

"I hope so."

"We should head back to town. My husband is expecting me for dinner at this new place that I absolutely dread going to. But what can you do?"

I nod awkwardly. I have never dreaded going to a fancy restaurant.

As we reach the end of the hallway, Jane pauses for a moment, turning to me with a curious look in her eyes. "Marie," she asks softly, "did you notice anything unusual at Elizabeth's party? Or perhaps something off about her brother?" Her voice is laced with an undercurrent of intrigue, as if she is piecing together a puzzle only she knows the shape of.

"No. Nothing unusual," I say.

She gives me a look. "Hm."

Jane follows me out the door and watches me as I lock it. My hands are shaking. She looks at me, her eyes softening.

"I can't believe Richard is still gone. We've got the yearly Cypress Estates country club charity ball coming up soon. I know it might sound silly, but I so wish Richard would come back in time to attend. We always go to it and have such a wonderful time. He never misses it."

I give her a smile and a soft nod. "Maybe he will."

"From your mouth to God's ears," she sighs.

I load my supplies into my car, my mind buzzing with dangerous possibilities. The information I've gathered today changes things—confirms suspicions, raises new questions. Could Elizabeth be right? Is Jane trying to frame her? Driving her insane so she can get rid of her? I can imagine Jane sending Richard off to that house in Savannah while she makes sure Elizabeth will be gone when he gets back. Admitted somewhere?

I start the engine, watching the beach house in my rearview

mirror. I pull away from the house, the photos I've taken burning a hole in my pocket. I came looking for leverage and found something far more complex—a family bound by secrets, money, and manipulation. And at the center of it all, Jane Wilson, pulling strings with cold precision.

SIXTEEN

JANE

I perch on the edge of the metal chair in Detective Mitchell's office, my back straight as a ruler. The fluorescent lights hum overhead, casting harsh shadows across the scratched wooden table between us. My purse sits on my lap like a shield.

"I wanted you to come in, because we've found something," he says.

My heart stutters. Found something. Not found *him*. I want to tell him so have I, but I want to hear what he has to say first.

"Could he have kept a secret life hidden from his family, and from you, Mrs. Wilson?"

"No, not Richard. Not from me. I've always known every-thing about my son—his favorite foods, his anxieties, the way he runs his hand through his hair when he's stressed. I was the one who taught him how to tie his shoes, who sat up with him when he had nightmares, who drove him to his first job interview. Richard doesn't keep secrets from me."

Except he has.

"He had a second phone that we found lots of information on. The phone was in his briefcase that he left in his office, and we found it when going through his things. We tracked that phone's location," Mitchell continues, pointing to a map on a printout. "He stopped at this apartment building the night before he disappeared. Stayed for three hours."

I stare intently at the little red dot on the digital map, my mind racing with images of Richard making his way toward that weathered brick building on the east side of town. It's nestled amidst a cluster of aging structures, a neighborhood marked by its faded signs and cracked sidewalks. I envision him entering the dimly lit lobby, the scent of dampness and old paint clinging to the air, before stepping into the creaky elevator that groans its way upward to the apartment. The thought of him crossing the threshold sends a surge of heat up my spine, and my fingers curl into my palm, nails biting sharply into my flesh as I wrestle with the unwelcome images in my mind.

"Now, we can't see which apartment he went into, only the building. Do you know who lives there?"

I stare at the address, my heart racing rapidly. I do know who lives there. I know exactly who she is. Yet I don't tell him this.

"No," I say. "This is not a part of town we frequent."

Mitchell's eyebrows lift, but he doesn't comment on my tone. "All right. I thought we'd at least ask."

I imagine Elizabeth finding out about this woman. Her perfect face crumpling, that polished exterior finally cracking. For a brief, horrible moment, I feel a dark satisfaction at the thought of her distress. Richard never should have married her. She's always been too cold, too controlled. Not right for my son.

The satisfaction is immediately followed by a wave of guilt so intense it makes me dizzy. My mouth fills with a bitter taste. What kind of mother takes pleasure in her son's failing marriage? In his pain?

But is it really his pain I'm concerned about, or my own? The thought slides into my mind, unwelcome and unsettling. I push it away.

"We'll find out which apartment he visited," Mitchell interrupts my thoughts, his tone firm but not unkind.

I clench my fists under the table, my pulse thundering beneath my skin. I want to scream, to demand that he understands what Richard means to me. That without my son, I am nothing.

Instead, I take a deep breath. "Can I take a photo?" I gesture to the folder.

Mitchell hesitates, then nods. "I guess you can take a photo of the location. But this doesn't leave this room, understand? If Richard is..." He pauses, choosing his words carefully. "If foul play is involved, we don't want to tip anyone off."

Foul play. The words hang in the air between us like smoke. I think of Richard in that awful apartment. Was *she* the last person to see him? Did she hurt him? The thought makes my hands shake. I know that the detective is trying to shut me up so I won't go to the chief of police and ask for more, or even worse, the mayor and complain about the entire police department as I have threatened to do before, but I will take it. I snap a quick photo with my phone.

"Thank you," I say, tucking my phone into my bag. "Please call me the moment you know anything more."

"Of course." He walks me to the door. "And Jane? Let us handle this. Don't do anything... impulsive."

I give him what I hope is a reassuring smile. "I just want my son back, Detective."

It's not a lie. I do want Richard back. But what Mitchell doesn't understand is that I'll do whatever it takes to make that happen.

As I leave, my mind is already racing ahead, plotting my next move. I slide into my Bentley. My hand trembles as I pull out my phone. Richard's face on the screensaver, illuminated by the harsh blue light, looks like a stranger's. I start the engine but don't move, transfixed by the image in my mind of my son with *her*.

My fingers grip the steering wheel so tightly as I move off and drive that my knuckles turn white. The leather creaks beneath my grasp. I've always prided myself on knowing everything about Richard—his habits, his moods, the subtle shifts in his voice that signal trouble.

It reminds me of when he was seventeen and started coming home late, smelling faintly of beer. I watched him for two weeks before confronting him about the senior parties he was attending. I remember his face—the shock that I knew, followed by shame.

"How did you find out?" he'd asked.

"I'm your mother," I'd replied, as if that explained everything. And to me, it did. Being Richard's mother means knowing him better than he knows himself.

A car cuts in front of me suddenly, and I slam on the brakes. My phone slides off the passenger seat onto the floor. I curse under my breath and reach for it at the next stoplight, my heart racing until I have it safely in my hand again.

The dashboard's lights dance over my face as I check the phone for damage. It's fine, but the picture is screaming at me from the screen. This is not my Richard. My Richard calls me every day without fail. My Richard has dinner at my house twice a month and tells me about his work, his investments, his plans.

Except he doesn't tell me everything, does he?

"She must have manipulated him somehow," I say aloud, the words a comfort in the silent car. Richard wouldn't willingly hide something this significant from me. This woman must have some hold on him.

The thought makes my breath come faster. Is that why he's missing? Is he hiding? Did she threaten him? Hurt him? Or is he with her right now, hiding from his life, from his responsibilities?

From me?

The low hum of the engine fills the car as I turn onto the highway that will take me home. I need to see this woman before Mitchell does. I need to look her in the eyes.

I glance again at my phone, at the address. North-east Jacksonville. I could go there tonight, wait outside, and watch her.

What would Richard think if he knew I was considering such a thing? He's always accused me of being overprotective, of getting too involved in his life. "Mother, I'm thirty-nine, not twelve," he said the last time I suggested his wife wasn't supporting his career properly. The hint of irritation in his voice had hurt, but I know him better than he knows himself. I've always protected him, even when he didn't realize he needed protection.

I remember when Richard was ten and broke his arm falling from a tree in the backyard. It was a crisp autumn afternoon, and the leaves crunched underfoot as he climbed higher, trying to reach the last apple clinging to the branches. When he fell, the sharp crack of his bone echoed through the yard, sending a jolt of fear through me. In the emergency room, with the sterile smell of antiseptic in the air, he'd looked at me with pain-glazed eyes and said, "Mother, don't let them hurt me." I'd held his hand through everything, glaring at the doctor who caused him pain, even while setting the bone to heal. The memory of his small fingers clutching mine so tightly is etched in my mind.

I've always protected him. Always.

Over the years, Richard has needed me in other ways too. There was that time in high school when he got into a scuffle with a classmate and ended up with a suspension. I was there, speaking to the principal, trying to understand what had happened, and making sure Richard was treated fairly. Then, during college, he struggled with his grades, and I found myself helping him navigate the chaos of assignments and deadlines, encouraging him to keep going despite the setbacks.

Financially, I've supported him more times than I can count. When he crashed his car while speeding and driving recklessly during his second year of college, leaving him stranded miles from campus, I didn't hesitate to cover the repair costs. And then there was the startup he was so passionate about. It was risky, but I believed in him and invested a significant amount to help get it off the ground. It failed, and he ended up working for the family company, even if he had sworn he'd rather die. That's when his father told me not to bail him out any more. That he needed to get by on his own. But then there was all the gambling. How could I not help him? I am still bailing him out of that again and again. His father doesn't know this. His father can't know this.

What if he's gone because of this horrible affair? What if this awful woman threatened to tell Elizabeth, and he panicked? What if she's blackmailing him somehow? The possibilities multiply in my mind, each more disturbing than the last.

Or what if it's simpler than that? What if he chose to be with her, to leave his life behind? To leave me behind?

No.

Richard wouldn't do that. It's always been Richard and me against the world. He knows that.

I may have failed to protect him from this woman once. I won't fail again. I turn the car around, and head east.

SEVENTEEN

MARIE

I press my back against the cracked plaster of my little living room, the one with the peeling wallpaper and the threadbare couch sagging under a pile of dirty laundry. A single bare bulb swings overhead, casting jittery shadows that feel as tired as I am. I'm halfway through sorting yesterday's dishes when the door flies open behind me.

Jane Wilson storms in, her presence filling the cramped space before her perfume even reaches my nose through the sour scent of stale takeout and damp carpet. She doesn't knock —she never does—and her heels click across the scratched linoleum like gunshots. I swallow hard, my heart slamming into my ribs.

"Marie," she says, her voice low and dangerous, "you owe me the truth."

Jane stands there, a striking figure in her tailored navy blazer and crisp white blouse, her hair cascading over her shoulders in waves. Her eyes, sharp and unyielding, fixate on me with an intensity that borders on madness. She sets her designer handbag on my rickety coffee table, its glossy leather gleaming under the dim light of my shabby apartment. The bag looks too expensive, a jarring contrast to the threadbare rug and peeling wallpaper. I stare at it, willing myself to stay still. I sit slumped in an old armchair, my dark hair pulled back in a messy bun. My eyes, wide and apprehensive, dart between Jane's face and the opulent bag, trying to gather the courage to speak.

"What... what are you doing here?" I manage.

"I'm here because you've been playing both sides." Her gray eyes narrow. "Spying on Elizabeth for me, feeding her little crumbs of information to keep her off balance. And all the while... you've been betraying me."

My throat goes dry. Betrayal. The word tastes like rust. "I—"

"You think I don't know?" Jane steps closer, the bulbs overhead flickering as if they can't bear her intensity. "I've seen how she looks at you. Heard the whispers. This"—she jabs a manicured finger at my chest—"this maid act, the dutiful little spy— you were never loyal."

I press my shaking hands into my jeans pockets. "I did what you asked. I—"

"Your lucrative little secret." Her lips twist into a bitter smile. "But now you've crossed the line."

The room shrinks around me. My pulse thunders. "What do you want?"

"I want the truth. No one crosses me and lives to tell about it."

"Wh... what? I have told you everything. I have done everything you asked me to."

"No, not everything, Marie, and you know it."

"What do you mean?"

Jane's gaze drills into me. "I know you're having an affair with my son."

The words land like stones in my gut. All color drains from my world. My legs go weak.

"You—" I can't find my voice.

"He came to your apartment the day before he vanished. He stayed for three hours, Marie."

"Y-yes."

"How could you?"

"You placed me there," I remind her, though my voice lacks conviction. "In the house."

"To watch *her*." Jane steps closer, the scent of her expensive perfume suffocating. "Well," Jane continues, her voice sharp as a blade, "I am going to tell Elizabeth. She's been harboring a snake."

Fear jolts through me. "Then I'll tell her you placed me there, to spy on her," I counter, surprising myself with my boldness. "How do you think that will be received? She'll never let you near the house again. You'll never know what happened to Richard."

I've crossed a line, and we both know it. Jane's face tightens, the skin stretching across her cheekbones.

The balance of power has shifted. I have something she wants.

She breathes in sharply. "What happened to my son?"

I look at her coldly.

"Get out of my house."

The door slams so hard the walls shake.

I sink onto the couch cushions, pressed between shame and fear. My hands curl into fists, nails digging into my palms. A tear shapes in the corner of my eye as I think about back in college, when I first met Richard.

EIGHTEEN

MARIE

Before

I slip through the heavy oak doors of the Wharton School Library, the leather satchel digging into my shoulder a constant reminder of my place here. Scholarship girl. Working-class interloper. The chandelier light catches on designer watches and pearl earrings as I move between tables, my secondhand blazer suddenly feeling like a costume in a play where everyone else received the proper wardrobe.

Three weeks into the semester, and I still haven't found my footing. The prestigious campus with its mix of ancient and modern buildings feels like a foreign country where I've memorized only the essential phrases but miss all the cultural nuances. Everyone else moves with the casual confidence of those born to belong.

The library, at least, offers some refuge. Books don't care about family names or trust funds. I run my fingers along the spines as I navigate toward the economics section, past study carrels occupied by students who probably summer in the Hamptons and winter in Aspen.

That's when I see him.

He sits alone at a corner table beneath a stained-glass window, the colored light painting academic halos across his dark hair. Even if I hadn't heard his name whispered in lecture halls, I would know he comes from money. It's in the precise cut of his navy blazer, the understated gleam of his watch—not flashy, but quietly expensive in that way only truly old money can be. His textbooks are arranged in perfect alignment with the edge of the table, his notes organized in neat stacks.

I pretend to search for a book while watching him from between the shelves. He adjusts his silver cufflinks—a habitual gesture, not born of necessity. His fountain pen makes quiet scratches against the paper as he works, and every few minutes, he runs his fingers through his hair, always between paragraphs, never mid-sentence. There's something mesmerizing in his methodical manner.

The library fills and empties around us, but he remains constant, focused. I've selected a book I don't need and claimed a table with a clear sight line to his. My own work sits neglected as I catalog his movements, the micro-expressions that flash across his face when he encounters something challenging in the text.

When he stands to retrieve another reference, I note how he straightens his already-straight tie, smooths his lapel. Every movement deliberate, controlled. He returns with a thick volume of economic theory—Schumpeter, from what I can glimpse of the spine—and settles back into his chair.

Minutes later, as he reaches for his water bottle, the book slides from his grasp, landing with a muffled thud at my feet. I hadn't realized I'd drifted so close to his table.

"I'm sorry," he says, looking up. His voice is warm.

I lean down to retrieve the book, my fingers tracing the embossed title. "It's fine," I say, handing it back. "Schumpeter is dense enough to bruise toes."

Something shifts in his expression—surprise, maybe, at my recognition of the text. "You're familiar with his work?" he asks, taking the book from me.

"'Creative destruction,'" I quote. "'The process of industrial mutation that continuously revolutionizes the economic structure from within.'" I've memorized the passage, highlighted it so many times the ink has bled through the page of my library copy.

He smiles, a small, restrained thing that nevertheless transforms his face. "Most people find him impenetrable."

"Most people don't have to understand him to pass Professor Harlow's midterm," I reply.

"You're in Harlow's Economic Development seminar?" He gestures to the chair across from him. "Please, join me."

I hesitate, acutely aware of my worn jeans beneath my blazer, the scuff marks on my shoes that no amount of polish can hide. He wears the kind of loafers that only really rich people can pull off.

"I don't want to interrupt," I say, but I'm already sliding into the seat, drawn by the focus of his gaze.

"I'm Richard Wilson." He extends his hand, and I note the manicured nails, the smooth skin that's never known manual labor.

"Marie Clements." My hand disappears into his briefly, and I resist the urge to check if my palm left a smudge.

"Scholarship?" he asks, and for a moment I stiffen, ready for the subtle condescension I've come to expect. But his tone holds only curiosity.

"Full ride," I confirm. "But I work on the side, cleaning and waitressing to cover rent and food."

He nods, and I wait for the obligatory comment about how "admirable" that is, the kind of thing rich kids say when they want to feel momentarily connected to the quaint struggles of the working class. Instead, he taps Schumpeter's cover.

"What did you think of his argument on the role of entre-
preneurs as disruptive forces?"

Just like that, we're discussing economic theory, and I forget
to be conscious of my secondhand clothes or the fact that I'd
skipped lunch to save money. I explain my critique of Schumpeter's blind spots regarding labor exploitation, and Richard
listens—actually listens—with his head tilted, eyes narrowed in
concentration.

"That's an interesting perspective," he says when I finish. "I
hadn't considered the power dynamics from that angle."

For the first time since arriving at Wharton, I don't feel like
an impostor. The way Richard leans forward, elbows on the
table, chin resting on his interlaced fingers—his entire body
language communicates genuine engagement with my ideas.

"Sorry," I say, suddenly aware I've been talking for several
minutes. "I tend to get carried away."

"Don't apologize for passion," he says. "It's refreshing."

The afternoon light shifts through the stained glass, casting
prismatic patterns across our books. I should leave—my shift at
the campus coffee shop starts in an hour—but I find myself
rooted to the chair, cataloging the precise blue of his eyes, the
way his signet ring catches the light when he turns a page.

"I should go," I finally say, gathering my neglected notes.

"Same time tomorrow?" he asks, and there's something in
his voice—a hint of eagerness beneath the cultivated calm—that
makes my heart skip.

"Sure," I say, aiming for casual and missing by miles.

As I walk away, I feel his eyes following me, and something
warm unfurls in my chest—a dangerous feeling of possibility. I
know the rules of places like Wharton. Boys like Richard
Wilson don't end up with scholarship girls from nowhere
towns. They date debutantes and marry within their tax
bracket.

But for a few hours, in the quiet space between economic

theories, the distance between our worlds felt crossable. And that's a far more intoxicating idea than I care to admit.

Over the next month, Richard and I carve out a rhythm between us, our study sessions becoming regular. Tuesdays and Thursdays in the library's west wing, where the afternoon light stretches lazy fingers across our shared table. Mondays and Wednesdays at The Grind, the campus coffee shop where I sometimes work evening cleaning after closing. I learn to read his moods in the arrangement of his pens, the careful way he aligns his notebook to the table edge when he's stressed, the slight relaxation of his shoulders when it's just the two of us.

On days when I work behind the counter, I catch him watching me, his gaze tracking my movements. When our fingers brush during the handoff of his Americano, I note the microsecond his touch lingers—a data point I file away with dozens of others. The slight forward tilt of his torso when I'm speaking. The way his formal reserve softens around the edges after our third or fourth meeting. The rare laugh I manage to draw from him when I tease apart the flaws in our professor's argument.

"That's not what Marx intended at all," I say one afternoon as we huddle over our textbooks, and Richard's laugh—a genuine one that reaches his eyes—feels like winning something precious.

The Grind hums around us, the air thick with coffee steam and the murmur of student conversations. Richard's Americano sits cooling beside my more economical drip coffee. I've stopped pretending I don't notice the difference. Instead, I make mental notes of everything—the way he holds his mug, the unconscious straightening of his spine when someone from his social circle walks by, the subtle softening of his expression when we're alone again.

"You're different," he says unexpectedly, setting down his pen.

"Different how?" I ask, suddenly self-conscious.

"You actually think about the material. Everyone else just memorizes enough to pass the exams." He runs a hand through his hair—right on schedule, I think, noting the time. "They're just checking a box on the way to whatever corporate job their parents have lined up."

"Isn't that what you're doing?" The question slips out before I can filter it.

Instead of taking offense, he smiles—a wry twist of his lips. "The Wilson name opens certain doors. In boardrooms, country clubs." He traces the rim of his mug with one finger. "My mother has my entire future mapped out, down to which corner office I'll occupy and which social register family I'll marry into."

"And you're okay with that?" I keep my tone light, but I'm cataloging every word, every expression.

"It's complicated." He looks out the window, where students cross the quad with the easy confidence of those who've never questioned their place in the world. "The family business has been built over generations. Duty. Legacy. These aren't just words to my mother."

"Your mother sounds... formidable." I test the waters.

"Jane Wilson doesn't just plan for contingencies—she elimi-nates them." He says this with a mix of respect and resignation that I file away for later examination. "Nothing happens without her approval."

"But what about you? What do you want?" I ask.

His eyes are lit up, and his smile suddenly bright. "I'd rather start my own company."

"Then you should."

He shakes his head. "I can't. They'll never let me."

I try to imagine growing up with such expectations. My

own childhood featured free lunch programs and secondhand clothes, my mother picking up extra shifts to keep our electricity on.

"What about you?" Richard asks, turning the conversation. "What's your family like?"

I shrug, stirring my coffee though the creamer dissolved long ago. "Not much to tell. My mom works at a hospital—administrative assistant, not doctor. Dad left when I was ten. We moved around a lot. This scholarship was my ticket out."

"That must have been difficult." His expression shows genuine interest, not the performative sympathy I often get from wealthy students.

"We managed." I pause, weighing how much to reveal.

Richard's eyes narrow, processing this information. I wonder if he's ever had to work a day in his life, or if words like "rent" and "utilities" exist only as abstract concepts to him.

"Is that why you always order drip coffee instead of lattes?" he asks suddenly.

I feel heat rise to my cheeks. Of course he's noticed. "Three-dollar difference adds up when you're on a budget."

He seems about to say something—perhaps offer to buy my coffee, which would embarrass us both—when his phone buzzes on the table. The screen illuminates with "Mother" and a perfectly composed photo of an elegant older woman.

The transformation is immediate and fascinating. Richard's shoulders square, his jaw tightens, his entire body language shifts like he's donning invisible armor. He answers with, "Hello, Mother," in a voice stripped of the warmth it held moments ago.

I pretend to focus on my notes while unabashedly listening to his side of the conversation. His responses are clipped, formal affirmatives: "Yes, Mother." "Of course." "I understand." His free hand has unconsciously aligned his pen perfectly parallel to his notebook edge.

"I'll be there," he says finally, eyes flicking to his watch—a Patek Philippe I've priced online during moments of weakness. "Six o'clock. Yes, I remember."

He ends the call and sits motionless for three seconds—I count them—before his body language gradually thaws.

"Sorry about that," he says, already gathering his things. "Family dinner I forgot about."

"No problem." I maintain a casual tone while noting every detail: the light tremor in his hands as he closes his textbook, the renewed formality in his posture, the way his accent has shifted to more patrician after speaking with his mother.

"I've got to run. Can we pick this up tomorrow?" He's already half-standing, his mind clearly elsewhere.

"Sure. Library at two?"

"Perfect." He offers a distracted smile that doesn't reach his eyes, then hesitates. For a moment, I think he might explain more about the call, about his mother, about the dinner that has him checking his watch again with barely concealed anxiety. Instead, he says, "Your point about labor alienation was brilliant, by the way. You should develop that for your final paper."

Before I can respond, he's gone, weaving between tables with the careful grace of someone raised in spaces far more exclusive than this campus coffee shop. I watch his retreating back—the perfect cut of his blazer, the set of his shoulders that has reverted to something stiffer, more formal after his mother's call.

A knot tightens in my chest as I gather my own things more slowly. I've always been good at watching people, at noticing the patterns in their behavior, the subtle tells that reveal what they try to hide.

But Richard Wilson isn't just anyone. And the way his entire being changed at the sound of his mother's voice sends a warning flare through me.

.　.　.

Richard guides me through polished brass doors with a light touch at the small of my back. La Maison d'Or unfolds before us—all amber lighting and white tablecloths that glow like small moons in the dimness. A chandelier casts fractured light across crystal stemware, and the soft murmur of expensive conversations hangs in the air. I tug discreetly at the hem of my dress—black, simple, purchased secondhand but carefully tailored to hide that fact—and follow the maître d' to our corner table, feeling every eye track our passage.

"Wine list, sir?" The server materializes beside us, addressing Richard as if I'm merely decorative. Richard doesn't seem to notice, accepting the leather-bound menu with a casual nod that speaks of familiarity with such rituals.

I settle into my chair, tucking my legs carefully to one side the way I've seen women do in films, and study the menu with mounting panic. No prices listed—the universal signal that if you have to ask, you can't afford it. My semester's textbook budget probably wouldn't cover the appetizers.

"The duck confit is excellent," Richard says, misinterpreting my silence for indecision rather than economic vertigo. "Or the seared scallops, if you prefer seafood."

"I trust your judgment," I reply, which is both true and a convenient escape from revealing my complete unfamiliarity with half the French terms on the menu.

A different server approaches, this one bearing a silver tray. His gaze slides over me with clinical assessment—taking in my dress, my hair, my lack of designer accessories—before turning to Richard with skilled deference.

"Good evening, Mr. Wilson. Lovely to see you again."

Richard smiles. "Thank you, James. It's been a while."

The exchange confirms what I'd suspected—this isn't just any expensive restaurant; it's one the Wilson family frequents. I wonder if Richard's mother has her regular table, if the staff knows her wine preferences without asking.

"The twenty fifteen Château Margaux, please," Richard says, and I suppress a wince at what I know such a bottle costs. "Marie, is red all right with you?"

I nod, smiling through the discomfort of being so thoroughly out of my element. The waiter retreats, and Richard reaches across the table to touch my hand briefly.

"You look beautiful tonight," he says, and the simple sincerity in his voice momentarily eases the tightness in my chest.

"Thank you. This place is..." I search for a word that won't betray my intimidation.

"Too formal?" he asks, surprising me with his perception. "We could go somewhere else if you'd prefer."

"No, it's fine." I straighten my posture, determined not to let him see how the crystal and silver make my hands want to tremble. "Though I suspect they don't serve ramen here."

He laughs, and the sound loosens something in the air between us. "Probably not. Though sometimes I prefer it to whatever deconstructed, foam-enhanced creation is currently fashionable."

The wine arrives with ceremony—the presentation of the bottle, the ritual of the cork, Richard's performative taste before nodding approval. I follow his lead through each course, watching which fork he selects, how he breaks his bread, the precise angle at which he holds his wine glass. I'm learning his world one detail at a time, filing away each observation like a survival guide to a foreign country.

Between the main course and dessert, Richard tells me about his childhood summers in Newport, about sailing with his father, about the weight of a family name that stretches back to the *Mayflower*. I share stories of my own—carefully edited versions of moving from apartment to apartment, of my mother's determination, of scholarships and weekend jobs through high school. We're exchanging more than anecdotes; we're offering maps to territories the other has never visited.

"Sometimes I envy you," he says unexpectedly as we share a chocolate soufflé.

"Me? Why?"

"Your freedom. Every decision I make has the weight of five generations behind it." He runs a finger around the rim of his water glass. "My mother reminds me constantly that I'm not just Richard—I'm a Wilson. Son of a senator."

"And who would you be, if you could choose?" I ask, genuinely curious.

He considers this, his fork paused midair. "I don't know," he admits finally. "That's the problem."

When the check arrives, he signs without looking at the total, an unconscious gesture that reminds me of the gulf between us. Yet as we stand to leave, his hand finds the small of my back again, and that point of contact feels like a bridge across impossible distance.

Outside, the night wraps around us, crisp and clear with early spring. Richard's car waits at the curb—a sleek German import with butter-soft leather seats. He opens my door, and I slide in, careful not to catch my dress on anything. The interior smells of his cologne and something else, a subtle leather-and-wool richness that I associate exclusively with him.

He joins me, closing his door with a solid thunk that seals us in a bubble of quiet luxury. Instead of starting the engine, he sits motionless, his profile outlined by the distant streetlights. For several breaths, neither of us speaks.

"I had a wonderful time," I offer finally, when the silence stretches too long.

He turns to face me, and something in his expression makes my breath catch. There's vulnerability there, something I've never seen on his carefully composed face.

"Marie," he begins, then stops. His fingers tap a gentle

rhythm on the steering wheel—one, two, three, pause, repeat. A nervous habit I've never observed in him before.

I reach up to brush a stray curl behind my ear, and his eyes track the movement with unexpected intensity. Then he's leaning toward me, crossing the divide between our seats with deliberate slowness, giving me time to retreat if I wish.

I don't.

His lips meet mine in a kiss that starts gentle but deepens as my hand comes up to rest lightly on his chest. I feel the steady thud of his heart beneath fine cotton, catalog the pressure of his mouth, the faint trace of chocolate from our shared dessert, the subtle catch of his breath when I respond.

My free hand finds the leather seat beneath me, fingers tracing the seam as if to anchor myself in a moment I want to remember in perfect detail. The warmth of his skin radiates through his shirt. The whisper of his breath against my cheek when we part slightly, only to come together again.

Time suspends in the dark cocoon of his car. Outside, the city hums and flows around us, but here there is only the sound of our breathing, the gentle exploration of his hand at my neck, my fingers curling into the fabric of his jacket.

When we finally separate, his eyes search mine in the dimness. Whatever he sees there makes him smile—a genuine smile that transforms his face from handsome to almost painfully beautiful.

"I've been wanting to do that since the day you picked up my Schumpeter," he confesses, his voice lower than usual.

I laugh softly, aware of the irony. "That's not a line many girls hear."

"You're not many girls." His thumb traces my bottom lip with a reverence that steals my breath. "That's what makes you impossible to ignore."

I store away every second of this moment—the texture of the leather against my legs, the pattern of shadows across his face, the precise cadence of his words. This is a memory I want to keep pristine, perfect.

What I don't tell him is that I've been rehearsing this moment for weeks in my mind, playing out every possible scenario, studying his expressions and movements for any hint of interest. What probably feels spontaneous to him has been anticipated by me in a hundred different variations.

His forehead rests briefly against mine, our breath mingling in the small space between us. Outside, the city continues its nocturnal rhythm, but inside this car, we've created our own private universe where class differences and family expectations temporarily dissolve into insignificance.

"We should go," he whispers eventually, though he makes no move to start the car.

"We should," I agree, equally motionless.

Neither of us is ready to break the spell, to return to a world where he is Richard Wilson, heir to generations of privilege, and I am Marie Clements, scholarship girl from nowhere special. For now, in this moment, we're just two people connected by something that feels startlingly like belonging.

Richard's apartment occupies the top floor of a pre-war building with a doorman who eyes my worn boots with the briefest flicker of judgment. Inside, floor-to-ceiling windows frame the city skyline like living art, the lights of downtown glittering against the darkening evening sky. The space is exactly what I expected—hardwood floors gleaming beneath artfully arranged furniture that manages to look both new and casually lived-in, the kind of "effortless" aesthetic that requires serious money to achieve.

"Not too many people," Richard had promised when he invited me. "Just a few friends from the investment club."

A few friends turn out to be about fifteen impeccably

dressed twenty-somethings, all radiating the particular confidence that comes from never having worried about money. They clutch crystal tumblers of amber liquids or delicate stemmed glasses of wine, forming conversational clusters that shift and reform as if choreographed.

Richard guides me through the room with a hand at my waist, introducing me with a simple, "This is Marie." No explanation of how we met, no qualifier about my scholarship status. I'm grateful for this small mercy, though I suspect many already know.

"Economics, right?" asks a tall blonde with a casual cashmere sweater, if that's even a thing. "Richard mentioned you're brilliant."

"She is," Richard affirms, squeezing my waist gently. "Marie's paper on labor market inequalities is being published in the undergraduate journal next month."

"How impressive," says another woman, her dark hair twisted into an elegant knot. "Such an... important topic."

I smile and nod, hyperaware of my carefully curated outfit —the nicest pieces I own, assembled into what I hoped would read as understated elegance but now feels hopelessly inadequate. My earrings are silver plated, not sterling, my dress from a department store's clearance rack, not a boutique.

Richard is pulled away by someone wanting to discuss summer internships, leaving me stranded near the marble-topped kitchen island. I sip my wine slowly, calculating how long I need to stay.

Two men in nearly identical blue blazers stand nearby, their voices low but not quite low enough.

"—Wilson's latest project," one says, glancing my way. "The scholarship girl."

"His mother must be thrilled," the other replies with a smirk. "What would Jane Wilson think about her precious heir slumming with the help?"

"Three months, tops," the first predicts.

They notice my gaze and smile blandly before drifting away. I remain by the counter, my wine glass a prop to keep my hands occupied. Across the room, Richard laughs at something someone has said, his head thrown back in a way I've never seen with me. He belongs here, among these people with their shared references and inherited connections. I am an exhibit—the interesting, temporary diversion from his real life.

A woman with a sharp bob and sharper eyes approaches, extending her hand. "I'm Alicia. Richard and I practically grew up together." Her handshake is brief, assessing. "Our mothers serve on the same charity boards."

"Nice to meet you," I say, though it isn't.

"Richard seems quite taken with you." She tilts her head, studying me like a curious specimen. "He mentioned you work at the campus coffee shop?"

"I clean and sometimes work behind the counter," I add, though I immediately regret volunteering this additional evidence of my need for income.

"How industrious." The word drips with condescension disguised as compliment. "I've always admired people who... work so hard."

I smile, teeth clenched behind my lips. "Some of us don't have the luxury of family connections."

Her eyes widen at my directness. "Well," she says after a moment, "connection or not, Richard always gets what his mother wants in the end." She sips her wine, her eyes holding mine over the rim. "And Jane Wilson has very specific wants for her only son."

Before I can respond, Richard returns to my side, his presence both a relief and a new tension. I wonder if he heard Alicia's thinly veiled warning. His easy smile suggests not.

The evening stretches endlessly, each conversation a minefield of subtle class markers and references designed to exclude.

By the time the last guest leaves, my face aches from maintaining my polite mask.

"They liked you," Richard says as he closes the door behind Alicia and her companion, whose name I've already forgotten.

I don't contradict him. Perhaps in his world, thinly veiled assessment passes for acceptance.

The next morning, I spot Richard through The Grind's window before I enter. He sits at our usual table, the morning sun streaming across his face, highlighting the shadows beneath his eyes. His jacket hangs open, uncharacteristically casual, and his hands cup a coffee mug that he doesn't drink from.

Something is wrong. I catalog the signs automatically—the slight furrow between his eyebrows, the way his shoulders hunch forward rather than maintaining their usual perfect posture, the untouched coffee growing cold before him.

"Hey," I say, sliding into the chair across from him. "You look tired."

He meets my eyes briefly before his gaze skitters away to some point over my shoulder. "I didn't sleep well."

The espresso machine hisses in the background, punctuating the sudden awkward silence between us. Richard's fingers tap a nervous rhythm against his mug—one, two, three, pause, repeat—the same pattern I noticed in his car the night we first kissed.

"My mother called." The words emerge barely above the ambient noise of the coffee shop. His voice is flat, stripped of its usual warm cadence.

My stomach tightens. "Oh?"

"She's concerned about my focus lately." He finally looks at me directly, his expression a carefully constructed neutral that doesn't reach his eyes. "My grades, my internship applications."

I wait, knowing there's more, knowing exactly where this is heading but requiring him to say it.

"You're brilliant, Marie." The compliment lands like a prelude to execution. "But we come from different worlds."

"Different worlds," I repeat, my voice hollow. "I see."

"It's not that simple—"

"It is, though." I fold my hands in my lap to hide their trembling. "Your mother doesn't approve of the scholarship girl."

A flash of something—pain, guilt, relief?—crosses his face. "I think it's better if we end things now, before..."

"Before it gets serious?" I supply when he trails off. "Before your mother has to actually meet me and confirm her suspicions that I'm completely unsuitable?"

"That's not fair."

"Isn't it?" My voice remains calm, at odds with the fracturing I feel inside. "Tell me, Richard. If your mother hadn't called, would we be having this conversation?"

He doesn't answer, which is answer enough.

"I understand," I say, and I do. I've always understood the temporary nature of whatever existed between us. Fantasy versus reality. A diversion versus a suitable match. "The Wilson name has standards to maintain."

"Marie—"

"It's fine." I cut him off, unable to bear whatever rationalization he's about to offer. "Really. We had fun. But you're right. Different worlds."

I stand, my movements controlled despite the chaos roiling beneath my skin. My face remains a mask of calm acceptance while inside, something essential shatters into jagged pieces.

"I am sorry," he says, and I believe him. Richard isn't cruel, just weak in the ways that privilege often makes people—unable to fight against the currents that have carried him comfortably his entire life.

"Goodbye, Richard." I turn away before he can respond, my steps measured as I walk out of the coffee shop, out of his life.

The sunlight outside feels obscenely bright. Campus life continues around me—students rushing to class, laughing in groups, utterly unaware that my world has just collapsed. I maintain my composure with rigid control, each step carefully placed as if the ground might crumble beneath me.

Only when I'm alone in the stairwell of my dormitory do I allow my expression to change, the mask slipping to reveal the raw devastation beneath. But I don't cry. Instead, I feel a strange, cold clarity descending.

Knowledge is power. And right now, I feel powerless in a way I haven't since I was a child watching my father walk out the door. I won't feel this way again. I can't.

Two weeks after the breakup, I'm positioned behind a stone column on the quad, ostensibly reading, when Richard emerges from his afternoon seminar. That's when I see her.

A woman approaches him with purposeful strides—tall, elegant, her silver-streaked hair swept into an immaculate chignon, her tailored suit the color of rich burgundy. Even at a distance, I can see the resemblance: the same straight nose, the same precise way of holding the shoulders. Jane Wilson in the flesh, every bit as formidable as Richard described.

She doesn't hug him, doesn't display any of the typical maternal warmth one might expect. Instead, she places a hand on his arm—a proprietary gesture—and speaks to him in what appears to be a low, continuous stream. I'm too far away to hear the words, but I can read the body language perfectly.

Richard nods deferentially, his posture straightening, his entire being adjusting to her presence like a flower tracking the sun. He becomes smaller somehow, more contained, as if folding himself into a predetermined mold. His mother speaks; he listens. She gestures; he follows her lead.

They walk past my hiding spot, close enough now that fragments of conversation reach me.

"—told the board you'd be ready by June—"

"—dinner with the Harrises next week—"

"—need to focus now, Richard, not get distracted again—"

Jane Wilson walks beside her son, her hand still on his arm, guiding him subtly but unmistakably. Her profile is aristocratic, her movements economical yet graceful. She radiates authority in a way I've only seen in the most powerful professors, but with an added edge of something colder, more calculating.

As they pass, Richard's gaze sweeps across my location without recognition. But Jane—Jane pauses, her eyes narrowing as they land on me. For one electric moment, she sees me— really sees me—with an assessment so penetrating I feel physically exposed. Then she dismisses me with the slightest tightening of her lips, turning back to Richard and steering him away with renewed purpose.

In that moment, something crystallizes within me. Richard isn't just Richard—he's the product of this woman, this family, this entire system that deemed me unsuitable. Richard Wilson has just taught me the most important lesson of my education: in his world, love is secondary to suitability. It's a lesson I won't forget.

NINETEEN

MARIE

Silence stretches in my small apartment. I'm brutally ripped back to my present reality by my phone vibrating in the pocket of my torn cardigan.

I fish it out. Caller ID reads "Unknown." My thumb hovers over "Answer," but I know it's them—always them.

"Marie," the voice snarls the instant I pick up. "Where's my money?"

I press the phone to my ear, chest tightening. "I-I don't have it yet. I need more time."

"Time's up. Today." His tone is colder than Jane's glare.

My vision blurs. No time. No money. Burst of panic. I clamp my hand over the mouthpiece, breathing so hard I'm afraid I'll hyperventilate. The line goes dead, leaving me alone in the flickering light, heart pounding, trapped between two ruthless women—and a debt I can never repay.

TWENTY

JANE

I stand at the edge of the room, champagne flute balanced between fingertips that haven't stopped trembling since I arrived. The country club ballroom gleams with wealth—chandeliers throwing calculated light onto calculated smiles. I've attended dozens of these charity galas, but tonight feels different. Then Elizabeth makes her entrance, and suddenly I understand why my skin has been prickling with anticipation all evening.

Elizabeth glides through the doorway in midnight blue silk that catches the light like water. Her blonde hair falls in a perfect sweep across bare shoulders, and her smile—precise, practiced—switches on like a lamp.

But it's not Elizabeth who makes me nearly drop my glass. It's the woman who follows her.

"Who on earth is that?" whispers Valerie beside me, the wife of some hedge fund manager whose name I can never remember.

I don't answer because I'm trying to process what I'm seeing. The woman trailing behind Elizabeth is slender and plain, with mousy brown hair pulled back in a severe bun. I recognize her immediately—it's Marie. I've only seen her once out of her cleaning uniform, and then she definitely didn't look the way she does in this moment. Tonight, she's wearing a dress I recognize as Elizabeth's—a Givenchy I'd complimented at a luncheon last month. On Elizabeth, it had been elegant, fitted perfection. On Marie, it hangs like expensive drapery on a discount rod, loose across her chest, the hemline awkwardly long.

"Is that her dress?" Valerie hisses, her surgeon-crafted eyebrows climbing toward her hairline.

I nod, unable to form words. My heartbeat quickens as I watch them move through the crowd together. Elizabeth's hand rests lightly on Marie's elbow, guiding her toward a cluster of the neighborhood's most esteemed residents. I drift closer, drawn by a curiosity that feels almost predatory.

"Marie, these are my dearest friends," Elizabeth says, her voice carrying that familiar melodic quality she reserves for social occasions. There's something in her eyes I can't quite place—pride? Challenge? The group responds with reserved smiles, hands extended in obligatory greeting.

"Lovely to meet you all," Marie says, and I'm struck by how she mirrors Elizabeth's diction, the slight tilt of her head as she speaks. It's uncanny, like watching someone try on another person's skin.

I circle the group, pretending to admire a floral arrangement while straining to hear their conversation. Marie speaks of art exhibits and foreign films with surprising fluency, but there's a mechanical quality to her knowledge, as though she's reciting from memory rather than experience.

"And how do you know Elizabeth?" asks Caroline Porter, whose husband owns half the real estate developments in Jacksonville.

A beat of hesitation.

Elizabeth intercepts smoothly: "Marie and I met through

my charity work. She has the most fascinating perspective on community outreach."

Lies slip from Elizabeth's lips like smooth stones, polished and unremarkable. I've heard her mention Marie before—always as "my maid" or "the cleaning lady." Never as a friend. Never as someone she'd bring to the Cypress Estates annual fundraiser, wearing her own designer dress.

I watch the ripple effect through the small gathering. Glances exchange like silent telegrams. A slight widening of eyes. A subtle tightening of smiles. These people—my neighbors, my social circle—are experts in the language of unspoken judgment. They won't say anything directly, not here, not now. But I can read their thoughts as clearly as headlines.

"You look wonderful, Marie," says Michael Jenkins, his voice carrying that particular tone men reserve for women they consider beneath them. "That color suits you."

"Thank you," Marie replies, running her hands down the loose fabric at her hips. "Elizabeth insisted I borrow it. She's generous that way."

Another beat of silence. Elizabeth laughs, a sound like crystal tapped with silver. "Marie is too modest. She's been such a blessing in my life."

The group dissolves into conversation about the recent renovation of the club's east wing, but the undercurrent remains. I drift away, needing distance to process what I'm witnessing. My glass is empty, though I don't remember drinking its contents.

At the dimly lit bar, I order another glass of champagne, the golden liquid bubbling up to the rim, as I try to steady my breathing, which has become shallow and irregular. The bartender, a tall man with a neat bowtie and a knowing smile, serves me with a nod, his eyes flickering briefly towards Marie. I watch as one of the waiters, a young woman with a crisp uniform and a cautious glance, pauses as she passes by, her eyes lingering on Marie with a mix of curiosity and something akin to recognition? Marie, once one of them, now stands on the other side.

What game is Elizabeth playing? The Elizabeth I know is absolutely obsessed with her image and social status. She once cut off all communication with a board member just because they dared to suggest using paper napkins at the prestigious spring luncheon. Individuals like Elizabeth don't usually dress their maids in high-end designer clothes and introduce them as close companions. It's completely out of character. What could possibly be going on here?

And what about Marie? Our conversation last night repeats in my head. I spent all night trying to figure out if she knows where Richard is. If she's done something to him. But why would she?

I was wrong to place my trust in Marie. But what does that realization mean for my future? I need to start questioning everything I thought I knew.

I turn back toward the room, scanning for Elizabeth's blonde head among the crowd. I find her near the grand piano, laughing at something the club president is saying. Marie stands a little apart, watching Elizabeth with an intensity that makes my skin crawl. Her posture is different now—shoulders back, chin lifted. She holds her borrowed finery with growing confidence, as though the longer she wears it, the more it becomes hers.

"Quite the interesting plus-one Elizabeth brought tonight," says a voice at my elbow. It's James Mercer, a divorced attorney whose interest in me has been as persistent as it is unwelcome.

"Mmm," I respond noncommittally, still watching Marie.

"You know," he continues, leaning closer than necessary, "sometimes I wonder what everyone here is hiding."

The comment lands between us like a lit match. I turn to look at him properly, noting the knowing gleam in his eyes, the slight curl at the corner of his mouth. Does he know something I don't? Or is he simply doing what everyone else is—speculating, theorizing, constructing narratives from fragments?

"What are you implying, James?" I ask, my voice sounding distant to my own ears.

He shrugs, tapping his wedding-ringless finger against his glass. "Nothing specific. Just an observation that people in glass houses..." He trails off, his gaze drifting meaningfully toward Elizabeth and Marie. "How's Richard, by the way?"

He knows very well that Richard is missing; the rumor around the neighborhood is that he ran off with his mistress. This is not a question because he cares. This is a jab at me for not controlling my son's behavior well enough. I choose to ignore it. I don't have time for these people and their rumors.

I turn back to watch them, my suspicion hardening into something more concrete. Marie is speaking animatedly to a small group now, her hands gesturing in a way that perfectly mimics Elizabeth's characteristic movements. It's subtle—the way she tilts her head when listening, the light touch on someone's arm for emphasis—but unmistakable to anyone who's spent time studying Elizabeth.

I find her presence highly inappropriate and can't help wondering why Elizabeth would bring her here. To make me angry? To show me she knows about our arrangement? To flaunt her close relationship with her in my face? Letting me know she belongs to her now? That her loyalties have shifted? Does she know who Marie is?

The evening progresses in a haze of forced pleasantries and sidelong glances. I find myself unable to focus on conversations, my attention repeatedly drawn back to the strange pairing of the society wife and her maid. Elizabeth moves through the room, touching bases with everyone who matters, while Marie—growing more confident by the hour—stands in small circles of conversation, nodding and smiling as though she's always belonged here.

My husband—Joseph—finds me eventually, his hand warm at the small of my back. "You look like you've seen a ghost," he murmurs.

"Do you see that woman with Elizabeth?" I ask, nodding in their direction. "That's her cleaning lady."

He follows my gaze, frowning. "Are you sure? Why would she—"

"I don't know," I cut him off. "But she's wearing Elizabeth's dress."

He gives me that look—the one that says I'm being dramatic again, obsessing over details that don't matter. "Maybe she's being charitable," he suggests. "You know how kind Elizabeth is. Maybe they're just becoming friends."

But that's just it. I do know Elizabeth. And something doesn't feel right.

Across the room, Elizabeth catches my stare and raises her champagne in greeting. Her smile doesn't waver, but something in her eyes makes my throat tighten. Marie turns to see who Elizabeth is acknowledging, and for a moment, our gazes lock. Her expression is placid, unreadable. But there's something in the set of her mouth—a slight curve, almost smug—that sends a chill through me.

I stand frozen, my mouth agape, my eyes flickering between the two women as conversations flow around me like water around a stone. In this moment, I'm certain of only one thing: whatever is happening between Elizabeth Wilson and her cleaning lady, it isn't charity. And I need to find out what it is, before something irreversible occurs.

I abandon my husband to another endless conversation about golf handicaps and weave through the crowd, my focus narrowing like a camera lens on the two women who've consumed my thoughts all evening. The champagne in my system has shifted from a pleasant buzz to a sharp clarity. Something isn't right. The way Marie moves in Elizabeth's dress, the way her gestures become more fluid, more familiar with each passing hour—it's as though I'm watching a transformation, a becoming. And Elizabeth, oblivious or complicit, continues to shine her spotlight on this strange understudy.

Elizabeth laughs at something the club president's wife says, her head tilting back to expose the long line of her throat, the diamonds at her ears catching light. I've seen this laugh a hundred times at a hundred functions—it's her social laugh, rehearsed and perfect, loud enough to be noticed but not so loud as to be vulgar. Her hand touches her collarbone briefly, another signature Elizabeth gesture.

Ten feet away, Marie stands with three women I recognize from the garden committee. As I watch, she laughs just like Elizabeth.

"Another champagne, please," I tell the bartender, positioning myself strategically near Marie's group while pretending to study the silent auction items displayed on a nearby table. My heart pounds against my ribs as I strain to hear their conversation.

"—must be so fascinating," one of the women is saying, her voice dripping with condescension poorly disguised as interest. "Cleaning other people's houses."

Marie's response is measured, her voice soft yet somehow commanding attention. "I find people endlessly fascinating in every context. Don't you?" There's a subtle emphasis on the "you" that makes the woman shift uncomfortably.

"Well, yes, I suppose," she responds, clearly wrong-footed.

"Elizabeth has been so kind to include me tonight," Marie continues, smoothing her hands down the borrowed dress. "She says true friendship transcends social boundaries."

I nearly snort into my champagne. In the years I've known Elizabeth Wilson, she's never expressed a sentiment remotely like that. As soon as she got into our family, she acted as if she'd been privileged all her life.

I move along the bar, closer now to where Marie stands. She holds herself differently than she did earlier in the evening—the initial awkwardness in the borrowed finery has vanished. Now she wears the dress as though it was made for her, despite the poor fit. Her posture mimics Elizabeth's regal bearing, her gestures fluid and assured. It's only when she thinks no one is watching that her eyes change—calculating, observant, taking in every detail of her surroundings.

A small group gathers near me at the bar—James Mercer, the divorced attorney, Caroline Porter and her husband, and the club's treasurer, whose name escapes me. They lower their voices, but in the momentary lull of music between songs, their words carry.

"—quite the bold statement Elizabeth's making," Caroline says, her crimson lips barely moving.

"Or maybe it's quite the midlife crisis," replies James with a smirk. "Her husband has run away, and now she's playing dress-up with the help?"

"You know," the treasurer interjects, leaning in closer, "does anyone else wonder what on earth happened to Richard?"

The comment hangs in the air between them, loaded with insinuation. My grip tightens on my glass.

"Richard's been gone an awful long time," Caroline muses, swirling her martini.

"And there's been a man coming to her house lately," adds her husband. "Late in the afternoon visits, we've noticed."

James chuckles, a low, knowing sound. "Maybe our perfect Elizabeth finally got bored playing by the rules."

I want to turn around and confront them, to defend Eliza-beth against their petty speculation—which surprises me, given that I've been doing exactly the same thing all evening. But it's not just Elizabeth they're smearing. It's also me. And my family name. It makes me want to say something. But before I can move, their conversation shifts to the upcoming board election, and I'm left with my racing thoughts.

Across the room, Elizabeth works the crowd with effortless charm. She touches an elbow here, offers a compliment there, her social choreography as precise as a ballet. She seems utterly unaware of the undercurrent of speculation flowing through her precious social circle.

I find myself drifting toward her, pulled by some need to warn her or question her—I'm not sure which. But as I approach, I notice Marie is also moving in her direction, and something about her purposeful stride makes me hang back.

Marie reaches Elizabeth first, touching her arm with casual intimacy. Elizabeth turns, her face lighting with what appears to be genuine pleasure. They speak for a moment, heads close together, and then Elizabeth laughs—her real laugh this time, the one I've rarely heard, unguarded and spontaneous. My jaw clenches involuntarily.

"They make an odd pair, don't they?"

I turn to find Sarah Thomson at my side her eyes fixed on Elizabeth and Marie.

"Very odd," I agree, my voice tight. "How long have you known Elizabeth?"

"Three years," Sarah replies.

"Has she ever done anything like this before? Befriended someone from... well..."

"The serving class?" Sarah supplies with raised eyebrows. "God, no. Elizabeth was always painfully aware of social divisions." She pauses, studying my face. "You seem very interested in this situation."

I realize my hand is twitching at my side, a nervous tell I've never managed to control. I force it still. "Just curious. It's so out of character."

"Mmm," Sarah hums noncommittally. "Well, people

surprise us sometimes. Especially when they're under pressure."

"What kind of pressure is Elizabeth under?" I ask too quickly.

Sarah gives me a strange look. "I mean, her husband missing, the scrutiny..."

There's something accusatory in her tone that makes me step back. "Of course, yes. I think that perhaps—"

"Jane," she cuts me off, her voice surprisingly gentle, "you might want to check your investment level here. You've barely taken your eyes off them all night."

Heat rises to my face. Am I being that obvious? I mutter something about being concerned about my daughter-in-law's well-being and move away.

Did Marie tell her? Does Elizabeth know I used her to spy on her?

No, she wouldn't keep her this close, then, would she? She definitely wouldn't if she knew about Marie's affair with Richard.

I position myself near a large floral arrangement where I can observe without being obvious. Elizabeth continues her social circuit, but I notice now that she keeps Marie in her sightline at all times. When Marie drifts too far away, Elizabeth finds a reason to move closer. It's subtle—no one who wasn't watching as intently as I am would notice—but it's deliberate.

And Marie. The longer I watch, the more unsettled I become. She studies Elizabeth—her movements, her expressions, her social patterns—with an intensity that goes beyond mere observation. When she lifts her champagne glass, her pinky extends slightly, just like Elizabeth's does. When she listens to someone speak, she tilts her head at the exact same angle Elizabeth favors. It's as though she's not simply wearing Elizabeth's dress: she's trying on her entire being.

A memory surfaces—Elizabeth mentioning to me last

month that she thought someone had been in her closet. Items moved; not missing but rearranged. I'd suggested Marie might have tidied up. Elizabeth had agreed, dismissing her own concern with a laugh.

Now I wonder: how often has Marie tried on Elizabeth's clothes when she wasn't home? How long has this strange mimicry been developing?

Has Elizabeth gotten to her? Dazzled her with promises of bettering her social status? Of becoming like her?

I'm so lost in these thoughts that I flinch when someone touches my arm. It's my husband, looking concerned.

"You okay?" he asks. "You've been stalking around the edges of the room all night like you're on some kind of reconnaissance mission."

"I'm fine," I reply automatically. "Just a headache coming on."

He doesn't believe me—I can tell by the slight narrowing of his eyes—but he doesn't press. "Want to head home soon? It's after ten."

The thought of leaving before understanding what's happening between Elizabeth and Marie makes my stomach clench. "Not yet," I say. "I need to speak with Elizabeth first."

He sighs. "I'll get another drink, then."

As he walks away, I see that the crowd has thinned considerably. The auction winners are being announced from a small podium at the front of the room, drawing most of the remaining guests in that direction. Elizabeth stands among them, her golden head easy to spot. But Marie is nowhere near her.

I scan the room, a prickle of unease crawling up my spine. Where did she go? My eyes sweep past the bar, the auction tables, the small groupings of lingering guests, and then I spot her, slipping through a side door that leads to the club's private offices.

I follow, keeping a safe distance. The hallway beyond the

door is dimly lit and quiet, the sounds of the party muffled. I hear the soft click of heels against marble flooring and quicken my pace, turning a corner just in time to see Marie enter a room at the end of the hall: the ladies' powder room.

I wait a moment, then push through the door myself. The powder room is expansive, with a separate lounge area featuring velvet settees and gilt-framed mirrors. Marie stands alone at the farthest sink, her back to me. She doesn't turn when I enter.

I hesitate, then move to a sink several spaces away from her, pretending to fix my lipstick while watching her in the mirror. She's studying her own reflection with an intensity that's almost frightening, turning her head slightly from side to side as though memorizing the angles of her face.

Then she smiles. Not her own smile: Elizabeth's. The precise curve of lips, the slight showing of teeth, the crinkle at the corners of her eyes. It's perfect, and it chills me to my core. Does she think she belongs here? Has Elizabeth told her she could be one of us?

"It's a lovely party, isn't it?" I say, unable to stand the silence any longer.

Marie's eyes meet mine in the mirror, and for an instant, I see something flash across her face, surprise, perhaps, or annoyance at being interrupted. Then her features smooth into pleasant blandness.

"Yes, very lovely," she replies, her voice soft. "Elizabeth has been so kind to include me."

"You two seem... close," I venture, applying lipstick I don't need.

"She's been a wonderful friend," Marie says, and there's something in the way she emphasizes "friend" that makes my skin crawl. "We understand each other. That's what you wanted, isn't it?" She smooths down the front of the borrowed dress. "Elizabeth feels invisible sometimes, you know. Even in a room full of people who claim to be her friends. She asked me to come today. She needed me to be here for her. She was concerned about meeting all these people and what they'd say about her, the looks they might give her now that Richard is gone. Especially from the people who claim to care about her."

I grab her arm and speak through gritted teeth, careful not to lose composure completely. "What are you up to, Marie? What is really going on here?" I ask.

"Nothing. Just doing what you told me to."

I snort. "This... is not what I told you to do."

She shrugs and pulls her arm out of my grasp. "Well, it comes with the job. Acting like a close friend. Plus, the food is good."

"The police have you on their radar, you know," I say. "I didn't tell them it was you who lives in that location, as it would reflect badly on me. But you need to keep a low profile. They will be knocking on your door before you know it. What are you going to tell them?"

She smiles, then shrugs. "The truth."

"Truth can be many things. What variant of it are you planning on telling them?"

"The true kind?" she says.

"Stop playing games."

"Okay, then I will tell them I was seeing Richard in college."

"That will make you look very suspicious," I say. "Don't you realize that? I mean, what are you even doing in his house, cleaning for him?"

She nods. "Yeah, you're right. That doesn't make me look good, I guess."

"And Elizabeth might find out, and then you're out," I say. "I need you in that house to be my eyes and ears. If you're out, then where does that leave you? You need the money, remember?"

"Okay," she says, her shoulders slumping. "I won't tell them

I used to know him. Just that we had a brief affair. Is that good? Are you happy then?"

Before I can respond, the door opens and a pair of laughing women enter. Marie gives me a final, inscrutable look, then slips past them and out the door.

I stand frozen, my lipstick still in hand, as the women move to the mirrors, chatting about the auction results. My mind races. Can I still trust Marie? She's very good at appeasing me, but is that all she does? When I hired her, I wanted her to help me pull Richard away from Elizabeth. I never thought they'd start an affair. An affair is so dirty, so sleezy, and it definitely doesn't look good on the family name. At least I assumed Marie would tell me if they started anything up again.

By the time I compose myself and return to the ballroom, things are winding down. Elizabeth stands near the exit, saying good-byes, Marie at her side like a shadow. I watch as guests approach them, how conversations falter and resume, how eyes linger on Marie in the ill-fitting dress a beat too long.

Elizabeth remains blissfully unaware of Marie's past with her husband. Or, perhaps, I think with sudden clarity, she's perfectly aware and simply doesn't care. Maybe that's what tonight was about. A deliberate social experiment. A test to see who would say what, who would judge, who would pretend not to notice. Maybe it is simply about giving them something else to talk about, besides Richard going missing.

I find my husband, signal that I'm ready to leave, and we join the farewell queue. When we reach Elizabeth, she kisses me on both cheeks, the scent of her expensive perfume enveloping me.

"Jane, darling, so glad you could come," she says warmly.

"Wouldn't miss it," I reply, then turn to Marie. "Lovely to meet you properly."

Marie's eyes meet mine, steady and knowing. "The pleasure was mine. I'm sure we'll see each other again soon."

Something in her tone makes the statement sound like a promise—or a threat. I swallow hard and fix a piercing look at her as my husband guides me away, his hand at the small of my back.

In the car, he asks what's bothering me, but I can't explain the unease that's settled into my bones. Instead, I stare out the window at the passing landscape of Cypress Estates: the manicured lawns, the stately homes, the carefully maintained facades behind which anything might be happening.

My phone vibrates softly in my pocket. I pull it out, and the glow from the screen illuminates my face. I quickly scan the message, my heart racing with each word. It's from the private investigator. It's about Elizabeth and what she did all those years ago—a secret so dark it changes everything. My heart rate quickens as I digest the information, the implications swirling in my mind like a storm on the horizon.

TWENTY-ONE

MARIE

Light bounces off the glass tables in Jane's living room, making me squint as I sit across from her. Jane has asked me to come. This is outside of our weekly meetings. My new notebook rests on my lap, a thin barrier between us. I feel so anxious sitting here. Everything feels different between me and Jane for some reason.

Ever since Elizabeth took me to the ball.

Elizabeth almost didn't go at all. I found her in her bedroom on the day of the ball, sitting on her bed, crying, the dress hanging in front of her. I asked her what was wrong, and she said she couldn't do it.

"This is the first time I'll attend this without Richard. They'll all look at me like I did something to him, just like Jane does."

I told her, "Don't let these people get to you. They're no better than you."

She looked at me with a glimmer of hope in her eyes and grabbed my hand, asking softly, "Will you go with me? Be my plus-one?"

I shook my head, replying, "I could never, I don't belong in a place like that."

But she squeezed my hand tighter and pleaded, "Please, I need you there with me."

She couldn't do this evening without me, she insisted, and she had just the right dress for me to wear. She then showed me the dress, and I was stunned. It was exquisite, a deep emerald green that shimmered like a thousand tiny stars had been sewn into the fabric. The neckline was adorned with delicate lace, and the skirt flowed like a gentle stream. I had never worn anything remotely like it.

"Marie, this will make you look like royalty," she said with a smile, handing me the dress.

I hesitated, memories flooding back. The last time I had worn something so beautiful was at my wedding to Carl, though that dress was nothing compared to this. My wedding dress was borrowed from a distant cousin, simple and modest, but enough to make me feel special on that day.

And then there was the night in college when Richard took me out to a very expensive restaurant. I wore a dress that was secondhand, yet I wore it with pride, hoping to impress Richard. Richard, with his wealth and charm, who had swept me off my feet.

"Are you sure about this?" I asked, nervously fingering the fabric. "I mean, won't people notice that it's not mine?"

She chuckled softly. "Marie, no one will care. Besides, you deserve to feel beautiful."

I nodded, still feeling a bit of unease. "I just... I don't want to look out of place."

"Trust me," she reassured, placing a comforting hand on my shoulder. "Tonight, you'll fit right in. And people will see the real you, the you that shines brighter than any dress."

So, I did it. I went, for her sake. And a little bit for mine, I guess. I'll admit I wanted to try it, to feel what it is like being one of them, to feel what it's like being Elizabeth.

But now Jane thinks I'm betraying her. I can tell by the way she looks at me. The room feels too cold, and Jane's gaze is colder still.

"You're late," Jane says, her voice like a paper cut. She doesn't check her watch. She doesn't need to.

"Traffic on Cypress Boulevard." My excuse sounds hollow even to me. It's a lie. I was sitting in my car outside, not wanting to go in. The closer I get to Elizabeth, the harder it gets for me to see her in the light of the villain her mother-in-law wants to paint her. I smile; it comes off as awkward, nervous. I don't feel like myself. I've been sleeping in my car for the past two nights, not daring to go back home, worrying that the goons would be back and kill me. I don't have the money they want. Not enough. I don't know how I'm going to get it.

My hands smooth my plain uniform skirt: the perfect servant's attire, chosen deliberately for this meeting. Today I need to be invisible Marie again, unremarkable Marie, the help that no one really sees.

Jane sits there now, silver hair arranged in a perfect coiffure that probably took her stylist an hour to achieve. Her cashmere sweater is the color of fresh cream, pearls at her throat catching the light. Everything about her screams old money, careful breeding, absolute control.

I hate how much I need her and her money.

"Marie." My name in her mouth sounds like an accusation. "I want to thank you for coming on such short notice."

I dip my head, the picture of deference. "Of course, Mrs. Wilson."

I perch on the edge of the couch, hands folded in my lap, shoulders slightly hunched—the posture of someone who knows their place. Jane studies me for a long moment, her gaze clinical, assessing. I wonder if she can see the pulse hammering in my throat.

"I assume you're wondering why I called you here," she says finally.

She slides a manila folder across the highly polished coffee table. "I've discovered something about Elizabeth that changes everything. I know you think she's your friend, Marie, but she's not."

I stare at the folder but don't reach for it. "What do you mean?"

"Open it," she commands. "See for yourself."

My heart pounds as I lean forward and flip open the cover. Inside are newspaper clippings, police reports, photographs. I scan the headlines: "Local Businessman Missing, Foul Play Suspected"; "Search Continues for Thomas Barrett"; "Missing Man's Car Recovered from Lake."

"I don't understand," I say.

"Keep reading." Jane's voice is tight with something like triumph.

I flip through more clippings, coming to a more recent article: "Cold Case Solved: Body of Thomas Barrett Found in Submerged Vehicle." The date is just five weeks ago. I scan the article, phrases jumping out at me: "stabbed multiple times"; "homicide investigation"; "persons of interest being questioned."

"Elizabeth was Thomas Barrett's wife when he disappeared seven years ago," Jane says, leaning forward. "Before she met Richard."

"And now they've found his body," I finish, my mouth dry.

"Exactly." Jane rises from her chair, moves to the window. "Do you see what this means? She's done it before."

I stare at a photograph of the recovered car being lifted from murky water, trying to reconcile this information with the Elizabeth I know. Elizabeth, who cries at sad commercials. Elizabeth, who nurses wounded birds back to health in shoeboxes on her kitchen counter. Elizabeth, who confides in me over tea about her loneliness, her fears, her dreams.

"This doesn't make sense," I whisper. "She's not... she wouldn't..."

"Murder one husband and then make another disappear?" Jane turns her head, her face hard. "The timing is too perfect to be coincidence. The police reopen her ex-husband's case, start asking questions again, and suddenly Richard vanishes? I'm not that stupid."

I flip through more pages, finding police interview transcripts. Elizabeth's answers are calm, measured, consistently denying any knowledge of her ex-husband's whereabouts. Just like her calm, measured denials about knowing where Richard might be now, if anyone pressed her.

"She seems so normal," I say, my voice barely audible.

"That's what makes her dangerous," Jane replies. "She's extraordinarily good at presenting exactly the face people want to see. The perfect wife. The gracious hostess. The kind employer." She pauses. "She's fooled you too, hasn't she, Marie? Made you feel special, confided in you, treated you like more than just the help? Made you feel like you could be like her? One of us?"

I don't answer, but she sees the truth in my face. A small, sad smile touches her lips.

"I thought as much. She's very good at identifying people's vulnerabilities." Jane looks at me, her eyes piercing through my bones.

The implications send a chill through me. "Are you saying...?"

"I'm saying Elizabeth Wilson is dangerous," Jane states flatly. "To my son, to you, to anyone who gets too close to whatever secrets she's hiding."

I close the folder, my hands trembling.

"Why are you showing me this?" I ask Jane, though I already know.

She studies me, eyes narrowed. "Because you clearly have Elizabeth's trust. And now you have a choice to make."

The weight of that choice presses down on me, constricting my chest. I've spent months watching the Wilsons, learning their habits, their secrets. I thought I knew Elizabeth, or at least, I thought I understood her motives. Now I'm not sure of anything.

"I need to think," I say, pushing the folder away.

"Of course." Jane nods, surprisingly gentle. "This is a lot to process. But Marie..." She leans forward, her eyes intent on mine. "My son could be in grave danger. If he's not already dead."

The words are terrible and final. I feel sick, caught between loyalties I never expected to have, truths I'm not sure I want to confront.

"May I..." I gesture to the folder. "May I take this?"

"Please do." Jane sits back, watching me carefully. "I have copies. Read it all. Consider what it means. And then we'll talk again."

I rise on unsteady legs, clutching the folder to my chest like a shield. The evidence inside burns against me, damning and irrefutable. A man is dead. Another is missing. And Elizabeth Wilson sits at the center of both mysteries, smiling her secret smile.

"Thank you for coming, Marie," Jane says as I reach the door to the hallway. "I know this can't be easy."

I pause, one hand on the doorknob. "Mrs. Wilson... what do you think has happened to Richard?"

Her composure cracks, just slightly, enough to glimpse the terrified mother beneath the imperious exterior. "I pray we find him before it's too late," she says. "Before she does to him what she did to Thomas Barrett."

I nod once, wondering if I've been cleaning for a murderer all this time.

In my mind, I see Elizabeth sitting at her kitchen island five weeks ago, reading the newspaper on her iPad, face pale as she read something that clearly disturbed her. When I asked if she was all right, she'd put the iPad down quickly, smiled that brittle smile that never seems like a real smile. "Just bad news from an old friend," she'd said.

Had that been the moment she learned they'd found Thomas Barrett?

"But she seems so... nice," I say. The words sound foolish even to my own ears. What does that even mean? I, of all people, should know how easily a convincing facade can be constructed, maintained, perfected. My ex did it to me. He put me in this situation, and now I have them hunting me down for money.

Jane scoffs, a sharp sound utterly devoid of humor. "That's what makes her dangerous. The truly dangerous ones always appear ordinary. You've spent more time with her than almost anyone else these past months. You know things have been off."

A dozen moments flash through my mind: Elizabeth crying in her bathroom, door locked, thinking no one could hear her; Elizabeth's hands shaking as she poured herself an extra glass of wine after a phone call; Elizabeth staring at Richard across the dinner table with an expression I couldn't quite name—not hatred, not quite, but something adjacent to it.

"Everyone has secrets," I say carefully. "Private moments."

"Secrets and private moments are one thing. Murder is quite another." Jane studies my face, apparently notices something concerning there. "You look pale. Are you okay?"

"I... I guess."

"I understand this is difficult to process," Jane says, her tone softening slightly. "You've worked for them for months. You've developed... attachments."

I think of the quiet afternoons when Elizabeth would invite me to sit with her, drink tea while she talked about books she was reading, dreams she'd had, places she wanted to visit. I think of how she noticed when I was ill before I'd even mentioned it, how she insisted I take extra days off with pay. I think of the birthday card she gave me, signed with "love" and a personal note about how much she valued our friendship. And, of course, I think of the ball, and the dress that she let me wear.

Was it all manipulation? A careful cultivation of loyalty from someone she needed to keep close. I nod mechanically, but inside I'm fracturing—Jane's evidence is compelling, yet I've grown fond of Elizabeth. She's the only one in this family who has treated me like a human being. I've seen her vulnerability, her loneliness, her quiet desperation. Could it all have been an act? Or is Jane the manipulator here, twisting facts to fit her long-standing dislike of her daughter-in-law?

My stomach churns with the implications. I think of Richard—distant, preoccupied Richard, always more focused on his phone than his wife. I try to imagine Elizabeth harming him, but the image won't form clearly. Then again, could I have imagined her stabbing her ex-husband? Watching his car sink into dark water with his body inside?

"I need to protect Richard, wherever he is," Jane continues, her voice taking on an edge of desperation that feels genuine. "He's all I have. The police will reopen their investigation into Thomas's murder. They'll question Elizabeth again. But that could take time, and if my theory is correct, Richard doesn't have time." She fixes me with a stern look. "You could save my son's life."

The weight of this responsibility settles across my shoulders. I didn't ask for this. None of this was part of my plan. But I do care about Richard. I really do.

"What if she suspects I'm working with you?"

A flicker of something cold passes across Jane's features.

"Then you'll be in danger too. Be careful. Be convincing. You can see yourself out now," she says, dismissing me now that she's planted her seeds of doubt. "I expect to hear from you soon."

"Yes, Mrs. Wilson."

I walk through the grand hallways of her mansion, past priceless artwork and antique furniture that have witnessed generations of Wilson family schemes and secrets. The folder in my hands seems to grow heavier with each step.

Outside, the bright sunlight feels offensive against the darkness of my thoughts. I walk to my minivan—sensible, unremarkable, like the persona I've cultivated all these years—and slide into the driver's seat. The folder sits on the passenger seat beside me, its contents damning and irrefutable.

Elizabeth's voice echoes in my memory: "Marie, you're the only one I can trust. The only one who sees me—really sees me." Had that been manipulation, or a genuine moment of connection?

I start the engine, my hands steady despite the turmoil inside me. The drive back to the Wilson house stretches before me, a journey toward a confrontation I never anticipated. With each mile, I'll need to decide: am I Jane's spy or Elizabeth's confidante? And what happens when I can't be both?

As I pull away from Jane's mansion, one thought crystallizes with terrible clarity: I've been cleaning for either a murderer or a woman being framed. Either way, I'm now caught in the middle of something far more dangerous than I ever intended.

TWENTY-TWO

JANE

The crystal chandelier casts sharp reflections across the sterling silver place settings. I sit rigidly at one end of our mahogany dining table while Joseph occupies the other, twelve feet of polished wood and unspoken accusations between us. The servants have been dismissed for the evening. It's just us now, picking at our food, the silence punctuated only by the scrape of knives against fine china and the occasional clink of his wine glass. I've been waiting for the right moment to bring up Marie, and I decide that moment is now.

"I spoke with Marie today," I say, my voice cutting through the silence like a blade. "The cleaning lady I told you about?"

Joseph doesn't look up from his plate. "Did you?" He slices into his steak, the knife gliding through with practiced precision. Everything he does has that same precision—calculated, controlled.

"She was acting strange." I watch his face carefully for any reaction. "Nervous."

"I thought you told me that Marie always acts nervous. It's her default state." He takes a bite, chews methodically. "That's why you hired her. Quiet, efficient, doesn't ask questions."

I swirl the red wine in my glass, watching it coat the sides. "I think Elizabeth is getting to her."

"How so?" His tone is bored, as if we're discussing the weather or golf scores.

"Our daughter-in-law has her ways. She knows how to manipulate people. This is exactly what I was afraid would happen. She's gotten to her. I can feel it. She's managed to make Marie think I'm the bad guy. She's really good at this game."

Joseph finally looks up at me, his eyes narrowing slightly. "What game? You're being dramatic, Jane."

"I can't trust her any more—I know exactly what Elizabeth is capable of. But no one else sees it." My eyes narrow in quiet fury. The words come out low, controlled, but there's no mistaking the heat behind them.

My husband swallows a mouthful of red wine and replies dismissively. "You're acting crazy. Richard left to be with one of his mistresses for a while. I'm sure he'll be home soon." He sets his glass down with deliberate care. "Or maybe he simply had enough of the women in his life." Each phrase is punctuated by the sound of his wine glass clinking and his steady sips. "For all I know, he might be the smart one of us."

My face twists in disgust—not just at his blasé attitude, but at the insinuation that our son's hurt is nothing more than a family quirk. I fiddle with my wine glass, forcing my tone to remain even as I argue, "Elizabeth hurt our son, I know she did."

"You don't know anything," Joseph says. "None of us do. That's the point."

"I know my son."

"You know the version of him he allowed you to see." Joseph cuts another piece of steak, his knife scraping against the plate with an ugly sound. "The same way I only know the version of you that you allow me to see. And vice versa, of course."

I shake my head. "This isn't about us."

"Isn't it?"

Outside our dining room windows, the carefully manicured lawns of the Cypress Estates stretch into darkness. Beyond them, the swamp waits, patient and ancient. Sometimes I think of our marriage like that swamp—what appears stable on the surface is actually shifting, treacherous ground.

"Our son wouldn't just leave," I say. "Not without telling us. Not without taking anything."

Joseph sighs dramatically. "Lord knows I can't blame him. I should have done the same years ago—I thought about it. Simply leave everything behind, take my money and go to the Bahamas, or the Virgin Islands." His voice takes on a dreamy quality that clashes sharply with my resolute glare.

"Is that what you want?" I ask quietly. "To leave everything behind?"

He chuckles, but there's no humor in it. "What I want stopped mattering a long time ago, didn't it?"

I think about the last time I saw Richard. The argument he'd had with Elizabeth the day before. The way she had looked afterward—scared, guilty. As I mull over this chaotic whirlwind of thoughts, I can't help thinking of Marie. The knowledge that she had kept her affair with Richard a secret gnaws at me, and I can't help but feel the weight of it all, a worry that festers and grows. I remember how I found her. I had my private investigator track her down, remembering her dating Richard back in college, and how he would often bring her up in conversations as if harboring feelings for her still. She was so eager and nervous, and I was offering her the position as a maid, believing I was helping her turn her life around. The irony twists like a knife; she kept the affair a secret from me, all while I thought I was doing something noble. Yes, she was helping me out too. Still, the betrayal gnaws at my conscience, a worry that rises again, threatening to drown me in its tide.

"Marie went into the beach house last week," I say,

changing tactics. "She claimed she was cleaning, but I saw her on the cameras. She spent forty minutes in the master bedroom."

Joseph's hand pauses halfway to his mouth. A flicker of something—it might be concern, I can't quite tell—crosses his face before he regains his composure.

"Is that why you've been checking the security footage? Looking for ghosts?" He resumes eating as if we're discussing nothing more significant than the weather forecast. "Maybe she was just being thorough."

"She was in there for forty minutes." I lean forward. "It doesn't take that long to clean in there. It hasn't been used in months. What was she looking for? Who told her to do that? Elizabeth?"

"How should I know what goes through the mind of the help?" He shrugs with exaggerated nonchalance. "Maybe she was snooping. People like that always do."

"People like that," I repeat.

"You know what I mean." He waves his hand dismissively. "The service class. They're always curious about how the other half lives."

I take a long sip of wine. "She went into the safe. I'm certain of it. The alarm went off on my phone telling me it was opened."

This time, Joseph can't hide his reaction. His hand tightens around his knife, knuckles going white. "That's impossible. She doesn't have the combination."

"Apparently, she does." I set my glass down carefully. "Or she figured it out. Either way, she was in there for twelve minutes. That's how long it showed the door was open in my safety app."

The tension in the room thickens. Joseph's jaw works silently, as if he's chewing on words he can't spit out. Finally, he asks, "Did she take anything?"

"I don't know. The camera doesn't show the inside of the safe." I hold his gaze.

"What's in there that has you so concerned?" he says.

"Nothing worth stealing."

"Then why are you worried?"

My laugh is short and sharp. "I'm not worried about what she might have taken. I'm worried about having to fire her and find someone new. Good help is so hard to find these days, especially someone willing to help out in ways that isn't in the job description, if you know what I mean."

I think about Marie Clements, with her mousy brown hair always pulled back in that practical bun. The way she moves through Richard's house like a ghost, present but not really seen. The way her eyes take in everything.

"There's something not right about her," I say. "Something has changed recently. I bet you it's Elizabeth. She has gotten her over to her side. Pretending like she needs her. Playing the victim and making me look bad."

"That's her job, Jane. To anticipate the needs of the people in the house she cleans."

"It's more than that." I push my plate away, barely touched. "Sometimes I catch her mimicking Elizabeth's gestures when she thinks I'm not looking. The way she holds her coffee cup, the phrases she uses. It's like she's... studying her. Either way, they're getting too close for comfort."

Joseph rolls his eyes. "Now you really do sound crazy."

"Don't call me that." My voice is sharp. "Don't ever call me that."

He sighs, places his napkin on the table. "I have work to do tonight. Is there a point to all this paranoia, or can I be excused?"

I stare at him, at this man I've been married to for forty-seven years. I used to know every expression that crossed his face. Now he's like a house with all the windows darkened—I can see the outline, but I have no idea what's happening inside.

"Our son is missing," I say slowly. "Marie is snooping around. Elizabeth was the last person to see Richard, and she's terrified every time I mention his name. And you sit there eating your steak like none of this matters."

Joseph dabs the corner of his mouth with his napkin. "Richard is a grown man who decided to take a break from his life. It happens. He'll come back when he's ready."

"It's been four weeks."

"So? I once disappeared to Europe for a month. Didn't tell a soul." He shrugs. "It's a family tradition."

"This is different," I insist. "He would have called me. He would have told his mother. He would have taken his things."

"Maybe he wanted a fresh start. Maybe he's tired of being under your constant scrutiny," Joseph says, pushing back from the table and standing up abruptly. He straightens his tie, glancing nervously around the room as if the walls themselves might be listening. "Not everyone wants to be watched all the time, Jane. It doesn't concern you."

"Everything that pertains to my son concerns me," I retort.

Joseph hesitates, his eyes narrowing slightly as he looks at me with a mixture of frustration and unease. "No," he replies, his voice suddenly cold and firm. "Not everything. And you need to make sure you keep quiet about all this, Jane. We wouldn't want any unnecessary gossip tarnishing the family's reputation, and my image, would we?" He turns away. "Good night, Jane."

I watch him leave the dining room, his steps unhurried, shoulders relaxed. As if we'd just had a pleasant dinner conversation about neighborhood gossip or vacation plans. As if our son isn't missing and his maid isn't digging through our secrets. I know what she found in there, in the safe. The papers I had hidden from my husband. The money I had spent to bail out our son from his growing debts. She found all that, and I worry she'll use it against me. Joseph will kill me if he finds out what I have done. Or maybe even worse, he'll divorce me. He made me sign a prenup when we married. I'll get nothing if we divorce. Just like Elizabeth will get nothing if Richard divorces her.

But if he is dead, it's a whole different story.

How's that for a motive, Detective?

I remain at the table, surrounded by crystal, the remnants of our meal growing cold. Outside, the Spanish moss sways from the ancient oaks, moving like slow, grasping fingers in the night breeze. The cicadas have started their evening chorus, a pulsing rhythm that seems to match my heartbeat.

My wine glass is empty. I reach for the bottle and pour until the crimson liquid nearly reaches the rim. The chandelier light catches it, making it glow like blood.

I need to act. Before Marie decides to use whatever she found in that safe. I should have known better than to trust her. I raise my glass in a silent toast to the empty chair where my husband sat moments ago.

I think about the private investigator's files on my laptop. All this information I have on Elizabeth. It all points in the same direction. Elizabeth is not to be trusted. She is capable of violence. She is dangerous. I know what to do now. I know exactly what I'm going to do. I'm always one step ahead.

The dining room falls into silence after Joseph leaves, but my mind is anything but quiet. I stare at his empty chair across the vast expanse of mahogany, the candles flickering between us like fragile, dying stars.

I down my wine in one decisive gulp, the alcohol warming a path down my throat. The emptiness of the grand dining room suddenly feels oppressive rather than elegant. I need something stronger, something to match the steel forming in my spine.

I press the small button hidden beneath the table's edge—a discreet way to summon the evening staff without Joseph knowing. He hates when I drink after dinner. Says it makes me erratic, unpredictable. What he means is that it makes me honest.

The door opens silently, and one of the younger staff members appears. She hovers at the threshold, hands clasped before her crisp uniform.

"A martini," I say, my voice low yet edged with urgency. "Extra dry. Two olives."

"Yes, ma'am." She nods and disappears.

My jaw sets slowly as I make my final preparations, mentally reviewing each step of what I'm about to do.

I sit hunched in my car across from Richard and Elizabeth's house, the next day, the morning sun beating through the windshield despite my efforts with the visor. I'm in my Mercedes, the one I rarely use. The oversized sunglasses press uncomfortably against my temples, and the wide-brimmed hat I've borrowed from my gardener makes my forehead itch. Still, I don't move. I barely breathe. I'm not taking any chances of being recognized.

The morning stretches into its third hour when the front door finally swings open. My fingers tighten around my binoculars.

There she is. Not in the elegant outfit she usually wears, but in casual wear—yoga pants and a light tank top. Her blonde hair is hastily pulled back under a baseball cap, the brim pulled low over her face. Elizabeth glides; this woman hurries, her gestures sharp and efficient as she locks the door behind her.

I sink lower in my seat as she approaches her car. No casual stroll today. She moves with unusual urgency, checking her watch twice before sliding into the driver's seat. The engine starts with a purr I can hear even from my position down the street.

I count to ten after she pulls away, then start my own

engine. The familiar dance of surveillance begins again—keep three car lengths back, don't use your turn signal until the last moment, avoid eye contact at all costs. I learned these tricks from a private investigator I hired during Richard's father's first affair. Funny how that knowledge serves me now, decades later, as I track what might be the most bizarre affair of all—my daughter-in-law.

We travel away from the manicured perfection of Cypress Estates, past the gleaming storefronts of the shopping district where Elizabeth buys her overpriced organic produce. I maintain my distance, grateful for the morning traffic that provides cover for my pursuit.

The neighborhoods gradually change as we head east. First subtly—homes with smaller lawns, fewer luxury cars in driveways—then dramatically. Cracked sidewalks appear, chain-link fences replacing the ornamental wrought iron of Elizabeth's world. Graffiti blooms across concrete walls like angry flowers. A group of young men lounge on a corner, watching cars pass with flat, evaluating eyes.

My hands tighten on the steering wheel. I know this area, though I've rarely had reason to visit. This is the same seedy district where Richard met with his affair, the day before he disappeared.

She slows, scanning the street before pulling into a small, potholed parking lot beside a three-story brick building. Its windows are covered with iron bars, the original color of the paint impossible to determine beneath years of grime and neglect.

I drive past, catching a glimpse of her hurrying toward a side door. Her head is down, shoulders hunched as if expecting a blow. Nothing like Elizabeth's usual confident posture. I circle the block, heart pounding against my ribs as I search for a place to park that won't draw attention to my luxury car—a fool's errand in this neighborhood.

The building itself reveals nothing—no signs, no indication of its purpose. Just another anonymous structure in a forgotten part of the city. But I've been here before. This is where Marie lives.

Whatever secrets that building holds, I'm about to discover them. And God help anyone who stands in my way.

TWENTY-THREE

MARIE

I've dared to go back to my apartment for the day, hoping the goons will leave me alone. I need to grab some stuff, and have the day off, so I don't really know where else to go. I open my notebook, the spine cracked from constant use. Inside, I've documented everything—Elizabeth's morning routine (coffee black, sometimes toast), her evening rituals (wine at 5:15, always one glass before dinner then one during and a third one after, never more), her tells when she's angry (the slight clench of the jaw, the way her left hand moves to the side). There's power in this knowledge, a currency I've been saving for the right moment to spend.

I flip to a fresh page in my notebook and begin scribbling in the measured handwriting I've cultivated to be both legible and anonymous.

A sharp knock at the door interrupts me. Three quick raps—insistent, demanding attention. I hold my breath and wonder who it could be. Is it the landlord coming to evict me? Is it someone else coming for money? My body tenses as I quickly gather the clippings, photos, and notebook, shoving them into a drawer beneath a stack of innocuous romance novels. I smooth my hair, check my reflection in the small mirror by the door—adjusting my expression into the bland, slightly anxious mask I wear for the Wilsons.

When I open the door, Elizabeth Wilson storms past me, her perfume—Chanel No. 5, always too much of it—invading my space before she does. Her face is flushed, her normally perfect hair disheveled underneath a baseball cap.

"Mrs. Wilson, I—" I stammer, injecting confusion into my voice. "Did I miss a work day? I thought today was my—"

"Stop it," Elizabeth cuts me off, turning to face me with eyes like shattered glass. "Just stop the innocent act, Marie. I know everything."

I close the door slowly, buying seconds to adjust. This isn't in my plan. Elizabeth was supposed to be at her charity luncheon today—she told me about it yesterday while I dusted the credenza outside the dining room.

"I don't understand," I say, keeping my voice soft, my posture curved—making myself smaller, less threatening. "Is something wrong? Has something happened?"

Elizabeth laughs, a harsh sound that bounces off the walls of my small living room. "That's an interesting question to ask, Marie. Very interesting indeed."

"I'm sorry, I—"

"I spoke with Detective Mitchell this morning," she says, her voice brittle. She paces the limited space of my living room. "He had some very enlightening things to tell me."

My mind races. Mitchell—the detective on Richard's case. What could he have told Elizabeth that would bring her here, like this?

"About Richard?" I ask, genuine curiosity slipping through my carefully constructed facade. "Has there been news about him?"

Elizabeth stops pacing and stares at me, her expression

hardening into something dangerous. "Yes, about Richard. My husband. The man you've been sleeping with."

The accusation hits me like ice water.

"Mrs. Wilson, I would never—" I begin, real indignation fueling my defense.

"Don't lie to me!" she shouts, her composure finally cracking. "Mitchell has phone records, showing Richard was here the day before he disappeared. He was here, in this apartment, for three hours. I saw the address and immediately recognized it from your paperwork."

My mind spins. This is not good. I open my mouth to respond when another knock comes at the door—faster, more measured. A knock I recognize immediately.

Before I can move, Elizabeth strides to the door and yanks it open. Jane Wilson stands in the doorway, her expression showing me she isn't shocked at finding her daughter-in-law here.

"Elizabeth," Jane says, trying to sound surprised, but it's obvious she isn't. "What are you doing here?"

Elizabeth's laugh is hollow. "Apparently the same thing you are. Having a chat with my husband's mistress."

Jane steps inside, closing the door behind her with deliberate care. Her eyes meet mine over Elizabeth's shoulder, and there's something there I've never seen before—a cold triumph mixed with fear.

"So, you know," Jane says softly to Elizabeth. "I was going to tell you myself who Marie really was. But I just found out. She used to date him in college, apparently. And the police believe that they have rekindled recently. I was as shocked as you when they told me. That's why I'm here."

My face betrays me then, genuine shock and anger breaking through. I stare at her, feeling the weight of her betrayal crash over me. After everything we arranged, after all her promises—

this is how she repays me. By making me the scapegoat, the distraction, the villain in her twisted family drama.

"Jane," I say, forgetting the deferential "Mrs. Wilson" in my shock. "What are you doing?"

Jane doesn't answer me. Her eyes are fixed on Elizabeth, watching her daughter-in-law's pain with the detached curiosity of a scientist observing a lab specimen.

I straighten my spine, abandoning the hunched posture I've maintained for months in their presence. If Jane wants to break our arrangement, then the time for pretending is over.

The three of us stand in my cramped living room, the air thick with accusations and lies. Jane's betrayal burns through my veins like acid, dissolving the careful plans I've constructed. She thinks she can discard me, use me as a convenient villain in her family drama. But she's forgotten something crucial—I know her secrets just as intimately as she thinks she knows mine. I take a deep breath and feel something shift inside me, cracking along invisible fault lines. If she wants to change the rules to this game, I'll show her what happens when you corner someone with nothing left to lose.

"You should sit down, Elizabeth," I say, my voice transforming from the meek, deferential tone they're accustomed to hearing. "Your mother-in-law has been lying to you."

Jane steps forward. "Don't listen to her. She's trying to distract from her own guilt."

"Am I?" I raise an eyebrow, abandoning all pretense. "Tell her, Jane. Tell her why you really hired me."

Jane's face hardens. "I hired you because you came with excellent references. Though clearly, they were as fabricated as your innocence."

I laugh, a sound I've kept carefully hidden from them both. "References? Is that what we're calling it now?"

I turn to Elizabeth, whose confusion is evident in her furrowed brow. "Your mother-in-law didn't find me through an agency. She sought me out specifically because of my past with Richard."

Elizabeth's eyes dart between us. "What is she talking about, Jane?"

"She's right," I explain. "I was his girlfriend once. Before you met him, Elizabeth."

Elizabeth stares at me, her expression unreadable. "Why didn't he ever mention this?"

"Because Jane made sure he wouldn't," I say, watching Jane's face contort with barely contained rage. "She orchestrated this entire situation."

"She's lying," Jane interjects, her voice sharp. "This is absurd. Elizabeth, surely you can see—"

"Let her speak," Elizabeth says, not looking at Jane, her eyes fixed on me with new intensity.

I fold my arms across my chest, feeling a strange power in finally speaking the truth. "Jane approached me. She knew about my history with Richard, and she made me an offer I couldn't refuse."

Jane takes a step toward me, her voice low and dangerous. "Marie, I'm warning you—"

"She wanted me to come work for your family," I continue, in words that are sharp and undeniable, ignoring Jane's threat. "To get close to Richard again. To give him what she believed you couldn't. A child."

Elizabeth's face pales. "What are you saying?"

"She wanted me to seduce your husband, Elizabeth. To replace you with someone she could control. Jane has always hated that she couldn't manipulate you the way she manipulates everyone else. So, she asked me to spy on you. And report back to her."

Jane drops all pretense of civility. "This is ridiculous. She's clearly unbalanced. Look at this place—" She gestures around my modest apartment with disgust. "Probably filled with delusions and obsessions. She's trying to turn us against each other."

I walk calmly to the drawer where I hid my notebooks, pulling one out—not the most incriminating, but damaging enough. "Jane made me report back to her once a week. She also gave me updates on Richard's schedule, his moods. Told me when you two were fighting, when he would be most vulnerable." I flip through pages of notes.

Elizabeth takes the notebook with shaking hands, scanning the pages. Her expression shifts from disbelief to growing horror as she recognizes Jane's handwriting. "These are your notes," she says to Jane. "I recognize your handwriting."

Jane's demeanor changes instantly, her body language shifting from aggressive to defensive. "It's not what it looks like, Elizabeth. I was protecting our family."

"You wanted me out," Elizabeth interrupts, realization dawning on her face. "You've always wanted me out."

"She never thought you were good enough for Richard," I add, watching Jane's careful composure crumble. "Too independent. Too unwilling to be molded into the perfect Wilson wife."

Jane's shoulders straighten as she abandons her denials. "You were never right for him. You never understood what it means to be part of this family. The sacrifices required."

Elizabeth stands perfectly still, absorbing this confirmation of her worst suspicions. I notice her hands trembling—the only outward sign of her inner turmoil.

"But your plan didn't work, did it, Jane?" I press on, unable to stop now that I've begun. "Because Richard wasn't interested in rekindling anything with me. He saw through your manipulations. He was here the day before he disappeared, yes. But only to tell me he didn't want me. That he loves his wife. He asked me to please quit. To respect his family life. He was here for hours, yes, but we just talked about old days."

Jane's laugh is cold and brittle. "Oh, please."

I watch Elizabeth carefully, seeing the pieces click into place behind her eyes. "So, there was no affair," she says slowly. "Detective Mitchell is wrong."

"Yes. Nothing ever happened. We just talked. Listen, Elizabeth, I hate what I have done to you, spying on you, but... it wasn't supposed to be like this. Jane said you were cold, uncaring. That Richard was unhappy. That I'd be doing him a favor."

I look down at my feet. "But you're not what she described. And Richard... Richard isn't unhappy with you. He's unhappy with himself."

Jane's silence confirms my words more effectively than any protest could have.

Elizabeth turns to Jane, her expression hardening from hurt to fury. "This is definitely something you would do to me," she says, her voice trembling with rage. "Destroy my marriage, my trust, everything—just to maintain your control."

The air in my small apartment feels charged, like the moment before lightning strikes. Three women trapped in the web of lies Jane has spun—one the architect, one the intended victim, and me, the puppet.

"Why now?" Elizabeth asks Jane, her voice steady despite the emotion clearly churning beneath the surface. "Why try to convince me that Marie and Richard were having an affair now?"

Jane's eyes flick to mine, and I see it—the fear that I'll reveal what I found in the safe.

"Ask her about the safe, Elizabeth," I say softly. "From the beach house. Ask her what I found."

The room seems to shrink around us, the walls pressing in as the balance of power shifts like quicksand. Jane looks like a cornered animal, dangerous and desperate. Elizabeth stands between us, a woman realizing that everything she believed about her life has been carefully constructed fiction.

"You don't need to listen to her," Jane says. "She's playing you against me."

Elizabeth's eyes flick between Jane and me. She takes off her cap and wipes sweat off her forehead with a sigh.

"Actually, Jane, I would like to know what she's talking about." Elizabeth's voice is steady, but there's a tremor in her hands she can't quite control. "Why don't you explain?"

"I'm afraid I don't know what you're talking about," Jane says.

Her eyes narrow and her hands clench at her sides. The perfect picture of righteous indignation.

"Your son." Elizabeth spits the words. "How do I know that you haven't just sent him somewhere to get him away from me?"

"She did send him a lot of money shortly before he disappeared," I say.

Jane turns to look at me, appalled.

"How do you know this?" Elizabeth asks.

"That's what I found at the beach house. I was cleaning it, and I found transactions. Bank statements, lots of money. Richard had a gambling problem. Lots of online casinos that demanded he paid his debt. He also borrowed money from a group of people he shouldn't have. I know this because my ex did the same and left me with a huge debt. That's why I took this job, Elizabeth. Because your mother-in-law promised me enough money to get rid of it. Not that I have seen a lot of that, though. But you must believe me when I say, I didn't know you. Now that I do, I feel awful for having spied on you. Just awful."

The silence that follows hangs thick between us.

"You went through his desk? That's where you found these papers?"

"In the safe. I was cleaning, ma'am," I murmur. "I didn't mean to pry."

"Dusting inside a locked safe? That tells me the exact opposite, Marie." Elizabeth stands now, her height allowing her to look down at both of us. "What else have you been searching through while I'm not home?"

"I've been gathering information. There's a difference."

I take a step forward. "Mrs. Wilson—Elizabeth—I've seen the phone calls. In the guest room. The way you check over your shoulder before you answer. The burner phone you bought recently."

Elizabeth's face goes white. "You've been listening to my calls?"

"Not listening," I say softly. "Just... noticing. Jane told me to. And then to report back to her."

"I've heard enough," Jane says. "I'm not going to stand here and listen to this."

Jane meets Elizabeth's glare steadily. "I do not trust you, Elizabeth. I never have. Marie has uncovered evidence of your unfaithfulness." Her tone is firm when she asks, "Is that why you got rid of my son?"

The color drains from Elizabeth's face. "What did you say?"

"You heard me. The phone calls. The hushed conversations, the burner phone. It all adds up to a very ugly picture. You were cheating on him, right? And you know you won't get a dime if you divorce him. So, you murdered him. Had him buried somewhere. Now you're just waiting for him to be declared dead after five years, as is the Florida law, and you can walk away with all his money. It's brilliant. Except you never accounted for me. I was on to you from the very beginning. I know that you have done it before. You murdered your ex-husband, stabbed him to death."

"You're crazy." Elizabeth shakes her head. "You're insane. You have no idea what you're talking about."

"I think I do."

"You had no right to spy on me." Elizabeth's voice trembles. "No right at all."

"A mother has every right to protect her son." Jane smooths

her skirt down again. A habitual gesture from years of society luncheons and charity galas. Appearance matters, especially in confrontation. Can't lose composure. "And I intend to find out exactly what happened to Richard."

"Nothing happened to Richard!" Elizabeth snaps. "He's left me. Read the darn note! He's done with me." Elizabeth's voice is cold, controlled rage now.

"I'm leaving," Jane announces.

As she storms out, slamming the door behind her, I stand there, watching Elizabeth in the living room. She looks frozen, hugging herself tightly as if bracing against the storm Jane has left behind.

The moment Jane is gone, I turn to Elizabeth, my voice trembling as I beg, "Please forgive me."

I can see the anger in her eyes, but after a tense pause, she finally relents. "You were just a victim of Jane's manipulation," she tells me. "It's not your fault. I appreciate your apology, Marie." Her voice carries a mix of weariness and understanding. She moves to the sofa, sinking onto the cushions with a sigh. "But we both know that Jane's actions aren't yours to bear."

I join her in the living room, perching on the edge of an armchair, my hands clasped tightly in my lap. The remnants of smoke from the burned notebooks still linger in the air, a bitter reminder of the secrets I've been complicit in uncovering.

"I should have stood up to her," I confess, my gaze fixed on a frayed edge of the carpet. "I should have told you about the surveillance, about everything."

Elizabeth's eyes soften as she looks at me, a flicker of empathy crossing her features. "You were trying to survive, Marie. We all are in our own ways."

The weight of her words settles over me. Survival—a concept that has driven me, consumed me for so long, making me blind to the pain I was causing in my quest to exist in the periphery of privilege. Elizabeth's forgiveness is a balm to my guilt-ridden soul, but it also serves as a stark reminder of the choices I've made and the person I've become.

TWENTY-FOUR

JANE

The park shimmers in afternoon heat, a green oasis bordered by oak trees with Spanish moss dangling from every branch, whose shadows offer little relief from the Florida sun. It's been five days since the incident at Marie's apartment, and I haven't heard anything from either Marie or Elizabeth. I don't like not knowing what is going on. I spot Sarah Thomson before she sees me, pushing a stroller along the winding path, her shoulders hunched as if carrying more than just the weight of motherhood. My throat tightens as I prepare to voice my concerns about Elizabeth. Some truths are better discussed under open sky, where secrets can dissipate into the humid air rather than fester in closed rooms. I know I'm taking a risk in trusting Sarah, but I need more evidence. I need to find my son.

I raise my hand in a small wave, and Sarah's face brightens with recognition. We've always been friendly, despite the tension between Elizabeth and me. I'm sure Elizabeth would have complained about me to Sarah, and yet Sarah has always been warm. Her pace quickens as she navigates the stroller over the uneven bricks of the pathway.

"Jane, hi," she says, offering a quick hug. The baby in the

stroller—a little girl with Sarah's warm brown eyes—gurgles contentedly, clutching a cloth toy. "Sorry if I kept you waiting. Maddie decided her diaper needed changing right as we were walking out the door."

"No problem. Thanks for meeting me." I gesture to a bench nestled between two magnolia trees. "Want to sit?"

Sarah nods, maneuvering the stroller into position before settling beside me. "It's nice to see you, but I'll admit I was surprised by your call. I take it this is about Richard?"

"Yes," I say, feeling tired.

"Right." She adjusts the sunshade on the stroller. "Almost five weeks now, isn't it?"

"Thirty-four days." The number falls from my lips automatically. I've been counting.

Sarah's eyes fix on mine, searching. "So, why did you want to meet? You sounded... concerned on the phone."

I take a deep breath, feeling the humidity fill my lungs. My cotton blouse sticks to my back. "It's about Elizabeth. I'm worried about her."

Sarah's fingers tighten around the stroller handle. "Well, that makes sense. After all, her husband vanished without a trace."

"Yes, but she's been acting oddly." I lean forward, lowering my voice though no one is nearby. "I've been watching her. Something doesn't add up. She's too... composed."

"Well, everyone processes grief differently—"

"It's not grief," I interrupt. "It's something else. Like she's performing normalcy rather than experiencing it. Has she said anything to you?"

Sarah's expression shifts, subtle but noticeable—a slight narrowing of the eyes, a tightening around the mouth. "Actually," she says slowly, "Elizabeth has told me she no longer wishes to entertain our friendship."

This catches me by surprise. "What do you mean?"

"I got a text from her a few days ago." Sarah pulls out her phone, scrolls through it, then hands it to me. "See for yourself."

The message is brief and cold:

Sarah, I need space right now. Please don't contact me for the foreseeable future.

"That doesn't sound like her," I murmur, handing the phone back.

"No, it doesn't." Sarah stands, gesturing toward the path. "Mind if we walk? Maddie gets fussy if we stay still too long."

I fall into step beside her. The path curves around a small pond where a pair of pelicans drift lazily across the surface. The air smells of cut grass and sunscreen.

"Have you seen her recently?" I ask. "Have you guys been having lunch like you usually do? Before the text?"

"Not for a while, no." Sarah's voice drops. "But I did stop by her house about three days before I got that message. I was in the neighborhood and thought I'd check in. I didn't call first."

"What happened?"

Sarah carefully maneuvers the stroller around a crack in the path, taking her time before speaking. "Marie let me in, but she seemed... anxious. Said she was in the middle of some washing and mentioned Elizabeth was too busy for visitors, so I couldn't stay long."

"That's not unusual," I point out. "Elizabeth has always been particular about her house."

"No, it wasn't that." Sarah shakes her head. "Marie excused herself to check something, but she was gone for several minutes. Maddie was asleep in her carrier, and I needed to use the bathroom, so I went down the hallway."

My pulse quickens. "And then?"

"The bathroom door was open, but Elizabeth wasn't there. When I went back into the hallway, I saw Marie. She was rushing toward me, looking worried, anxious. I asked her what was going on, and she looked at me with those big eyes. She told me she heard noises from the guest room." Sarah's pace slows, her voice dropping to nearly a whisper. "She wasn't trying to spy, Jane. She swore she tried to let Elizabeth know she was there. But that's when she saw it."

"What did Marie see?" The question comes out sharper than I intended.

Sarah's knuckles turn white on the stroller handle. "Marie said Elizabeth was in the walk-in closet. The door was wide open, and she was on her knees, frantically shoving something into a duffel bag. Elizabeth didn't see her."

"What was it? What did she say Elizabeth was putting in the bag?"

"Clothes. But Marie said they had... what looked like blood-stains on them." Sarah stops walking entirely, turning to face me.

My stomach tightens. "Is Marie certain it was blood?"

"I guess so. She said she was uncomfortable in the house and didn't know what to do. I could tell she was worried for her own safety."

"What did you do?"

"I backed away. Went back to the kitchen as quietly as I could. When Elizabeth came in a few minutes later, I pretended I'd been with Maddie the whole time. I pretended like I didn't know anything and hugged her as usual, then we had a cup of tea, but I could barely swallow it." Sarah's eyes fill with tears. "I've never been so frightened in someone's home before. Elizabeth looked... different. Composed but cold. Like she was wearing a mask of herself."

A jogger passes us, nodding politely. We wait until he's well beyond earshot before continuing.

"Is that why you didn't tell anyone?" I ask.

Sarah's laugh is brittle. "Tell who? The police? 'Excuse me, officer, my friend's maid saw some bloody clothes in her house'? It's not like I saw it for myself, but Marie seemed very concerned..." Her voice trails off as she stares at the path ahead. "And so was I, to be honest."

"But then Elizabeth sent that text," I prompt.

"Three days later, yes." Sarah's lips press into a thin line. "I'd been debating whether to call her, trying to convince myself I'd misinterpreted what I heard. That maybe I got it all wrong. Then I got that message."

"Did you respond?"

"Once. I wrote back asking if everything was okay. Asked if maybe we could talk." Sarah's fists clench at her sides. "Then I texted again the next day. I was worried, Jane."

"Did she answer?"

"Nothing." Sarah shakes her head. "Complete silence."

I consider this information, fitting it into the puzzle I've been assembling since Richard disappeared. "You said the clothes were put in a duffel bag. Could Marie tell if it was a man's or a woman's clothing?"

Sarah furrows her brow. "I have no idea."

"Did you notice anything else unusual? Any other changes in the house since you'd last been there?"

Sarah thinks for a moment. "Richard's study door was open. It's always closed when I visit. Elizabeth says he's particular about his workspace. I think she was cleaning it out, getting rid of some of his things. Like she isn't expecting him to come back."

"What about Elizabeth's behavior when you've seen her at neighborhood functions? Before the text, I mean."

"Quieter than usual. But everyone assumed it was grief." Sarah adjusts the baby's blanket unnecessarily. "There was one thing, though. At the community center fundraiser last month, someone mentioned Richard's name, and Elizabeth didn't react at all. Not a flinch, not a sad look. Nothing. Like hearing her missing husband's name didn't register."

My mind catalogs these details, organizing them into a narrative that grows more disturbing by the minute. This fits with my own observations—Elizabeth's too-perfect composure, the way she maintains her routine with mechanical precision, the absence of the frantic energy that usually accompanies a loved one's disappearance.

"Jane." Sarah's voice breaks through my thoughts. "What are you thinking? You don't believe Elizabeth had something to do with Richard's disappearance, do you?"

I feel a weight in my chest, an uncomfortable heat that I recognize as the burden of suspicion.

"I don't know," I say finally. "But there are too many inconsistencies. The police have found nothing—no trace of Richard, no activity on his accounts, no evidence of foul play. They're still suggesting he simply left."

"But you don't believe that."

"I don't think he wrote that letter. Richard wasn't the type to walk away from his life, leaving me devastated. Or his work. His business partners are baffled." I watch a leaf spiral down from one of the oaks. "And Elizabeth... I've learned things about her. Lies and secrets. Lots of them."

We've reached a fork in the path. Sarah checks her watch. "I should get Maddie home for her nap."

I nod, understanding our time is up. "Thank you for telling me this. I know it wasn't easy."

"What are you going to do with this information?" Sarah asks, her voice tight with concern.

"Follow it," I say simply. "If there's a connection between what Marie saw and Richard's disappearance, I need to find it."

Sarah studies my face. "Be careful, Jane. If this means what we both think it might..." She doesn't finish the thought. "I really don't like to talk badly about my friend, but... you never know, right? Anything can happen? I mean, it could have been an accident?"

I touch her arm lightly. "I'll be discreet. And Sarah? Maybe don't try to contact Elizabeth again for now."

"Trust me, I won't." She shivers despite the heat. "Will you let me know if you find anything?"

"If I can," I promise.

We part ways at the fork, Sarah pushing the stroller toward the parking lot while I continue along the path that loops back toward the park entrance. My mind is already racing ahead, plotting my next move. If what Marie saw was indeed evidence of violence—of Richard's blood—then I finally have what I need to prove that the Cypress Estates is harboring a killer behind its manicured hedges and wrought-iron gates. Elizabeth might be exactly what I thought she was.

And then it hits me.

Marie might be in danger.

I know that Marie went back to the house after the blowout we had, and I assume that Elizabeth forgave her. She texted me that our arrangement was over. She would no longer spy on her for me, and report to me. Of course, she wouldn't tell me about the clothes. Not after all that went down. I was surprised that Elizabeth would take her back. But in this moment, it suddenly occurs to me that maybe that's why she did it? To get Marie back in the house, to get revenge for her betrayal?

To kill her.

I polish the rim of each crystal glass until it sings when I tap it with my fingernail. The Wilson family crystal—heirlooms passed down three generations—catches light from the chandelier and throws tiny rainbows across the mahogany table. My reflection fragments in each piece: dark eyes, tight lips, hands that never stop moving. Elizabeth likes things just so. After what happened, the least I can do is make sure everything gleams.

The dining room stretches before me, a space designed for performance as much as for eating. Twelve high-backed chairs wait silently around the table. The chandelier—all crystal teardrops and gold filigree—hangs heavy. I've polished every piece of silverware twice already, but I start a third round. Thoroughness is my penance.

I raise one of the wine glasses to the light. A fingerprint mars the bowl—mine, from handling it. I buff it away with my cloth, watching the smudge disappear. If only all mistakes could vanish so easily.

The grandfather clock in the hall strikes two. I move to the silverware, checking each piece for water spots. The weight of the silver feels good in my hand—substantial, valuable. Unlike my position here, which feels increasingly tenuous despite Elizabeth's forgiveness. She told me I could move in when I told her about the money people coming after me and the fear I live with. She understood, she said. That was my motivation for betraying her, and it was forgivable.

"Besides, I know it was all Jane," she then said. "Believe me, I know my mother-in-law. And you will actually be doing me a favor too. I don't want to be alone in the house right now."

It was a strange sensation, being absolved by someone I have deceived. I felt a peculiar mix of gratitude and unease, my heart racing with the realization that I couldn't look at Richard in the same way.

I line up the dessert forks, their tines catching the light. Six settings tonight. The Braxtons are coming for dinner—another couple from the Cypress Estates.

I set down a butter knife and flex my cramping fingers. I think about Jane, and wonder if Elizabeth will ever forgive her the way she did me. I hardly think so.

"I was never good at keeping house," Elizabeth told me once, in a rare moment of candor. "I never learned how to."

"You manage beautifully," I'd replied, the expected response.

She'd laughed—a brittle sound. "I manage to hire people like you who know what they're doing." Then, after a pause: "Don't ever leave us, Marie."

It wasn't a plea. Elizabeth Wilson doesn't plead. But there was something in her voice—a thin thread of vulnerability—that surprised me.

"Never," I'd said.

I move to the china cabinet, selecting the good plates for tonight. Bone china so fine that light passes through it. I set each place with meticulous care, measuring the distance between plate and silverware with my eye. Elizabeth notices these details.

A bead of sweat trickles down my temple, and I wipe it away with my wrist. The house is always kept at a perfect seventy degrees, but perfection makes me sweat. My humming fills the silence—an old habit that Elizabeth tolerates. The tune is something my mother used to sing, though I can't remember the words any more.

I step back to assess my work. The table gleams with potential energy—glasses, plates, and silverware waiting to fulfill their purpose. In three hours, this room will fill with conversation, judgment, and secrets wrapped in pleasantries. The Braxtons will smile and compliment and never suspect the currents running beneath the surface.

Sometimes I wonder what they would do if I spoke up during dinner. "Did you know," I might say, "that Richard's company is hemorrhaging money? That Elizabeth has a separate account with nearly two hundred thousand dollars? That Jane has been paying Richard's gambling debt behind her husband's back?"

But I won't say anything. My job is to serve and vanish, to know without knowing, to see without seeing. I give the table one final inspection, adjusting a fork that's a millimeter out of alignment. The silverware catches the light, sending bright reflections dancing across the ceiling. I allow myself a small smile of satisfaction. This, at least, I can control. This small universe of domestic perfection.

The back of my neck prickles suddenly—a sensation of being watched. I turn quickly, but the doorway is empty. Still, the feeling lingers. In a house this size, with its maze of hallways and rooms, someone could be anywhere.

"Just checking on your progress," Elizabeth said to me once, materializing behind me as I arranged flowers. I'd jumped, nearly dropping a crystal vase. She'd smiled.

I shake off the memory and return to my work. One last check of the table settings. One last polish of the crystal. One last adjustment of the centerpiece—white roses, Elizabeth's favorite. My fingers linger on a petal, soft as satin. In this house of hard edges and sharp corners, these flowers are a rare softness.

The silver salad fork slips through my fingers and clatters against the porcelain plate. I never drop things. The sound feels offensive in the empty dining room, like a scream at a funeral. But it wasn't the fork that broke my concentration—it was something else. A sound from elsewhere in the house. Something that doesn't belong in the afternoon silence of the Wilson home. I hold my breath and listen, wondering if my nerves are finally fraying at the edges.

There it is again. A soft thud followed by what might be a creak. Not the normal settling sounds of this aging mansion—I know those intimately after months of service here. This is different.

My hand hovers over the next glass in line, suddenly unsure.

Elizabeth isn't home.

No one should be here but me.

"Hello?" I call out, my voice sounding thin and uncertain.

I place the polishing cloth carefully beside the silverware, making sure it's perfectly aligned with the edge of the table. Elizabeth notices a detail like that—a cloth askew, a glass slightly out of place. Even in potential danger, I can't abandon my standards. Especially not after what happened.

The sound comes a third time. Closer now, or am I imagining that? It's coming from the main hallway, the one that cuts through the center of the first floor like a spine.

I should call someone. Security, perhaps. The Cypress Estates has a patrol that circles the neighborhood every thirty minutes. But what would I say? That I heard a noise? That I'm jumping at shadows in a house too big for comfort?

Elizabeth's words from last month float back to me: "We need someone steady, Marie. Someone we can rely on completely."

Steady people don't call security over creaking floorboards. Reliable people investigate strange noises themselves. I move toward the hallway, my stockings silent against the hardwood. The door between the dining room and the main hall is heavy oak, ornately carved with vines and flowers. I push it open just enough to peer through.

The hallway stretches before me, dim despite the afternoon sun. Heavy curtains filter the light into a sepia glow that makes the space feel like an old photograph—frozen in time, melancholy. The walls are lined with portraits of Wilson ancestors, their eyes following me as I step fully into the corridor.

Another creak. Ahead and to the right, near where the hallway opens into the front sitting room. I move toward it, keeping close to the wall. My heart pounds a rhythm against my ribs that feels too loud in the silence. The sitting room door is ajar, a slice of darkness visible through the gap. I push it further open with my fingertips, wincing at the slight squeak of the hinges.

Empty.

The furniture—all antiques selected by Victoria Wilson, Richard's grandmother, decades ago—sits in perfect arrangement. The silk drapes hang motionless. Nothing disturbed, nothing out of place.

I exhale slowly, only now realizing I've been holding my breath. Maybe it was just the house settling after all. Or perhaps—

The sound comes again, sharper this time. Not from the sitting room but further down the hall. I whirl around, my back pressing against the doorframe. At the far end of the corridor stands the grandfather clock. A Wilson heirloom, handcrafted in England in the 1800s, according to Elizabeth's frequent explanations to guests. It looms in the shadows, its dark wood absorbing what little light filters through the curtains.

As I watch, the pendulum swings behind the glass door. Tick. The mechanism shifts. Tock. A sound I've heard a thousand times before, but never quite like this—never when I'm alone and on edge.

I make my way toward it, drawn despite my unease. The clock stands nearly seven feet tall, its face adorned with gold numerals and elaborate hands. The pendulum gleams as it swings back and forth in its hypnotic rhythm.

Tick. Tock. Tick. Tock.

But there's something wrong. The clock shows 2:37, but it can't be later than 2:15. And the clock—a timepiece that Richard winds religiously every Sunday evening—never runs fast. Its precision is a point of pride for the Wilson family. After Richard disappeared, I have been rewinding it to keep it going.

"Swiss movement," Richard told guests at the last dinner party he was here for. "Keeps time better than the atomic clock in Colorado." An exaggeration, but one that no one challenged.

I reach out, my fingers trembling as they near the glass door protecting the pendulum. The brass key that winds the mechanism hangs on its little hook inside. But as I touch the glass, the pendulum stops.

Mid-swing.

The silence that follows feels heavier than the ticking. The hair on my arms rises, and a chill crawls up my spine like cold fingers.

"Don't touch that," Jane had told me during my first week here. "The clock is temperamental. Only Richard handles it."

Those words still echo in my mind, a stark reminder of how drastically my life has changed. Once, I was on track to become the lady of this house, dating Richard, the man I thought I would marry. But Jane, with her domineering presence, orchestrated our breakup, viewing me as unworthy of her precious son. Her manipulation pushed me into the arms of Carl, a decision I regret deeply.

Carl was nothing like Richard. He was a disastrous boyfriend, deceitful and untrustworthy. He siphoned money from me, always promising to return it, yet never managing to do so. Our relationship was a whirlwind of lies and betrayal, culminating in his sudden disappearance one cold night. He vanished without a trace, leaving me to deal with the aftermath. I haven't heard from him since, yet his shadow looms over me. I am haunted by calls from his creditors, menacing voices threatening violence if I don't pay his debts.

Now, instead of being the housewife I once envisioned, I am the help, reduced to following Jane's orders. The irony is not lost on me. Every tick of that temperamental clock feels like the heartbeat of my new reality, a constant reminder of how far I've fallen from the life I once imagined I could have.

I pull my hand back as if burned. The pendulum remains frozen, defying gravity in its suspended state.

Then, as I watch, it begins to swing again. But in the opposite direction.

My breath catches. That's not possible. Pendulums don't change direction on their own. I blink hard, wondering if my eyes are playing tricks on me. When I look again, the pendulum swings normally, its soft tick-tock resuming as if nothing had happened. The clock face now shows 2:14—the correct time.

Something cold settles in my stomach. A feeling I recognize from childhood—the certainty that something was hiding under my bed, despite all rational evidence to the contrary.

"You're being ridiculous," I whisper to myself. The sound of my own voice steadies me somewhat. "It's an old clock. They do strange things sometimes."

But my hands are cold, and my heart still races. I back away from the clock, unwilling to turn my back on it just yet. Three steps, then four.

A floorboard creaks beneath my foot, and I nearly jump out of my skin. The same sound I've been hearing. Just the old house settling, the wood expanding and contracting with temperature changes. Nothing sinister. Nothing unexplained.

I laugh then—a short, sharp sound that echoes in the hallway. The portraits seem to judge me for my momentary lapse into superstition. Wilson ancestors with their stern expressions and perfect posture wouldn't approve of such nonsense.

"Pull yourself together," I mutter. Elizabeth needs everything perfect for tonight. The Braxtons are important connections for Richard's business—especially now, with the troubles I'm not supposed to know about. We must keep the wheels turning even in his absence.

As I head back to the dining room, a shadow moves at the far end of the hall. Just a trick of the light, I tell myself. The curtains shifting in the air conditioning, perhaps. But my feet freeze in place, unwilling to move forward or back.

"Hello?" I call again, hating how my voice wavers.

Nothing.

"Mrs. Wilson?" I try.

Still nothing.

I force myself to move, one foot in front of the other, back toward the dining room. My sanctuary of order and purpose. Away from trick clocks and shifting shadows. The hallway seems longer than before, the portraits watching my retreat with painted eyes that suddenly seem too knowing. I imagine them whispering to each other after I pass: "She knows too much. She's seen too much. She doesn't belong here."

I push the dining room door open with more force than necessary, letting it swing wide until it bumps against the wall. The sound is grounding—real and immediate.

The dining room looks exactly as I left it. Sunlight streams through the tall windows, illuminating the perfectly set table. The crystal glasses catch the light, throwing rainbows across the white tablecloth. The silver gleams. Everything in its place. Everything controlled.

My breathing slows as I step back into my domain. I glance at my watch—2:15. Less than a minute has passed since I first heard the sound. It feels like hours.

I return to the table, picking up my polishing cloth. The fabric is soft between my fingers, familiar and comforting. I resume my work, lifting the next glass to the light to check for spots. But my hands aren't steady any more. I can feel a tremor running through them, slight but persistent. The glass wobbles in my grasp, and I set it down carefully before I drop it.

Behind me, the hallway door stands open. I should close it—return to the perfect isolation of my work. But something keeps me rooted in place, staring at that rectangle of shadow.

The grandfather clock chimes the quarter hour, the sound floating down the corridor like a reminder. I flinch.

I force myself to cross the room and close the door firmly. The soft click of the latch is reassuring. I press my forehead against the wood for a moment, gathering myself.

"Just nerves," I whisper. "Just an old house and frayed nerves."

When I return to the table, I resume humming—louder now, filling the silence with sound of my own making. The tune is still my mother's lullaby, though the words continue to elude me. Something about safety and sleep and watching over.

I pick up the glass again, more carefully this time. My reflection stares back at me from its curved surface—eyes a little too wide, mouth a little too tight.

"Everything is fine," I tell my fragmented reflection. "Everything is under control."

But even as I say it, I can't help glancing toward the closed door, half expecting to hear the sound again. And I can't shake the feeling that somewhere in this vast house, someone—or something—is watching, waiting for me to make another mistake.

It's okay. Everything is under control.

I polish the glass until I can see nothing but light reflected in its surface. No shadows, no distortions. Just pure, perfect clarity. If only everything could be so easily perfected, so thoroughly controlled. The clock in the hall strikes the half hour, and I count the chimes reflexively. One. Two. Correct timing now. Nothing strange or unexplained. Just an old house with old things that sometimes behave unpredictably.

I set down the glass and reach for another, forcing my attention back to the task at hand. Everything must be perfect. No time for ghost stories or wandering thoughts. But even as I work, my ears remain attuned to the hallway beyond the door. Waiting, despite myself, for the next unexplained sound.

When I'm finally satisfied, I gather my cleaning supplies. The dining room is perfect now. As I turn to leave, I catch my reflection in the china cabinet's glass door. I barely recognize myself sometimes—this careful woman with watchful eyes and measured movements. I wonder what Elizabeth sees when she looks at me. A trusted employee? A necessary convenience? A potential threat?

I close the dining room door behind me, leaving everything flawless. Everything in its place.

Including me.

TWENTY-SIX

JANE

I push open the heavy oak door, my breath catching as it swings open to the silent foyer. The house feels different tonight. Empty, yet occupied. Cold, yet alive with an energy that makes the fine hairs on my arms stand at attention. I have come to have a talk with Elizabeth. I am worried about her state of mind, and whether Marie might be in danger. The chandelier casts fractured light across the marble, and for a moment, I see her—Elizabeth—moving through the living room. I blink, and the figure turns a little. My breath is caught in my throat.

It's not Elizabeth.

It's Marie.

But why is she wearing my daughter-in-law's dress again, pale blue silk this time?

My keys clink against the silver dish by the door—a sound that should announce my presence—but Marie doesn't turn. She continues moving through the living space with an unsettling grace, her back to me, her posture perfect. The air feels thick with expensive Chanel No. 5 Elizabeth's signature scent, not the unobtrusive soap smell that usually trails Marie.

"Marie?" I call out, my voice smaller than intended.

She turns, and my stomach drops. It's Marie's face, certainly —those unremarkable features I've seen countless times during my visits—but her hair... Her usual mousy brown bun is gone, replaced with a blonde wig styled exactly like Elizabeth's shoulder-length cut. The color matches perfectly, the part on the exact same side, even the way it curls slightly at the ends.

"Mrs. Wilson," she says, Elizabeth's slight inflection on the "son" infiltrating her usually flat tone. "I wasn't expecting you this evening."

I step further into the room, willing my face to remain neutral. "What's going on here?"

"Nothing." She smiles—Elizabeth's smile, the one that never quite reaches her eyes—and gestures toward the sitting room. "Would you like some tea?"

My mouth is dry. "No, thank you."

I watch as she turns away, moving toward the kitchen with Elizabeth's characteristic gait—the slight swing of her right hip, the measured steps that never rush. My daughter-in-law's dress hangs perfectly on Marie's frame. I'd recognized it instantly. I'd given it to Elizabeth last Christmas.

My hands brush against the side table, and I notice the vase of fresh white roses—Elizabeth's favorite—arranged exactly as she always does them, with the fullest blooms facing outward toward the center of the room. Marie appears in the doorway, watching me with Elizabeth's patient smile.

"Where's Elizabeth?" I ask, moving toward the built-in bookshelves.

"She's out," she replies, each syllable measured exactly as Elizabeth would say it.

I nod, afraid my voice might betray me. The family photos on the wall catch my eye—Richard and Elizabeth at their wedding, on their trip to Greece. In every picture, Elizabeth stands with the same poised elegance that Marie now mirrors with frightening accuracy.

She doesn't move from the doorway. "Would you like to stay for dinner? I've made coq au vin."

Elizabeth's specialty. The dish she makes for special occasions.

"I can't tonight," I say, nervous. "I have plans."

Marie nods, her expression somehow both blank and knowing. "Another time, then."

I move toward the exit, but curiosity pulls me toward the stairs. "Where did Elizabeth go? When is she coming back?"

Something flickers across Marie's face—a momentary slip in her performance. "She's out of town. She'll be back when she's ready."

The vagueness of the answer sits like a stone in my stomach. Something definitely isn't right here.

I stare toward the foyer, noting that the silver picture frames on the mantel have been rearranged—Elizabeth always places them chronologically, but now they're jumbled. The orchid in the corner is dying, its leaves yellowing, something Elizabeth would never allow. And there's a faint smell beneath the lavender—something chemical and sharp.

Marie follows me to the door, her footsteps falling in Elizabeth's characteristic rhythm—left foot a little heavier than the right. I turn at the threshold and catch her adjusting her posture, straightening her spine to match Elizabeth's statuesque bearing.

"Please tell her I stopped by," I say, fighting to keep my voice steady. "And tell her to call me when she gets back. I have been trying to reach her, but she doesn't answer her phone."

"Of course," she replies with Elizabeth's slight tilt of the head. "Have a lovely evening."

As I walk to my car, my legs feel unsteady. Through the front window, I see Marie return to the living room. She stops before the large mirror by the staircase, studying her reflection. I watch as she adjusts the blonde wig, practices Elizabeth's smile, and straightens the dress with Elizabeth's precise movements.

The heat in my chest intensifies—not guilt, but fear, sharp and insistent. Where is Elizabeth? And why is Marie wearing her life like a second skin?

I sit in my car but don't start the engine. The house looms before me, its perfect facade concealing whatever twisted scenario is playing out inside. I should call the police, but what would I say? That my son's maid is playing dress-up as his wife? That something feels wrong, but I can't articulate what?

My phone buzzes with a text from Joseph:

Did you get your book?

My fingers hover over the screen. I told him I went to get the book, *How to Win Friends and Influence People,* by Dale Carnegie, that I loaned to Elizabeth one time long ago. It was never about the darn book. I was worried about Elizabeth, but for the wrong reasons, I now fear. I should tell him something is wrong. That Marie is behaving strangely. That I'm concerned about my daughter-in-law.

Instead, I type:

Got it. Everything at home okay?

His reply comes quickly.

All fine. Busy with work.

All fine. But it isn't.

I start the car but don't drive away. Instead, I watch as lights click on and off in the house—Marie moving through the rooms, practicing being Elizabeth. In the upstairs bedroom window, I see her silhouette as she holds up what must be one of Elizabeth's other dresses, examining it against her body. Then she puts it on, along with a set of high heels.

The front door opens, and I shrink down in my seat. Marie steps out, still in Elizabeth's clothes, and walks to the mailbox. She moves with such perfect imitation that, for a moment, I question my own sanity. Maybe it is Elizabeth. Maybe I'm seeing threats where none exist.

But then she turns, and the porch light catches her face at an angle that reveals the uneven application of makeup—an attempt to contour her features to look more like Elizabeth's. The blonde wig shifts slightly in the evening breeze.

Then she waves at me.

She returns inside, closing the door with Elizabeth's characteristic soft click.

I finally pull away from the curb, my mind racing. I imagine Marie adjusting that vase on the side table, arranging the roses—with careful precision and deliberate mimicry. Elizabeth always arranges flowers with her left hand guiding the stems while her right hand adjusts the blooms. I imagine Marie doing exactly the same, as if she'd studied this specific movement for hours.

The thought sends chills down my spine.

I drive slowly through the streets of the estate, past the perfect homes with their perfect lawns. The Spanish moss hanging from the oak trees seems to reach for my car, ghostly fingers trying to stop me from leaving. In my rearview mirror, Richard and Elizabeth's house grows smaller.

My hands grip the steering wheel tightly as I make a decision. I won't go home. Not yet. I'll wait, watch, find out what's happened to Elizabeth. Because one thing is certain—the woman in that house is dangerous.

I circle the block three times before finding the courage to return. The afternoon has grown thicker, a blanket of humidity, dark clouds gathering above, punctuated by the rhythmic chirping of cicadas and the occasional rumble of distant thunder. I grip my phone in my hand—no response from Elizabeth to my follow-up texts. No reasonable explanation for any of this. I know she's angry at me for what I did, but somehow, I think that's not the reason she's not answering me. My hands tremble as I approach the front door again, determination propelling me forward where caution fails.

This time, I don't use my key. I ring the doorbell, counting the seconds it takes for footsteps to approach: seventeen; exactly how long Elizabeth takes to reach the door from the kitchen. The soft click of the lock, the measured swing of the door—all Elizabeth's movements recreated with disturbing accuracy.

"Mrs. Wilson." Marie's eyes widen, not in surprise but in a perfect imitation of Elizabeth's expression when confronted with an unexpected situation. "You've returned." The blonde wig catches the hallway light, gleaming in a way that emphasizes its artificiality.

"I forgot to ask about Elizabeth's birthday dinner next week," I lie, stepping forward without waiting for an invitation. My heart hammers in my chest as I cross the threshold, but I keep my voice steady. "I wanted to coordinate with her."

Marie doesn't step back far enough. It's a subtle power play Elizabeth often employs—maintaining physical proximity to assert control of her space. "As I mentioned, Elizabeth is away. I'd be happy to pass along any messages when she calls."

I move past her into the hallway, noticing how Marie adjusts her stance to mirror Elizabeth's typical posture—weight shifted a little to the left, right hand resting lightly against her collarbone. The hall light flickers, casting momentary shadows across her face that reveal the foundation caked along her jawline, simply too dark for her natural skin tone. Elizabeth's shade, not hers.

"Why are you wearing her clothes and her perfume?" I ask, my voice low but firm. No pretense now.

Marie blinks twice—Elizabeth's tell when formulating a careful response. "I don't understand what you mean."

"The dress." I gesture at her outfit. "That is Elizabeth's. That's her perfume. And that awful wig. That's her hairstyle you're attempting to recreate."

The silence stretches between us, thick with unspoken tension. Marie's expression doesn't change, but something in her eyes shifts—a hardening, a calculation.

"Elizabeth gave me these clothes," she says finally, her voice taking on that peculiar cadence that belongs to my daughter-in-law—the slight emphasis on the ends of sentences, the barely perceptible uptick in pitch when she's being defensive. "She said they no longer fit her style. As for the hair"—she touches the wig with Elizabeth's characteristic light fingertip adjustment—"I've been considering a change. Elizabeth suggested I try something similar to hers."

"When did she suggest this?" I press, noting how Marie's right foot taps once against the floor—another of Elizabeth's unconscious habits when cornered.

"Before she left."

"To visit her sister in Maine."

Marie nods, her lips pressing together exactly as Elizabeth's do when confirming something she considers obvious. "Yes."

"Elizabeth doesn't have a sister. I told you this."

Marie's expression doesn't change, but her eyes flicker toward the stairs for a fraction of a second.

"Perhaps I'm mistaken about where she went," she says, her voice maintaining that perfect Elizabeth timbre. "She mentioned visiting family. I didn't ask for specifics. Now I do think you should leave. Elizabeth doesn't want to see you," she adds suddenly, her tone shifting to something colder. "She made that very clear before she left."

An involuntary shiver runs down my spine. Not from the words themselves, but from the eerie manner with which she delivers them—the exact cadence and inflection Elizabeth uses when establishing boundaries.

"Did she?" I ask, taking a step closer. "When exactly did she leave, Marie?"

"Three days ago," she answers without hesitation.

"And yet her car is still here." I gesture toward the window where Elizabeth's cherry-red Mercedes sits in the driveway, visible under the security light. "Did she take a cab to the airport? Or perhaps you drove her?"

Marie's fingers find the delicate gold necklace at her throat—Elizabeth's necklace, the one Richard gave her on their anniversary—and fiddle with it in Elizabeth's nervous manner.

"I arranged transportation for her."

"Did she take suitcases?"

"Elizabeth isn't home," Marie says, each word clipped. "Come back later."

"Where is my daughter-in-law, Marie?" I ask, my voice barely above a whisper.

Her face remains impassive, but her pupils dilate. "I've told you. She's away."

"And what did you do to her?"

The question slips out before I can stop it. Marie's expression doesn't change, but her posture shifts subtly.

"I don't know what you're implying," she says: Elizabeth's exact intonation when she's buying time. "But I find it extremely offensive."

"This isn't the first time you've done this, is it?" The realization crashes over me as I connect dots I didn't know existed until this moment. "The way you move, speak, gesture—you've been studying her for months."

"I work closely with Mrs. Wilson," Marie says, a fake smile

forming. "Perhaps I've unconsciously adopted some of her mannerisms. It's not unusual."

My eyes catch her hand, and that's when I see it. The diamond on her finger.

"You're wearing her wedding ring."

Marie's left hand twitches almost imperceptibly. The platinum band with its princess-cut diamond catches the light.

"She gave this to me," she says, the lie smooth. "For safe-keeping while she is away. I figured she doesn't want to wear it any more now that Richard has left. It only reminds her of him."

I laugh, a short, sharp sound that cuts through the tension. "My daughter-in-law would never ask you to wear her wedding ring."

"You'd be surprised what she asks of me. She trusts me with many things," Marie says, Elizabeth's slight sardonic edge creeping into her voice. "We've grown quite close in Richard's absence."

The implication settles like ice in my stomach. I take another step forward, and this time Marie retreats a step.

"What have you done with Elizabeth?" I ask again, my voice stronger now. "Where is she?"

Marie's facade finally slips—just for a moment—her eyes darkening with something primal and frightening. Then Elizabeth's polite mask slides back into place.

"I think you should leave now, Mrs. Wilson," she says, Elizabeth's diplomatic dismissal tone perfect down to the slight lowering of pitch at the end. "You're clearly upset, and I wouldn't want to have to tell Elizabeth about this unfortunate conversation."

"Tell Elizabeth what?" I counter. "That her mother-in-law is concerned because the maid is walking around in her clothes, wearing her wedding ring, and what else... sleeping in her bed?"

Marie's eyes narrow, not Elizabeth's expression now, but something entirely her own. Something calculating and cold.

"Elizabeth knows all of that," she says quietly. "She's trusted me with everything. She knows I'm the only one who cares for her."

The implication threatens to knock me off balance, but I stand my ground. "I don't believe you."

"Believe what you wish," she says, Elizabeth's dismissive hand gesture accompanying the words. "But I think you should consider why she hasn't returned your calls. Why she told me she didn't want to see you here again."

The whole conversation sends a wave of nausea through me, but I push it aside.

"Now, if you'll excuse me, I have dinner to prepare."

Dinner? For whom?

I don't move. "What did you do to her, Marie? Where is she?"

Something flickers across Marie's face—a micro expression of irritation that belongs entirely to her, not to Elizabeth. "As I've explained repeatedly, Elizabeth is away. Your persistence is becoming tiresome."

"I'm calling the police," I say, reaching for my phone.

Marie's laugh is a perfect recreation of Elizabeth's—light, almost musical, with that distinctive catch at the end. "And tell them what? That you don't like my outfit? That you're upset I'm house-sitting while your daughter-in-law is away? That you're having trouble finding your son?" She shakes her head, blonde wig shifting slightly. "Do you hear how that sounds? Maybe they just don't want to talk to you. Maybe they've had enough of you."

She's right, and we both know it. I have suspicions but no proof. Nothing concrete to tell the authorities.

"Come to think of it, Elizabeth has mentioned that you've been... confused lately," she says. "Having trouble distinguishing between reality and your anxieties. I probably should disclose that to the police when they get here, right?"

The accusation stings because Elizabeth has indeed mentioned concerns about my mental state—subtle suggestions that I might be imagining problems, seeing threats where none exist. And so has the detective. My obsession with my son, the constant probing for answers. A growing pattern over the past few months that now casts my current suspicions in a troubling light.

"Where is she?" I ask again, my voice barely audible.

Marie's smile is Elizabeth's, perfect in its practiced insincerity. "Safe," she says simply.

The word is laden with implications too terrible to contemplate.

"If you've hurt her—"

"Mrs. Wilson," Marie interrupts, Elizabeth's authoritative tone shutting me down, "I think you should leave now. Before you say something you'll regret." She adjusts the blonde wig with Elizabeth's precise movements. "I'll tell her you stopped by again. I'm sure she'll call you tomorrow."

She moves toward the door, opening it in a clear dismissal. Outside, thunder rumbles closer, and the first heavy drops of rain begin to fall, tapping against the walkway like impatient fingers.

I step toward the door, then pause, turning to face her one last time. "This isn't over."

Marie's smile never wavers. "It was over before it began," she says softly. "Elizabeth understood that. Eventually, you will too."

The door closes behind me with a decisive click—Elizabeth's way of ending a conversation, executed with perfect fidelity.

I stand on the porch as rain begins to fall in earnest, soaking through my light sweater. Through the frosted glass panels flanking the door, I see Marie's silhouette move away, her gait an uncanny recreation of my daughter-in-law's distinctive walk.

My phone buzzes with a text. Joseph:

I thought you were coming home? Everything okay?

I stare at the message, not knowing what to do next. The rain falls harder now, plastering my hair to my face as I type a response with trembling fingers:

Something is wrong. Elizabeth is missing now too.

His reply comes quickly:

What do you mean by missing?

I hesitate, then type:

She's not here. Only the cleaning lady is at their house.

Three dots appear, disappear, then appear again. Finally:

Elizabeth is fine. She's just taking some time away. Stop worrying.

I look back at the house. Through the living room window, I see Marie adjusting a photograph on the mantel, and suddenly doubt creeps in. Am I seeing something that isn't there? Is my mind creating connections, manufacturing suspicion? Maybe she did go away, and Marie is just playing around? Playing dress-up?

Then I remember the wedding ring. The car in the driveway. Elizabeth's non-existent sister.

I know she's not away.

I send another one.

I know something's wrong.

Joseph doesn't respond.

I walk to my car, rain soaking through my clothes, my resolve hardening with each step. If Joseph won't help me find Elizabeth, I'll have to do it myself. I'll uncover what Marie has done.

Through sheets of rain, I take one last look at the house. In the upstairs window, Marie stands watching me, her silhouette a perfect imitation of Elizabeth's statuesque posture. She raises one hand in a familiar wave—Elizabeth's wave—before slowly drawing the curtains closed.

TWENTY-SEVEN

JANE

I stand rigid beside the detective's sedan, my gaze fixed on Richard and Elizabeth's house as if it might disappear should I look away. The evening air presses against my skin, heavy with unspoken accusations. Inside that house, behind those tasteful curtains I helped Elizabeth select, something is terribly wrong. I know what I saw. I know.

"Mrs. Wilson." Detective Mitchell's voice pulls me back to the present. He stands beside me, his weathered face etched with the impatience of a man interrupted on his way home. "You said this was urgent."

"It is." My voice comes out sharper than intended, but I don't apologize. One doesn't reach my position in society by softening one's edges unnecessarily.

Mitchell sighs, checking his watch with deliberate slowness. "It's after five. I was heading home for dinner."

"I wouldn't have called if it wasn't important." I straighten my spine, drawing myself up to my full height. The pearl necklace at my throat feels suddenly tight. "I saw something... disturbing."

"So you said on the phone." He doesn't hide his skepticism,

but at least he's here. Arnold Mitchell has been in law enforcement long enough to know the Wilson name carries weight in this community. "You want to tell me what exactly you saw that couldn't wait until morning?"

I turn back toward the house, with its perfect landscaping and warm golden windows. From here, it looks like any other evening at my son's home. That's what makes it so unsettling.

"I came by earlier to attend to... family matters."

I don't elaborate; Mitchell doesn't need to know the details. "I have a key, of course. When I let myself in, I called out, but no one answered."

"And that's unusual?" Mitchell pulls out a small notebook, more out of habit than necessity, I suspect.

"No. I assumed Elizabeth was upstairs." I pause, collecting my thoughts. "I walked inside. That's when I saw her."

"Saw who?"

"Marie. Their cleaning lady. But she wasn't dressed as Marie." I turn to face him fully, my eyes searching his for understanding. "She was wearing Elizabeth's clothes. Not just any clothes—her favorite blue dress. Her hair was different, a blonde wig that was styled like Elizabeth's. She was wearing Elizabeth's jewelry and even her wedding ring."

Mitchell's pen pauses above his notebook, his brow furrowing with a mix of curiosity and suspicion. "Maybe she was just trying things on? Not great employee behavior, but—" He hesitates, then leans forward, lowering his voice. "I know, Jane. I know that you hired Marie."

I blink, caught off guard by his revelation. "What do you mean?" I say, my heart pounding in my chest.

Mitchell's gaze is steady, unwavering. "That you hired her to spy on your daughter-in-law, Elizabeth. You thought she was hiding something, didn't you? You wanted someone on the inside."

"Spy on Elizabeth?" I repeat. The weight of Mitchell's

accusation settles around me, suffocating. "I don't know what you're talking about."

Mitchell sighs, his expression unreadable. "Don't insult my intelligence, Jane. I know Richard was at her apartment for three hours the day before he disappeared. Before he came to your house for dinner. I spoke to her, and she told me about how she got hired for the job. That you sought her out, Jane."

I swallow hard, trying to compose myself. "I hired her as a cleaning lady," I say, my voice regaining a semblance of control. "Nothing more."

The detective fixes me with a penetrating look. "If you say so. But I must say that I am getting a little tired of all your games. And now you've called me here because the cleaning lady tried on some clothes?"

"No." The word cuts between us like a knife. "You don't understand. She wasn't just trying on clothes. She was becoming Elizabeth. The way she stood, the tilt of her head. Even her voice when she muttered to herself. She was practicing being Elizabeth."

A flicker of something passes across Mitchell's face—not quite belief, but perhaps less dismissal.

"When she saw me, she turned around and smiled. Not like someone caught doing something wrong. Like someone interrupted in the middle of a task." My hands tremble, and I tuck them into the pockets of my slacks. "She said, 'Oh, Jane, I didn't hear you come in.' But she said it as Elizabeth would say it. The same tone of voice."

I can hear how crazy I sound, but can't stop myself. I know there's no way this man will believe me. But he has to. Right? I'm not just seeing things?

Right?

No, I'm not. I must get him to see it for himself, then he'll know I'm not just paranoid or insane, the way I feel he thinks I am right now.

Am I babbling?

"What did you do then?"

"I confronted her. She said Elizabeth was away. There was something in her eyes." I look away, hating how it sounds. Like something from one of those cheap paperbacks Elizabeth reads or pretends to be reading, I don't know any more... "Something... wrong."

Mitchell exhales slowly. "Mrs. Wilson, have you been in touch with your daughter-in-law recently?"

"I've called her multiple times. No answer."

"That could mean anything. Maybe she found out you've been spying on her and simply doesn't want to talk to you any more."

I feel the familiar irritation at having to explain myself. "Elizabeth's car is in the driveway."

"So maybe she took a cab somewhere? Or an Uber?"

"Then where is she? And why is Marie there, dressed like Elizabeth?"

Mitchell doesn't answer immediately, and in that pause, I feel a flutter of validation.

"Look," I continue, "I know how it sounds. But I know what I saw. That woman"—I point toward the house—"is not just a maid with boundary issues. She has hurt Elizabeth, I know she has, and Richard. She's done something to them both."

The silence between us feels like its own presence now, a third party weighing our next move.

"When was the last time you spoke with your daughter-in-law?" Mitchell asks, finally.

"Five days." I don't mention our last conversation was strained, that she's actually angry with me for what I did. "But I know her. This isn't normal."

"That doesn't really justify—"

"Detective, please." I rarely plead, but extraordinary circumstances call for extraordinary measures. "Something is wrong. Go to the door. Ask to speak with Elizabeth. See for yourself."

Mitchell glances toward the house, then back at me. His eyes, I notice, are tired around the edges. The kind of tiredness that comes from seeing too much of human frailty. At least I guess so. I wouldn't really know.

"Mrs. Wilson, do you know how many welfare checks I've done that turned out to be nothing? Family misunderstandings, overreactions, miscommunications."

"I am not overreacting." I enunciate each word. "I am not some hysterical old woman imagining things."

His expression softens. "I didn't say you were. But you have to understand my position. I can't just go barging into people's homes because something *feels off*."

"Then don't barge in. Knock. Ask questions. Do your job." I regret the words as soon as they leave my mouth. Antagonizing him won't help.

But rather than take offense, Mitchell gives me a long, appraising look. "You're really worried, aren't you?"

For once, I allow myself to show it. "Yes. I am."

He sighs, tucks away his notebook. "All right. Let's walk up to the house. I'll ask a few questions, see if we can get a look at Mrs. Wilson—your daughter-in-law, I mean. And the maid. But if everything seems in order, we leave. No scenes, no accusations. Agreed?"

"Agreed." I would promise anything to get inside that house right now.

As we start up the long driveway, I feel a strange hollowness in my chest. I've walked this path countless times—for dinner parties, for impromptu visits that Elizabeth pretends to welcome, for family gatherings where the tension sits like an uninvited guest. But never like this. Never with dread pooling in my stomach.

"Detective," I say, my voice lower now that we're approaching, "thank you for taking this seriously."

He doesn't respond directly. "How long has Marie worked for your son and his wife?"

"A little over four months now."

"Any problems before?"

"No." I hesitate. "She's always been... efficient. Quiet. The perfect employee, really."

"But?"

"But there's something about her. The way she watches. The way she's always there but somehow invisible." I struggle to articulate what has always bothered me about Marie. "She knows too much about us. About the family."

Mitchell nods without commenting.

We've reached the front steps now. Through the side window, I can see a lamp burning in the living room. All perfectly normal. If it wasn't because everything was all perfectly wrong.

Mitchell raises his hand to knock, and I hold my breath, uncertain what I'm more afraid of—that Marie will answer, or that no one will.

Three sharp knocks from Detective Mitchell's knuckles against the heavy oak door. I find myself holding my breath, counting the seconds until it swings open. When it does, Marie stands before us in her standard uniform—crisp, gray, professional. No blonde wig. No blue dress. No jewelry and no wedding ring. Her face reveals nothing beyond mild surprise, as if we're unexpected dinner guests arriving at an inconvenient hour.

"Detective," she says, her eyes flicking to his badge before settling on me. "Mrs. Wilson." No warmth in the greeting, but no animosity either. Just the perfect professional distance of a good servant. A performance I've seen a hundred times before.

"Good evening," Mitchell says. "I'm Detective Arnold

Mitchell. We've met before, if you recall. I was hoping to speak with Mrs. Elizabeth Wilson."

Marie's expression doesn't change. "I'm afraid she's not available at the moment."

"But her car is here, look." I point toward the driveway where Elizabeth's red Mercedes sits. The words tumble out before I can stop them, my composure slipping. "Right there. She never goes anywhere without that car. Or at least put it in the garage."

Marie's eyes follow my gesture, then return to us. "Yes, Mrs. Wilson is correct. The car is here." She smooths an invisible wrinkle from her uniform. "Mrs. Elizabeth is out of town. I took her to the airport earlier today."

"The airport?" Mitchell asks.

"Yes, sir. She went to visit her family. Some kind of emergency, I understand." Marie's face shows just the right amount of polite concern. Too perfect. Too practiced. "She asked me to drive her so she could keep the car here. For safety, I believe. And to house-sit while they're away."

"They?" Mitchell catches the word immediately.

"Mr. Wilson is with her." She offers this information freely, as if it explains everything. "Mrs. Elizabeth received a call three days ago and had to leave suddenly."

"So, Mr. Wilson is no longer missing?" the detective says. "I don't understand."

"He left her," Marie says. "But called, and I guess they reconciled. I don't know everything, Detective, I'm just the cleaning lady and now a house sitter as well."

I study Marie's face, searching for cracks in her composure. Her mousy hair is pulled back in its usual practical bun. No makeup to speak of. Nothing like the vision I saw earlier, yet I'm certain it was her.

Am I going insane?

"That's very convenient," I say, unable to keep the edge from my voice. "Both of them gone, just like that."

Marie doesn't rise to the bait. "Family emergencies rarely come at convenient times, Mrs. Wilson."

Mitchell shifts his weight, the porch boards creaking beneath him. "Did Mrs. Wilson mention which family member was having an emergency?"

"Her mother, I believe. In Savannah." Marie answers without hesitation. "She was quite upset when she got the call."

I feel a flicker of doubt. Could I have been mistaken? No. I know what I saw.

"That's odd," I interject. "Elizabeth never mentioned her mother was ill. Besides, I thought she was dead."

Marie's eyes meet mine, unflinching. "It may have been her sister—again they don't tell me everything. I don't believe Mrs. Elizabeth shares every detail of her family matters with the household staff, ma'am. But they should have told you. Are you sure they didn't mention this to you? How inconsiderate of your feelings if they didn't. Or maybe you forgot? Elizabeth did mention you've been struggling a little lately, with memory and... well, paranoia. Or maybe they didn't want to tell you? How awful that must be for you."

The subtle reminder of my place—outside my son's marriage, not privy to their intimate conversations—lands like a slap. Marie has always been skilled at these small, perfectly deniable jabs.

"When do you expect her back?" Mitchell asks, his tone neutral.

"She didn't specify. A few days, perhaps." Marie glances at her watch—Elizabeth's watch, I realize with a jolt. A delicate gold thing Richard gave her for their fourth anniversary. "She was in quite a hurry."

"And you're staying here while they're gone?" Mitchell continues.

"Yes. Mrs. Elizabeth asked me to."

"May we come in?" Mitchell asks suddenly. "I'd like to verify a few things, and I'm sure Mrs. Wilson here would feel better seeing that everything is in order."

A flicker—something so quick I almost miss it—crosses Marie's face. Annoyance? Fear? It's gone before I can name it.

"Of course," she says, stepping back. "Though I'm not sure what there is to verify."

We enter the foyer, and I immediately scan for anything amiss. The house is immaculate as always. The familiar scent of the lemon polish Marie uses on the antique sideboard. Everything in its place.

Mitchell makes a show of looking around casually. "Looks nice."

"Yes, the Wilsons have beautiful taste," Marie agrees, her tone suggesting she has no particular role in maintaining that beauty, though we all know otherwise.

"When exactly did you say Mrs. Wilson left?" Mitchell asks.

"Yesterday morning. Around ten."

"I see."

I move toward the living room; drawn by some instinct I can't name. The room is perfectly arranged, not a cushion out of place. I move toward the staircase. "I'd like to see upstairs."

"Mrs. Wilson." Marie's voice takes on a new edge. "I'm not sure that's appropriate while the family is away."

"Elizabeth is my daughter-in-law," I remind her coldly. "This is my son's home."

"Jane," Mitchell intervenes, using my first name in a way that grates, "maybe we should respect the boundaries here."

"Boundaries?" I turn on him, my voice rising imperceptibly. "I was in this house earlier today. I saw—" I stop, aware of Marie watching me with those calculating eyes.

"You were here earlier?" Marie asks, her tone perfectly puzzled. "I didn't realize. What time was that?"

"Around three," I say, watching her closely. "I let myself in with my key."

"How strange. I was here all afternoon. I didn't hear anyone come in." Marie's brow furrows in what looks like genuine confusion, but I know better.

"I saw you, Marie. I spoke to you," I say with frustration.

"That can't be true. I was upstairs for a while, organizing the guest room where I have been sleeping. Perhaps that's when you came by?"

"Perhaps," I say, though we both know it's a lie. But I know it's no use to fight it. She'll just lie some more.

Mitchell checks his watch again, more deliberately this time. A small sigh escapes him—the sound of a man who has better things to do with his evening than mediate a family disagreement.

"Detective," Marie says, turning her attention to him. "I understand Mrs. Wilson's concern for her family. It speaks well of her devotion." The compliment slides off her tongue easily. "But I assure you, everything is as I've explained. If you'd like, I can give you the contact information for Mr. Wilson's office. They can confirm his travel schedule."

No, they won't! He hasn't been to the office in five weeks!

"That won't be necessary right now," Mitchell replies, though I can see he's making mental notes. "You mentioned Mrs. Wilson went to Savannah. Do you have an address or phone number where she can be reached?"

Marie hesitates for the first time. "I'm afraid not. She didn't leave that information with me. Only that she would call when she knew more about her mother's condition. I can call once she checks in."

"Mrs. Wilson," Mitchell says. "I think we've taken enough of Ms. Clements's time this evening."

"But—" I begin.

"Everything appears to be in order," he continues firmly. "I understand your concern, but there's nothing here to suggest any problem beyond a family emergency and a woman stepping in to help out in a time of need."

Marie offers a small, sympathetic smile. "I'll be sure to let Mrs. Elizabeth know you were concerned when she calls. I'm sure she'll appreciate your thoughtfulness."

The condescension in her tone is so subtle that Mitchell misses it completely, but it burns through me like acid. This woman—this nobody—standing in my son's home, wearing my daughter-in-law's watch, speaking to me as if I'm some doddering old fool.

"I'd like to look upstairs," I repeat, more firmly this time.

Mitchell places a hand lightly on my arm. "Mrs. Wilson—Jane—we should go."

"It's quite all right," Marie says smoothly. "If it would put Mrs. Wilson's mind at ease, she's welcome to look around. Though I'd prefer to accompany her, of course. For propriety's sake. I am, after all, responsible for this house till the family returns."

"That won't be necessary," Mitchell says before I can accept her offer. "We've imposed enough this evening."

Marie inclines her head slightly. "As you wish. Please don't hesitate to call if there's anything else I can help with."

The family. As if she isn't just the help. As if she belongs here.

"Come on, Jane," Mitchell says quietly. "We should go."

I allow him to guide me toward the door, every instinct screaming that we're making a terrible mistake. As we step back onto the porch, Marie remains in the doorway, framed by the warm light from inside.

"Good night, Detective. Mrs. Wilson," she says, her hand

already on the door. "I do hope you'll be able to set your mind at ease."

The door closes with a soft click, and I hear the deadbolt slide into place. I stand there, staring at the polished oak, feeling as if I've just lost a battle I didn't even know I was fighting.

Mitchell's expression as he turns to me is carefully neutral, but I can see the skepticism in his eyes. "Well," he says, "that was certainly interesting."

I look back at the house, at the perfect facade hiding whatever secrets lurk within. "She's lying," I say simply. "I know she is. She told me Elizabeth left three days ago. To you, she said today at first, and then yesterday. Her mother is dead, and she doesn't have a sister. She's from Tallahassee, not Savannah. It's all made up. Can't you see it?"

Mitchell sighs, rubbing a hand across his weathered face. "There were a few inconsistencies to the whole thing, I will agree to that. But is that enough? I hardly think so. What I know is that without evidence of a crime or reason to believe someone is in danger, there's not much more I can do tonight."

The finality in his tone tells me I'm losing him. Losing my only ally in whatever strange game Marie is playing.

"Detective," I say, my voice low and urgent as we walk back toward his car. "I know what I saw. That woman is not who she pretends to be. And my family is in danger. I feel it."

He stops, studies me for a long moment. He sighs. "Look, if you haven't heard from your son or daughter-in-law in the next forty-eight hours, call me. We can file another missing person's report then. In the meantime, go home. Get some rest."

"I'm not going home," I say, my voice steady despite the rage and fear churning inside me. "I'm staying right here."

Mitchell's expression hardens. "Mrs. Wilson, if you harass Ms. Clements further tonight, she would be well within her rights to call the police. And the responding officers might not be as understanding as I've been."

"I won't approach the house again. But I'm staying in my car, watching." I meet his gaze unflinchingly. "That's not illegal."

He holds my stare for a long moment, then shakes his head. "Your choice. But don't do anything that might complicate matters if there really is something going on."

"There is something going on," I insist. "And I'm going to prove it."

"As I said, it's your choice."

Mitchell gets into his car without another word. I watch his taillights disappear down the curved driveway before walking to my own car, parked just outside the property line where the road curves away from the house.

From here, I have a clear view of the front entrance and part of the driveway. I settle in, adjusting the seat for what I know will be a long night. The dashboard clock reads 7:47 p.m. Outside, the evening has deepened into full darkness, broken only by the security lights illuminating the front of Richard and Elizabeth's home.

Hours pass. I keep my vigil, fighting against exhaustion, against the doubt that creeps in with each passing minute. What if I'm wrong? What if Elizabeth really did rush off to tend to her ailing family member? What if Richard is simply with her, and they have found one another again?

But I know what I saw. That woman, wearing Elizabeth's clothes, practicing Elizabeth's mannerisms. And now, installed in their home as if she belongs there.

The dashboard clock reads 1:26 a.m. when movement at the house catches my eye. The front door opens, spilling light across the porch. A figure emerges—a woman, but not in a maid's uniform.

I lean forward, straining to see in the dim light. The woman locks the door behind her, then turns toward the driveway. Her hair catches the security light—blonde, styled in the loose waves Elizabeth favors. She's wearing what looks like a tailored jacket, her posture straight and confident.

As she moves toward Elizabeth's car, her face becomes visible, and my breath catches in my throat. It's Marie—but not Marie as I've ever seen her. Her transformation is complete now, from the elegant sweep of her hair to the precise way she carries herself. She walks exactly like Elizabeth, moves exactly like Elizabeth.

She unlocks the Mercedes with a casual press of the key fob, slides into the driver's seat. The engine purrs to life, headlights cutting through the darkness as she backs out of the driveway.

I sit frozen, watching as the car passes my hiding spot. Through the window, I catch a glimpse of her profile—perfect, poised, a flawless replica of my daughter-in-law.

The car continues down the road, taillights glowing red in the darkness until they disappear around a bend. Only then do I realize I'm shaking, my knuckles white against the steering wheel.

Where is she going at this hour, dressed as Elizabeth? And more importantly—where are Elizabeth and Richard?

I reach for my phone, scrolling to Mitchell's number before stopping myself. What would I tell him? That I saw Marie dressed as Elizabeth again, driving Elizabeth's car? He'd dismiss it as more evidence that Marie is house-sitting as claimed.

No, I need more than suspicion now. I need proof.

I start my engine quietly, keeping the headlights off until I'm well away from the house. Then I accelerate, following the route Marie took. Whatever game she's playing, whatever she's done to my family, I'm going to find out.

And God help her when I do.

TWENTY-EIGHT

JANE

This is where she's going? The beach house? I can't believe it. I stare at it, looming against the pitch-black sky, a shadow darker than the night itself as I watch her park the Mercedes and rush inside. I pause at the edge of the property, fingers brushing the shape of the gun Joseph once bought for me for protection, nestled in my purse. This place—once a sanctuary, a proud family legacy—now feels like a trap waiting to spring. The wind carries salt and secrets across my face as I stare at what used to be our haven, what became Richard and Elizabeth's, and what might now be their tomb.

No stars tonight. No moon. Just darkness and the rhythmic crash of waves I can hear but barely see. Perfect cover, I suppose, though I'm not sure who's hiding from whom any more.

I step forward, my heels sinking into the cool, wet sand that borders the manicured lawn. The sensation is familiar—how many summers did I spend running barefoot across this same stretch? But tonight, each step feels like moving through a dream.

A nightmare.

"You shouldn't have come alone," I whisper to myself, the words immediately stolen by the wind. But who would come with me? Joseph? He thinks I've lost my mind. I've been alone since Richard disappeared. All alone.

The house stands three stories tall, white clapboard now gray in the darkness, wraparound porch, empty of the rocking chairs usually lined up. It was built by Richard's great-grandfather, passed down through generations of Wilsons, a symbol of our family's enduring presence on this stretch of Atlantic coastline. I remember the day we gave it to Richard and Elizabeth—my proud smile, the champagne toast on this very porch, my careful explanation that this was tradition, that the house should always belong to the family heir.

"A wedding gift," I had called it, though it felt more like surrendering a piece of myself.

Richard had nodded solemnly, understanding the weight of the gesture. Elizabeth had been less excited, and talked about redecorating it, which I had refused her.

The steps to the porch creak under my weight. They always have, an unintentional alarm system Richard's grandfather refused to fix.

"Keeps the teenagers honest," he used to joke. Now the sound feels like a betrayal, announcing my arrival to whoever might be listening.

I pause at the door, pressing my ear against the weathered wood. Nothing. The house holds its breath, waiting. The key slides into the lock. One turn, two, and the door swings inward on silent hinges—at least those have been oiled. The familiar smell hits me immediately: salt water, old wood, the faint trace of lemon polish. But underneath lurks something else, something wrong.

Tension, perhaps.

Fear.

I step into the foyer, my hand returning to my purse, to the gun. The space unfolds around me, high ceilings disappearing into shadow, decorative beams cutting across like the ribcage of some great beast. The chandelier—three generations old and shipped from Europe—hangs unlit above me, its crystals dull without light to bring them to life.

"Richard?" I call softly, my voice sounding foreign in the emptiness. "Elizabeth?"

The names hover in the air, then dissipate. No answer.

To my right, the grand staircase curves upward into darkness. To my left, the hallway leads to the kitchen and dining room. Straight ahead, the living room opens onto the back deck and the ocean beyond. Where would they be?

I reach for the light switch, then hesitate. Darkness is my ally right now. Or is it hers?

My eyes adjust slowly, picking out shapes in the gloom: the glass display case filled with seashells collected over decades; the row of nautical paintings my mother-in-law insisted on keeping despite their mediocrity; the antique console table where we always tossed our keys and sunglasses.

I take another step forward, and my heel catches on the edge of the Persian rug—the one Joseph's mother insisted was "too good" for a beach house but installed anyway. I stumble a little, catching myself against the wall, and that's when I hear it.

A floorboard groans somewhere to my left.

Not the natural settling of an old house.

A footstep.

I freeze, my breath caught in my throat. The gun is in my hand now, though I don't remember drawing it. My finger rests beside the trigger, not on it—not yet.

"Who's there?" I demand, my voice steadier than I feel.

Silence answers me. Then another creak, closer this time.

I spin toward the sound, gun raised, heart hammering against my ribs like it's trying to escape.

And there she is, emerging from the shadows of the hallway.

Marie. Her slim figure almost disappears into the darkness, except for the pale oval of her face and the metallic glint in her hand—a gun, pointing directly at me.

"Hello, Jane," she says, her voice soft but carrying easily in the quiet house.

Her words bounce off the wooden beams, the glass cases, the walls that have witnessed generations of our family's joys and sorrows. The echo seems to multiply her presence until I feel surrounded by her, trapped.

I tighten my grip on my own weapon, grateful for the hours at the shooting range, for the lessons my father insisted upon. "Where are they, Marie?"

She tilts her head. Even in this moment—this insane, terrifying moment—she maintains the appearance of the perfect imitation of my daughter-in-law. Except for her eyes. They've always been watchful, but now they burn with something I've never seen before. Something hungry.

"They're here," she says, taking a step closer. "Safe and sound. For now. Once they sign over the house and all their money to me, they will be dead, of course. Well, maybe not Richard. I'm considering keeping him."

"I want to see them." My voice doesn't waver, and I'm proud of that small victory.

Marie smiles, and the expression transforms her unremarkable features into something truly unsettling. "Of course you do. The devoted mother-in-law, coming to the rescue. How touching."

"What do you want, Marie?" I ask, trying to keep her talking, trying to think. The house is large, with plenty of places to hide two people. Are they bound? Gagged? Already—no, I can't think that. They're alive. They have to be.

"What do I want?" She repeats the question like it's a fascinating philosophical proposition. "I want what everyone wants, Jane. To be seen. To matter." Her free hand gestures around at the opulent foyer. "To have all this."

I take a careful step to the side, testing whether she'll follow my movement. She does, her gun never wavering from my chest.

"This isn't the way to get it," I say as calmly as I can manage.

She laughs, the sound startlingly loud after our hushed conversation. "Isn't it? It seems to be working perfectly well so far."

My mind races through options. I could shoot her now, but if I miss—or if she fires simultaneously—or if I actually kill her, I might never find Richard and Elizabeth. I could try to reason with her, but the gleam in her eyes suggests she's beyond reason. I could attempt to distract her, but with what?

"Why the beach house?" I ask, trying to trick her into telling me where they are, despite the fear coursing through me. "Why bring them here?"

Something flickers across her face—a shadow of emotion I can't quite place. "It seemed fitting," she says after a moment. "The place where it all began."

"What began?"

"Their perfect life." She practically spits the words. "The life I've been cleaning up after, invisible in the background. Did you know Elizabeth leaves her wet towels on the marble floor every single day? Every. Single. Day. And Richard never puts his coffee mug in the dishwasher. Never."

The mundane complaints sound absurd in this context, with guns pointed and lives at stake, but I sense there's something deeper beneath them. Some festering wound I can't see.

"I'm sorry they weren't better employers," I say carefully.

Her laugh is harsh. "Employers? Is that what you think this is about? God, you're just like them. So self-centered. So blind."

I shift my weight, feeling the aged floorboards beneath me.

In my youth, I knew every creak, every groan of this house. I could navigate it blindfolded. Does that knowledge still serve me, or has time rewritten this map too?

"Then tell me," I say. "Help me understand."

Marie takes another step forward, close enough now that I can see the rise and fall of her chest, the slight tremor in her hand that belies her calm exterior. "It's about taking back what should have been mine," she whispers. "Starting with this house."

The statement lands like a physical blow. This house? What claim could she possibly have on our family home?

"Marie," I say slowly, "this house has been in the Wilson family for generations."

Her smile widens, revealing teeth that seem too sharp in the darkness. "Yes," she agrees. "It has."

And suddenly, horribly, I begin to understand. I thought she accepted the end of her relationship with Richard all those years ago, but she never did.

"You told Richard to get rid of me. That I wasn't good enough for him, Jane. That I could never be a part of this family. That's why he broke up with me."

I wrinkle my forehead, thinking about this. "No," I say. "I never said that he shouldn't be with you."

"Yes, you did. Richard told me when he broke up with me."

"Well, he lied, then. I never meddled in your relationship with him. Why would I think you weren't good enough then, if I thought you were now? He must have told a lie, Marie, maybe because he didn't want to be with you?"

"You're lying! He wants to be with me. I will get rid of you and Elizabeth and then take him home with me. We will be a family."

As I said, pure madness. There's no reasoning with her any more, I realize.

I don't think. I just move. My body launches into motion

before my mind catches up, a primitive survival instinct taking over as I bolt from the foyer. The familiar corridors of the beach house—where Richard and I would play tag when he was a boy, where Richard and his father would go fishing down on the beach—now stretch before me like a labyrinth. My heels clatter against hardwood, each step an announcement of my location. I kick them off without slowing, bare feet silent now on the cool floors that have supported generations of Wilsons. Behind me, Marie's voice calls out, mockingly sweet, "Running won't help, Jane. This house remembers who belongs here."

The gun weighs heavy in my hand as I round the corner into the main hallway. I know this house intimately: every closet, every hidden alcove, every squeaky board. At least, I used to. Five years of Richard and Elizabeth's ownership may have changed things.

A bullet smashes into the wall beside me, sending splinters of wood and plaster into the air. I flinch but don't slow down. Marie's accuracy leaves much to be desired, thank God.

"Where's my son?" I shout over my shoulder, hoping to distract her, to buy time, to learn something—anything.

Her laugh follows me down the corridor. "Somewhere safe. Somewhere waiting for you."

I duck into the library, a grand room lined with bookshelves Richard's great-grandfather installed himself. I've always loved this room. The smell of old paper and leather bindings usually comforts me, but tonight it's just another reminder of what's at stake. Our history. Our future.

My mind races as I crouch behind a leather armchair, heart hammering against my ribs. Richard. Elizabeth. Are they here? Are they alive? The thought that my son and his wife might be hurt—or worse—sends a fresh wave of adrenaline through me.

"Richard once told me he always thought this house was haunted," Marie's voice drifts from the hallway. "Did you know that? He told me during one of our... conversations."

I clench my jaw, hating the way she emphasizes the word, the implication hanging in the air. She's trying to get under my skin. I won't let her.

Instead, I focus on escape. The library has two doors—the one I entered through, and another that leads to the sunroom. If I can reach the sunroom, I can access the back staircase. From there, the second floor, where most of the bedrooms are located. Where Richard and Elizabeth might be.

I take a deep breath and run.

Marie appears in the library entrance just as I'm halfway across. Our eyes meet for a split second. She looks wild. Unhinged.

She fires again. The bullet tears through a row of first editions my father collected. I duck instinctively, continuing my run in a crouch.

"You're making this harder than it needs to be," she calls out, her voice eerily calm despite the violence of her actions.

I slam the sunroom door behind me and scan the room for something to block it. The white wicker furniture is too light. The potted palms too unwieldy. I settle for tipping a small side table against the doorknob—not much, but it might slow her down.

The sunroom glows with ambient light from the beach, where the moon is rising, the darkness outside somehow less oppressive here with the wall of windows facing the ocean. In daylight, this room is magical—sunlight dancing on glass surfaces, the horizon stretching endlessly blue. Now, it's all shadows and reflections, the glass making me feel exposed.

I hear a thud against the door. Then another.

Marie is trying to break through.

The back staircase is across the room, a narrow spiral of wrought iron that leads up to the second-floor gallery. I make a dash for it, just as the sunroom door bursts open, sending the side table skidding across the floor. Marie stands in the doorway, silhouetted against the light from the library. She raises her gun.

I dive behind a chaise longue as the shot goes wide, shattering one of the floor-to-ceiling windows. Glass rains down, tinkling against the tile floor like wind chimes in a hurricane.

"That was my mother-in-law's favorite window," I say, surprising myself with the inanity of the comment in this life-or-death moment.

"I know," Marie responds, stepping carefully over broken glass. "She commissioned it from an artist in Charleston. Paid a fortune. Richard told me."

The casual knowledge of my family history on her lips feels like a violation. How many stories has Richard shared with her? I underestimated how close they got all those years ago. How attached she was to him.

I scramble toward the staircase, staying low. Another shot, another miss. The spiral stairs vibrate under my feet as I climb, the metal cold against my bare soles.

From this elevated position, I can see Marie crossing the sunroom, stepping deliberately through the debris of broken glass and pottery. She doesn't hurry. She moves like she has all the time in the world.

I reach the second-floor gallery and pause for a split second, orienting myself. A long corridor stretches in both directions, bedrooms branching off like the ribs of a skeleton. The master suite—where Richard and Elizabeth would naturally stay—is at the far end. But would Marie keep them there? Too obvious.

The guest rooms, perhaps? Or maybe the old nursery, where Richard once spent his carefree childhood summers. I remember it well, with its faded wallpaper and the lingering scent of lavender. But then, I recall my own steps echoing through these halls since the day Richard went missing. Could it be that I had unknowingly passed by the very room that held him, so painfully close yet out of reach? As Marie's footsteps resonate on the spiral staircase, I am jolted from my thoughts and force myself to move. The weight of those memories, of being so near to my son and yet not finding him, presses heavily on my heart.

The hallway stretches before me, the walls lined with photographs—generations of Wilsons at this very beach house. Weddings. Christenings. Birthdays. My own face smiles from several frames, younger, happier, unaware of what the future holds.

A sudden crash from below startles me—Marie must have stumbled on the stairs. I use the momentary advantage to duck into the nearest room, my brother-in-law's old bedroom, now converted to a generic guest room with nautical décor.

The door closes quietly behind me, and I press my ear against it, listening for Marie's approach. My breathing sounds thunderous in the silence. I try to control it, counting inhalations like I used to teach Richard to do when he had nightmares as a child.

One, two, three, inhale. One, two, three, exhale.

I turn slowly, scanning the room, gun still clutched in my damp palm. The space is tidy, impersonal now without the old posters and tennis trophies that used to be here. A double bed with a blue and white quilt. A dresser with seashells arranged artfully on top. A closet with louvered doors.

The closet. Something about it catches my attention. A shadow beneath the door that shouldn't be there? A scent that doesn't belong? I approach cautiously, heart pounding.

Before I can reach it, footsteps echo in the hallway.

I freeze. The doorknob to the hallway turns slowly. I dive beneath the bed, pressing myself against the dusty hardwood floor, gun extended toward the door. The door swings open. Marie's sensible shoes appear in my limited field of vision.

She takes two steps into the room, then stops.

Her feet stop moving, pointing directly at the bed. "Found you."

I roll out from the other side as she fires, the bullet tearing through the mattress where I had been. I scramble to my feet, raising my own gun, but Marie is already moving, backing toward the door.

"You won't shoot me," she says confidently. "Not until you know where they are."

She's right, damn her. I adjust my aim, pointing at her leg instead of her chest.

"Tell me now, or I'll make sure you can't walk to wherever you're keeping them."

For the first time, uncertainty flickers across her face. She hadn't considered this possibility. A noise from somewhere down the hall distracts us both—a thud, followed by a muffled sound that might be a voice. Marie's eyes widen fractionally before she regains control. "Seems like someone's getting impatient," she says with forced lightness.

I lunge toward the door, but Marie is quicker, slamming it shut as she backs into the hallway. I hear the key turn in the lock—a key she must have taken from the utility drawer in the kitchen, where we've always kept spares.

"No!" I slam my shoulder against the door, once, twice, but it holds firm. These old houses were built to last.

"I'll go check on our guests," Marie calls through the wood. "Sit tight, Jane."

Her footsteps recede down the hall toward the sound.

I spin around, searching the room for another exit. The windows are an option, but I'm on the second floor, and the drop to the dunes below could break an ankle—or worse. The closet catches my eye again. The old houses along this stretch of coast were built with secret passages, ways for the wealthy to hide their valuables—or themselves—during hurricanes and, if family legend is to be believed, prohibition.

I wrench open the closet doors. Empty hangers click against each other like wind chimes. The back wall is solid cedar, aromatic even after all these years. I run my hands along the panels, searching for the catch I know must be here. My husband showed me once, decades ago. A hidden button, a pressure point, something—

There. A small knot in the wood gives under my fingers. I press harder, and a section of the wall swings inward, revealing a narrow passageway.

I slip inside without hesitation, pulling the panel closed behind me. The passage is pitch black and smells of dust and forgotten spaces. I feel my way forward, one hand on the rough wall, the other still gripping my gun.

The passage slopes gently downward. It must connect to another room, perhaps even to the first floor. I move as quickly as I dare in the darkness, ears straining for any sound that might guide me.

After what feels like an eternity but is probably less than a minute, I hear voices—muffled but distinct—coming from somewhere ahead. It's Marie's controlled tones, now with an edge of panic.

"—doesn't matter any more. She's here. She knows."

I pause, pressing my ear against the wall. Where am I? Which room lies beyond?

A sudden, high-pitched laugh rings out—Marie, but transformed, her usual restraint completely abandoned. "You should see your faces! The great Wilson family, tied up like Christmas presents. What would your country club friends say?"

My blood turns to ice at the confirmation. They're alive but restrained. And Marie is unraveling. I feel along the wall, searching for another panel, another way in. My fingers brush something metal—a hinge, nearly invisible in the seam of the wood. I push gently, and a small viewing port opens, allowing me to peer into the room beyond.

It's the old nursery. And there they are—Richard and Elizabeth, bound to chairs, pale and disheveled but alive. Marie paces before them, gun waving erratically as she speaks. A flood of relief goes through me. Richard is alive. There's a cut on his forehead, dried blood crusted along his temple. Elizabeth's makeup is streaked with tears, but her eyes are fierce, defiant.

I take a deep breath, steadying my hand on my gun. I need to get to that room. I need a plan. Marie is between me and everything I love, but for the first time since entering this nightmare version of our family home, I feel something beyond fear. I feel ready.

TWENTY-NINE

JANE

I burst through the door, then stand frozen in the doorway, my eyes adjusting to the dim light filtering through dusty blinds. Marie's wild eyes find mine across the cluttered room. The gun in her hand doesn't tremble—only her finger does, hovering over the trigger with terrible certainty.

Behind her are two figures slumped in wooden chairs. Elizabeth's blonde hair catches what little light there is, and beside her, Richard's broad shoulders are hunched forward in defeat. Rope binds their wrists and ankles. Their mouths are covered with duct tape, but their eyes—wide with terror and pleading—scream volumes.

As I take in the scene, my heart shatters at the sight of my son, who has been trapped here for weeks. A sob catches in my throat, and questions race through my mind. What horrors has he endured during this time? How have they changed him? He looks so much skinnier now, his cheeks hollow and his eyes sunken. Has he been eating at all, or has hunger become his constant companion?

Every instinct screams for me to rush to my poor baby boy, to cradle him in my arms and assure him that everything will be all right. But I restrain myself, my body trembling with the effort. Marie stands between us, a menacing figure with a gun clutched tightly in her hand, an insurmountable barrier separating me from the child I long to comfort.

"Marie," I say, my voice steadier than I feel, though my heart pounds like a drum. "You need to put the gun down."

As the tension thickens in the room, Richard's eyes roam and land on me. Our eyes lock, a silent exchange passing between us. I can see the fear etched deep in Richard's eyes, mirroring my own. The room feels like it's holding its breath.

She shakes her head, a small, jerky motion. "You shouldn't have come, Jane." Her voice has lost the soft, timid quality I remember. Now it's sharp—the voice of someone who's been acting for a very long time. She places the gun on Richard's forehead. "You put your gun down or he is gone."

Seeing the panic on my son's face, I do as I'm told. I place the gun on the floor.

"Now kick it away," Marie says. "All the way to the corner."

Again, I do as she tells me to. For Richard.

"You can't have them," I tell her, my gaze darting between the gun and the bound couple. My son and his wife. "This ends now."

I don't give her time to respond. I lunge forward, driven by a surge of adrenaline that momentarily blinds me to reason. My body moves ahead of my thoughts, propelled by raw instinct.

Marie's eyes widen in surprise. She wasn't expecting this—not from me. The gun swings toward my chest, but I'm already crashing into her. My fingers close around her wrist, pushing the weapon up and away. The cold metal grazes my cheek as we stumble backward together.

Elizabeth's scream is muffled behind the tape, but the panic in it pierces through.

Richard shouts something unintelligible, the wooden chair creaking as he struggles against his restraints.

Marie and I fall against a side table. A lamp crashes to the floor, glass shattering. We're a tangle of limbs and fury. Her free hand claws at my face, nails raking across my skin. I feel the hot sting, then the warm trickle of blood down my cheek.

"Let go," she hisses, her face inches from mine. Gone is the meek maid, replaced by something feral and desperate.

I tighten my grip on her wrist, twisting hard. "Never."

The gun is still between us, caught in the vise of our struggling hands. My heart pounds so loudly I can barely hear anything else. A single misplaced finger, a moment of lost control, and everything could end.

Marie brings her knee up sharply into my stomach. The air rushes from my lungs, and my grip loosens for just a second. It's enough. She wrenches her hand free and swings the gun toward me.

I throw myself sideways as a deafening crack splits the air when her gun goes off. A white-hot pain explodes in my left shoulder. The force spins me around, and I slam into the wall, sliding down to my knees.

Elizabeth screams again, and both she and Richard twist frantically.

I press my hand to my shoulder. It comes away slick with blood. The pain is immediate and blinding, radiating outward in pulsing waves. My vision blurs at the edges.

I've been shot.

"I didn't want to do that," Marie says, taking a step toward me. There's something almost regretful in her tone. "You could have just left us alone. They're not worth it, Jane. They're not worth dying for."

I force myself to look up at her, past the gun now pointed directly at my face. "You're wrong," I manage through gritted teeth.

Behind her, Elizabeth and Richard continue to struggle

against their bonds. The sight of them—frightened but fighting —renews something in me.

I can't stop now.

I push through the pain, gathering my feet under me. Marie watches, curiosity mixing with contempt on her face.

"You don't give up, do you?" she asks.

I launch myself at her again, this time aiming low. My good shoulder connects with her midsection. The gun goes off again, the bullet splintering wood somewhere above us. We crash to the ground together, rolling across the cluttered floor.

My shoulder screams in protest, but I hang on, pinning her gun hand to the floor with my knee. Her face contorts with rage, and she thrashes beneath me. Her free hand finds my injured shoulder and digs in.

I cry out, vision temporarily whiting out from the pain. Marie uses the moment to roll us over, reversing our positions. Her weight settles on my chest, crushing the air from my lungs.

"Why couldn't you just stay away?" she demands, her face flushed with exertion. "They don't care about you. They don't care about anyone but themselves. Richard belongs to me."

"No, he doesn't, Marie. And he never will," I say. "He will never love you. Just because you went to one charity function in a borrowed dress doesn't make you part of our world."

I struggle beneath her, but my strength is fading. The room spins slightly. I need to end this—now. My eyes dart around, searching for something, anything.

There—about an arm's length away—a shard of the broken lamp, its edge jagged and gleaming.

I stretch my fingers toward it, straining. Marie's attention is on my face, on my eyes. She doesn't notice my hand creeping across the floor until my fingers close around the glass.

"You're dying for nothing," she says, raising the gun once more.

I bring the shard up in a swift arc, slashing across her forearm. She shrieks, the gun tumbling from her suddenly nerveless fingers. I kick it away, sending it skittering across the hardwood floor.

Marie clutches her bleeding arm, her face a mask of shock and pain. I push her off me, scrambling to my feet. The room tilts alarmingly, and I have to steady myself against the wall.

"You bitch," she spits, but there's fear in her eyes now. She backs away, eyes darting between me and the discarded gun.

I ignore her, stumbling toward Elizabeth and Richard. They're watching me with wide, desperate eyes. Elizabeth's mascara has run in black trails down her cheeks. Richard's usually immaculate shirt is soaked with sweat.

I drop to my knees beside Elizabeth first, fingers fumbling with the knots binding her wrists. My left arm is nearly useless, and blood continues to seep from my wound, making my hands slippery.

"Hold on," I murmur, working the rope loose. "Almost there."

Behind me, I hear Marie moving. I work faster, my fingers clumsy with urgency. The knot finally gives, and Elizabeth's hands spring free. She immediately tears the tape from her mouth, gasping for air.

"Jane, behind you!"

I whirl around to see Marie lunging for the gun. I push to my feet, intending to intercept her, but my injury makes me slow. Elizabeth is already moving. With her ankles still bound, she throws herself forward off the chair, crashing into Marie's legs.

They tumble to the floor together, buying me precious seconds. I turn back to Richard, attacking the ropes at his wrists. Tears well up in his eyes, tracing clean paths down his dirty cheeks. Exhaustion takes over as he slumps forward, his body dropping heavily against mine. He has been held captive for weeks, his once strong frame now frail and weak. I can feel the tremors of fatigue coursing through him as I frantically work to free him, my heart aching at the thought of what he has endured.

The rope finally comes loose. "Get your ankles. Help Elizabeth."

He nods, bending to untie his feet. I turn back to the struggle on the floor. Elizabeth and Marie are grappling for control, rolling across broken glass and scattered papers. Marie's stronger than she looks, and Elizabeth is still handicapped by her bound ankles.

I lurch forward, diving into the fray. My shoulder burns with fresh fire as I collide with Marie, knocking her away from Elizabeth. We roll together, coming to a stop with me on top. I pin her arms down, my blood dripping onto her face.

"It's over, Marie," I pant.

She stares up at me, her chest heaving. "It's never over," she says, and there's something in her eyes—something beyond the rage and fear—that chills me to the core.

Behind me, I hear Elizabeth gasp as Richard finally frees her ankles. They're both loose now. They can run.

"Go!" I shout, not taking my eyes off Marie. "Run! Go, now!"

"Jane—" Elizabeth starts.

"Now!" I don't have the strength to hold Marie much longer. My vision is starting to fade at the edges, black creeping in. I need to know they're safe.

I hear movement behind me—footsteps, the rustle of clothing, Richard's low voice urging Elizabeth toward the door.

Marie sees it too. The fight seems to drain out of her, her body going slack beneath mine.

"They're leaving you," she whispers. "Just like they leave everyone. They don't care about you, Jane."

"Shut up," I growl.

The footsteps stop. "Mother." It's Richard's voice, closer than I expected. "We're not going without you."

Relief floods through me, so intense it's almost painful. I look up to see Richard and Elizabeth standing a few feet away, disheveled but determined.

"We're all leaving," Elizabeth adds, her voice steady despite the tremor in her hands.

Marie laughs, a brittle sound. "How touching. The perfect couple comes to the rescue."

I press down harder on her wrists. "Don't move," I warn her.

She smiles, a strange, knowing smile. "Or what, Jane? What will you do?"

I don't have an answer. My strength is fading fast, blood soaking through my shirt, and the room won't stop spinning. Every heartbeat sends a fresh wave of pain through my shoulder.

"Jane," Elizabeth says, taking a step closer. "We called for help using the landline. The police are coming. Thank God we kept the old landline for emergencies like this."

As if on cue, the distant wail of sirens cuts through the silence. Marie hears it too. Her smile fades, replaced by something harder, more desperate.

"You think this is over?" she asks, her voice barely above a whisper. "This is just the beginning."

I stare down at her, trying to understand how the quiet, efficient cleaning lady I knew could have transformed into this. What happened to her? What drove her to this point?

The sirens grow louder. The room darkens further around me, narrowing to a pinpoint of light with Marie's face at its center.

"Mother!" Richard's voice seems to come from very far away. "Mother, stay with us!"

I feel hands on my shoulders, gently pulling me away from Marie. The sudden movement sends a fresh wave of agony through my wounded shoulder, and the darkness rushes in, consuming everything in its path.

The last thing I see is Marie's face, watching me with those knowing eyes as Richard and Elizabeth pull me away from her. The last thing I feel is their hands, steady and sure, holding me up as my legs give way beneath me.

Then, nothing.

THIRTY

JANE

When I regain consciousness, I realize we're outside. It's cooler than I expected, or perhaps that's the blood loss talking. This is, after all, Florida. It's never cool out. The world tilts and shifts around me, the flashing lights of the police cars bleeding into streams of color. Officers approach, their faces serious, their words a jumble of sound that I can't process.

Elizabeth is speaking rapidly beside me, explaining something. Richard's hand presses against my uninjured shoulder. I try to focus on his touch, on the fact that he's here, that he's safe.

"Ma'am, can you hear me?" A new voice, a paramedic kneeling in front of me. When did I sit down on the porch steps? I don't remember.

"Yes," I say, or try to say. My lips feel numb.

"You've lost a lot of blood. We're going to take care of you, okay?"

I nod or think I nod. More figures in uniform appear, moving past us into the house. Securing Marie, securing the scene. Someone presses a gauze pad against my shoulder. The pressure sends a bolt of pain down my arm, and I gasp.

"Sorry," the paramedic says. "We need to stop the bleeding."

Elizabeth hasn't let go of my hand. Her fingers are cold against mine, or perhaps mine are just too warm. Shock, probably. I know the symptoms distantly, academically.

"You saved us," she says, her voice breaking a fraction. "Jane, you saved our lives."

I look at her, trying to focus on her face through the encroaching darkness. "You would have done the same."

Her eyes fill with tears. "I don't know if I would have. I don't know if I could have."

"You did," I remind her. "You helped me fight her. You didn't run when I told you to."

Richard kneels beside us, his face pale but composed. There's blood on his shirt—mine, probably. "None of us ran," he says. "We stayed together."

Their faces swim before me, hazy through my darkening vision. Elizabeth's elegant features now bruised and tear-streaked. Richard's stern countenance, usually unyielding, is now softened by exhaustion and relief, his eyes shadowed with fatigue. They're battered, traumatized, but alive. We all are. The police glance at Richard with a mixture of pity and disbelief. His skin is pallid, drawn tightly over his cheekbones. The ropes that had bound his hands for weeks left angry, raw wounds, and as they are carefully examined, the extent of the horrors he has endured becomes painfully apparent.

The paramedics are moving me now, lifting me onto a stretcher. The sudden shift sends a wave of pain through my body, and I can't hold back a cry.

"We're coming with you," Elizabeth says firmly to the paramedic. It's not a question.

"Family only in the ambulance, ma'am," he responds, adjusting something on my IV.

Elizabeth and Richard exchange a glance, some unspoken

communication passing between them. Then Elizabeth turns back to the paramedic. "We are family," she says, her voice leaving no room for argument.

I feel a warmth in my chest that has nothing to do with my injury, or the shock blanket they've draped over me. Family. The word is new and yet somehow right.

Richard squeezes my hand. "We'll go with you in the ambulance," he promises. "We won't leave you alone."

I try to respond, but the words won't come. The darkness is closing in faster now, the sounds around me fading into a distant hum. The last thing I see before unconsciousness claims me is their faces, watching over me with a fierceness that speaks of something beyond gratitude or obligation.

We survived Marie's obsession. We fought together and won. Whatever comes next—the questions, the investigations, the long process of healing—we'll face it the same way.

As the ambulance doors close and the sirens wail to life, I let go of consciousness, carried away on a tide of pain and exhaustion. But beneath it all, there's a strange sense of peace.

For the first time in longer than I can remember, I don't feel alone.

The darkness takes me completely then, but it's not frightening any more. Not with them waiting on the other side.

I close my eyes and let go, knowing they'll be there when I wake up.

THIRTY-ONE

JANE

The antiseptic smell of the hospital room burns my nostrils, and my shoulder throbs beneath the stiff bandage. Elizabeth sits beside my bed, her fingers resting lightly on my arm. Richard paces near the window, his shoes making soft tapping sounds against the linoleum as sunlight catches the worry lines etched around his eyes. Joseph just left to get some coffee.

The beeping of the heart monitor fills the silence, marking time in this strange limbo we've entered. Three days ago, we were trapped together, certain we wouldn't make it out alive. Now we're here, safe but broken in ways that can't be wrapped in gauze.

"The doctor says you can go home tomorrow," Elizabeth says finally, her voice carrying that smoothness she uses at charity galas. Her blonde hair is pulled back in a loose ponytail —a far cry from her usual perfect styling. Dark circles shadow her eyes.

I nod, not trusting my voice yet. Home. The word feels hollow after everything.

Richard stops his pacing and turns to face us. The expensive fabric of his suit hangs differently on him now.

"It's all my fault this happened to us. When I realized it was Marie you had hired as our cleaning lady, I thought I would be able to handle it," he says, the words directed at Elizabeth but his eyes darting toward me. "I feared you'd find out, Elizabeth. Every day."

He swallows hard, Adam's apple bobbing beneath the stubble on his throat. "But I had never foreseen this would happen. That she would actually try to hurt us. She tried to get back with me, and I rejected her every time. I even went to her apartment the day before she kidnapped me, and argued with her for three whole hours, telling her she needed to stop this, she needed to quit her job, or I would have to make up an excuse to fire her. She finally said she would resign the next day. I believed her."

His hands are trembling. He stuffs them into his pockets in a gesture I recognize—Richard hiding his vulnerabilities.

Elizabeth's fingers tighten almost imperceptibly on my arm. "We all made mistakes," she says. Her wedding ring catches the fluorescent light, throwing tiny prisms across the thin hospital blanket covering my legs. I'm glad to see it back on her finger again. So much more fitting on her than Marie.

I close my eyes briefly, wishing I could shut out more than just the sight of them. The pain medication makes my thoughts foggy, a thick haze that clouds my mind, but not foggy enough to erase the piercing echo of Marie's laughter as she held that gun with a chilling confidence. It's not enough to forget how she almost killed us, leaving a scar deeper than any physical wound. I turn to my son, his eyes searching mine for answers I have long hidden.

"Hiring Marie was a mistake, a terrible mistake, and I can only hope you can forgive me." An apology lingers on my lips, fragile and sincere, as I brace myself for his reaction.

He stares at me, his expression a mix of shock and confusion, absorbing the revelation like a sponge soaking in water. For a moment, silence separates us, thick with unspoken emotions. Then, slowly, his shoulders relax, and a flicker of understanding passes through his eyes.

"We all make mistakes. And a lot of mistakes were made."

"I, for one, made a lot. I was stupid enough to go to the beach house when I received a text from Marie," Elizabeth says, her gaze fixed on some middle distance. "She said she thought she saw Richard at the beach house and urged me to hurry down there." Her voice catches.

Richard nods, halting his restless movement for a moment. "Marie also sent me a message telling me to come to the beach house immediately," he explains, his tone unnaturally calm and measured. "I thought something terrible had happened to Elizabeth or the house. I also feared she was going to blackmail me and threaten to tell Elizabeth that we used to be together, and maybe even lie and say we had an affair. That's why I went. That's also why I deleted the text immediately after receiving it. And didn't take the phone since I worried my mother would track me and know where I was. But Marie was the only one there when I arrived." His jaw tightens. "She was waiting there, holding a gun, and then she tied me up."

"She knew our schedules," I say. "She knew so much about all of us. Including the fact that none of us ever go to the beach house any more."

Elizabeth nods, her composed mask slipping for just a moment. "She watched us for months. In our own home." A shudder runs through her. "All those times I spoke to her about dinner parties, about my schedule, about—" She stops abruptly.

About her secrets, I think but don't say. About the hushed phone calls she didn't want Richard to know about.

"Did she say anything to either of you about why?" I ask, though I already know the answer. Marie had been explicit about her reasons during those long, terrifying hours.

Richard and Elizabeth exchange a look loaded with meaning.

"She thought we had everything," Richard says finally. "The perfect marriage, the perfect home, the perfect friends." His laugh is hollow. "She wanted to have it all. She wanted to be us. Take over Elizabeth's life. When I rejected her, I guess she lost it. Went mad."

The silence that follows is heavy with unspoken truths. Yes, Marie succeeded in exposing all our careful lies—the affairs, the financial deceptions, the false identities we've constructed to face the world. She held up a mirror and forced us to look at our reflections, distorted but recognizable.

"We're alive," Elizabeth says firmly. "That's what matters now."

Is it, though? I wonder as the pain in my shoulder flares again. The bullet has been taken out of me, but sometimes I think I can still feel it burning through my flesh, still hear the deafening crack of the gun firing when I lunged at Marie. I still see the surprise in her eyes—she hadn't expected me to fight back.

"The police said they found evidence at her apartment," Richard continues. "Photographs of us. Journal entries dating back months. She'd been watching all of us, learning our patterns, our weaknesses. She was manipulating you all along, Mother. She was watching us long before you even contacted her about the maid job. That just happened to land right in her lap. A perfect opportunity for her to get really close."

Richard comes to stand at the foot of my bed. "The detective wants to speak with you again tomorrow," he says. "They need to corroborate our statements."

Our statements.

"I'll tell them what happened," I say. "That Marie trapped you there for weeks. That she threatened to kill us." I meet Richard's gaze directly.

"We need to be careful," Elizabeth says, her voice barely above a whisper. "About what we share."

My heart clenches at the familiar words. How many times have we said that to each other over the years? Be careful what you share. Be careful what you reveal. Keep the secrets, maintain the facade, protect the illusion we've all invested so heavily in. Elizabeth wants to protect me, hide the fact that I employed Marie to spy on her and knew who she was this whole time.

"I'm tired of being careful," I reply, surprising even myself with the edge in my voice.

Richard's expression shifts, something like respect flashing across his features before disappearing behind his careful mask. "We all are," he says. "But there are some things the police don't need to know. Some things that won't help their case against Marie."

Like the fact that Elizabeth has been living under a false identity for years. Like the debt that is draining all my accounts when constantly bailing Richard out. Like the reason Marie targeted us specifically.

"My mind reels at the thought," I say, "that despite the terror of the past days, we might finally be on the path to rebuilding, to honesty."

Elizabeth's eyes widen in recognition. Richard stiffens.

"And have we?" Richard asks, his voice strangely vulnerable. "Been honest?"

All the secrets we've kept, all the lies we've told each other and ourselves, laid bare by a woman we barely noticed as she cleaned our homes and observed our lives.

I look from Richard to Elizabeth, these two people who have shaped my existence for the past five years.

"Not yet," I answer finally. "But maybe we can start."

Elizabeth's hand slides from my arm to my hand, squeezing gently. Richard's posture relaxes, his shoulders dropping from their defensive height.

The hum of the hospital equipment fades in and out of my awareness like a distant tide. I stare at the ceiling, counting the tiny holes in each acoustic tile to keep myself anchored in the present. Thirty-six, thirty-seven, thirty-eight... It's better than dwelling on the beach house, on Marie's voice, on the weight of the gun when I finally managed to grab it. The fluorescent light flickers once, casting strange shadows across Richard's face as he resumes his restless pacing.

"They should fix that," he mutters, glancing up at the light fixture.

Always focused on the practical, the fixable.

Elizabeth sits unnaturally still in the chair beside my bed. Her posture remains perfect—spine straight, shoulders back—but her usual elegant composure has frayed around the edges.

"Jane," she murmurs, her fingers curling back around my arm. "There's more you should know—before tomorrow's police interview. Both of you. You will find out anyway after I talk to them."

I turn toward her, wincing as the movement tugs at my injured shoulder. "More secrets?" I say, my voice rough with fatigue.

Richard stands by the window, his back taut, shoulders squared as if bracing for impact. Even without looking at us, I can feel his tension.

She inhales slowly. "My maiden name isn't Elizabeth Turner. It's Elizabeth Keller. I changed my identity years ago."

I nod, though I already know this.

She closes her eyes for a heartbeat, then continues. "Before I became Turner, I was Elizabeth Barrett. I was married once before—no one here knows about him. He was... controlling, violent. The first time he hit me, I was too stunned to fight back. But one night he cornered me in the kitchen, knife in hand, threatening to kill me. I grabbed a fire poker to defend myself. A neighbor called the police. When they arrived, they found me standing over him, poker in hand—and him bruised, me pale and silent. They never asked about the knee and rib bruises I'd gotten moments before, or the blood on my shirt. They saw me with the weapon and him with the marks, and they arrested me as the aggressor."

Her voice trembles. "He dropped the charges the next day and came to 'rescue' me. He told me I should be grateful. I wasn't."

She glances at Richard—still watching, still silent—and presses on. "The abuse continued. So, one day, I ran. I hid in a cabin by the lake under a new name: Elizabeth Spencer. For months, I thought I was safe. Then he found me. He stood at the foot of my bed when I woke up, grabbed me by the hair, dragged me to his car, and drove like a madman, swerving, nearly killing us both. He didn't know I'd slipped a pocket knife into my car, hiding it between the seats for situations like this. He hit me again and again, screaming that he'd kill me. I pulled the knife out and stabbed him. Once. Then again. The car veered off the road and plunged into the lake. Everything went under. I managed to get out somehow. I swam to shore, left him —or his body—in the dark water. I didn't wait to see if he lived. I ran."

She pauses, her breath catching. "The police later questioned me about his disappearance. Every day I feared he'd show up in town. So, I left. I changed my name so he could never find me. I thought the nightmare was over until shortly before Richard disappeared, when I heard they'd recovered a body from that lake. I was terrified the police would come for me, accuse me of murder. My brother helped to arrange for me to disappear all over again if needed. I've been using a burner phone, talking in hushed tones to my brother, or Sarah, trying to keep this hidden until... until we sort everything out."

Silence settles between us. The single lamp casts trembling shadows on her face. I rest my hand on hers, trembling too, as we both realize how far the truth has brought us—and how much farther we still must go.

Those phone calls that I had experienced myself and that Marie had reported to me. I'd known something was wrong, but I'd never pushed for the truth. Instead, I had judged, assumed she was cheating on my son, or worse, planning to kill him.

A real good mother-in-law indeed.

"Why didn't you tell me, Lizzie? Did you think I would judge you for surviving? For doing what you had to do?" Richard says.

Elizabeth looks down at her hands. "I didn't want you to look at me differently. To see me as damaged. And... I was afraid your mother would find out."

Ah, yes. The formidable Mrs. Wilson senior, with her rigid ideas about family reputation and social standing. That would be me. A woman who would undoubtedly find a daughter-in-law with a false identity and a violent past to be utterly unacceptable.

I shift slightly in the hospital bed, trying to find a position that doesn't send pain shooting through my shoulder.

"What about the bloodstained clothes Marie saw you hide in the closet of the guest room?" I ask. "She told Sarah about it?"

Elizabeth looks at me, her brow furrowed in confusion. "I... I don't know what you're talking about. I never hid any clothes. Why would Marie say that?"

A sudden realization hits me. Marie must have concocted the whole story. She wanted to make us think Elizabeth had hurt Richard. That's why she went to Sarah with this information, not me.

"I guess it was all part of her game. Making us think we were hiding things from each other. Playing us against each other, all of us."

Richard stops and looks directly at me, his gaze surprisingly steady. "Marie may have revealed things we were hiding from each other. But she underestimated what we mean to each other."

I think of the scars I've glimpsed on Elizabeth's back when zipping up her dresses—thin white lines she always dismissed as childhood accidents. I wonder what other scars she carries that aren't visible.

"I already knew," Richard says, his voice soft but firm. "About your real name. About why you left." He meets Elizabeth's shocked expression with calm resolve. "And that's okay. I still love you."

Elizabeth's composure cracks, tears welling in her eyes. "How long have you known?"

"Since before we were married," he admits. "I hired a private investigator when we started dating. Standard procedure for someone in my position—my family insisted."

She stiffens. "You investigated me?"

"Yes," he says without apology. "And when I learned the truth, I made sure all records were sealed. I created additional protections for your new identity." His expression softens. "I never said anything because I was waiting for you to trust me enough to tell me yourself."

"So you knew," Elizabeth says slowly, "and you married me anyway."

"I married you because of who you are, not despite it," Richard replies. "Your past is part of you, but it doesn't define you."

Their fingers brush as he moves closer to her chair, and I see a spark pass between them—not passion exactly, but recognition. Two people seeing each other clearly, perhaps for the first time. I'm trapped in this moment, witnessing something intensely private yet unable to look away. The past days have been filled with relentless tension and fear, with the growing certainty that one or all of us would die. Now, in the sterile safety of the hospital room, truth continues to spill out, but by choice rather than coercion.

"And Marie?" Elizabeth asks, her voice small. "What will happen to her? Will any of what she found out about us be revealed?"

"Marie will be facing multiple charges of kidnapping, assault, and attempted murder," Richard says calmly. "Her credibility is non-existent. And anything she claims we 'confessed' under duress would be inadmissible and irrelevant."

Always the lawyer, even though he never formally practiced. Richard's father made sure he understood the law well enough to skirt its edges without crossing over.

Elizabeth's hand squeezes my arm gently, a subtle reminder of our connection. Every squeeze underscores our fragile unity—the three of us bound by secrets and survival.

"So we just... move on?" I ask, the words tasting bitter on my tongue. "Pretend none of this happened?"

"Not pretend," Richard says, coming to stand at the foot of my bed. "But we choose what parts of this experience define us going forward."

Elizabeth nods. "We rebuild," she says. "Together."

I study their faces—Richard's careful confidence, Elizabeth's determined vulnerability. Both looking at me with a mixture of concern and something else. Something like need.

"Together," I repeat, testing the weight of the word.

Richard's hand finds mine, his fingers warm and steady. Elizabeth's grip on my other arm tightens just a little. We form a triangle of touch, of connection.

Maybe now we can be a family? The thought surfaces unbidden, hopeful, and dangerous. Not the conventional kind—I harbor no illusions about that. But something real, nonetheless. Something honest, built on the ruins of our carefully constructed facades.

The pain in my shoulder pulses in time with my heartbeat.

A reminder of what I risked to save them, to save us. A reminder that some wounds heal clean, while others leave scars that change us forever.

"Yes," Richard says, as if reading my thoughts. "Let's try to be a normal family now."

Elizabeth's slight nod confirms it. The secrets are out, the lies exposed. Marie's plan to destroy us has instead stripped away the barriers we built against each other.

"Well, normal might be a stretch," I say with a smile. "After all, we are The Wilsons, a highly esteemed family name. We have to live up to that. Normal won't exactly cut it."

That makes them laugh.

I close my eyes, suddenly exhausted by it all. The pain medication pulls at me, drawing me toward sleep. But for the first time in years, I don't resist the vulnerability. I let myself drift, anchored by their touch, by the desperate hope that from these broken pieces, we might build something true.

THIRTY-TWO

JANE

I adjust the arrangement of white lilies in the crystal vase, turning it a quarter inch to the right. The renovated living room gleams around me—white walls, polished floors, tasteful furniture in shades of cream and pale blue. Perfect. Immaculate. Just as I've worked so hard to make it. Just as everything in this house should be.

Sunlight streams through the floor-to-ceiling windows, casting long rectangles of light across the newly installed hardwood. Three months of renovation dust, contractors tracking mud, and the constant din of power tools have finally yielded this serene space. I have spent night and day monitoring the renovation of my son and daughter-in-law's refuge within the Cypress Estates, where appearances matter more than most care to admit. This time because they asked me to.

And I have done a darn good job at it, if I may say so.

My fingers smooth an invisible wrinkle in the throw draped across the arm of the sofa. The interior designer suggested "casual elegance," but I insisted on perfection. In this neighborhood, casual isn't an option—not when the ladies from the garden club drop by unannounced, their eyes scanning for flaws behind their rehearsed smiles.

"The room has wonderful bones," the designer had said, "but it needs to be livable."

Livable. As if imperfection should be embraced rather than corrected.

I step back to survey my domain. The built-in bookshelves—filled with leather-bound classics I've actually read, unlike some of the neighbors—frame the limestone fireplace. Above it hangs an abstract painting in blues and grays, selected not for any emotional resonance but because it complements the room's color scheme perfectly.

My phone buzzes from the side table. I pick it up, seeing a notification from the cleaning agency.

Good afternoon, Mrs. Wilson. This is to confirm that your new maid, Marta, will begin this Monday at 8 a.m. as requested.

I tap out a reply, each word measured and precise:

Thank you for confirming. Please remind Marta that I expect punctuality and attention to detail. The security code will be provided upon arrival.

As I set the phone down, my gaze falls on the collection of family photographs arranged on the console table beneath the window. I approach them, adjusting one frame that sits a millimeter too far to the left. Richard stands tall in each image, his posture straight, his smile controlled.

Just like his father. Just like I taught him.

In the largest photo, taken last week in Santorini, Richard has his arm around Elizabeth. My daughter-in-law's blonde hair catches the light, her smile wide. Between them, a sliver of space, barely noticeable unless you're looking for it. For once, I'm not filling it.

I pick up this frame, running my thumb across the glass. The photo taken last year captures what appears to be a perfect moment—sunset, cliffside restaurant, expensive wine. But I see what others miss. The slight tension in Richard's jaw. The way Elizabeth leans almost imperceptibly away from him. The careful performance of marital bliss.

In another photo, Richard stands beside me at his firm's holiday party. His eyes—so like his father's—contain that familiar distance. He's present but elsewhere, a trait he developed in childhood that I never managed to correct. Elizabeth isn't in this picture. She had a migraine that night, or so she claimed. The third time that month her headaches had coincided with events important to Richard's career.

My finger traces the outline of my son's face behind the glass. Handsome, successful, respected. Everything I raised him to be. Everything his father has expected.

I set the frame down precisely where it had been and move to the next—Richard and Elizabeth at their last anniversary party. I'd organized it myself, transforming the club's ballroom into an elegant recreation of their wedding reception. Elizabeth had wanted something "more intimate," but anniversaries, like weddings, aren't really about what the couple wants. They're statements made to society.

And the Wilsons make grand statements.

In this photo, Elizabeth wears the diamond necklace Richard gave her that evening. Her fingers touch it in what could be interpreted as a gesture of appreciation, but I recognize it as a nervous habit. She touches her jewelry when she's uncomfortable. I've cataloged all her tells over the years.

The final photograph shows the three of us at Christmas. My arm links with Richard's, while Elizabeth stands a little apart, her smile tight at the corners. I'd noticed her drinking more that evening, her third glass of wine making her laugh too loudly at the neighbor's tasteless jokes. When she excused herself to the powder room, she was gone long enough that Richard glanced at his watch twice.

I straighten this frame with deliberate care, feeling a familiar tightness in my chest that I've come to recognize as concern, not dislike. Despite what Elizabeth might think, I've never disliked her. I've simply seen what Richard refuses to— the inconsistencies, the small deceptions, the careful performance.

She's not perfect.

From the kitchen comes the sound of laughter: Richard's deep chuckle followed by Elizabeth's lighter tone. The sound stops me, a discordant note in the quiet house. Genuine laughter. Not the polite social kind, but the intimate sound of shared amusement.

I return the frame to its place, my reflection ghosting across the glass. Still in my sixties, I remain what people call "well-preserved"; my silver-streaked hair is always perfectly styled, my clothing expensive but understated. I've maintained the discipline of regular exercise, careful diet, and monthly visits to the dermatologist. Age may be inevitable, but its visible signs are often negotiable with the right resources.

The laughter continues, drawing me slowly toward the kitchen like a skeptical moth to an unexpected flame. Before I move, I take a final survey of the living room, noting with satisfaction its flawless appearance. If only people were as easily arranged as furniture, as readily polished as silver.

My phone buzzes again. Another message from the agency with Marta's credentials attached: background check, references, experience. All immaculate, all carefully vetted. I skim the information, noting her five years with the Hendersons before they relocated to Charlotte. The Hendersons, known for their exacting standards.

Good.

I slip the phone into my pocket and listen again to the sound of my son and his wife sharing a moment I wasn't invited to join. Their voices rise and fall in a rhythm that sounds like intimacy, like connection.

For a moment—brief, unwelcome—doubt flickers. Perhaps I've misread the signs. Perhaps the distance I've perceived is merely a projection of my own concerns, my own disappointments.

But no. I've always been observant. It's both gift and burden to see what others miss, to notice the small betrayals, the tiny fractures that eventually become breaking points. Richard's father never saw it coming when his business partner embezzled funds. I had noticed the man's new watch, his sudden vacations, the way his eyes shifted during conversations about finances.

"You're paranoid, Jane," he'd said.

Until I was proven right.

I won't make that mistake with my son's marriage. The stakes are too high: his position in the community; his standing at the firm; his future. Our family name.

The laughter from the kitchen fades, replaced by the murmur of conversation. Words I can't quite make out, but tones I recognize. There's a cadence to Elizabeth's voice when she's trying to convince Richard of something—a lilt at the end of sentences, a deliberate pause before key points. I've heard it when she suggested they "invest" in her brother's startup. When she wanted the house in Oakwood Heights rather than the equally prestigious but more established Cypress Estates. Well, she lost that one, and I won.

I pause at the kitchen doorway, one hand resting on the frame. Richard leans against the marble island, wine glass dangling from his fingers, while Elizabeth stands across from him, her hair caught in the pendant lights above. They haven't noticed me yet. These unguarded moments reveal more than hours of dinner conversation ever could.

The kitchen gleams with stainless steel and quartzite, another recently renovated space that cost more than my first house. Elizabeth insisted on the six-burner professional range she rarely uses. Richard wanted the wine refrigerator programmed to maintain exact temperatures for different vintages.

"You can't be serious," Elizabeth says, her voice carrying a lightness I rarely hear when I'm present. She's cut her hair recently—a sleek bob that emphasizes her cheekbones. The style looks expensive. Everything about Elizabeth looks expensive, as it should.

Richard swirls the burgundy liquid in his glass. "Dead serious. Benson took one look at the brief and nearly spilled his coffee."

Elizabeth laughs, not the controlled social laugh she employs at benefit galas, but something more genuine. My son responds with a smile that reaches his eyes. A rarity I catalog automatically. His posture has softened from the rigid bearing he maintains in public. His suit jacket hangs on the back of a barstool, his tie loosened. Signs of comfort. Or carelessness.

I clear my throat and step into the kitchen. "Something amusing?"

Richard straightens immediately, an instinctive response to my presence that I've never discouraged. "Just work stories. Nothing important."

Elizabeth's smile remains, though it recalibrates into something more polite. "Richard was telling me about a mishap at the firm. Would you like some wine, Jane? We opened a lovely Bordeaux."

"Just a small glass," I say, moving further into the kitchen. "The living room is finally complete. Not a speck of dust or single item out of place."

"The designers did a beautiful job," Elizabeth offers, reaching for another glass from the cabinet. She moves with the careful grace of someone who took ballet lessons as a child. I realize I still don't even know if she did. She doesn't talk about her childhood.

"The designers provided options. I made the final decisions." I accept the glass she extends, our fingers not quite touching in the exchange. "As it should be."

Richard clears his throat, a signal I recognize as discomfort. "Mother has excellent taste. Always has."

"Of course," Elizabeth agrees, too quickly. She turns to the refrigerator, extracting a cheese plate I hadn't noticed earlier. "I picked this up from that new specialty shop in the plaza. The owner sources everything directly from small European producers."

I examine the arrangement—Brie, something blue-veined, a hard cheese with a rind I don't recognize. Expensive crackers. Red grapes. Artfully arranged, I must admit.

"Thoughtful," I say, selecting a grape. "Though I hope you didn't overpay. These specialty shops often mark up their products for the neighborhood."

Elizabeth's smile doesn't waver. "The quality speaks for itself. Richard, could you grab the honey from the pantry? Apparently, it's supposed to pair wonderfully with the Manchego."

I watch my son move across the kitchen, the careful way he navigates around his wife, maintaining a distance that's neither too intimate nor too formal.

"I received confirmation that your new maid starts Monday," I say, setting my glass on the counter without drinking.

Richard returns with a small jar of honey. "That's good news."

"Marta comes highly recommended by the Hendersons." I

watch Elizabeth's reaction carefully. "She'll be here three times a week, full days."

Something flickers across Elizabeth's face—a tightening around the eyes, perhaps. "I thought we discussed twice weekly. The house isn't that large, and I work from home most days. I can manage the day-to-day upkeep."

"The Cypress Estates requires certain standards," I reply, meeting her gaze directly. "Three days ensures nothing slips through the cracks. Besides, you should focus on your consulting work, not housekeeping."

Richard places a hand on Elizabeth's shoulder—a gesture that appears supportive but also silencing. "Mother's right. Your clients need your full attention, especially with the Taylor project deadline approaching."

Elizabeth's shoulder shifts minutely under his touch. Another tell. "Of course. Three days is fine."

I sip my wine, observing them over the rim of my glass. Richard arranges plates while Elizabeth slices the cheese. I set down my barely touched wine glass. "I should let you enjoy your evening."

"You're welcome to stay," Richard offers, but his relief when I shake my head is palpable.

"Another time," I say, "I have some correspondence to attend to."

As I turn to leave, I catch a glimpse of them in the reflection of the microwave door—Richard moving closer to Elizabeth, her body relaxing incrementally as I prepare to exit. The shift is subtle but unmistakable. They are different when I'm not present. Freer, perhaps. Or simply more themselves.

And what versions of themselves might those be?

I pause at the doorway, watching Richard refill Elizabeth's wine glass, their fingers brushing in a way they never would if they knew I was observing. The contact lingers a second too long. Elizabeth says something too quiet for me to hear, and Richard laughs—that same genuine laugh I'd heard earlier.

A thought crystallizes as I turn away. The new maid, Marta, will have access to the entire house. She'll observe Elizabeth during the day when Richard is at the office. She'll notice patterns, behaviors, perhaps visitors that come and go. She'll hear phone calls, note Elizabeth's movements, the hours she keeps.

If properly motivated—perhaps with generous holiday bonuses and the occasional confidence shared over coffee—Marta might become my eyes when I cannot be present. A casual question here, an observation there. Nothing inappropriate, nothing direct. Just another layer of awareness in a house that already contains too many secrets.

I move silently back to the immaculate living room, the decision forming with each step. Monday, when Marta arrives, I'll establish the relationship carefully. I'll explain our family's need for discretion, for attention to detail, for loyalty. I'll ensure she understands that sharing observations with me is part of her role.

After all, I'm only protecting my son. His career. His reputation. His future.

If Elizabeth has nothing to hide, there's nothing to fear.

I straighten a pillow on the sofa and glance toward the kitchen, where laughter again floats through the doorway.

"What harm could it do?" I whisper to myself.

In the perfect stillness of the room, there is neither question nor answer, but something in between.

Dear reader,

I want to say a huge thank you for choosing to read *The Woman He Married*. If you did enjoy it, and want to keep up to date with all my latest releases, just sign up at the following link. Your email address will never be shared and you can unsubscribe at any time.

www.bookouture.com/willow-rose

The idea for this book came to me one day when thinking back at my own life, and when I was seventeen and I used to clean houses to make extra money. I worked for a very rich family living in a beautiful beach house, and they quickly grew to become like family to me. They'd invite me to family gatherings, and I'm pretty sure the son had a thing for me for a little while, or maybe I had a thing for him, who knows. We flirted. But there was something else I used to do. I was always alone in the house when cleaning it, and sometimes I'd try on the woman's jewelry and look at myself in the mirror while dreaming of one day living in a house like that. The memory made me laugh, but it also made me think. What if someone took it too far, wanting to be a part of the family she was cleaning for?

And that's how this book was born.

As always, I am so happy for all your support and want to

give a huge thank you to my editor, Jennifer Hunt, and all her tremendous work in making this book happen.

Take care,

Willow

https://www.willow-rose.net

facebook.com/willowredrose

x.com/madamwillowrose

instagram.com/willowroseauthor

bookbub.com/authors/willow-rose

PUBLISHING TEAM

Turning a manuscript into a book requires the efforts of many people. The publishing team at Bookouture would like to acknowledge everyone who contributed to this publication.

Audio
Alba Proko
Sinead O'Connor
Melissa Tran

Commercial
Lauren Morrissette
Hannah Richmond
Imogen Allport

Cover design
Eileen Carey

Data and analysis
Mark Alder
Mohamed Bussuri

Editorial
Jennifer Hunt
Charlotte Hegley

Copyeditor
Janette Currie

Proofreader
Lynne Walker

Marketing
Alex Crow
Melanie Price
Occy Carr
Cíara Rosney
Martyna Młynarska

Operations and distribution
Marina Valles
Stephanie Straub
Joe Morris

Production
Hannah Snetsinger
Mandy Kullar
Nadia Michael
Charlotte Hegley

Publicity
Kim Nash
Noelle Holten
Jess Readett
Sarah Hardy

Rights and contracts
Peta Nightingale
Richard King
Saidah Graham

Dear Reader,

We'd love your attention for one more page to tell you about the crisis in children's reading, and what we can all do.

Studies have shown that reading for fun is the **single biggest predictor of a child's future life chances** – more than family circumstance, parents' educational background or income. It improves academic results, mental health, wealth, communication skills, ambition and happiness.

The number of children reading for fun is in rapid decline. Young people have a lot of competition for their time, and a worryingly high number do not have a single book at home.

Hachette works extensively with schools, libraries and literacy charities, but here are some ways we can all raise more readers:

- Reading to children for just 10 minutes a day makes a difference
- Don't give up if children aren't regular readers – there will be books for them!

- Visit bookshops and libraries to get recommendations
- Encourage them to listen to audiobooks
- Support school libraries
- Give books as gifts

There's a lot more information about how to encourage children to read on our websites: **www.RaisingReaders.co.uk** and **www.JoinRaisingReaders.com**.

Thank you for reading.